OBEDIENCE

Writing as Dee Cheers

Capricorn: Speculative Fiction Inspired by the Zodiac (The Zodiac Series) Deadset Press
(15 December 2019)

Aquarius: Speculative Fiction Inspired by the Zodiac (The Zodiac Series) Deadset Press
(17 January 2020)

D.E. CHEERS

OBEDIENCE

BOOK ONE IN THE ABOMINATION SERIES

To my family. Thank you all for your support and love and patience. Special thanks to my son Chris, who listened, suggested and advised me along the way.

CONTENTS

CENTRAL

One

The soldier the Xi called Oryelle Tey forced back a gasp of pain as another shudder aggravated her barely healed femur. She tried to keep her breath shallow and slow, if only to avoid the icy air surrounding her in the lightless metal box of her cell. It was already more than twenty degrees below the ice point of water, and it was growing colder still with each passing moment.

The chill brought with it a numbing sensation, one she welcomed at first. But soon enough, it began to reach deep inside her bones and threaten to take away all feeling from them altogether — a sensation too close for comfort when she considered what brokenness could lay ahead if her captors felt inclined.

"Prisoner?" came an artificially melodious voice. "Prisoner, wake up."

Ori stirred, dragging herself back from the beckoning darkness. "What do you want? Can't you let me die in peace?" she whispered as another wave of shivering racked her body. The remains of the mattress, stinking of stale sweat and a mélange of malodorous body fluids, couldn't hold back the cold seeping up from the bare synthecrete floor.

"Your core temperature is dropping toward critical levels," the AI observed.

"Just let me go," she muttered into the darkness.

Let me die.

She curled herself tighter on the fetid lump of foam and calculated how long until hypothermia killed her. Not soon enough, her interface told her, projecting a display of dropping core temperatures and rising physiological distress onto her field of vision. The animals — her jailers — would not summon the medic for anything short of an emergency and they knew from experience how much abuse her body could take. Hypothermia at least granted an easy death; certainly, Ori knew all the hard ways to die.

"I cannot," the machine replied, sounding almost apologetic. The primitive machine couldn't override the guard's authorization and whoever thought her suffering entertaining was no doubt enjoying themselves. "You must raise your core temperature," chided the AI, in incongruously soft tones for a prison monitor.

The icons in her peripheral vision pulsed in sullen amber or red, warning of the damage from exposure, starvation, and pain. Her body spasmed again. And this time she couldn't stifle the cry.

Her grumbling stomach also reminded her the next meal was another five hours away — if it came at all. Water would help. Ori ran her tongue over her bleeding, swollen lips, calculating how much energy moving would cost her. Too much, warned her systems. She couldn't waste the small ball of warmth she hoarded in her aching body on water, no matter how thirsty she became.

Despair settled on her; a darkness more absolute than this small, cold cell. Ten years as a prisoner of the Republic, condemned without a trial to life imprisonment with no possibility of freedom, except in death. Ten years of solitary confinement, subjected to constant abuse and torture.

If she moved, if she squandered these last shreds of warmth, wasted these last vestiges of energy, gave into the persistent urge to sleep, perhaps she would hasten the fall into unconsciousness. To inevitable death. The prospect no longer terrified her; the idea of dying at the hands of animals, so far away from her family, her people. Once, Ori had considered such a fate the ultimate failure for a soldier of her Line, but now, as the temperature dropped further, she allowed her imagination to drift toward acceptance. To finally rest, to be done with the pain and the humiliations and abuse would be a relief. Exhaustion swept over her; blissful, unending darkness called her.

Choices. There weren't many left now. Either let go and hope death came quickly, or struggle one last time to survive.

So, choose.

With a mental nudge, the interface increased her metabolic rate, stripping her metabolism of critical calories. She ignored the multiple warnings scrolling across her vision.

"Go and get Twari. Remind him if I die, he'll lose all his money," she said, struggling to stay conscious. The plan was still viable, all she had to do was stay alive.

The AI's voice jerked her back out of dangerous drowsiness.

"Captain Twari says he is returning the environmental controls to normal. The individuals responsible for altering them will be punished."

Punished? She had been on the receiving end of Twari's punishments herself; the depth of the captain's cruelty matched the spiders' sometimes. Whichever fool decided to have some fun with the prisoner would be regretting their choices about now. Twari's interest in her well-being extended only to her ability to fight; her injuries didn't concern him.

Wisps of warm air drifted down from the vents. The temperature began to creep higher, although the cell remained in total darkness. Ori didn't need the thermal imaging to find her way around her prison. Ten steps to the waste unit, one step further to the sink and its single tap with its trickle of metallic-tasting water. Another two steps to the shower. All under the ubiquitous monitoring of the AI and the guards' constant source of amusement. Nothing apart from the remains of the filthy mattress. No windows, no openings at all, except for one heavily armored and reinforced door.

If her plan worked, if the nanites completed their repairs on time, tomorrow might be her last fight. The medic had sworn he could smuggle her out of the house undetected. More importantly, he claimed he could remove the ID chip without alerting the AI — all she had to do was live long enough to make it to the infirmary.

Cramped muscles protested as Ori uncurled her body and climbed unsteadily to her feet, grimacing at the pain. Her leg was well on its way to healed, but it would be another ten or twelve hours before it would be able to fully bear her weight. Limping and cursing, Ori dragged her protesting body to the sink. The foul-tasting water, still icy, at least slaked her thirst and took the edge off her hunger.

Unable to bear the stench of the mattress again, she slumped into a corner, as far away from the stinking foam as possible, the cold metal walls eating through her thin overalls.

Get to the infirmary.

A straightforward goal, made almost impossible by Twari. She'd hoped that the last fight, responsible for more broken bones than just the femur, would be sufficient reason, but the captain had ordered her returned to her cell. The hard truth was she might have to risk everything — to lose — and accept the possibility of permanent damage, or death.

The idea that Twari might again refuse her medical help and abandon her for days or weeks in the dark while her blood and tears and waste soaked into the lump of foam, terrified her, and it took far too long for the neuro-suppressors to return her to some level of calm. Her reliance on them was a weakness she couldn't afford. And while she lay helpless, the medic might change his mind, or be replaced. His continued cooperation couldn't be relied on, bought with the only currency she possessed — her body. Every sordid encounter, every abuse, ate away at her, leaving nothing behind but her hatred and growing despair. She had to escape, and accept she might die in the attempt.

Despite her training, Ori felt her resolve weaken. Why was she spared in that last engagement, instead of being ejected into the unforgiving vacuum as the enemy ripped her ship apart? Why hadn't the ship jumped in time? She'd felt the drives engage in those last desperate minutes searching for survivors. And the most important question of all — where in this vast galaxy was home?

Home. The virtual icon nestled in the corner of her visual interface. Unlike all the others, still pulsing red, or glowing amber, this icon resembled time-worn silver. Behind it lay digital memory; precise, date-stamped, unyielding data, every second of her existence recorded. With one mental nudge, she could be with her siblings again, but the memory she needed didn't reside in the quantum computer embedded in her brain. In those first few years of training, you learned fast how to hide the precious, or the forbidden, in the tenuous network of organic memory, imprecise and fluid, and inaccessible to the monitors. The cold, dark cell disappeared, the pain ebbed away as Ori held the memory to herself like a flame.

The animals were hairy and brown with large yellow spots, and their long tails flicked back and forth, chasing the tiny flies gathered in clouds around them. In the memory she holds out her hand, her chubby fingers clutching a piece of fruit, the beasts nuzzling at the treat with noses as soft as velvet. Their big brown eyes regard her with no fear as their tongues chase the sticky juice across her tiny palms.

Tszcienna laughing. It was the only time she ever heard him laugh. He asked her what they smelled like and she had struggled with the concept. "They smell...warm?" she'd said, and feared this was another test and she had failed.

"Warm is a perfect description," he'd replied, picking her up and enfolding her in his arms.

There were three guards this time, all armed with stun sticks, their fingers hovering close to the triggers. They herded her through the drab, green-gray corridors leading past the infirmary to the innocuously named training room. Ori slowed as much as she dared as they passed the infirmary doors, earning a vicious jab to the ribs, but infrared only revealed a body heat signature, which told her nothing.

Another warning jab forced her into the brightly lit training room. The arena took up two-thirds of the long rectangular room, bits of plaster flaking off the poorly rendered stonework where they'd torn down the dividing wall. Thick black bars disappeared into the floor and ceiling, forming a circle over ten meters in diameter, with a floor of syntheplaz matting. The guards clustered around the arena like flies on a corpse, jostling and yelling; the insults escalating to the particular and the obscene as soon as they caught sight of her.

"My money's on the fucking bot," the guard said, as he shoved Ori through the arena gate and slammed it shut behind her. "Going to be sweet, watching it take you apart."

She ignored him, taking up her position on the mat, the glare of the overhead lighting casting sharp-edged shadows across the mat. The forfeit line, marked in fresh black paint, stood out against the worn and stained matting under her bare feet. This would be her third fight in eleven days, and despite Twari giving her over fifty hours to recover, a bone-deep weariness enveloped her, beyond the abilities of her neuro-chemical enhancements to alleviate.

The crowd noise grew into a roar as the bot lowered into position, bobbing on its anti-grav field, the sensor ring set into the matte silver-and-blue casing already feeding real-time tracking to the house AI. Instead of weapons, the bot now sported two articulated pincers. Hadn't she destroyed this one last time? No, this was the bot from four fights ago – she recognized the knife score down the left side, back when they'd still allowed her a weapon. The lazy animals hadn't bothered painting over the gouge. Twari passed the engineered graphene fighting staff through the bars and the bot grasped its almost two-meter length tightly.

The guards pressed close, yelling insults and obscenities while Twari worked the crowd, collecting bets, and slapping backs. After all these years, weren't they getting tired of the spectacle? At a sign from the captain, everyone hushed.

"Begin," one of Twari's henchmen yelled.

The word scarcely left his mouth before the bot flew across the mat, guard high, the staff raised above its ovoid body. The weapon hissed through the air, missing her by millimeters, cracking into the mat with a sound like gunshot. Ori rolled to one side, only to be forced to leap in the opposite direction as the staff slammed down again.

Without a weapon, her only strategy was to keep as much distance between herself and the bot as she raced across the arena, the machine in close pursuit, the slight hum of its field almost lost in the shouts of the crowd.

The line of black came into view and she dropped to the mat, flattening herself, exhaling as the anti-grav field passed over her prone body, squeezing the last breath out of her. Moving at such speed, the bot failed to compensate and slammed into the bars, the entire edifice shaking with the impact. Ori swung up and around, her foot describing a lethal curve, slamming into the bot before the machine had a chance to recover, its shielding crackling red. It fell back to the edge, wobbling erratically, the hum not quite as smooth as before.

It came at her again, the rod slashing at her, the rush of its passing ruffling her hair, missing her skull only by luck, as the staff hissed by in an inhuman blur.

The mechanoid turned, faster than any human opponent, attacking without respite now. Twice Ori landed a strike, catapulting her opponent across the mat and into the bars again, to the shouts and yells of the crowd.

The staff blurred through the air, sweeping to take out her legs. She hit the floor and rolled but the maneuver took her too close to the edge and she stumbled into the bars, only to recoil in agony as a guard rammed his stun stick into her leg.

For long moments the bot chased her back and forth across the arena, as Ori repeatedly pushed it to the forfeit line, but each time the AI avoided the trap and escaped. She swore she could feel its anger at being thwarted. Sweat glued her clothes to her body and left treacherous patches on the mat, so she had to watch both her footing and the bot.

The yelling rose as the crowd became impatient; now if she got too close, the guards thrust their stun sticks through the bars, uncaring whether they hit her or the machine. The bot took a charge and wobbled back across the arena, sensor lights flashing as it adjusted.

In the desperate seconds it took for the machine to regroup, Ori weighed and discarded all the available strategies. Her systems screen flicked into view, activating the sub-dermal armor, the graphene mesh running sharp and prickly under her skin as it hardened. Apart from her speed, and skill in hand-to-hand fighting, the armor remained her last and only defense. She rushed the machine, her body a blur of motion, giving no quarter, pressing the bot relentlessly as the AI fought to adjust.

Now

Her foot came down on the slick, wet patch, sliding out from under her as she lost traction. The intended strike missed completely. One of the guards yelled a warning, far too late.

The bot spun, fast and deadly; its stave smashed into her side, only the mesh preventing her rib cage from shattering. For an instant, agony rendered her paralyzed, deaf and blind with pain.

Not quite long enough, however, to save the bot. In pressing its advantage, the mechanoid left itself vulnerable; she was inside its guard. Her hand shot out, fingers wrapping around the metal arms, severing one of the pincers, and sending the stave spiraling through the air to land in her palm with an audible smack.

She struck down with the staff; through the shielding, through the battered casing, to bury it in the machine's core in a shower of sparks, and the bot crashed to the mat, dead.

Whoops of excitement and groans of defeat ran around the room, depending on which of them the guards had placed bets on.

"Right, out," Twari ordered, motioning his men into position. "You know the drill." The door swung open, and she stepped out, her hands laced at the back of her head. The others kept their weapons trained on her every second — they'd learned quickly not to take chances.

"See, Salber? Told you it could take out the bot. Pay up," said Twari, to the new guard, a tall, brown-haired man with a slight trace of an Orchetti accent. Evidently, he hadn't been informed about Twari and his little business ventures, as he stared at Ori with a mix of anger and bewilderment.

"Still say it's a trick," Salber said. "No one should be able to take out a bot at that setting, and with no weapon." He pulled his sheet out from a pocket, thumbed the interface to active and poked at the transparent syntheglass for a few seconds, with angry jabbing motions.

"Yeah, well it can. You remember that, in case you start getting all sympathetic," said Twari, grinning. As captain and in charge of this prison, the twin privileges of both running the betting pool and fleecing the newbies were his — a situation he took full advantage of.

"There, done," the newbie replied, in a tone of restrained aggrievement.

Twari grinned and gave the other guard a friendly punch on the arm. Dark, thickset and cold-eyed, Twari was an ex-Imperial Guard, although the Imperium had ceased existence as a political entity nearly three hundred years ago, destroyed by the Great War and subsequently replaced by the Republic. They kept the Guard though, and a few other reminders of lost glory, holdovers from an empire long gone.

Guarding her was his punishment — as it was for all these animals, these eijen, who tormented and abused her during her imprisonment. Dismissed from the Guard for a range of disciplinary issues, they ended up here, in this remote house, and under the control of the Directorate of Protection, to be her jailers. Some took out their resentment on her; some, like Twari, used it to make money.

For Twari, torturing her was merely a perk.

"Never take your eyes off it," Twari continued, gesturing toward where she stood with blood soaking into her clothes, "and never underestimate what it can do. You'll live longer than some previous guards."

The suddenly much poorer Salber frowned but wisely kept his opinions to himself.

Perhaps this one might be amenable to some manipulation? Over the last week, his covert glances had begun to morph into outright staring, followed by his embarrassment at having been caught watching her. He looked like a possible candidate; her last conquest disappeared months ago. The guards were often easy to suborn, but their usefulness was all too limited. Only Twari and the medics had sufficient authority to be useful. Twari was immune to seduction — he took what he wanted. The medics were unpredictable and transient.

She often wondered if they shot them or only imprisoned them; either way, they were better off than she was. Warnings populated her vision; blood loss, nerve damage, pain — all beyond her abilities to control. Now she had to wait, and hope.

"What about her?" Salber asked. "Shouldn't we call in the medic?" He kept giving her sideways glances, half fear, half interest.

In answer, Twari peeled the blood-soaked shirt away from her body. She didn't need to imagine the damage; the pain was beginning to blot out all rational thought.

Keep your head down, be good, don't antagonize them. Please, just let them take me to the medic.

"Nah, waste of time," he said, deliberately lifting the shirt higher, exposing her breasts. Salber blushed bright red at the violation. "A couple of days and you won't even see the scar." Twari poked the muzzle of his weapon into her side and white-hot pain shot through her, vision blackening at the edges, consciousness sliding away. "Only a scratch for it, isn't it, bitch," he continued, grinning at her.

No. No, I can't go back to the cell. They have to take me to the infirmary today.

She fixed Twari with a look of absolute contempt. "Get your hands off me, filth."

Two

The scarlet drops splattered onto the worn synthecrete floor as her toes smeared a wavering line from the training room, along the hallways, to the infirmary.

Consciousness became an elusive concept, sliding in and out in sync with the waves of pain. The restraints holding her arms behind her back bit deeply into both wrists, a counterpoint to the crunching shift of broken bones and the unceasing trail of blood. Her head swung, hanging between Salber on one side, and the fat eijen Adlai on the other, although she could only see Salber's feet in a blood-tinged blur of burst blood vessels. Adlai she perceived only by his grunting and muttered cursing, her left eye now swollen closed, weeping its own contribution to her bloody progress. The interface still worked, although nearly every peripheral strobed red, and a constant stream of system warnings scrolled across her screens. She'd stopped reading the damage report after the second page.

Behind her, in the training room, Twari continued to bellow threats and orders with equal intensity, as booted feet clattered back and forth amid the voices raised in fear and panic.

If you listened carefully, you could still hear the screaming.

The infirmary doors swung open at their approach, too slowly for Adlai's temper. He slammed the door back with a crash, jerking her body, bones grinding on bones, her barely suppressed scream eliciting a snort of amusement from the fat eijen.

The floor changed, the scarlet line of blood scribing itself across smooth white tiles, reflecting the bright lighting. Their little group came to a stop. Adlai let her drop, and Salber, with a yelp of surprise, couldn't prevent her headlong crash onto the infirmary floor.

When she struggled back up to consciousness, with a throbbing head to add to the rest of her injuries, a raging argument was underway. Someone, the voice unfamiliar, was yelling at the guards.

"What in the name of the Blessed Mother are you doing?" the voice demanded.

A male voice, Ori concluded after a few seconds. The medic. She had made it, she had succeeded. Now she only had to wait until he dismissed these two and she would be free. She lay perfectly still, feigning unconsciousness, her one barely functioning eye taking in an expanse of white tiles and one set of boots.

Stay awake, stay conscious. Soon, soon.

"Fuck off, medic," retorted Adlai. "This fucking thing just killed three of our mates and injured the captain. It ripped Fergo's arm off. I should have kicked its fucking head in."

"I don't know how the previous medic handled things," the voice replied, "but I will not tolerate such mistreatment, regardless of the provocation. This is inhumane."

It isn't him. It isn't his voice. It isn't him.

In response, Adlai's boot landed in Ori's side; the sub-dermal mesh absorbing most of the impact. "The captain's orders are for you to patch it up. Those Imperial pricks will be here in two days to take it away. I hope it's an execution. Something slow. I'd pay to see that." He punctuated this statement with a precise glob of sputum landing mere millimeters from Ori's nose.

If it isn't him, what do I do? How do I escape?

"Where are the other injured? I'll need to assess their injuries."

Whoever this medic was, he certainly wasn't backing down. Ori had never heard anyone stand up to the guards like this.

"You're here," Adlai said, contempt in every syllable, "to keep it alive." The kick this time was harder. Staying silent, staying conscious took every shred of strength she possessed. "Our people are being evacuated. To a proper medic, who isn't a fuck-up or deregistered or whatever your story is."

"I'd have a better chance of keeping her alive if you stopped kicking her, and I can't treat her in restraints. Take them off."

"Fuck you, medic. The damned thing will kill you without blinking," Ori heard Salber say from the other side. "You've no idea what it can do. It ripped them apart, right in front of me. The training room is a slaughterhouse. You know what it is, it doesn't deserve your kindness."

"She can't kill me, she's unconscious. I'll take full responsibility, and I'll decide who does and doesn't deserve kindness."

Do not give up. This one may be just as corrupt. Stay conscious.

She lost the thread of the argument as Salber and Adlai debated the consequences of releasing her. Finally, with obvious contempt, Adlai complied — but not without one final kick. Blood filled her mouth as she bit down hard to suppress any sound.

"We've warned you, medic. If it pulls your arms right out of your sockets, it'll serve you right," the fat eijen said, laughing and spitting obscenities when the medic asked for help to lift her. The infirmary doors slammed shut behind them, and Ori was alone with the stranger.

A hand rested gently on her shoulder. "You can move now," he said, "they've gone."

Ori froze, waiting. What would this new medic do? What price would he extract for his silence, or his help?

"Unconscious bodies don't tense up when they drop, and you flinched slightly when I touched you," he explained. "Can you stand? Do you understand me?" the medic added, uncertainly.

"I understand you, I can speak Standard," she said, levering herself up enough to bring the medic within the range of her one functioning eye. He was younger than the previous medic; much shorter, and rounder, with a mass of dark curls. Soft flesh padded out a face of high cheekbones and a pointed chin. He spoke Standard like some of the officers and handlers she'd run into over the years, all rounded vowels and clipped sentences. The Central AI provided her with an extensive database of all the Republic's major languages; however, it took a few days to reach full fluency.

"Clever. They would never have released me if they knew I was conscious." She took his arm and, with his help, rose unsteadily to her feet. "*Ikoulos,*" she muttered, as the room swung around her in sudden vertigo, forcing her to clutch at him. She expected him to push her away, but instead he slid his arm around her, taking her weight.

"Come over here," the new medic said. "Lie down on the scanner bed."

She had to know. Before she took another step, she had to know whether it had all been worthwhile.

"Where is the other one?" she demanded, unmoving. It was possible the other medic was here, somewhere. Or might return.

"The other one? You mean the previous medic?" He was struggling to hold her; she was much taller than the average citizen, and he was too short. "It's all right, my name is Keren. I don't know about anyone else, sorry. I only started a few weeks ago." He moved his arm for a better grip, hastily shifting his hand when she jerked away.

"You have been here for weeks?" No, that could not be right. He was lying.

"I'm qualified," he said, sounding defensive. "I'm sorry your regular medic isn't here."

"Weeks," she repeated, to herself. "Weeks. For nothing."

"I'm sorry, I don't understand, please come over to the scanner, lie down."

She didn't answer him immediately, instead pulling away. "Leave me alone. I don't need your help," she said, swaying on her feet.

"Yes, you do," he said firmly. "You have numerous injuries— "

The words died on his tongue as she slammed him into the infirmary wall, her hand tightening around his throat, her bloodstained fingers digging into his soft flesh.

"I have been waiting for weeks," she said, the anger and fear boiling to the surface, "and instead of him, I get you. Where is he?" She looked around the infirmary, as if hoping he might materialize, but it was unchanged from all the other times she'd been here.

The scanner bed still occupied most of the space, its head against one wall, the little cart packed with supplies parked beside it, the desk and a worn chair in the corner. The bank of cabinets, in too-bright polished steel filled the opposite wall, and between them ran a bench with a sink, and the one high, narrow window, triple locked, barred and monitored, overlooking the overgrown garden. But no medic.

"Please," he managed to choke out, "I don't know anything." She loosened her grip a little, and he drew in a desperate gulp of air. "Tell me what you want, and maybe I can help." She caught his desperate glance toward the AI monitoring point.

"The machine will not help you," she said. "The medics bribe the guards generously to disable the cameras."

All that time wasted. The pain, the humiliation, the despair. For nothing. Had that other medic been lying the whole time? Had she put her entire trust in a lying, filthy eijen? The warnings from her system were getting more strident as the blood now dripped from her sodden clothing and coalesced into a pool around her. She let him go and the medic slid to the floor, panting with fear.

"I don't know what happened to the previous medic. I'm sorry," he said, dragging himself upright, and massaging his throat. "You're in danger of bleeding out, the longer you hold me. I can help. Let me help."

Her arm fell to her side as the world spun, consciousness sliding away.

"Let's get you up on the bed," he said, catching her as her legs crumpled, the effort of staying upright beyond her.

Ori let him take her weight, despair crushing her. "Do not pretend sympathy. You are still my enemy." Now she would have to start again. Right now, it was simply too great a task.

Just let go.

"I'm not your enemy. I'm here to treat you," he said, huffing at the effort of helping her up on the scanning bed.

"Why do you care?" She sank back on the pillows, unable to stifle the gasp of pain. "Tell me you do not work for the Directorate and I may reassess your status."

Still puffing a little, he unfolded a light cover and draped it over her. "It's hardly a secret, and working for the Directorate of Protection doesn't make me an enemy," he said, pulling the little medical cart closer. He rummaged around in the drawers before retrieving two pain patches, stripping off their coverings. As he moved to apply them, she caught his wrist, making him jump.

"You are here to put me back together, just enough so I am useful for Twari's schemes. And since when have medics been permitted those?" She nodded at the pain relief. "You risk punishment for me?"

He frowned in confusion. "What punishment?" His face cleared, becoming dark with anger. "Did they withhold pain relief? I'm the medic, I'll decide how to treat you. And I will speak to Captain Twari about your treatment in this facility later."

After a second, she dropped her hand and let him apply the patches, one above each fold of her elbow. What did it matter? Let him explain his disobedience to Twari. This medic was delusional if he thought the captain would pay any attention to his protests. The pain began to ebb away, replaced by the rising wave of sedatives and muscle relaxants.

The scanner activated, the faintly bluish beam passing up and down her body. Beside her, the medic watched the progress on his sheet, his frown deepening as the images appeared.

"Blessed Mother," he said, incredulously, "how did you survive with so few internal injuries? You should be dead."

"Yes, they all react the same, the first time. Do none of you read the briefing material?" she said, "Or look at the previous scans at all?"

"I. I didn't believe it. I thought it was some sort of joke. Or something. It's not possible."

There were always a few who didn't believe, even when the evidence was staring them in the face. One medic had run screaming from the infirmary, insane with fear. She had been able to hear him, babbling hysterically, all the way down the hallway, until one of the guards put an end to it.

"This," he said, pushing the sheet into her one-eyed field of vision, and pointing to the thoracic region of her skeleton. "Does the two extra pairs of ribs give you greater lung capacity?"

"And room for all the rest of the hardware," she said, with a laugh halfway between pain and derision. If this eijen didn't hurry up, she would bleed out here on this bed. He could try explaining that to the Xi.

"I'm sorry, you aren't a science experiment. I forgot my manners," he said, administering a professionally reassuring pat. "If you're ready, I can start repairing the damage." He selected a medi-scalpel from the tray beside him, adjusted the settings and began cutting away her clothing.

Perhaps she could gain further assistance if she engaged his interest in her enhancements. "Give me the sheet," she said, motioning with her other hand.

The medic considered her for a moment, clearly wary of her motives, before handing her the sheet.

"Enhanced lymphatic and endocrine systems, carbon-fiber reinforcement of the bones and cartilage," she explained, flicking the image around with effortless dexterity. "An entire chemical factory staffed by nanites, regulating my blood, filling me with neuro-enhancers or suppressors. Whatever is required."

He glanced at the pain patches.

"Everything except pain blockers," she said with bitterness, pushing the sheet back at him. "The Xi said it was beyond their ability to repair that function."

"You don't believe them?" he asked, wiping the smears of blood off the synthe-glass screen.

No, she didn't believe them, but self-delusion had never been part of her character either. The truth was Ori had given both the Hubnae and the Xi more than enough justification for their actions.

She owed her rescue and consequent survival to the Hubnae, although she hadn't understood that the time. When consciousness returned, Ori had found herself in a strange room, connected to unfamiliar machines and surrounded by black, slug-like creatures with twinkling gems embedded in their thick, glistening hides. Her reaction, under the circumstances, was understandable.

The Hubnae had not seen it that way, especially after the third escape attempt. They were a peaceful race, they explained, their huge, all-black eyes regarding her mournfully.

We don't have cells strong enough to hold you, and we don't approve of judicial murder. We will send you to our allies, the Xi. They have both cells and executions. Take our advice: Do not test their patience.

"It's convenient if you want your torture to be effective." She hadn't listened to the Hubnae advice. The Xi indeed had cells. And skilled torturers.

"I was told the Xi captured your ship. They said you attacked first."

"If I had come to this sector voluntarily," she said, half rising from the bed, her voice swelling in anger, "I would be with my fleet, and you and all the rest of the Republic, and the Xi, and the Hubnae, would be dead or enslaved." Ori slumped back, emotion draining out of her as the powerful medications overwhelmed her. So now would come the lecture on the Republic's strength, or anger at her criticism. She braced herself for the inevitable retaliation.

Instead, he patted the cover back over her. "So, you haven't told me your name," he said, his tone light and conversational as the tiny laser sliced away the blood-soaked cloth.

Ori stared at him, confused.

Does this one think he can win me over by pretending friendship?

"You are eijen, an animal. You should address me as aoteh."

An infuriating smile quirked one corner of his mouth. "I'm guessing that's master or something similar. Well, this eijen animal is looking after you, so maybe you might make an exception?"

The silence stretched out as he removed sections of fabric. She watched him warily, unsure of how to approach this one; he was so unlike any of the previous medics. She made a sound that would be a sigh in anyone else.

"You are not afraid of me. Not like the others."

"You haven't met my mother," the little man said, with another smile, but Ori saw the brief flash of pain underneath.

"You would not understand my Line designation, and I do not give my private name to eijen. The Xi call me Oryelle Tey."

He nodded, as if he understood. "So, what should I call you?"

"Ori is close enough," she said, struggling against the pull of sedation. To rest, to sleep. Warm and safe. She could, with a thought, sweep the sedatives out of her system, but she lacked the time and the knowledge to differentiate between them and the painkillers. What did it matter what he called her? She knew who she was.

"And you, medic. What did you do?" she asked, curiosity warring with drowsiness. "Are you deregistered, disgraced, as the fat eijen said? They only use those they have power over. I know what they have on the guards. What do they have over you?"

Keren didn't answer at first, it looked like he was trying to find the right words. "The usual. Drugs. Inappropriate relationships. With students."

"You don't look the type," she pronounced, a little surprised.

A piece of bloodstained cloth hit the floor and he peeled back the remains of her shirt.

"Let me see," she demanded, shifting awkwardly on the bed.

Keren gently pushed her back down and handed her the sheet. With a few flicks, Ori found the images from the scanner.

The extent of the damage made her wince. The staff had come in from the left, its impact leaving a long, deep mark at an oblique angle to her ribs, rising toward her back. A bloody rupture, where the skin split open, marked the center of the strike. Either side of the injury the flesh swelled, black and purple, weeping blood along the edges. This had been meant to kill. Anyone else would be dead, their rib cages a mass of splintered bone and mangled flesh, their lungs destroyed. It had been a calculated risk to allow the hit, one she now realized was pointless and ill judged. Like many of her decisions over the years. Keren caught the sheet as it slipped from her hand, returning it to the cart.

"Is there a type?" he asked. As the laser scalpel cut through what remained of her clothing, he pulled the cover up to maintain some privacy for her.

She nodded slowly. "Oh yes," she said, wiping a string of blood and snot with the back of her hand. "There have been more than one through here. So, they said they would make it all go away if you did this?"

Keren made a noise of irritation and grabbed her hand, wiping away the mess. Startled by this solicitousness, Ori didn't pull away.

"No. They said they would make it all disappear for my brother."

"Your brother? Ah, see. I knew you weren't the type." It pleased her to be proved correct. "You risk much for him," she said. Didn't he grasp that the Directorate would never let him leave this house alive? What guarantee did he have they would keep their word?

The little medic laid down the scalpel and selected a large, hand-held tissue regeneration unit. Without pain blockers or large doses of sedatives, the repair of extensive injuries like her own was excruciating; she had endured more than her fair share of such treatments. This time, the combination of sufficient pain relief, and the medic's skillful touch, healed her ravaged flesh almost instantly. When he was done with each section, a pale red scar was the only trace of her injuries, which her own systems would eliminate in hours.

"I don't expect you to understand," he murmured, intent on his work.

"I understand family," she answered, fighting through the fog of medication. "I have a family, a Line. Just because it does not conform to your idea of it does not make it less."

He took a half step back, startled by her anger.

How dare this animal dismiss her like this? Her people had demonstrated their superiority against countless lesser civilizations. Cleansing the galaxy of the eijen filth was a sacred duty; Ori, and all her siblings had been part of the vast military machine tasked with accomplishing that task. The breeding centers turned out thousands, hundreds of thousands, like her, every day.

"So, you are from a cell line? That's what you said. Cell lines are like clones."

"I am not a clone," she snapped. "The clones are stupid, bred for strength and obedience. I am a Command Line, designed to lead."

Millions of warrior clones were incubated, force-grown, and imprinted with sufficient knowledge to follow orders. An enormous army of obedient organic machines, who would not question, or doubt or rebel.

"I'm sorry," he said. And she could see he was genuine, or at least thought himself so. "I have no right to judge; my family barely qualifies as functional on a good day."

"Is he guilty? Your brother?" Ori knew enough about Republican justice to estimate his brother's crimes were considered quite serious.

The regeneration unit turned in his hands; Ori saw again a spasm of pain pass across the medic's face.

"He is. I know he is. But— "

Beside him, the sheet pinged, the sound sharp in the quiet of the infirmary. "Sorry, I have to check my sheet," he said, pulling the cover up to her chin and stepping away from the scanner bed.

Ori nodded again, closing her eyes, and letting herself sink into chemical lassitude, a blissful cessation of all the despair and fear, at least temporarily.

The medic made a little noise, and her eyes flew open. The sheet clattered to the floor; his face white.

"It appears I also need to check the neural port."

Neuro-enhancers swirled through her bloodstream flushing away the soothing, deceiving sedation. The sub-dermal armor activated, running hard and prickly under her skin, the flash of pain under her barely healed rib cage ignored. The scanner head bit into her back as she pressed herself against the wall, hands clenched, the bed covering crumpling under her. She would not submit without a fight.

"No, Ori, it's all right." He reached out, his palms towards her in a gesture he thought must be reassuring. "I'm not going to do a scan. I promise."

"You lie," she screamed at him. "You all lie. They will make you do it." She recoiled from him, her head snapping back and forth as she sought an escape route. "You will do it; the monsters will make you."

"It's all right." He stepped away, arms still outstretched, his voice low and calming, as if he spoke to an animal, or a frightened child. "I will only check the port remains intact, that's all. I promise."

She did not believe him. None of the others ever cared, they all lied, seeing her as nothing more than a thing. A thing you could hurt, or abuse or experiment on, without consequences. For who in the Republic would care about the fate of one such as her?

"Here." She flung the cover off. "Take what you want. You eijen are all the same."

He took another step back, until he was up against the opposite bench, and shook his head, averting his eyes from her naked body. "No. I'm going to stay over here. I won't touch you or come closer until you are comfortable."

His response confused her. Previous medics had either taken advantage of her vulnerability or simply called for the guards to subdue her. "Why?"

"I'm not a monster," he said. "I've seen the feeds from previous attempts. I didn't believe they were real at the time. Now I know." He paused, looking stricken. "It is inconceivable cruelty to subject anyone to such abuse. And I won't use this position to inflict more pain on you, regardless of what they say you are."

"And what did they say?" she asked, torn between curiosity and derision. "Do they say the word? Or do they skirt around it, too terrified to utter it, even to themselves?"

"They said engineered. Enhanced. Augmented. Not, not the other," he answered, quietly.

"Abomination." The Republic's last, and only, taboo. On some worlds, to express any admiration or sympathy for the long-extinct engineered might bring a substantial fine, or imprisonment.

She leaned forward, watching to see how he would react. Salber was right. She could kill him without hesitation if she chose. He was frightened, she could see it, but despite his fear, he hadn't called the guards back, or attempted to coerce her, or drug her. Was this the mistake she had been waiting for? Had the Directorate finally blackmailed the wrong person?

She shifted forward, slowly, carefully, alert for betrayal, but the little medic stayed unmoving on the other side of the room until at last she reached the edge of the bed, her hands in her lap, letting her legs dangle off the end. "You wish only to look?" Her bloodstained feet swung back and forth with nervous energy.

"Yes. I promise. No scan. I won't touch you or do anything unless I have your permission."

She regarded him for a long while, assessing him. "So, look." She shifted around on the bed, letting her legs hang over the opposite side so her back was toward him. His footsteps sounded behind her, hesitant and soft, and she half flinched as Keren touched her left shoulder, the reflex aborted as she asserted control.

"I'm going to touch the back of your neck. Yes?" It took all her courage to meekly nod and bow her head. He pressed on each cervical vertebrae, making his way methodically from the base of her skull. "Here?" he asked. "This space between C3 and 4?"

"Yes. If that is what you call them," she said, as his fingers lingered, brushing over her skin. This she understood. No matter what they said, it always came to this eventually.

"You have been kind," she said, her voice soft. "You heard what the guards said. The Imperial Guard will be here in two days. I have seen how the Republic dealt with the engineered, during the purges."

"I can't help you escape," he said, but his fingers remained on her skin.

"You can," she said again, more softly, turning to face him, edging closer, assessing his willingness to flout the rules. He didn't move away, although his eyes stayed resolutely above her collarbones. "You have all this equipment, drugs. You could remove the chip."

"Did the previous medic promise you freedom?" he asked. "Because he lied. It's impossible without the Directorate AI authority. It would be easier to remove your arm."

"But you are happy to see me executed? Shot? Or worse? Keren, I do not have any other options. They have taken them all away, over the years."

"I can't," he said, firmly, "it's impossible. But I do promise I will complain to whoever will listen about your treatment. I would have done it anyway. I won't stand by and see anyone mistreated."

Her shoulders slumped momentarily in defeat, then she raised her head in defiance. "I should not have expected anything better from animals."

"Let's see about fixing up the rest of the injuries." Keren moved the medical cart closer to the bed, and she noticed his hands were trembling. "Can you lay down again?"

The guards returned her to the cell with uncharacteristic restraint. The little medic refused to let her leave until every injury had been treated, even when Salber and fat Adlai demanded she be turned over to them, half-healed and naked. He had planted himself between her and them, a short, round man with a mass of dark curls, and defied the guards with their weapons and sneering condescension, ordering them to bring her clean clothes. She thought they would hit him or shoot him, the way their fingers twitched on their weapons, but they backed down, to return a few minutes later and toss a pile of clothes on the floor.

The door slammed shut behind her, plunging the cell into darkness again. Not that it mattered; optics flicked over to thermal imaging and the cell appeared in gray-green clarity. There would be no food for hours, so she lowered herself to the rancid mattress. There were times when she would give up everything for a blanket, to pull the cloth up over her head and hide. Hide from the guards watching her, the AI monitoring her, the Xi manipulating her.

With no reason, no explanation.

Her fingers slid across her side, probing expertly for pain, but the medic had been thorough. Only one other of these animals had ever defended her before, and such kindness disconcerted her. The shame of pleading for his help hit her, threatening to overwhelm and destroy the last shreds of her self-control. She did not need their pity, these animals who imprisoned her. Her enemies. It didn't matter anymore. They would be here in two days to take her away. The medic's promise to obtain better treatment for her was yet another attempt to manipulate her into compliance. None of these eijen could be trusted.

She sighed into the darkness and wondered if she should be glad it was ending. Ori curled up into a defensive ball, a habit acquired over her years of imprisonment, and reached down into her memories. As she slipped into drowsiness, in her imagination she was once again a small child, with Tszcienna's arms holding her.

Three

The palace AI chimed melodically. "Lord President?"

Tel Rossim dragged his attention away from the scenes below. "Yes, what is it now?" It had better not be the stupid bitch from Xi Liaison; he had enough problems to deal with today.

"You have a call from Xia."

He felt the blood drain from his face as icy tendrils of fear raced up his spine. *What the fuck do they want?* He gave significant thought, for about a nanosecond, of refusing the call, or pretending he was out, until sanity re-established itself.

Trying to avoid the Xi was pointless and possibly career-ending; he had begun to suspect his overlords were making plans to replace him. One more reason for the urgency of his scheme.

Rossim took his position in front of the desk, smoothed the silk jacket into position and took a deep breath.

The AI gave another melodious chime and the hologram sprang into life. Rossim had no idea how the Xi maintained a live, instant feed from their home world Xia, hundreds of light years away, to his office, without any degradation or lag. Generations of Republic scientists had toiled their entire lives to replicate the technology, with zero success. Questioning the Xi was another pointless exercise — they ignored any questions they didn't want to answer.

He bowed, as deeply as he thought necessary. "Great One, I am honored," he began as the hologram snapped into existence. "How can I serve— "

Across two hundred and thirty-five light years, the hologram Xi was just as, or perhaps even more terrifying than the real, live individual. The light glittered off a triangular head of black, glossy chitin with its obscene, prehensile palps of naked, translucent flesh.

"Rossim, we are busy," the Xi Matriarch answered in rasping, clicking speech. "There is a new batch of males hatched. We have decisions to make." The Matriarch loomed over him, the two back legs covered in shining silver hair, the vestigial pairs tucked under her body. Malevolent, glittering eyes stared down at him. Telling himself it was a hologram did nothing to soften the horror.

Rossim's skin crawled, imagining what those decisions might be. Xi males did not have long lives.

"My apologies, Matriarch." Rossim bowed again, lower this time, trying to hide his anger. *Fucking spiders.* "How may I serve?"

"It is about the Brightstar. We have received disturbing news."

If the thing was dead, he would have heard about it. Perhaps it had escaped? That would be perfect; he could have it killed off at last and put this nightmare behind him.

"I'm sorry, Great One," he said, bowing slightly lower, "I assure you; it is still— "

"What were your instructions?" the Matriarch demanded. "What did I say to that creeping filth, Garrett?"

Rossim froze with shock. In his six years of service to the Xi, he'd seen them amused, irritated or impatient. Never angry. And the Matriarch was not just angry, she was incandescent with rage.

"To keep her safe— "

"Yes, safe." Across more than two hundred and thirty-five light years, Rossim felt that rage. "Did I authorize torture? Did I permit rape? Does 'safe' include using her for illegal fights? You hide this information from us. From me."

The icy tendrils became a raging river of fear and he had to clench his fists to hide the shaking. *Who the fuck has betrayed me?*

"It is an Abomination, Great One," he said, keeping his voice servile, "what do you care how we treat it?"

"Abomination?" The hologram lowered herself on those monstrous legs until the horror of her face loomed over Rossim. "You use the words of children. Your Republic is here only by the barest of luck. Your continued existence rests entirely with us. We gave you specific orders. Orders you appear to have disobeyed. Ensure the Brightstar remains untouched, undamaged from now on, or I will find a Lord President who will follow orders. And I will make personally sure you will regret your disobedience."

"I'm sorry, Great One. I will obey," he said, trying to sound sincere and contrite, but the anger threatened to overtake him and he'd never been adept at hiding his emotions.

The silence dragged out. With dawning horror, he realized what the Matriarch was waiting for. He risked a quick, upward glance. Malice shone in every dark eye.

Rage and terror fought for control, freezing him in place. It took all his will to lower himself, his knees sinking into the soft rug. He kept hoping she would call an end to it, but the monster waited, towering above him in holographic obscenity. Rossim prostrated himself, extending his arms out across the bright wool, in imitation of vulnerable palps. He remembered the first time he had done this; in the Nest, cool and dark, the smell of decay, the clawed, hairy foot resting on his arm, the crack as the bone fractured. The hard, sharp agony.

One silver-haired leg moved, touching in ghostly detail onto his left arm. He kept his face pressed to the floor. Off-screen, something laughed.

"You are a servant of the Nest, Rossim. You would be wise to remember that."

"Yes, Great One." His voice shook with the effort to maintain control.

"Let us be extremely clear. Pain, pleasure, freedom, imprisonment. These are our gifts to dispense. Your job is to keep the Brightstar contained and available. That is all. Your infantile revenge fantasies do not interest us. Am I understood?"

Fucking Abomination.

"Understood, Great One."

"We will select a new Xi Liaison. Clearly, this woman Babima is useless. I want her gone. I want her to disappear into obscurity and never be seen or heard of again. Am I clear?"

"Perfectly, Great One."

"Good. You will receive new orders shortly. Do not disappoint me again."

Rossim remained prostrate until the hologram winked out, before climbing slowly to his feet, shaking with rage. "I want a full list of all traffic in and out of the safe house," he screamed at the AI. "Now."

He would find out who had been giving information to the Xi, and they would be sorry. "And get me the head of the Directorate."

Four

"**N**o!" Her scream echoed around the cell, bouncing off the gray walls and ceiling as her heart hammered hard enough to burst from her chest. The lights came on, too bright and she winced away from the harshness.

"Do you require assistance?" inquired the AI.

The words stuck in her throat. Go away, she wanted to scream, as her arms covered her head as if shielding her from an unseen assailant, every muscle rigid with terror. *Go away and leave me to die. I can't do this anymore.*

She had begged for his help, like an animal. Six days later, and her skin still crawled with shame at the memory; now she was awake and hunger gnawed at her. According to her interface, synced to Central time, it was midmorning, and in all those six days only three of the rations these animals' called food had appeared.

No, she would not give in. Not yet. Regardless of the cost, she had to keep functioning. Still shaking, Ori stumbled across the cold floor to the tiny sink and its foul water, forcing herself to drink, as her systems once again flooded her bloodstream with neuro-suppressors.

"I'm fine," she managed to rasp out, "go away." The AI didn't respond, but the lights dimmed to a soothing ambiance, an unexpected mercy. Two days, the fat one had said, and that time had come and gone. Perhaps, finally, they may simply lock her in here and forget her.

The thin mattress welcomed her back, cold sweat gluing her clothes to her body. Hours passed, as Ori drifted in the artificial calm of the suppressors, the absolute silence enclosing her.

The beast nuzzles at the treat with a nose as soft as velvet.

The door crashed open to reveal an armed contingent of the Imperial Guard in matte-black tactical armor. A faded green prison jumpsuit landed on the floor at her feet.

"Put it on," one of them ordered.

Another humiliation to add to the list. How many times did they have to see her naked body before they tired of it? Ori stripped off the dank and evil-smelling clothing and slipped into the jumpsuit. Another guard tossed her a pair of slippers. So, they were going outside. They motioned her out into the hall. A curt command, reinforced at gunpoint, told her to turn and hold her wrists together behind her back. From behind came the familiar clink of restraints, the cold harshness of the metal. The restraints tightened before another set of fingers took over as the metal bit into her skin. Blood trickled down between her fingers, slippery and warm, dripping to the gray floor.

The leg shackles came next, the guard's hands probing between her legs, fingers pressing the thin cloth into her, while the others stood around laughing.

One day you will pay for this.

They marched her through the house, along halls that went from dull, green synthecrete to faded, peeling frescoes. This had been a holiday home or country retreat she guessed; a remnant of the mighty Imperium, or some long-dead senator's estate, far enough away from the capital to be bucolically rural, but not too far from its luxuries. Sometimes Ori tried to imagine what the house used to look like. Were there painted rooms, with elegant drapes at the windows, tables of exotic woods, and seats of padded silk?

Unlikely. If the decaying hallway was anything to go by, everything beautiful and elegant had probably been ripped out of the old house decades ago, and replaced with military starkness and utility. The areas she was permitted to enter certainly fitted that description: her cell; the training room, with its barred arena; and the infirmary. Despite this, it still represented a significant improvement on her imprisonment on Xia.

Please, do not send me back there.

The one outer door opened, heavily armored and AI-monitored, and a rifle-butt propelled her out onto the drive, the gravel crunching beneath her thin slippers. Eleven months had gone, taking with it spring and summer. Orange and gold leaves skittered across the surrounding lawns, the breeze bringing the scents of long-forgotten things: rain, and earth and late-blooming flowers. The tall tree still stood in the middle of the sweep of lawn, the too-long grass under its majestic sweep of branches now covered in a deep pile of russet and purple. Ori couldn't remember the last time she'd seen spring. Three years ago?

The transport van, a featureless white rectangle on wheels, originally designed for automated parcel transport, stood sandwiched between two armored vehicles, both emblazoned with the Imperial Guard crest — another remnant from an Imperium long gone. Armed troops in matte-black tactical armor maintained a tight cordon, preventing any escape attempts.

The van door stood open to reveal the cage inside, unchanged from previous trips, its heavy mesh welded to thick bars of black-painted steel, the door barely wide enough for her to crawl through. The addition of multiple layers of reinforcing and armor plating had reduced the roomy interior to a tiny box.

A familiar figure stood awkwardly beside the van; Salber, trying unsuccessfully to look like part of the team, and sporting an impressive black eye. It seemed he had run afoul of Twari's temper, in more ways than one. Twari always selected a "victim" to ride with her, working on the principle — demonstrated more than once — that said victim would be the first to die, should she attempt another escape. From Salber's pallid face and darting, nervous expression, he was well aware of this.

I might be going to my execution, but looks like I can have some fun on the way.

"Still no blanket? Or a cushion?" she joked, as they herded her toward the van.

An old jest repeated too many times over the years. It didn't provoke a reprisal beyond another jab from the rifle, although she caught a quickly suppressed grin from Salber.

No one offered assistance — they'd only made that mistake once — as they forced her to crawl in, her knees bruising on the metal floor. The heavy mesh door swung shut behind her and the guards checked and rechecked every lock with meticulous care.

"Hands."

Twisting around in the narrow space left her with more bruises, but finally, she was in position, the restraints against the mesh. A heavy chain, with another lock, anchored her to the cage structure. She waited to see if they would tighten the restraints again, but they appeared content with this small level of cruelty.

"Well, get in," came the voice of one of the black-clad figures from behind her, "and don't fucking ask for a cushion, either. We're already running late; that fucking demonstration at the palace has stopped traffic all through the city."

Another voice chimed in. "Firing squads get cranky when they get stuffed around. They might not aim so well." Laughter all round.

"Don't I get a weapon?" Salber whined as he crammed himself into the space between the mesh and the doors, his body warmth seeping through the thin stuff of her clothing.

"Fuck, no. If it gets hold of a weapon, there's no stopping it." The doors slammed shut, plunging them both into darkness. Salber cursed and Ori heard him fumble around until a small interior light came on. The van took off sharply, tossing Salber against the doors with a satisfying thump. The AI-controlled vehicle would convey them to their destination. To her execution.

If she turned her head and pressed her cheek against the mesh, she could see half of Salber's face. "So," she said after a few minutes, giving the guard time to settle back down, "what did you do to get this duty?"

"Shut up. I was ordered not to talk to you."

"Very well. I understand obeying orders." Ori leaned back against the hard mesh and waited. The silence dragged out; Ori could almost feel the guard struggling to not speak.

"The others said you're going to be shot," Salber finally blurted out.

It was the logical end to her imprisonment. Surely the Republic must grow tired of the death toll and injuries it cost to guard her. Logic also told her they could have carried out her execution at the house with less effort and fewer witnesses. Of course, there was always the option of a public execution, a scenario she refused to entertain.

"I've been threatened enough times with execution. It appears it's happening today." In truth, Ori had never understood why they had continued to keep her alive all these years.

"You don't sound frightened about it." Salber sounded more curious than angry.

Ori shrugged, as much as the chains and restraints would allow. "I'm a soldier," she said, philosophically. "Death is always a possibility. At least I will have the satisfaction of knowing you will all join me in death."

Salber laughed. "And just how do you think you're going to kill us all, locked up and chained?"

How did they maintain a galactic empire, even one as insignificant as the Republic, with such stupid soldiers? Her Line's warrior clones were cleverer than this.

"If they execute me," she said, speaking to him as the animal he was, "what use do they have for you? All of you have seen too much to simply be let loose." She twisted around as far as her torn and bloody wrists would allow, to catch his expression. Salber's face had gone quite pale, under the bruises. "Surely you knew this?"

Five

"Lord President, Central network confirms the convoy left the house an hour ago. No issues reported," said the AI, in irritatingly musical tones.

Rossim took a deep breath and put his hand against the cool glass that was vibrating in sympathy with the noise from outside. "Well, that's something, I suppose. Inform me the moment they arrive."

"Yes, Lord President."

Rossim turned back to the window. In the square below, the demonstration in the capital had moved into its tenth day. On the side nearest the sprawling Law Courts, a seething mass of banners, holo-placards and flags replaced the quiet restraint of government workers and tourists. Rossim frowned, reading messages ranging from demands for the government intervene, to calls for the entire Senate to resign, to outright threats against Ma'al.

Hostility toward Ma'al and their supporters was growing as the escalating tensions between the Republic and the Ma'ali government began to spill over into ordinary people's lives. The imposition of visas was bad enough, but the abrupt denial of entry to Ma'al space to anyone who was not a citizen had managed to provoke a substantial portion of the ordinary citizenry to public displays of rage.

Piali Eidress, founder of Ma'al, had been a lawyer, they said, among other things. Rich, powerful, head of one of Cimmili's oldest families, with dynastic wealth going back for hundreds of years, she'd given it all up and persuaded twelve hundred men and women to follow her to an isolated, icy ball of rock, with one small landmass, no animals, few plants and little sunlight. While Admiral Danizitia's fleet rained nuclear death down on the twelve billion people of Da Chet, Piali and her followers carved out her vision of the perfect society in the lava tunnels and magma domes of Ma'al.

Nominally, legally, Ma'al and its tiny, empty system, were part of the Republic and subject to the same laws. In reality, countless Republic governments had allowed Ma'al ever greater exemptions from those same laws, to the point where Ma'al now existed as an almost independent state within the Republic.

Historians all agreed that the Ma'al colony was doomed from the beginning. The one planet in the system was a Marginal — a world trapped in eternal winter, its orbit grazing the limits of habitable distance from its star. Technology should have given the colony an extra decade, maybe two of existence, they said, before the struggle to survive underground drove all of Piali's followers back to civilization. The arrival on the market of Ma'al silk changed all that. No one had seen a textile like it before, and the fabric quickly became the preferred signifier of immense wealth, next to Polini silver. And once the potential military graphene-silk composites were apparent, Ma'al could barely keep up with the supply. The mystique surroundings its origins just made it more desirable, and the colony went from merely surviving to thriving virtually overnight.

The immense wealth generated by the silk gave Ma'al unimaginable leverage and power, which they used — with increasing regularity — to restrict movement into and out of the system. They chose which transport companies had access and had now imposed further conditions on the freighter crews, causing long delays. Sometimes Rossim wished the Ma'al colony had collapsed, and Jared Ansissi had never found the source of the silk. Piali and all her cultists would have starved to death in the dark, and the Republic would have been none the wiser.

The Senate was divided into those who had grown rich on the silk monopoly, and those who would like the same opportunity. Outside, the crowds steadily increased, mainly students and other concerned citizens. It had been noisy, but generally peaceful — the few minor clashes were more to do with large crowds herded together rather than real animosity.

Of course, Ma'al had its supporters, from those who romanticized the culture to the point of fetish, a few who were concerned about the legal and moral implications, and finally those who made a profession of opposing whatever was popular on any given subject. Palace security patrolled around the edges, barricades keeping the crowd corralled and segregated according to political allegiances. There had already been clashes between the many groups; nothing major, a few insults hurled, followed by the occasional fist. AI-controlled drones from palace security flittered overhead, fighting the news feeds for airspace.

On this side, closest to the palace itself, the crowd consisted of mainly soberly dressed citizens. In one corner, a small group held up "One Republic", "No Exceptions" and

"Throw Them Out" placards, waving them defiantly at a nearby Ma'al supporters' group, wearing faux plaits and cheap silver house rings in homage or imitation of their idols and carrying "We Love Ma'al" signs, adorned with bright, glittery hearts.

Rossim viewed them all with equal derision. He would like nothing better than to shut the entire thing down and clear the square, but the Senate continually overruled him. There had to be some semblance of democracy, at least, where public actions were concerned, the Speaker of the Senate advised him. Anyway, it suited Rossim's purposes to have public feeling running so high. The populace was so much easier to manage when frightened or angry.

He sighed and strode back to his desk. His sheet still lay where he'd thrown it, the end of its trajectory marked by a long gouge in the priceless frescoes. Palace maintenance would be all over him for that. He stared balefully at the sheet for a few minutes, before retrieving it and tossing the clear syntheglass sheet back onto his desk. Despite its treatment, the sheet remained undamaged, the message still perfectly readable. Why did the Xi want the abomination sent there? The timing was too perfect to be coincidence — they were just starting to get results.

"Fucking Xi. Treacherous fucking spiders," he muttered and followed it up with an obscenity of requisite vileness. He forced himself back into calmness, fighting down the impulse to embed the sheet in one of the walls again. Nearly a year of planning could be in jeopardy now.

And on top of everything else he had the new Xi Liaison to deal with.

"Is Reinnor here?" The Matriarch threw the last leg to the pack of squealing males, who leaped on it, chattering angrily at each other as they fought over the scraps. This hatching looked promising; strong, aggressive, virile. One bold male tried climbing her, squeaking excitedly, begging for sex. She swatted him across the chamber, into the enclosing webs, where he scuttled off, chattering in outrage.

"Yes, he is waiting outside. I have put him in the main corridor. So far, he has not fled." First Sister bent her triangular, chitinous head to observe the males at play, their excited chitters rising and falling as they scurried among the webs.

"I'm surprised he made it this far. He might actually be of use. Better than the last one, selected by that incompetent Rossim." The Xi Liaison was simply one more in a long line of bureaucrats the Nest had seen come and go over the centuries. Normally, incumbents were either incredibly ambitious or they had been posted to Xia because someone in the higher levels of the Republic government was seriously annoyed with them. The situation now demanded a different approach.

"Intelligence suggests our Lord President is plotting something; we are monitoring the network," First Sister said, as the males squabbled over the last morsels of their former Nest-mate. The Nest did not tolerate weaklings. "It is perhaps time to replace him, given this latest failure. Did he really think he could hide such behavior from us?"

"If I could, I would rip his head from his body and feed him to the children." The Matriarch wiped her sensitive prehensile palps on the cloth a servile junior handed her. "The problem is he succeeded, and we would not have known except for the medic. We — I — trusted his fear to keep him compliant. Now his anger will drive him to greater disobedience in retaliation."

First Sister made an obscene gesture with one foreleg. "It would not be the first time we have removed an inconvenient president. I doubt anyone would miss him."

"Unfortunately, with the current instability across the Republic, we can't be precipitous. They need order, and for all his many deficiencies, Rossim can provide that. There will be plenty of time to remove him once the Brightstar is successful," said the Matriarch, taking the time to swat the junior too slow to catch the used cloth. "Although this limited operation skirts dangerously close to violating the accord. But this is the only way we can give them a chance. I won't stand by and watch another civilization swept away while we do nothing." As the disciplined junior female limped away, clutching one of her palps, the Matriarch returned her attention to First Sister.

"It is your decision, Great One," First Sister said, "and you still command a majority in the Nest, but when our allies discover the truth, their anger will be truly terrible."

The Matriarch gazed across the restless webs and the young males, and sighed. "I know. But she was my friend. I made a promise. Send in Reinnor, and let us hope this time luck favors us."

Jak Reinnor tugged his jacket of pale green watered silk into position for the third time in as many minutes and ran through the breathing exercises the psych tech had recommended — with precious little improvement. He should have taken the posting on

Central instead of letting his ambition get the better of him. Coming here to the eternal gloom of Xia, surrounded by the webs, shifting and heaving with the scuttling inhabitants of the Nest, bordered on insanity. But he wanted to be Lord President more than he'd ever wanted anything else, and the quickest way was as Xi Liaison — the highest diplomatic position in the Republic, despite what some naysayers proclaimed.

Monstrous females, three times his height, stalked past, their glossy black hair shimmering in the dim light brought down from the uninhabitable surface nearly a kilometer above him. The males were the worst. Mindless beasts, forever searching for food or sex; they used all their legs, having never developed the ability to stand upright, which only made them more disgusting. Jak tugged fretfully at the ephemeral lace of his cuff and fervently wished this was over.

Jak couldn't remember a time when he hadn't been obsessed with the enigmatic and frankly terrifying Xi. While the rest of his siblings, half siblings, cousins and friends recreated the highlights of the Great War — including one memorable re-enactment of the destruction of Da Chet that ruined his mother's conservatory — the young Jak spent every spare moment reading and watching countless articles and feeds about the aliens. At one point the household staff wouldn't come into his room, as every surface held replicas of the distinctly spider-like race.

Although everyone called them spiders, there was always more than one "Xi expert" who would point out their evolutionary history aligned more with marine arthropods rather than arachnids, although the Xi themselves made no commentary on such theories. Jak supposed a race several million years old may not remember what their ancestors were. Or care. A mature female could grow to over three meters tall, with the two primary back legs covered in thick black hair that aged to silver-gray, two sets of vestigial legs held tucked up under a bulbous abdomen, a set of forelegs, and the naked, translucent palps that functioned as elongated fingers.

Inanimate models and e-feeds were one thing, but the reality of the Nest proved to be too much. For the past two days he'd barely left his room in the laughingly named "Visitor's Center": a squat collection of buildings at the edge of the Nest. Apart from the diplomatic staff, a few hardy academics, and himself, the center remained empty. Those tourists who made it as far as the viewing platform, conveniently situated off the arrivals lounge, took one look at the heaving, restless webs and their scuttling inhabitants, and turned around and ran, often literally, straight back to the shuttles.

His own breakdown had been only marginally less humiliating. He'd marched out of the shuttle, secure in his almost-encyclopedic knowledge of Xia and its many-legged rulers, only to be paralyzed with terror at the nightmare confronting him.

The psych tech called in to treat him clucked sympathetically at Jak's distress, explaining that Xi Derangement Syndrome was only tangentially related to common arachnophobia, and its onset almost impossible to predict. She'd offered him a selection of sedative patches and suggested neural realignment, all of which Jak refused. He had to do this without medication, without assistance. The Xi had no patience for weakness.

A juvenile female appeared, to escort him to the center of the Nest, her clawed feet clicking on the polished stone floor, multiple eyes glittering with open contempt. As the junior moved away, Jak noted how she held the other palp awkwardly, a rising bruise covering most of the limb. Life in the Nest was brutal; thirty percent of females didn't make it to adulthood, and for the males, the mortality rate was much higher, even without considering their much shorter lifespans.

A circle of light illuminated the only open space in the vast chamber, the edges lost in a wall of webs, punctuated by the entrances to the network of silken tunnels. A thousand eyes watched him from the gloom, in a nightmare of scuttling claustrophobia. More Xi, wearing brightly colored sashes over matte-black body armor, ringed the central space. Soldiers or ceremonial guard? The curved blades they carried in highly decorated scabbards looked more than ceremonial.

"Reinnor, welcome to Xia." The Matriarch loomed above him, a forest of legs and gleaming chitin, the naked palps elongated and prehensile like skinned tentacles. Beside her stood a smaller, darker individual Jak assumed was First Sister. Jak dragged his attention away from the guards, forced down a glob of nausea, and tried to do the mental exercises again.

"Thank you, Great One," he said, swallowing bile and lowering his head less in obeisance than to delay looking at the Matriarch for as long as possible. To his horror, he saw he was standing in a pool of slimy gore.

"So, you wish to be our new Liaison?" she asked, gesturing with one of the translucent palps at the heaving web surrounding her.

Surrounding him. Eyes glittering in the strands. Watching.

"Yes, Great One," he finally managed to spit out, although his tongue felt glued to the roof of his mouth.

Blessed Mother, give me strength.

The Matriarch made another gesture, and Jak lowered himself to the cold stone floor, flinching at the chill. Jak extended his arms out in front of him, his skin crawling as the cold slime seeped through the thin silk of his favorite suit, his fists clenched to conceal his shaking hands. The gore stank of sewage and rotten meat, and it was all he could do to keep his stomach contents under control.

The Matriarch's clawed foot, with its bristling hairs, pressed heavily into his flesh; Jak couldn't suppress a shudder of revulsion.

"Then be one with the Nest, Xi Liaison," the Matriarch said, and transferred her entire weight onto his arm. The crack of bone, like a stick breaking, echoed around the chamber. It took a moment for his brain to register the pain, sharp and bright, exploding in his arm. Nausea followed, as he heaved up an already empty stomach on the stone floor. A smaller Xi, waiting on the edge of the web, scuttled over and administered a pain shot with professional speed.

"Now we have the formalities out of the way," said the Matriarch, as the Xi medic began healing the bone with a hand-held medi-scanner, "we have some briefing material for you. So you are fully informed as to your responsibilities."

Jak closed the door, shutting out both the professionally concerned psych tech with her offers of medication, and his staff with their requests for decisions.

"Lock it," he commanded the center's AI, unable to suppress a half sob of relief as the lock engaged with a metallic click. The lights across the apartment dimmed.

"No," he yelled. "No, brighter. I want every light on." No more gloom, no more shadows and shifting, restless webs.

No more Xi.

The AI complied, flooding every room with light. The official rooms of the Xi Liaison. Room after room of exquisite furnishings and meticulously placed art works.

His rooms.

"How dare they?" he whispered.

He stank. The beautiful green silk reeked of dead Xi, or whatever it was they'd made him kneel in. The cuffs of delicate lace, ragged and coated in drying gore, shed flakes of indescribable filth with every movement, the fabric irreparably ruined by ugly orange and green stains. His arm ached, despite the painkillers, encased in an immobilizing cast he had to keep on for a whole twelve hours.

In a fury, Jak tugged and tore at his clothing, ripping away the filthy cloth, flinging it across the room, cursing at the spasms of pain, until he stood naked, gasping with exertion and shock. Tattered remains hung from light fixtures and draped themselves over furniture.

"How fucking dare they?" he snarled again to the empty room. All those years spent studying, venerating the technologically superior (morally superior?) Xi, only to discover they were not the benign partners of the Republic, but ruthless and cruel overlords.

How could he have been so naive?

"Excellency," the Center's AI broke in. "Do you require assistance?"

Jak Reinnor regarded the destroyed suit, the stinking rags festooning everything within range, as a cold, dark anger began to rise.

"Get housekeeping in here, I want this place spotless," he commanded. His stomach grumbled. "And food. Now."

An hour later, clean and dressed, and with two strong drinks in him, he no longer wanted to bury himself in a corner and scream. Center housekeeping had come through while he was dressing; no sign of his loss of control remained. After a decent meal, washed down with more alcohol, the shaking finally subsided, and his mind began to process the insanity he found himself in.

An Abomination. An engineered, enhanced, and augmented soldier. Here. In the Republic. And he, Jak Reinnor, Xi Liaison, was responsible for it. Her.

He leaned back in the chair, nursing another generous shot, and contemplated what that meant. Illegal, certainly. Blasphemous, if you were a traditionalist. Uncle Amordo, who spent nearly two decades serving as a Brother, would have a stroke if he knew. Terminal, in every sense of the word, if this became public knowledge.

"Return the lights to normal," he said, sipping at the calming liquor.

Yes, illegal, and hideously dangerous. But the possibilities ... Jak set the glass down and leaned forward, elbows on his knees, his uninjured hand rubbing the smooth, blue syntheplaz cast, as he contemplated the advantages.

Power, for one. Immense power. Unlimited funds, access to the Directorate and the Imperial Guard. Answerable to the Xi alone, not the Senate, and not Rossim. That last benefit alone was worth the threat of execution.

He rose and walked to the window, pulling back the curtains shielding him from the Nest. Terror still licked at him, an icy roiling in his stomach and sweaty palms. The Matriarch's instructions had left Jak under no illusions — if the prisoner was to escape, or be injured or, worse still, die, he wouldn't live long enough to be tried for treason. And more terrifying still, the Matriarch warned, punishment would also fall on his family.

Jak dismissed both threats. He wanted power. Now he had more than he could possibly imagine. And he had never been short of imagination. Now to decide what to do with it.

The first order of business was returning to Central. And find a way to meet his new charge. *Oryelle Tey*, the Xi called her. The second task was to find out everything he could about her, and attempt to work out what the Xi wanted. They would pay for today's humiliations. He returned the empty glass to the table, running through in his mind everything he needed to do once he returned to Central.

I wonder what she's like?

Six

The van slowed to a halt. Salber, silent for the last hour of the journey, stirred behind her.

"Looks like we're here," he said, more to himself, than to Ori. She waited for him to open the door, to put as much distance between himself and her, but he didn't move. "I'm sorry," he said at last. "It doesn't seem very fair."

"I don't need your pity," she said shortly. Where were they? Some underground bunker, or military facility where the presence of a firing squad would be unobserved? Rossim would be there, for certain. He wouldn't miss her death for anything. Would they make the little medic attend? "They have been threatening this for years; it was only a matter of time."

Please, let it be quick. Peripheral icons strobed red, finally ebbing to sullen amber as her systems pumped more suppressors into her bloodstream. She would not go to her execution shaking with fear.

Salber said nothing as the AI network unlocked the door, artificial light flooding the interior as he pushed it open. The van dipped and rocked slightly as the guard climbed out, cursing under his breath as his stiff limbs unfolded. "For fuck's sake," she heard him exclaim, but couldn't turn enough to see what the problem was.

"What?" she called, feeding more suppressors into her bloodstream. "Where are we?"

"We're at the fucking main entrance to the administration wing of the palace," Salber yelled back. "This isn't right. The captain was real specific about where to go."

The wire mesh bit into her spine as Ori slumped against the cage door in relief. They were at the palace, and alone, by the sounds of it. She would never get a better chance than this, but they wouldn't be alone for long.

"While we're waiting for the guard to turn up, how about loosening this chain a bit. I've been stuck like this for hours." Metal bit deep into her flesh, as she jerked the chain as hard as she could, tearing her already lacerated wrists. Blood dripped down between her fingers, warm and slick.

"No fucking way," Salber said, from the van's doorway. "The captain gave me specific orders not to unlock you until the Guard were in position. I'm not going to risk another punishment session. And remember, I saw what happened to the guys at the house. I mean, yeah, they shouldn't have done that to you, but you tore their arms off."

Ori took a deep breath, and tried to inject as much reasonableness as possible into her voice. "I'm not asking to be released, only to loosen the chain a little. I can't get out of the cage. I've tried, more than once." Which wasn't exactly true. With her hands chained, escape was impossible, but if she could persuade Salber to release her...

"You aren't like them, I can see that," she continued. They were animals, and like all animals, sometimes they needed the whip, sometimes a reward. "You took me to the infirmary. I'm grateful." Although her skin crawled at the thought, seducing Salber wouldn't be the worst thing she'd endured.

The van dipped a little. "The other guys, they said you deserved it. That you kill anyone who gets near you."

A reasonably accurate assessment, under the circumstances.

"I didn't kill the medic. I didn't harm you," Ori pointed out. Which had more to do with Salber retreating to a safe distance while Twari and his subordinates beat her into unconsciousness, than any restraint on her part. The medic had been no threat, and had even been useful.

The van dipped again, and Ori could feel his body heat behind her.

"I'm just going to give it bit of slack." The chain moved. "Blessed Mother, what did they do to you? The bastards." Salber shifted behind her and unexpectedly gentle fingers released the chain. "I'm going to remove it. But I don't want any trouble, all right."

"Thank you, Salber," Ori said, moving as slowly as she dared. There would be only one chance. "The Guard enjoy hurting me. I haven't done anything. I don't even know why I'm being held prisoner." It had to look natural, a simple movement across the floor of the van that would put her facing the cage door.

Salber crouched in the confined space on the other side of the mesh wall, confusion creasing his brow into furrows. "Yeah, none of the other guys knew why, either. The captain said— "

Whatever wisdom Twari had imparted was lost as Ori kicked out with both feet, dead center of the cage door. Salber careened back, arms flailing helplessly, through the van door, and onto the synthecrete concourse, the twisted remains of the cage door landing on top of him. The sickening crack of his head hitting the ground echoed through the underground space.

Her clothes caught on the broken edges of the cage as she struggled to the doorway of the van and scanned the immediate area. Salber was correct, this was one of the entrances to the palace, although not the main one. The enormous synthecrete space was empty now, except for a line of AI-controlled vehicles lined up to one side. But palace security and staff would be here somewhere, so she didn't have much time. Now to find cover, get the restraints off, and find some way to remove the chip —even if it meant amputating her hand.

The column not five meters from her exploded in a spray of synthecrete chips and dust.

"Go on. Make one more move and I'll blow a hole straight through you," came a hard, cold voice behind her.

The Imperial Guard had found her. Slowly, she lowered herself to her knees, and braced herself.

The guards propelled her at gunpoint into the office. With her hands bound, she had to struggle to avoid crashing head-first into the floor. Another blow, this time to the back of her legs, drove her to her knees. The Imperial Guard were unimpressed at her latest escape attempt and proceeded to deal out her punishment with the same dispassionate brutality as all the other times she'd annoyed them.

Rossim stood at his favorite position at the windows overlooking the square, the noise from the demonstration irritatingly audible, even up here. Surveying his domain, watching the other animals pretending to be free.

Tel Rossim, Lord President of the Republic. My jailer.

"What the fuck happened?" Rossim demanded, striding down the length of his office. "Weapons discharge in the palace grounds? The Senate is going to have my fucking balls for this."

One of the guards pushed Ori's head into the carpet, the muzzle of his weapon pressed painfully into the back of her neck. She took the opportunity to smear blood and snot across the antique carpet.

"There was an issue, Lord President." The shrug in the guard's reply was almost tangible. They obeyed Rossim, and gave him the respect he demanded, but they didn't fear him. "We caught it trying to escape. Again. The stupid AI rerouted the van to the wrong location. We had to subdue it."

There was no mention of the fact she was still in restraints when this subduing took place. No mention either, she noted, of Salber's fate. Ori couldn't see the Lord President's face, but she had no problem imagining his incredulity at this display of incompetence. Patience wasn't one of Rossim's virtues.

"And where the fuck were you?" Rossim shouted at them. "You were supposed to stay with it at all times."

A different voice answered, with more than an edge of impatience. "The demonstrations, sir. We were caught in traffic; we couldn't force our way through. Not without attracting attention."

With a rapidly swelling black eye, and her face pressed deep into the woolen tufts, it was difficult to estimate, but Ori thought a respectable pool of blood had now gathered under her head. She hoped the entire rug was ruined.

"By the Mother's cunt, I'm surrounded by idiots. Get it up." Rossim's footsteps came closer. "I swear I'll have you all court-martialed for this."

The guards dragged her by her injured hands to her feet, sending the pain singing through her arms.

Couldn't they shoot her and end the whole farce now?

Rossim regarded her with a mix of hatred, disgust, and something else that slid away too quickly for her to quantify, his jaw clenched with suppressed emotion. She'd thought he would look happier at the thought of finally being rid of her. Rossim lifted his hand and she reacted instinctively, shying back out of range, as she braced herself for the inevitable blow; instead, Rossim waved away the guards.

"Release it and go," he ordered.

"With respect, Lord President, are you sure?"

The guards were as confused as her. Every encounter with Rossim began and ended with her on her knees, aided by the attentions of the Guard, and sometimes Rossim himself.

Release me? What new humiliation is this?

"I'll be fine. I have the Xi's assurances. If it gives us any more trouble, I can send it back to the nests. And it knows what will happen then."

He didn't need to see her reaction. It didn't have to be true. Reluctantly the guards removed the restraints and left. She massaged her numb hands until the feeling returned, wary of Rossim's intentions. He'd never ordered them to uncuff her before.

"What do you want, Rossim?" she asked, looking around. Rossim's office was larger than the combined area of the entire training room and most of the infirmary. The ceiling soared above her, intricately painted frescoes covering the entire area from the windows overlooking the square to the double doors of dark wood. Directly above, a massive blue beast, with horns wreathed in flowers, looked mournfully down on her. The semi-naked nymphs gamboling in accompaniment looked bored, as though they'd rather be somewhere else.

Rossim obviously liked his comforts. His desk of exotic golden wood, elaborately carved with leaves and fruit, stretched between the two floor-length windows overlooking the square. On the desk sat a line of meticulously positioned curios. Sunshine streamed through the windows, illuminating a substantial crystal sphere, its multicolored layers sparkling in the light.

On a whim, she removed it from the wooden mount and flicked the ball into the air. It landed back in her palm with a weighty smack.

"Put it down. It's an antique." His voice betrayed no fear, although the orb would make an excellent weapon and he had seen firsthand what she was capable of.

"It is a pretty thing. Old too, I think," she said, turning the sphere in her hands. The glass looked worn in places, as though many fingers had traced the layers across its cool surface. Each layer appeared to merge seamlessly into the next, each color chosen to enhance the preceding layer and highlight the succeeding one.

"It's from Da Chet. Now put it back."

Da Chet? That made the globe over three hundred years old, and highly illegal. "So, do you keep such a pretty thing as a memento of all those dead billions?" No doubt there was a thriving trade in artifacts from the burned world; the long prison sentences and hefty fines would mean nothing to the circles Rossim moved in.

"I keep it as a reminder my side won. Now put it back."

The glass sparkled as Ori flicked it into the air. His voice filled with impatience. "I can always call the guards back. Perhaps a few hours with them might remind you to behave." She replaced the ball with delicate precision, bloody fingerprints marring the smooth surface. This sudden leniency was more than likely a trap. Was he expecting her to attack him, an excuse for the guards outside to come to his rescue?

"There. Your toy is back," she announced, and made herself comfortable in one of the commodious chairs facing the desk. She would play along, see what he was up to. May as well enjoy a little luxury before they shot her.

"Do you want to go back to your cell. Or better yet, perhaps I should send you back to the Xi and be done with you."

"Do it," she spat, launching herself back out of the chair, disregarding all the consequences, her decision to face whatever this latest development held dissolving in rage. "Ten years I've been a prisoner. A slave kept in check with torture and abuse and dragged out to kill on your behalf whenever you please."

"Don't pretend killing disgusts you," Rossim shot back. "I was here, remember? In this office. When you killed Garrett. If it hadn't been for my intervention, they would have executed you immediately."

Lord President Garrett had only recently been appointed, and was still enjoying his new privileges when Rossim was made Xi Liaison. A tall, well-built man in an immaculate handmade suit, with a mane of dark hair, Ori had hoped Rossim might be an ally. Or at least a moderating influence on Garrett's cruelty. That hope died quickly, as the new Xi Liaison demonstrated a malevolence the equal of his president.

Garrett's mistake had been overconfidence. After she'd suffered nearly three years of uninterrupted brutality, he'd thought her beaten and cowed into submission. He'd turned his back on her, believing her unconscious. A fatal error.

"You only intervened because it suited your lust for power. You are nothing but their puppet, their toy. They have bought your obedience with this office and all these trinkets." She flung out one arm, encompassing all Rossim's privileges. "You cannot buy mine, or beat it out of me. Throw me to your guards. What can they do that has not already been done? But I will never yield. I will die first."

"And you have made that abundantly clear over the years."

She sank back into the chair and stared blindly across the room. "So, you have set a date then. For my execution?"

"Oh, I wish." He tossed a sheet over the desk, knowing she would catch it. "But no. They sent through orders for you."

She thumbed the sheet into active and scrolled down the message list. *Send the Brightstar to Ma'al, we have a task for her. Tell her to await orders. Tell her if she does this, she is free.* She read it twice, convinced this was either a perverse jest or some sort of bizarre test. "Free? Is this a joke?" She threw the sheet back across the desk, barely missing the crystal orb. "What do they mean, free? They will let me go? Just like that? After all these years?" The sheet clattered as it hit the desk.

"I don't know. You'd need an Eidress lawyer to parse that message. That's all they sent."

"And you think I will fall for this trap? Do you think me so stupid? That I believe you will allow me to walk away as though nothing has happened?"

"As you are so fond of pointing out, I answer to them. Do you think I'd be foolish enough to defy them?"

"And Ma'al? What have they done to earn your masters' attention? I cannot imagine the Xi lust after their wealth."

Rossim took his seat in his overwrought chair. "I don't know," he said, with a dismissive wave. "I don't know what this is about. Unlike you, I am expected to obey without question."

The bitterness in his voice surprised her. *Free.* Never, in all the years of imprisonment, had the Xi made this sort of offer. Bribed, yes, with promises of soft beds and real food and a limited sort of detention, in exchange for her cooperation. To her, it sounded a lot like imprisonment on a slightly longer leash. Freedom, real freedom, had always been denied. She reminded herself not to trust any of them. Not the Xi, not Rossim, not the gentle medic. They were all eijen, all animals. "And if I chose not to take this offer, this bait? Then what will you do?"

Rossim grinned, an expression of cruel glee. "I have explicit orders to put you on the first ship back to Xia. Personally, nothing would make me happier than seeing you defy them. Go ahead. I hope they let me watch your torture."

Seven

"Are you sure this is safe?" Betan Casar peered around the enclosed garden, his round face full of suspicion as though the shrubbery concealed unknown assassins and spies. "Couldn't we have met in your office?"

Rossim kicked a small stone across the path, where it struck one of the ornate planters with a satisfying crack. "My office? Are you insane? The entire fucking palace is in an uproar with the demonstrations. Security everywhere. At least out here I know we won't be observed." The dark-gray planter now sported an ugly scar of exposed synthecrete. "Show some fucking backbone, Casar. If we pull this off, they'll be erecting statues in our honor."

The gravel crunched under the Lord President's boots. Out of the wind, the garden was surprisingly warm, no doubt the reason why it still held some scattered flowers long after every park in the capital lay bare. At the end of the path, a small gazebo of pale wood offered some welcome shade. Casar hesitated for a moment, grumbling under his breath, before joining Rossim in the dappled light, a bead of sweat tracing its way down his florid cheek before dropping on the lapel of blue silk. A semicircular bench ran halfway around the gazebo's circumference, liberally covered in autumnal leaves. Casar brushed fretfully at a handful of withered leaves, before settling himself, hands over his stomach, looking for all the world like someone's dyspeptic uncle.

Just goes to show you how deceptive appearances are.

"And if we are unsuccessful, we will be shot for treason. Our families will be ruined. Are you absolutely certain you want to court such a risk?"

"There is only a minimal risk," Rossim said, biting down on his anger. Trust Casar to bring up family ruin. "The Directorate is loyal to me, and Pesek is competent and discreet," he said, sending the leaves flying with one decisive sweep. "We can make this work, and finally rid ourselves of the Ma'al problem once and for all." He would have much preferred to pull off this plan without Casar, but the man had power and influence in areas Rossim's family no longer did. Rossim eyed a pebble and wondered if he could hit the planter from this distance, or better still, Casar's fat head.

"We're orchestrating a coup, Rossim," Casar said, rubbing one thumb along the other, a sure sign of his ambivalence. "How many will die?"

Casar wasn't asking from a humanitarian perspective. This was merely risk assessment. "No one is going to die," Rossim said. "Well, not many. We'll continue to covertly supply troops and armaments; when it all goes to shit, Cimmili 'intervenes' with the support of the Senate, and order is restored. Ma'al returns to the full control of the Republic, in line with all the other systems, the silk production moves to Polinia or some other suitable world. We control the monopoly and all is well."

No one needed to know Rossim and a few select friends had several discreetly positioned companies waiting to step forward and take up silk production. If they controlled the release of finished product half as well as Ma'al, they would all be exceedingly wealthy. Then let the Xi try and threaten him.

"And this puppet you have on Ma'al? What if this Karis Samara suspects he's being played?"

"He's too stupid, and greedy, and we have sufficient insurance to make sure he behaves." The file on Karis Samara made for some interesting reading. The man was, in the Directorate's opinion, a complete psychopath — a diagnosis rarely seen in the Republic. Mental illnesses had been one of the first targets of mankind's enthusiastic but ill-judged steps in genetic engineering. That thought brought him immediately to the Abomination, now on its way to Ma'al at the most inconvenient time possible. His anger must have showed because Casar gave him a quizzical look.

"I haven't been Leader of the Senate for all these years, Tel, without knowing you're holding something back. And what do we know about the new Xi Liaison? It looks like he was dropped into the role without any Senate input."

Rossim tried to imagine the look on the fat fool if he did tell him the truth. With any luck he'd have a heart attack, although from which revelation? That the Republic had kept an alien abomination as prisoner or that the Xi had the ultimate authority to decide who became Lord President, or Xi Liaison?

"Betan, Jak Reinnor comes from a good family. I decided we need someone capable and stable in the job, given the current uneasiness gripping the populace." Rossim assumed his most reassuring persona. "All you have to do is keep anti-Ma'al sentiment bubbling along in the Senate. Encourage that idiot from Cimmili a bit more."

If you were looking for mental illness, the Cimmili paranoia over Ma'al must be a textbook case of collective rage. Useful though, it made them vulnerable to manipulation and easy scapegoats should it prove necessary. Casar fretted away at his hands, in increasing anxiety.

"You know the Ma'al government aren't all lunatics like Samara, or spineless puppets like Tylis Mathani. Shizuri Eidress won't sit idly by and let a coup happen," Casar warned.

No, the old man wouldn't. But the Ma'ali government was riven with factional infighting, the reason why Tylis, a weak and ineffectual head of her own hanjile, had found herself elevated to ruler of nearly thirty million people and the richest commercial enterprise in the history of the Republic.

Rossim shrugged. "We have it covered."

Rossim tossed his sheet onto the desk with satisfaction. Good, one more problem taken care of. The Directorate had moved with its usual efficiency, taking out the remainder of the house guards with little opposition.

The interfering little medic was another problem altogether. Rossim had toyed with the idea of shooting him as well, and dumping his body into the same mass grave as the guards, but this solution was far more elegant, and with luck the interfering little prick wouldn't see the outside of a prison cell for years.

Pesek had moved with admirable speed and manufactured enough evidence for a swift arrest and trial. This Keren Ha'haru hadn't even put up a defense, so now he and his pervert brother would both rot in prison for the same offenses. The irony of it pleased Rossim. What pleased him more was the progress Pesek had made in undermining the Abomination's mission. Simply ordering its assassination was never going to work; the Xi would enact a terrible revenge for disobedience. Over the years though, Rossim had assessed a great deal of insight on how the Abomination thought, and acted when provoked. All it would take was a series of setbacks, and when it reacted as planned, well, the Directorate might have to act. For the safety of innocent citizens, of course.

Rossim poured himself another large drink and sauntered to the window. Outside, the square was silent and empty at this time of day. He liked it this way.

Quiet. Peaceful. Under control.

Eight

O ri sank back into the comfortable bench, as outside the café a flight of seabirds wheeled and dipped over the rooftops of L'seitwan, capital of the world of Six Jump. It was pleasant to be out, away from her prison in the Directorate safe house, despite the overcast weather and intermittent squalls.

This late in the afternoon, the café held only a few customers: an elderly couple arguing over something on their sheets, two engineers in the next booth loudly discussing thruster linings, and not far away, her two Directorate handlers, pretending to be friends as they sipped on messil and toyed with a small pile of cakes, all the while never taking their eyes off her. There would be another team outside, waiting and watching, and a contingent of Imperial Guard somewhere close by, in case she got any ideas.

The jump from Central, in a fast cruiser seconded from Fleet, was remarkable in its lack of violence. Something had happened, that much was clear. The guards hadn't returned her to the house. Instead, the van, its mesh repaired and reinforced again, took her straight to the shuttle, and then to the cruiser, waiting in orbit. Yes, they'd still locked her in the brig, but they didn't starve her, or abuse her, and she'd had a blanket, and a medic to treat her injuries — an unheard-of luxury.

Now they were here, on Six, and Ori was allowed out for a few hours a day to walk along the seafront of Old Town, full of winding laneways and quaint buildings, or to climb the interminable stairs to this little café, where she ordered what she wanted and almost convinced herself she was free. So long as she didn't attempt to evade her handlers, or cause trouble, they treated her with a degree of grudging respect. Ori found it very unsettling.

A gust of wind dashed a spray of raindrops against the window. Outside, cut into the native rock of the mountain range, a small park of more mud than grass held the obligatory monument to the Great War, although she was sure the war had never reached this far out. A scattering of bushes, long since stripped of their autumn leaves by the relentless wind, hugged the stone wall on the seaward side. Beyond the wall, the roofs of the lower town poked up; farther out, the sullen winter skies merged into gray sea and wind-tossed breakers. Behind the café, the urban sprawl continued up the mountain range, clinging to increasingly vertical surfaces until only sky remained.

The wind battered at the window again, raindrops pattering against the glass in waves while above, the birds whistled and dove in the cold sea air. This far out on the border, systems like Six Jump were usually struggling backwaters, filled with the tired and desperate, or perhaps a mining operation with a floating population of workers looking for quick money. Fate, or whatever forces shaped the universe, had been kind to Six as the locals called it. Its nondescript system of two habitable worlds and three gas giants was fortunately in the exact position to serve as the sector's hub. The vast spaceport that sprawled across the plains behind this mountain range serviced the rich agricultural worlds of Tersen and Corelli, and, crucially, the Republic's only privately owned system and its fabulously wealthy planet — Ma'al.

She pulled her gaze back from the vista of rainy skies, windswept seas and brown roofs of the old quarter, as one of the café staff laid out a steaming mug of fragrant rakosh, a tiny dish of cerrisma powder and a bowl of crispy deep-fried Orchetti root on the artfully distressed tabletop.

"Are you sure you don't want farei with your chips?" asked the woman, J'nni, according to her name tag. She would be from any one of the dozen races who called Six Jump home. This had originally been a Sanctuary world, a refuge for those displaced by the Great War. As the fighting raged back and forth across the remains of the Imperium, refugees fled the conflict to the border colonies. In the years after the war ended, many attempted to return to their homeworlds, to find their previous homes and businesses occupied by others. It became yet another source of conflict in the fledgling Republic that continued to this day.

"No," Ori said, bringing her attention back to the eijen. "I prefer them plain," she continued, eyeing the small pendant the woman wore, a clear syntheglass disc containing a tiny circle of Ma'al silk. A gift, perhaps, from a captain, or navigator; they were the only ones likely to have the income to buy such an expensive piece. Ori tapped her wrist — containing her ID chip, complete with its false information — on the woman's sheet. There was a tiny ping as the transaction went through.

"Thank you, ma'am," J'nni said with a professional smile, before turning away to her other customers. Ori took a spoonful of the dark red cerrisma and stirred it into the mug as a lone bird hopped across the tiny patch of grass by the path. She'd been here for nearly two weeks, shuttling between the safe house near the old fish docks, and the port. With her went the two handlers, with a discreet backup of Directorate agents and the lurking Guard, while she trudged from one labour hire agent to another, searching for a berth that would take her to Ma'al. The Directorate had refused to falsify captain's papers for her, another insult to add to all the rest, but finally accepted she could fulfil a navigator's position, given that the run from Six to Ma'al was simple enough for a cadet to plot.

It should have been straightforward; she was more than qualified and the Directorate of Protection provided generous bribes, but the berth she needed kept eluding her. As the days passed, with no result, Ori found it harder to push down the rising anxiety. What if the Directorate lost patience and decided to abandon the mission?

The dim afternoon light suddenly vanished in a blaze of fire rivaling mid-summer, the vibration rattling her food across the table. The roar of a heavy shuttle lumbering toward orbit made speech or thought impossible for a few seconds. No one else in the café reacted apart from the necessary corralling of their food, although her watchdogs had to divert their attention for a few seconds.

While they were distracted, Ori pulled up the position listings from the port network, the list scrolling past her vision as the interface updated the information. Good. Nothing had changed; only one name separated her from a navigator's berth on the *Havali's Hope*, a medium-sized freighter on the Six Jump– Corelli–Tersen–Ma'al run.

The seabirds scattered as the sky lit up again. One of the agents wasn't quite as fast as she should be and her mug crashed to the floor, pale green messil spreading across the faux wood. Ori wisely did not show any amusement and turned back to pretending to use her sheet, while the feed scrolled on her interface.

Captains of the small freighters had absolute control over who worked on their ships, a privilege they protected ruthlessly. The larger freighters, carrying millions of tons of cargo, were owned by a handful of transport conglomerates and took their crews from a pool of applicants. A pool that had a waiting list of months, if not years. Small freighter crew — haulers, or pod-jockeys — were far more transient, and every port had multiple companies sourcing crews for captains too busy to pick through applications.

None of these factors accounted for the delay in finding a ship for her. Bribes, threats, pleas — nothing worked. The usually plentiful cargo-hand work disappeared the moment she applied. Her suggestion, to "accidently" remove the navigator of the *Havali's Hope*, was rejected out of hand, and her one attempt to revisit the topic brought not only refusal but an explicit threat to revoke her privileges. Ori acquiesced reluctantly; the few hours of unrestrained freedom were too precious.

That didn't stop her handlers arguing about it, after they returned her to her locked room. The male (she had never concerned herself with their names), seemed content to wait until something turned up; his colleague was adamantly and loudly opposed to staying on Six Jump any longer than she had to. If she'd had her way, Ori would be back on Central.

A gasp from one of the engineers pulled her away from her research. The café screen, playing a local entertainment feed, abruptly switched to the news channel. The audio announced this was direct from Freedom Square, albeit on a sixteen-hour delay from Central. As Ori moved closer to the screen, her watchdogs followed her, taking up a station at each shoulder. J'nni turned up the sound as the feed cut to the drone footage of the demonstrations in front of the palace. The newsreader, an AI-generated avatar, explained the senator for the Ma'al system was addressing the Senate, and this speech was being broadcast live throughout Central. A ribbon of information ran along the bottom of the screen listing the latest in a string of Ma'al government "provocations".

The news drone dipped in closer; everyone in the crowd, including some of palace security, turned to watch the two-story-high screen, which took up a large section of the palace wall. A striking woman, the Ma'ali Senator, in Eidress-green silk, the informative swirls of thread covering nearly the entire surface of her knee-length che'b'ni. She faced the Senate calmly, not once betraying the fact she was addressing billions of people.

"Honored members of the Senate, Lord President," she began, bowing elegantly from the waist. The feed cut to Rossim, catching him shifting uncomfortably on his presidential throne. "The people of Ma'al are citizens of the Republic, good citizens, hardworking and honorable." The square erupted into loud derision and shouted obscenities.

"We reject completely the suggestion that these steps, taken by the Ma'al government, are in any way provocations." Another roar of dissent filled the air. "We, as a government, have the right to control access to our system."

Whatever else she might have said was drowned out as missiles hit the screen, sending shudders across the image. Palace security, caught off guard, milled in confusion.

"Don't just stand there," the woman agent said, in a murmur, presumably to the frozen security personnel onscreen. The Ma'al supporters with their glittery banners began to huddle together as the angry crowd coalesced around them, waving their own signs and fists in rage. A glitter bomb arced across the barriers, exploding among a group of citizens calling for Rossim's resignation, engulfing them in a whirlwind of multicolored particles. The barriers strained to hold back the crowds as security still failed to act.

"Palace security doesn't know what to do," Ori pointed out to the agents. "I would have sent in my troops, splitting up the crowd, taking those" —she pointed at the screen— "troublemakers. They are going to lose control soon."

"We're a democracy," snapped the other agent, a lean man with a sharp face. "No one is going to lose control. Palace security has it in-hand."

The news drones zoomed-in en masse as a Ma'al supporter dropped his pants and wiggled his bare ass at the other side. The response was an edging stone from the palace gardens, hurled into the faux Ma'ali. A spray of blood fountained across the heaving bodies, screams of terror spread as the barricades collapsed, and palace security fled from the sudden maelstrom of violence.

"You were saying," Ori said, knowing full well she shouldn't provoke them, but opportunities like this were rare. "I would flog whoever was in command. Why haven't they ordered security back in?"

To her immense satisfaction more than one in the café muttered agreement. The female agent cursed and grabbed at Ori's arm.

"We're leaving. Now," she ordered as the feed shifted focus to a disturbance at the far end of the crowd, at the gates near the Law Courts.

A line of black appeared like a line of ink drawn across the scene. A ripple, a wave front, propagated through the crowd in reaction. Someone had ordered in the Imperial Guard. Even though they were hundreds of light years away, Ori couldn't control the shiver of fear that ran through her.

"What the fuck," the man murmured. For once, Ori had to agree. This was a vast overreaction. Someone should be rallying palace security, restoring order, but whoever that someone was, they had fled as well. She could pinpoint the exact moment when it all fell apart. A missile, thrown in the heat of the moment, hit one of the armored figures. It didn't matter that the Imperial Guard wore silk/graphene composite armor— almost impenetrable to all but the highest caliber weaponry. It mattered only that it happened.

The Guard retaliated, storming through the crowd, rifle-butts slamming into bodies, driving the guilty and innocent alike to the ground. Panic spread and the crowd stampeded, crushing bodies underfoot in the rush to escape. The drones swept in closer and someone, in a control room a long way from the conflict, decided to zoom in on the carnage, closer to the bloodstained flagstones, the broken bodies, the screaming injured.

Bodies strewn across the cleared areas around the pens. The screams and the cries and the stench of death. Blood clotting everywhere in thick, dark pools. Peripherals shrieked warnings as Ori's heart rate rocketed, stress hormones howling through her bloodstream. Harsh, bitter vomit welled at the back of her throat

"Do you need a medic?" the waitress asked, her voice full of concern.

She had to scramble for control, forcing the enhancements to flood her body with neuro-suppressors, peripherals flashing red at the distress. Her handlers were there in seconds, hands locked hard on her body, although still pretending concern.

"She's fine," said the woman agent. "She's delicate, doesn't like the sight of blood," she continued, not bothering to hide her derision. The hard jab of a weapon dug into Ori's ribs.

"Come on." The male had his arm under her, pulling her toward the door. "You're going back to the house."

Nine

"You can't drag me back just because I felt ill," Ori protested, as she exited the café, with a Directorate agent on either side, and a gun jammed into her ribcage. "I'm fine now." What if they decided to drag her back to Central? Or give up completely and send her back to Xia? The fear raced through her, forcing her to release more neuro-suppressors.

The sun was dipping toward the distant horizon, shadows lengthening across the patchy grass. Across the city, the lights were coming on, revealing the long sweep of civilization squeezed between the sea and the mountains, spreading along the coast for hundreds of kilometers in both directions. The wind was full of salt, and the metallic tang of shuttle exhaust fumes. At least it had stopped raining.

"We can do whatever we want," replied the male agent, tugging her across the park toward the stairs. "You were warned. If you gave us any trouble, we would pull the plug on this little excursion. We're going back to the safe house for more orders."

She could take them both and the agents that came after her, and the Guard, but she would never escape this world. The AI link to her enhancements was unbreakable, both the Xi and the Directorate had demonstrated that more than once. Her only hope was that berth and a ship.

"I don't want to be sitting around here waiting for a berth either. But I have been given this assignment. I don't have a choice about carrying it out."

If they decided this was too difficult, these Directorate agents might decide that returning to Central while alternatives were explored might be the safer route.

"This could be our last chance," Ori said, trying not to sound desperate. "The Lord President will not be pleased if this mission fails."

The two agents slowed and stared at each other; uncertainty writ large on their faces. The man fumbled in his jacket for a sheet, maybe for directions to a quiet spot to shoot her.

Stand by… The message scrolled across her vision, a direct link from the city AI network. This had never happened before; the planetary AIs responded to queries, they never initiated them.

The scene in the café, what happened? Why did you react like that?

Who was this? This wasn't the AI, this was someone who had access to the network, and who knew how to contact her directly. A disturbing new development.

Who is this? she sent back.

Just answer the question. The reply was almost instantaneous. Was she being watched remotely? How else did this unknown person know about her collapse? Neither of the agents, still arguing with each other on their next course of action, appeared to be reporting to anyone in real time. Whoever it was must be accessing the city network and watching her through the AI monitoring points.

A side effect of the Xi interrogations. Close enough to the truth. There was a long silence and then the female agent's sheet pinged, and she had to juggle both it and her weapon.

"Fuck. It's the boss. He wants us to bring her to him. Now."

Ten

From his vantage point at the library window, Jak Reinnor waited impatiently as the vehicle ascended the winding driveway and came to a precise halt at the house entrance. Behind him on the table, his sheet still displayed the vehicle's movements since it left the café, tracking his new charge and his two agents up the narrow coastline and into the elegant houses and parklands favored by L'seitwan's wealthier citizens.

The house, one of many owned by the Directorate, made a convenient base of operations as the exasperating struggle to find a berth for the prisoner dragged on. He was beginning to suspect that the Directorate themselves were behind the obstructions, probably on Rossim's orders. A dangerous path to take, to risk aggravating the Xi. They would not be merciful should Rossim, or himself for that matter, screw up again.

This would be his first meeting with his prisoner. With an engineered being. He was surprised to find his palms slick from apprehension. The vehicle doors opened, but only Finn and Mardia got out. It appeared that his agents were having difficulties persuading their prisoner to leave the vehicle. Both had drawn their weapons; Finn looked like he was on the verge of shooting her.

With a sigh of exasperation, Jak thumped his glass down and went down to sort out yet another mess.

"I said out." The male agent waved his weapon at Ori again.

"I'm not leaving this vehicle until you tell me why we are here." Every icon on her interface still glowed amber or sullen red after the episode in the café, and her anger simmered just below the surface, waiting for an excuse. After weeks spent trying to find a berth, these two idiots decided to drag her halfway up the coast, to this house.

Whoever they were supposed to be meeting, it could not be their "boss". The head of the Directorate would hardly be out here, so far away from Central. She supposed it could be some sort of section chief, although she had never met one before. Her only points of contact had been Rossim and Garrett.

"And I told you to get out." The agent's voice rose in anger. "I swear, if you don't move now, I'll fucking shoot you where you sit." He certainly looked angry enough to do it. How far could she push him?

"Finn, stand down," came a voice from the building. Both agents froze, before slowly lowering their weapons. "By the Blessed Mother, I gave straightforward orders, and you two make it into another drama." The speaker was short, with a thin, nervous face, his hair falling in precise auburn ringlets to his shoulders. The long coat, cut back to display a slender, but well-formed body, was of pale-blue silk with some sort of finish that made it shimmer in the light from the house. Tightly styled trousers of black silk clung to every curve of calf and thigh and groin. You could buy a small freighter with the jacket alone.

The bureaucrat waved a tiny, delicate hand at the male agent, who apparently was called Finn. "Leave her alone. No wonder she won't cooperate, the way we treat her."

To Ori's utter amazement, the overdressed fool sketched a serviceable court bow in her direction and held out his hand. "My apologies, Oryelle. Please, would you join me in the house?"

Ori gave serious consideration to snapping the idiot's neck before the agents had a chance to fire, but regretfully abandoned the idea. Getting off this world remained the only viable option for escape. Once again, she forced down her rage in the name of compromise. "And you are?" she asked, pushing past him to stand and look around the house and grounds. Full night had fallen thirty-five minutes ago, according to her interface.

From her position on the hillside, Ori could see the ribbon of light delineating the sweep of urban sprawl from one end of the coastline to the other. Both agents bristled at her movement, caught between their instincts to keep her contained, and their superior's orders. She expected indignation, or a demonstration of his power; Rossim would have had her on her knees by now for her insolence. Instead, the man gave a snort of amusement and waved irritably at the two agents, who lowered their weapons again with ill grace.

"I am Jak Reinnor," he said with another bow.

"Aren't you a long way from Central? They must be missing you at some court function."

Reinnor ignored the insult, gesturing toward the house. "Come with me," he said, "and we can talk, like adults."

Ori eyed off the two agents who looked quite alarmed at this suggestion. "What about your pets?" she asked, pushing to see how far she could annoy him. Reinnor looked at both of his agents as though selecting furniture.

"They can stay here. On guard, if they wish. You know the Six Jump AI network is tracking your position. And you can't escape off-world, or out of the city, without detection." The agent, Finn, began to object, but Reinnor shut him down with a gesture easily interpreted as *stay*. Both agents stepped back scowling, as Ori followed the strange little man into the house.

"I could kill you," Ori said, as Reinnor proceeded up the wide flight of stairs. "Your pets wouldn't be able to stop me." Subdued lighting flickered on, illuminating each tread with a warm glow. From somewhere in the dark, a night-blooming flower sent its perfume adrift on a breeze sharp with the scent of the sea and fragrant herbage. Reinnor didn't turn around or slow his pace.

"The Xi would find someone else. You would be punished, and you'd still have to complete your mission. I don't think I'm worth it, do you?" The substantial wooden door, solid enough to resist armed invaders, opened silently at his approach.

As much as she hated to admit it, he had a point. The Xi would indeed punish her — severely. Not for killing someone, but for inconveniencing them. Ori didn't imagine there was a line-up of people willing to serve the aliens.

Reinnor paced into the house, continuing to treat her as a guest rather than a prisoner. Ori didn't expect that charade to last long. The door swung shut silently behind her. Before her stretched the foyer, alternating squares of black and cream marble stretching off toward the rear of the house. Instead of the overdone frescoes of the palace, deeply polished wood paneling ran waist-high around the walls, with plain ivory-white walls above. Lamps placed with military precision on matched tables pushed the warm shadows back into the corners, and caught the highlights on somber paintings. Stairs with ornate metal balustrades swept up to a second floor, a chandelier of scintillating crystal prisms taller than herself hung in the space. Everything breathed restrained, expensive elegance. *Threat analysis?* Only the low hum of electronics from the surveillance points for the house AI tucked up into the cornices. Her interface briefly flicked optics from visible to seven hundred nanometers, transforming the glow into pulsing blobs of orange and purple, but not detecting any other surveillance equipment.

Underfoot, jewel-toned rugs muffled their footsteps to a bare whisper as Reinnor made for another door, this time designed to look like interlocking puzzle pieces. "Come in," he said, with another sweeping bow. "Would you like a drink?"

It wasn't a large room, not by palace standards, anyway. More of the wood paneling covered the walls, interspersed with largely empty shelving and glass-fronted cabinets. For all its luxury, the room had an unused, abandoned quality, as though it lay unoccupied for long stretches of time. The only window, a single floor-to-ceiling expanse of syntheglass, overlooked the entrance and beyond to the twinkling ribbon of close-packed civilization. To one side a small table held an abandoned tumbler, an expensive looking decanter of amber liquid, and a sheet.

"Please, take a seat," he said, waving at a set of chairs that rivaled Rossim's in size and plushness. Ori ignored him, choosing to pace the length of the room, her interface flicking through wavelengths and frequencies, until she was convinced the room was reasonably safe. Reinnor clucked disapprovingly. "Please, come and sit down. No one is going to harm you."

She remained where she was, her back to him. "You aren't the first one, you know," Ori said to the reflection in the cabinet door. She knew this dance, the fake concern, the semblance of empathy. *We're both civilized humans. We can find common ground, work together.* Work together. When would they accept that he and his kind were nothing, less than animals? Not even close to human. Certainly not her equal.

"The first one? Oh, yes. Others no doubt have pretended friendship, before turning on you when you refused to be compliant?"

"Get straight to the threats, whoever you are. Do not waste my time with attempts to charm me into submission."

The reflection placed another glass on the table, pouring a measure of alcohol from the decanter into both glasses and positioned himself in one of the chairs so she could still see him. "Do you ever wonder," Reinnor said, in a tone of polite curiosity, ignoring her, "why the Xi want you kept as a prisoner?"

All the time.

"I'm sure they have given you their reasons." Ori turned to face him, the cabinet glass hard and cold at her back.

"No." Reinnor raised his tumbler to his lips, the light sparking off the etched crystal. "They have never explained their motives to anyone, as far as I know. We are simply expected to obey."

"And you do this? You obey? Without question?"

"Oh, we question," Reinnor answered, draining his glass. "We simply don't receive any answers."

Ori had asked the Xi once, in a brief interregnum between the pain, why they didn't simply enslave the humans. Her torturer, a small, dark and glossy haired female, had laughed. "It's exhausting and it always ends badly. Better to let them think they rule themselves."

Better to let them think they rule themselves. These fools thought they were the equal of the Xi, when they were nothing but slaves. "So, do you have a theory? As to why I am kept a prisoner?" Despite her instincts, a faint thread of curiosity was forming.

"No," said Reinnor, refilling his glass. He nudged the other glass, her glass, across the table. "I hate drinking alone."

She could stay here, at the other end of the room, pretending she had any sort of control, or she could drink the doubtless excellent liquor, in the comfortable seat, and listen to this eijen's lies. The man made no comment, or changed expression as Ori lowered herself into the chair's enveloping embrace and drained the glass in one swallow.

"But I think, with your assistance, we could find out," Reinnor continued, leaning forward, his narrow face alight with enthusiasm. "I know you don't have a very high opinion of us, and I can't say I blame you, but we're just as interested in getting out from under the Xi control as you are. I'm convinced that if we found out what their purpose is for you— "

"Their purpose?" Her chair scraped loudly across the floor as she sprang to her feet. "What purpose do they require except the need to inflict pain? They did not torture me for information. Your masters did not ask about the strength of our military assets, or the extent of our empire, or our intentions. They tortured for the pleasure of it, the joy of it, then they gave me over to you to continue the job."

Amid her rage, Ori noted that Reinnor had not moved, neither in reaction to her anger, or to remove himself out of range. The enthusiasm, though, had fled, replaced by horror and dawning comprehension.

"Do not," she warned, stepping back, away, until she felt a solid wall at her back. "I do not want your pity, your sympathy." Black despair flooded up, a wave of grief colder and sharper than the darkness between worlds.

"I want my freedom. Let me go." Shame filled her, as once again she succumbed and pleaded. That she had been reduced to this, begging for her freedom from an eijen. Her Line would be disgusted at her weakness.

Reinnor replaced his glass on the table with exquisite care, as if a wayward motion might catapult her into action. "I can't. I'm truly sorry. I have also been a target of their cruelty, but you know the Xi. You know what would happen if I disobeyed them. Their revenge would be terrible; it wouldn't only fall on me, but on my family as well."

If she killed him, took out the two agents, made it to the port. Perhaps she could steal a shuttle ... No. There were other agents, more guards. The AI network tracked her position second by second. Reinnor was correct. No matter what she did, the Xi would make sure she obeyed.

"The Xi manipulate and terrorize," Reinnor said, his voice soft, like the medic's. "But always, always for a reason. I have spent my entire life researching them. They did not torture you for pleasure, they do not keep you prisoner for entertainment. It may not be easy, but if we find out what they want you for, maybe that will give us both enough leverage to obtain our freedom."

"You say this so I will go to Ma'al without protest." The Xi may very well have a plan, but the Republic would never let her return to her people, even if she did complete whatever mission they had for her.

Reinnor sighed, an expression more of exasperation than anything. "I want you to go to Ma'al, yes. Because what they want is there. I'm sure of it. I promise, as soon as I know their orders, I will tell you."

"You forget," she said, now back on more familiar ground. "I do not have a berth. I thought the Directorate oversaw that, but weeks have gone by and nothing has happened. I tried to persuade your agents to take out the navigator of the *Hope*, and now that chance is gone, because you dragged me here."

The sound Reinnor made this time was of resigned patience as he retrieved the sheet. He made no attempt to come closer, simply holding out the sheet to her. She took it, resisting the urge to snatch it from him like a piqued child.

The sheet activated as her thumb found the depression in the unadorned syntheglass, instantly springing into life with a feed that she guessed came from the city AI, taken from a series of surveillance points — proof that this strange little man had been watching her. She recognized the area, a maze of tiny lanes and unexpected courtyards in the old town, below the café.

With nightfall, the mist had risen from the seafront, wreathing the streetlights in a dim yellow gloom, muffling and distorting every sound. A man came into view, shorter than her, but not by much, with a heavy build, and blond, short-cropped hair. No doubt he stank of beer, and spicy food, and sweat as he left the pub, pulling the collar of his heavy coat up against the nighttime chill. The feed switched seamlessly to Main Street where he turned left into a side street, past houses with flowerpots at the brightly colored doors, and into the poorly lit lane that led to the stairs connecting the lower town to the sad little park and the adjoining café

The lights across the lower end of town blinked off, and the feed switched to thermal imaging. The man cursed softly under his breath as he stumbled past the doorway of a closed shop. The drone appeared out of the mist, hovering silently for a second or two as it acquired its target; the dart took him in the neck. For a moment the navigator of the *Havali's Hope* stood, a puzzled expression forming, as he took in one ragged, desperate breath. His heart stopped, his lifeless body crumpling to the cold ground. The lights came back up and the feed ended.

"Now you have your berth, Oryelle."

Eleven

"ID?" She waved her wrist under the scanner and waited while the labor-hire rep plodded through the information populating his screen. Outside, the frigid wind swirled and gusted across the port and around the collection of temporary offices at the edge of the small freight area. At least she could escape the cold in the small demountable. After the interview with Reinnor, Finn and the other agent had wasted no time bundling her back into their vehicle, in which they'd then stayed warm after depositing her within visual range, confident she could not escape them. At no time had the overdressed little man ever told her who he really was. Directorate was the most likely answer; in reality, it didn't matter. It was yet to be seen if he had kept his promise and sent through her orders.

"Hmm…" The rep pecked at his screen. "Oryelle Tey, homeworld Orchetti Prime, says here you're a licensed navigator, certified to S5."

She was beginning to think that the reps were like warrior clones, all designed to a simple template and turned out in vast incubation facilities, somewhere dark and cold. They had been, nearly without exception, fat, greasy, avaricious, and lascivious, happy to take bribes, even happier to accept other trade, involving her and whatever body part they fancied.

"I know what it says. I have a berth, the *Havali's Hope*, bound for Ma'al, stopping at Corelli and Tersen. I had confirmation sixty-five minutes ago. Something about their regular not showing up."

The office reeked of stale air, stale food, sweat and dust. In one corner sat a shrine to the Old Ones, the name most of the Republic called the three non-humanoid races of Hubnae, Meian and Xi, a cluster of melted candles and wilted flowers laid out as offerings. Even in such an innocuous form, the thought of them made her skin crawl. Although she had never seen the Meian, every image she had seen depicted them as some sort of winged insect. Ori had met the Hubnae. The black, slug-like creatures were unlikely ever to forget her, either.

"Ah, yeah, fucking loser is probably drunk somewhere. But good news— " He scratched a spot in his greasy mop of hair. "You're booked on the *Sirius Nova*, sixteen weeks, bound for Polinia. It's just come up. They need a decent navigator and they'll pay above rate. That system is murder to get in and out of." He leered suggestively. "So, like, don't thank me for getting you a fantastic gig."

It took her a second to process the information. They'd assigned her to another ship? "I checked the feeds twenty minutes ago. I didn't get a notification." Her fists clenched, the nails digging into her flesh as disbelief warred with anger.

"Yeah, well their navigator got picked up for floess possession thirty minutes ago. It hasn't hit the job feed yet. I saw your profile on the feed." He leaned back in his chair, hands behind his head. "Thought to myself, that girl looks like she deserves a nice gig. That loser won't see the outside of a rehab clinic for at least a year."

A string of invectives ran through her mind. Would nothing on this assignment go to plan? "I want the *Havali* berth. I do not want to go to Polinia. I am not interested in extra pay. " She tried to keep calm; she couldn't afford to alienate another rep.

The man's fat, greasy face fell. "Hey, I'm doing you a favor here." His voice rose in anger. "I'm supposed to prioritize navigators, especially ex-Fleet. You signed up to the general pool, you can ask for a route, but I have full discretion to reassign anyone."

"So, who's on the *Havali*?"

"A navigator with less experience than you. You'd better not be one of those fucking Ma'al groupies. Freighter captains don't want your sort, thinking you're going to score big on Ma'al."

"I am not whatever a groupie is. I want the Ma'al run." She paused, knowing what would happen next. "I'll take anything."

"Well . . ." He leaned back again and gave her that look she'd had to endure too many times already on this mission. "A pretty girl like you should be able to persuade me." His hand drifted down to the bulge in his crotch. "If you really want to."

"Indeed, I think I might be able to do that." She leaned across the desk and the rep moved toward her, grinning in anticipation. Her hand shot out, latching into his greasy hair and slamming his head violently into the desktop.

"Bitch! Let me— "

She slammed his head again. Blood splattered from his broken nose and a tooth bounced to the floor.

"Now. Have I persuaded you? Or would you like more?" The little demountable didn't have the almost ubiquitous AI monitoring point, so Ori was spared the lecture about hurting civilians. She could kill him and no one would know until they found the body. Of course, the security cameras outside had captured her entering the building, and the two agents weren't far away, so it wouldn't take long before law enforcement would come after her. Whether Reinnor intervened to save her was too great an unknown. "Find me a berth to Ma'al. While you still have a face."

"All right, all right." He wiped the blood and snot from his face and pulled the screen toward him with trembling hands. "It was just a fucking joke. Fucking Fleet psychos." He tapped angrily at the screen while his broken nose dripped blood onto his uniform in thick, dark spots. "All right, I've an opening on the *Avadora*. As a general hand. That's less than half of what you'd get as a navigator. And she's old and slow, so have fun on a six-week run to Ma'al. Bitch. Ship runs on Central time, twenty-six hours, two thirteen-hour shifts."

"There, not much persuading needed after all." The small ping confirmed the addition of the ship assignment to her profile. A general hand was the lowest rank on a freighter, unskilled and poorly paid, but her plan would not work if she couldn't get a ship. This would have to do.

"Cunt." He spat at her. "Shuttle leaves soon, over on the other side of the loading bay. Don't ever fucking come back here."

The sun had long since set, descending into the gray sea behind a bank of equally gray clouds without fanfare. All along the coast, the city lights delineated the curve of the bay and the narrow strip of land, in a bright band hundreds of kilometers long. Inland on the vast plains, the evening wind carried the scents of engine exhaust and coolant and heated metal, while the undersides of the gray clouds glowed with the brilliant glare of the port. Icy gusts swirled around the gantries and the shuttles lined up on the tarmac and battered the sprawl of buildings containing the Six Jump Port Authority, while the intermittent rain created sodium-yellow halos around all the lights.

Yaol Zarr, junior cargo hand on the freighter *Avadora*, pulled his collar tighter and thrust his hands deep into his jacket pockets. The walk from home to the authority's office complex was a cold and lonely one, through dark, empty streets. Anyone with any sense stayed inside once the winter night came; the sea wind, wet and salty, bit through clothing and sent freezing bursts of rain to soak the unlucky. Anyone with any sense wouldn't have got into a raging argument with his family and stormed out of the house.

Zarr pulled out one hand and scrubbed away tears. "Damn you, Jacie," he whispered into the wind. Except it wasn't his sister's fault. "Second promotion in a year," his mother pronounced at dinner, while Jacie stared at her plate and Dad glowered at him from the other end of the table. *Why can't you be like your sister*, was the unspoken comment. *Why did you leave school, to go off to work the freighters?*

He knew it wasn't only that. If he'd had aspirations to get his own ship, signed up for his navigator's certificate — or even a Cargomaster's license — or took work on the larger freighters working inbound to systems like Polinia or Central, his family might have grudgingly accepted it. But working as a junior cargo hand on the old, slow *Avadora* just so he could spend a few days on Ma'al? That, his parents wouldn't tolerate.

"There you are. I've been looking for you."

Zarr gave a small, inward sigh and turned around. Ilsa Van, the *Avadora*'s engineer loomed over him.

"Hi, Van," he said, shoving his hands deeper into his pockets. "I just got here."

Van grunted, frowned, and scratched at his arm.

Great. He's got another implant. Which means in the three weeks since the last run, he's fallen back into the drinking again. Wonder how long this one will last?

"Have you signed in?" Zarr asked, jerking his head at the line that snaked across the synthecrete forecourt and up to the doors of the Port Authority's offices.

Van shook his head. "No. Thought Jen would be here, too."

Knowing Jen, they'd be lucky if she turned up on the right day. As the ship's maintenance officer, Jen struggled to keep the *Ava* going. She also treated the entire crew like they were overgrown children.

"Hey, Yaol," called a voice with the flat nasal twang of a Corelli native. "I missed you last trip."

Van swore under his breath. Zarr gave a sigh of annoyance and a brief, non-committal smile. "Hey, Minci," he said, eyeing off the line ahead of him, and calculating how long before he could evade the other man. "Yeah, missed you too." Minci headed toward them, and Zarr winced as the lanky figure stumbled over an unseen obstacle, but that was Minci; the man could fall over his own shadow.

"Hey guys," said Minci to the line, his too-large head bobbing on a scrawny neck that appeared barely capable of holding it upright. Van made a neutral grunt of acknowledgment. Minci had a habit of attaching himself to anyone who showed the slightest bit of interest. That had been Zarr's mistake.

"So off to Ma'al again?" Minci asked, as though this was a novelty. Minci had attached himself to Zarr nearly a year ago, and he asked the same damned thing every damned time.

"Yeah, off to Ma'al." Zarr took a quick look at the line, a few more minutes and he'd be inside. The ground shook and the night sky illuminated in brilliant light as a shuttle passed overhead, so close Zarr thought he could touch it if he'd been on the roof. No one in the group gave it the slightest attention.

"Hey, Zarr." Minci stuck his hands in his overall pockets in a blatant parody of Zarr's habit. "How's the fan club going?"

"I'm not in a fan club, I've told you that before." Zarr didn't try to cover his annoyance.

"So, you're not going to Ma'al and spend all your leave hanging out with other losers talking about an e-feed?" asked Minci with feigned innocence. Zarr opened his mouth, to launch into a defense of his obsession, as Van nudged him, nearly knocking him off his feet.

"Come on, Zarr, we have to sign off."

"Yeah, sure. Sorry, have to go. The shuttle leaves in a few hours and we're still short a fourth cargo hand, so it's going to be a busy trip."

"Yeah," said Minci, taking his hands out of his pockets and waving them around. "When are you guys going to find another hand? The last one left months ago."

Why the man had any interest in the crewing of the *Avadora* escaped Zarr. Hundreds of ships plied the Six Jump, Corelli, Tersen, Ma'al route. None of them captured Minci's attention. Or it could be that those crew had more sense than to allow him anywhere near them.

"He didn't work out," he said, shortly. The search for a fourth cargo hand for the Ava was a perennial source of frustration. The last one, whose name Zarr couldn't recall, was just the latest in a line of failures.

"Yeah, he turned out to be a bigger Ma'al groupie than Zarr here," Van said, with a half laugh. "Would not shut up about it. Even wore one of those fake plaits when he was off-duty. Captain couldn't wait to get in-system to dump him."

Despite the cold, Zarr felt himself go bright red. E'efi, that was his name. A total waste of oxygen. Couldn't do even the simplest tasks, although he'd told everyone he'd spent years on freighters. And his vocal and irritating cosplay had led to the captain cracking down on all on- and off-duty behavior. Now Zarr was banned from even mentioning his entertainment feed, *Hearts of Maal*. Totally unfair. Season Three had some really intense plot lines; it wasn't just lightweight crap like Van thought. No one stopped Davey from going on about his e-feed girls.

"I don't know why you keep signing up for that piece of junk, Zarr," said Minci, waving one hand in the air to punctuate his words. "Drop the Ma'al crap, and take a few runs out to the frontier; there's, like, five systems out there now with regular runs. Or go in-system, to Polinia, or one of their colonies. Nax'tl is nice, I hear. For a mining camp. I mean, doesn't your dad work here?" Minci's gesture encompassed the port buildings.

"It's not a piece of junk, and I don't need your advice. You live on Ma'al, where do you get off telling me I can't go there?" Zarr's voice rose in anger, loud enough to attract the attention of a few stragglers hanging around the entrance.

"For fuck's sake, Zarr, shut up," Van said, clamping his hand hard down on Zarr's shoulder and turning to the port worker. "Look, we've got to sign in and catch the shuttle. See you maybe on Ma'al."

"Yeah, sure, bo," Minci replied, suddenly aware the conversation had taken a turn for the worse. "Meant no harm, bo." His hands flapped awkwardly as if trying to bat away the uncomfortable feelings. He stomped away into the darkness, muttering to himself.

"He's fucking weird," said Zarr to Van, who shrugged, fumbling in his jacket as his sheet pinged loudly.

"Finally. Looks like we've got a fourth cargo hand," Van said, brightening for the first time. "We might have a good run this time."

"Let's hope it's someone with sense," Zarr spat back.

The bitter wind howled through the brilliantly lit cargo gantries, and around the piles of abandoned equipment, a counterpoint to the constant grumbling reverberations of the port that set the ground vibrating under Ori's feet. Another deep roar split the night air, and the glare of thrusters from a cargo shuttle lit up the night sky, the trail of fire rising into the darkness to the freighters in orbit. To space. To freedom.

Ori tracked its flight until it disappeared. The light pollution from the sprawling port complex prevented any glimpse of the night sky, so she couldn't even begin to try and pick out a familiar star, futile though she knew that to be. Home. If she could get a ship, she could escape and return to her people. Wherever they were.

Tears spread across her cheekbones to be dashed into the night by the wind. Fatigue tugged at her, making the cold wind and bright lights too intense. This wouldn't help. With a sigh of resignation, she released a dose of stimulants into her bloodstream and scrubbed at her face with the sleeve of her jacket. In the absence of sleep, that would have to do. She pulled her jacket closer and headed over to the makeshift shelter on the edge of the shuttle pick-up point where two long-abandoned cargo pods had been shoved into a rough L shape to give some protection from the wind. The freezing gusts tormented a ragged piece of tarp suspended between the pods, and drove sparks up into the darkness from a fire set in an old drive bearing.

The Directorate had subverted the Port Authority weeks ago, surveilling everywhere she went and everyone she had contact with. It wasn't all one way; she could access the AI directly and get information denied to an ordinary citizen.

Requesting access to crew files.

Hold, requesting authorization ... It took a real effort to contain her impatience while the AI sought approval from its human masters.

Which ship? the AI finally asked.

The Avadora. *Out of Six Jump, Corelli, Tersen, Ma'al route.* Another delay, infinitely slow for the AI, while it checked again.

Complying ... Crew files downloading now.

Ori dropped her bag to the ground and dragged an almost clean shipping crate closer to the warmth, grateful to be out of the cold. Four crew members sat around on a collection of discarded crates and barrels, all immersed in their feeds and illuminated by the fire. She pulled out her sheet, thumbed it to active and pretended equal interest. The entire area was suddenly as bright as day as another shuttle took off with an earth-shattering roar. None of her companions reacted, although Ori suspected they were all discreetly watching her to check her reaction.

"Hey, you going up to the *Ava*?" asked one. Ori inspected him from across the fire. He was about half a meter shorter than her, with a face that verged on skeletal, the usual close-shaven head, and faded Fleet tats that snaked down his neck to disappear into the top of his overalls, marking him as a general crew hand. One of the icons on her interface pulsed softly. A mental nudge and a screen opened, populated with the crew files. *Taedus Lart. Home world Corelli.* A string of minor public nuisance charges. Over forty years' service in Fleet, before his discharge twenty-three years ago for his part in a fight that put a cadet in hospital. His file contained line after line of ships he had served on. A very long list. Even with access to the best anti-aging meds, Lart should have retired over a decade ago. He was also the ship's representative for the conventions — a labyrinthine framework of regulations agreed to by most of the smaller freighter companies and all the independent ships. Designed to regulate life in space, where everyone had to work, and sleep and coexist, in vulnerable metal containers surrounded by the pitiless environment of hard vacuum.

"No, I like hanging around ports in the rain," she responded. The only other woman in the group laughed. *Jen Sukin. Home world Corelli. Maintenance officer on the Avadora for two years. Married, wife and two sons.* Again, another string of ships, all at low-level maintenance positions, none of them of sufficient seniority for her to be the maintenance officer. Sukin had a mass of dark curly hair, a round face and the sigil of the Blessed Mother, cupped palms holding a stylized flame, slung on a cord around her neck. She waved in the general direction of the rest of the group. "You can call me Jen — maintenance officer. That's Lart, cargo leading hand. The big guy is Van, the engineer— "

"Hey there, I'm Zarr," interrupted a young man, with close-cropped brown hair, and large ears that stuck out too far. He leaned over and held out his hand — to her obvious confusion. "Oh, sorry. I'm from Dimzi Ja. We shake hands there."

"Dimzi Ja? In the Kwali Sector?" She had never been there, but as far as she knew, no one in the Republic touched hands. *Yaol Zarr. Home world Six Jump.* This time, the list was a lot shorter, but only because he had barely two years of experience.

"Fuck off, Zarr," retorted Lart. "Your mum still lives down on Tressel Road, not twenty k's from here. You've never even been to Polinia, let alone DJ."

The boy blushed bright red and slumped back in his seat. "Ignore Zarr," explained Sukin. "I'm sure that's a line from his entertainment feed. *Hearts of Maal.* He's obsessed. Don't let him bore you to death with it." She patted the boy's leg fondly, and he turned even redder, folding his arms across his chest.

"So, who are you, again?" asked the final member of the group, Van the engineer.

He was about her height, wide shouldered and displaying far more recent Fleet tats, this time the curving glyphs of the engineering corp. She had found the Fleet obsession with their distinctive tattoos perplexing. Each division had its own unique designs, added on and embellished over years of service; if you were fluent in reading them you could track a person's entire career. Except for officers. For reasons she had never been able to discover, the service tattoos were banned for them. *Ilse Van. Home world Central. Fifteen years in the Fleet. Discharged four years ago in the last round of downsizing.* His records showed the same pattern — multiple ships, often for only one run, before being "let go". A euphemism for any number of issues all easily filed under the general heading of "Unreliable".

"Oryelle Tey, general hand," she replied.

According to the files, she had yet to meet the other hand, D'vai, and the navigator, Jwali ve Dev. D'vai again bounced from one ship to another. Jwali had been on the *Avadora* for years. He had his license, and a string of minor drug offenses, but nothing out of the ordinary for freighter crew. Why was he on a ship like this instead of something far more lucrative? Her unease turned into concern. How well maintained was this ship? How dysfunctional were the crew dynamics?

"I was on the Araedia III to O Prime run for a while," she replied, parroting her cover story, "but it's getting tight there for small haulers." If the story failed, this could be a very short trip.

"Yeah, we've heard." Sukin shook her head. "Lots of people coming in from that run. Hard to find work, even if you have papers." The maintenance officer knotted her hands over her plump stomach and shook her head again. "Not sure there's enough work for all us as it is. May the Blessed Mother protect us," she said, as she touched the pendant again.

"I just missed out on a berth to Polinia. The *Ava* was the first one I could get." Torture may have taught her how to survive in the no man's land between pain and oblivion, but imprisonment had taught her the necessity of subterfuge, as much as she might despise it.

Above them came the roar of engines.

"Shuttle's coming." Van picked up his bag. "Welcome to the *Ava*, Tey."

SIX JUMP

One

The shuttle, nothing more than a re-purposed cargo pod under the control of the port network, engaged with the *Avadora*'s airlock with a slight shudder. On the trip up, the maintenance officer, Sukin, attempted some random small talk, and there was more than one probing question from Engineer Van, but her briefings were thorough and eventually both withdrew into silence, apparently satisfied with Ori's answers. The boy, however, would not shut up; his inept but relentless interrogation irritating her until Lart, also losing patience, cuffed him into silence. The rest of the trip proceeded in blissful silence.

Ori hung back as Van and Sukin exited, lugging overstuffed bags — her own half-empty carryall hanging limply from her clenched fist. Lart impatiently waved the boy through ahead of him, before gesturing to the airlock coaming. "Mind your head on the hatch," said Lart. "Don't want you knocking yourself out on your first day."

Zarr giggled loudly. The hatch wasn't particularly small, but she still had to duck a little, suppressing irritation at the man's patronizing tone and the boy's obvious amusement. According to the files, the *Avadora* was twenty-five years old; Ori swore the bones of the ship creaked as she stepped through the airlock hatch and into the main corridor, the military-gray paint chipped and scratched. A strong metallic tang pointed to a malfunctioning recycler, most likely a clogged filter. Doubt gripped her. Had she made another terrible mistake?

"Hey, Jen," the boy yelled, "the air smells funny and Taddie here hasn't been on board more than five minutes!" He jabbed the old man with his elbow, overcome with laughter again at his own cleverness.

"Have some respect, boy." Lart only half-jokingly swiped at Zarr's head, and the boy dodged, still smirking, and collided with Van. The big engineer pushed the boy away with restrained irritation.

"That damned filter. You lot go stow your gear, and I'll go fix it. Again," the maintenance officer said, hefting her bag to her shoulder and heading off down the corridor. Van peeled off with her, without a word, although Ori caught his thoughtful glance directed at her as he left.

Lart and the boy headed off in the opposite direction. Ori followed, comparing the route to the schematics provided by the Directorate. So far everything matched up, location wise, as the pulsing blue light in her left field of vision traced their progress forward of the cargo bays and drives. Of all the possible problems with the ship, the condition of those drives now concerned her the most. The *Havali's Hope*, her original target, was only a few years old, with a crew of twelve; as her navigator Ori would have had almost unlimited access to the ship's systems. A successful escape plan required two elements — a ship capable of making the border in one jump— and access to the navigation and drive systems. She reached out to the ship's AI.

Ship?

Ava online.

At least the response time was acceptable. Perhaps this wreck was in better condition than she thought.

Requesting access, ship's navigation system.

Input access codes.

So, despite being old, someone on board was competent enough to set up decent security protocols. Ori would have to extract the codes from the captain before she killed all the crew. Without the correct codes, only the public areas — recorded entertainment feeds, backups of the news, some books and music, depending on the tastes of the crew, and the captain's budget— were accessible to the crew. There would be no comms once they jumped, so whatever was in the ship's data banks would be all the entertainment available in the long weeks between systems.

"Here we are: home for the next three months." Zarr pulled open a hatch. "It's no luxury liner, and it can be a bit crowded, but I've been on worse."

The compartment held four bunks, two against each bulkhead, with a small table bolted into position between them. Against the far bulkhead, four narrow lockers gave everyone personal storage space. Every surface was painted in varying tones of gray, chipped and worn in places, but clean. The bunks held a real blanket and two pillows. A young man lounged in one of the bottom bunks, ear buds in, watching something on his sheet. Ori guessed this was D'vai, the other cargo hand, and from the speed at which he killed the display, she suspected a sex feed.

Lart kicked the bunk. "This is Davey," the old man said, swinging his bag onto the other bunk. "Stop jerking off, this is Tey, she's new."

"Last in gets the last pick," the boy grumbled, rolling off the bunk with ill grace. D'vai wore his dark red hair cut close to his skull like all haulers, with a mass of freckles fanning out across pale skin. His ship's issue overalls were rumpled and bore more than one food stain down the front. A wash of neuro-suppressors controlled her disgust at the prospect of sharing space with these animals for weeks.

"Me and Davey are in the bottom two, you and Zarr have the top ones." Lart started unpacking his belongings, making neat piles of clothes and personal items. Ori debated throwing her bag into one of the lockers, before deciding she didn't care if they saw how little she had. The small pile of clothes, in the cheapest print run available, and an equally small bag of toiletries, was all Reinnor's agents had allowed her. Whether this was out of general spite or payback for humiliating them in front of their boss, Ori had no idea, and less interest. What else would you expect from eijen?

The general chatter and noise abruptly stopped as a woman appeared at the hatch, sharp-faced, her frown etched into her bones. A mental nudge at the ship's files identified this was Cargomaster Lianna, co-owner of the ship with her wife, Captain Marissa. Lianna surveyed the room as if suspecting mutiny.

"Get changed, stow your crap and report to the mess for the briefing," Lianna ordered, turning her attention to Ori. For a long moment, the cargomaster stared at her. "Change into your uniform, this isn't a cruise ship," she said, contempt dripping from every word. No one said anything, but Ori heard the boy's suppressed mutter from his place in the corner.

"Yes, Cargomaster," Ori replied, as she pulled out a standard ship's overall from the pile. Lianna looked around the cabin once more, made a disgusted noise and left. Lart spat an obscenity, although Ori noted he waited until Lianna was well out of earshot.

"That's Lianna," said the boy, sidling up to her, one eye on the vacant hatch, "stay out of her way if you can. Otherwise, you'll find yourself scrubbing out storage lockers forever." He paused. "Um," he continued in a whisper, hands thrust down into the pockets of his overalls, and a bright red blush extending up to his ears, "the showers are down the hall, if you want to get changed."

Ori looked around the cabin and found Lart busy at his locker, slowly rearranging his clothes, while the other cargo hand, D'vai, lounged on his bunk studiously avoiding looking at anything. If eight years of training, and another three decades of military service had not disabused her of the notion of privacy, ten years of imprisonment certainly had. They were probably waiting for her to make a mistake; if she left to change, doubtless the crew would mock her for her squeamishness. Without a word, she began to strip down, ignoring Zarr's strangled yelp of surprise.

"Yes?" she said, arching an eyebrow. Zarr blushed a deep scarlet, obliterating the freckles and igniting his ears in flames.

Lart smacked the boy, hard, rocking him on his feet. "What have I said?" the old man demanded.

"No looking, no touching. Sorry," Zarr mumbled, rubbing the back of his head, while the older cargo hand, D'vai, smirked.

"Sorry, we don't, you know, see many like you." Lart waved his hand at her. "You can lodge a complaint."

Zarr stood rubbing his head, not looking at her. Aggravating the crew over such a small thing had no strategic advantages. There'd been no shortage of guards who enjoyed forcing her to expose herself for their amusement. One ogling child didn't count.

"Make sure he keeps his hands to himself."

"Thanks," said Lart, with obvious relief, nudging Zarr hard in the ribs. "Say you're sorry."

"Sorry," he mumbled, going bright red with embarrassment, as Ori turned away and continued dressing.

Nothing more was said as they all filed down to the mess. D'vai clearly enjoyed tormenting his younger crewmate, nudging him into hatches and protruding bulkheads, or attempting to trip him until Lart lost his temper again and smacked both. The boy, Zarr, said nothing, continuing to keep his head down, and accepting Lart's blow with nothing more than a hiss of pain. Ori made no attempt to interfere. None of these animals would have survived her own training.

The mess conformed to the schematics Reinnor's agents had given her, much to Ori's relief. Her cover story of being a long-haul navigator would be seriously questioned if she couldn't find the mess or work a reheater. There were three tables with bench seats, all painted in the same overlapping tones of gray as the rest of the ship, cold stores for the pre-packaged meals, a drink dispenser, and a bank of reheating chambers.

Everyone either took a seat or, like Van and herself, lounged against the bulkheads. Amid the general chatter and banter, Van kept glancing in her direction. Interest or suspicion? She didn't need anyone asking questions. Reinnor's agents had provided an extensive cover story, designed to cover most eventualities, but one mistake could unravel the entire mission. Once they reached Tersen, it wouldn't matter anyway.

On one wall, a screen played a constant loop of information feeds from the Port Authority. A news update slid across the bottom. The death toll from the Freedom Square riot was now at thirty-four. Three systems were threatening to secede over the chaos. Good. They might hang Rossim from the palace gates. There was something about Ma'al, then Ori's attention was snatched away as the cargomaster banged on a table for quiet.

"Right, we finally have a fourth cargo hand. Tey's over there." She pointed generally in Ori's direction. "Tey, this is nearly everyone. Captain Marissa is on the bridge; you'll meet her later. This is Jwali, our navigator."

Jwali's thin, sharp features and short-cropped brown hair bore an unmistakable resemblance to the Cargomaster's. Then she caught his gaze. Predatory. Cold. The sort of look she'd received from too many guards. Her skin crawled, the response provoking her automatic systems to alert. Peripherals flashed amber, warning of rising stress hormones. Refusing to be provoked, Ori returned his gaze with contempt and the navigator flushed red with anger, much to her amusement.

"We're currently waiting for the cargo pods to be loaded," Lianna continued. "Our present schedule gives us only one shift to complete that, so no slacking. Our jump window opens in exactly fourteen hours. Corelli is our first stop. The usual procedure: we wait for clearance, do the small jump into L5, and from there into our assigned slot and drop our pods. Next jump is the usual set up — refuel and cargo exchange at Tersen. And before anyone asks, no, no one is going dirtside until Ma'al. Any questions? No? Right, go and eat, whatever. First shift starts in an hour. Tey and Zarr, you're up first. Cargo pods. Davey and Lart, you're down with Van in engineering and Jen in maintenance."

The meeting broke up. Jwali left with Lianna, but not before giving Ori one last venomous glare over his shoulder. The rest of the crew milled around, rummaging for a meal, filling mugs with rakosh or messil, arguing over access to the reheaters. Ori took her food and mug and found a seat, expecting to be left alone. To her discomfort, Zarr and

D'vai joined her, food trays in one hand, screens in the other. A few seconds later, Lart slid in beside her, dropping his tray with a loud clatter onto the tabletop with its hagiography of scratched initials and chipped edges. She kept her attention fixed on her food, taking occasional covert glances around the room. Van and Sukin sat at an adjacent table, eating and chatting with the familiarity of shipmates. A pang of some emotion, part loss and part anger, bubbled up like acid in the back of her throat and she stabbed viciously with her fork at a lump of unidentifiable cultured protein until D'vai's surprised grunt distracted her from the attack.

"They found Jerris, the navigator for the *Hope*, dead in an alley. Brain anu— something." He read out the report in a tone of surprise and disgust. "By the Blessed Mother, that sucks. He was a good guy."

"Aneurysm," Lart corrected, in obvious distress, "I saw him in the pub a few days ago." He shook his head in disbelief. "He was seeing that lovely girl up at the café. J'nni."

Zarr leaned forward as if imparting some great secret. "You know ..." He paused. "I did read there were people who could make you drop dead. Or control you with their minds. Make you do anything they wanted."

"Yeah, sure, Zarr." Lart nudged Ori conspiratorially. "Someone telepathically killed a hauler and made out it was a terrible accident. Is that because he had information the Abominations are going to return to avenge Da Chet or that he knew the secret to Ma'al silk? Or, no, what about that one where the Old Ones still rule the Republic in secret?"

"Just because they're on conspiracy feeds doesn't make them any less true," Zarr said with an air of defensiveness. "I mean, some of them are shit, obviously."

"Zarr." D'vai didn't bother looking up from his sheet. "They're all shit. All the engineered died in the purge. That old story about some of them escaping is crap. And don't get me started on all those pathetic losers claiming they're a long-lost Imperial heir. The same goes for those fucking creepy spiders. The whole thing is shit."

For a second, Ori gave serious consideration to telling D'vai the truth: that the *fucking creepy spiders* did indeed rule the Republic, but dismissed the idea. The animals did not deserve the truth. As for Jerris, no doubt J'nni would find a new source of expensive jewelry. Across the table, Zarr poked at his food, gripping a chipped "I heart Maal" mug tightly. Stupid boy couldn't even get the spelling correct.

"OK, so what about Fried'nz then?" he said, in a tone of aggrievement.

Everyone at the table began to laugh, except Ori, who didn't understand the joke, and the boy, who went redder still.

"Fried'nz?" she asked, drawn into this conversation more than she wanted.

"A nutter," said Lart.

"Yeah, a nutter," agreed D'vai, nudging the boy roughly, so that his utensil clattered to the deck.

"He wasn't a nutter, he worked for the Directorate of Protection," Zarr said, retrieving the spoon and wiping it on his overalls, "in the Antiquities department."

D'vai caught her raised eyebrow and launched into an explanation. "The department in charge of hunting down Da Chet scavengers and confiscating the stuff they find, and he was a cleaner."

I wonder if he ever saw the glass orb? Even weeks later, she didn't need digital memory to recall the smooth, cool surface, or the flash of color in the sunlight.

"No, he was an archivist; the feeds started saying he was a cleaner afterwards." Zarr's voice rose in pitch and volume.

"So, what did he do that causes such amusement?" Ori asked, her curiosity unexpectedly piqued.

"He wrote a book," began Zarr.

"Yeah, a work of fiction," noted Lart, who collapsed into laughter again.

"He said he found a data storage unit, like a primitive sheet, and he said he retrieved data from it," answered Zarr, glaring at Lart.

"I don't understand what's so surprising about that," Ori said. "Technology hasn't advanced so far in a few hundred years." In fact, you could make the case that technology had regressed since the end of the war. The ban on genetic engineering also extended to the many enhancements and augmentations that Ori carried within herself, including the microscopic nanites. All these technologies were banned; long prison sentences, and sometimes the death penalty, was imposed for law breakers.

"It was messages; normal, ordinary texts between two Abominations, complaining about stuff. Boring. Can you imagine?" D'vai adopted high-pitched sing-song type speech, "Oh, my vat is sooo slimy this morning, and did you hear what my clone did?"

"I still don't see the point," said Ori, beginning to take a real dislike to D'vai.

"Ignore Davey, he's an idiot," said Zarr, and received an elbow in the ribs from the older boy. "The real controversy is his chapter about the thefts."

"Thefts?"

"Yes, Fried'nz wrote that most of the messages were an investigation into a theft from a research facility. Remember, this was months before the attack on Da Chet.

"Yeah, when we slagged those Abominations to ash," crowed D'vai.

Ori had little sympathy for the long-dead engineered of the Imperium. The civil war had raged for decades, displacing entire planetary populations; the death toll had reached billions long before Da Chet's annihilation. They had lost, proving they were inferior. There was only one race of True People in the galaxy — hers. The rest were just animals. "We have work to do," she said, losing interest in the story. "The cargomaster has given us our assignments and I have no wish to be disciplined on my first shift." She threw her tray and mug into the cleaning unit and headed toward the cargo bay. After a minute, the boy followed, trailing silently behind her.

Two

Zarr remained silent on the way down to the hold. Ori, immersed in calculations, ignored him. Factoring in the cargo drop at Corelli, it would be at least five weeks until the *Ava* dropped into Tersen space given how frustratingly slow this ship was. Five weeks of living with animals. Five weeks before she could kill them and take the ship. All she had to do was not arouse any suspicions. That shouldn't be too difficult; they all appeared remarkably stupid.

They came to the end of the corridor, and Ori, distracted by her planning, did not at first comprehend that the boy, Zarr, was looking at her strangely.

They were in the wrong corridor.

"Have you ever served on anything this old before?" Zarr asked, his voice tinged with amusement.

"No," Ori replied, pushing the anger back down. "I didn't think the layouts would be so different." She had the schematics, there, ready, waiting. How could she be this incompetent?

"It's this way." He pointed down a side corridor. A faded sign on the bulkhead pointed the way to the cargo holds. Seething with humiliation, Ori followed the boy to a hatch marked CARGO HOLD — PORT in Standard and Polini, and through to the walkway overlooking one half of the *Avadora*'s hold. The bulkheads in this section loomed heavy with reinforcement, as did a series of hatches that ran the length of the walkway.

The walkway followed the main axis of the ship. At a fraction over two hundred meters long and massing nearly a quarter of a million tons fully loaded, the *Avadora* resembled nothing more than a fat cylinder, with a lumpy nose at one end and a bundle of thruster cones at the other. The forward section held mainly water and supplies, protected from any impacts by an incredibly thick and reinforced hull. Behind that were crew facilities, then crew quarters, and finally the bridge and the captain's quarters. At the end were the drives and the engineering sections.

All of that took up only a small percentage of the *Avadora's* bulk. The rest was cargo bays. Two hemispheres running the length of the ship, with a combined circumference of over thirty-five meters. Each section of *Avadora's* hold could be vented individually as loading and unloading proceeded. In the cargo bays, enormous reinforced rails ran out at ninety degrees to this spine in a three-hundred-and-sixty-degree arc. Each rail could hold twenty standard-sized cargo pods, full of everything from Orchetti root to machine parts and consumer items.

AI-controlled cargo shuttles ferried the pods up to the ship where the cargo hands would guide each pod into its correct position on the designated rail. When Ori and Zarr entered, half of the slots were empty, awaiting their loads from the surface. Also waiting for them was Cargomaster Lianna, sheet in one hand, with a scowl that could curdle milk.

"Take the scenic route, did you?" Ori waited for the boy to blame her for the delay, but he remained silent. Lianna gave them both an icy glare. "Move your asses; the first delivery is on its way." The cargomaster surveyed Ori, clearly searching for something to complain about. "Do you know your decompression protocols?"

"I am quite competent in all ship functions." Ori doubted that any of this crew were proficient in decompression protocols, let alone knowing how to function in one. "I know what to do." On a freighter, such incidents would be rare.

The cargomaster glowered at her. Ori met her gaze without reaction. The older woman scowled and shoved a sheet into Ori's hands. "Tey, forward position, Zarr, you're aft. Move."

The boy scurried off to the other end of the walkway.

"Ava," ordered Lianna, "prepare for cargo transfer."

"Acknowledged. Crew standby. Venting cargo bay," warned the AI. Orange warning lights flashed, accompanied by the obligatory warning sirens. "Cargo bay clear, opening bay doors." The entire walkway shuddered as the massive doors of the cargo bay swung open.

It seemed the cargomaster intended to supervise her new cargo handler as the older woman followed Ori to her station. Ori logged in with her ID chip, but the expected holo-controls didn't materialize. Lianna cursed under her breath and hit the side of the panel with her fist. The display spluttered into life; thruster controls for the pods, cargo information and schematics on the screen, showing her where each pod should go.

"Tey, are you ready? Don't cock this up," warned Lianna.

"No, Cargomaster. I'll try not to," she said, struggling to keep the anger from showing. Children could handle pod docking, even an idiot like Zarr should be capable of carrying it out without too many mistakes.

The first shuttle arrived and, with a series of maneuvering thrusts, positioned itself parallel to the cargo hold. A quick glance at the screen confirmed the pod's intended position.

"Ready port, relinquish control," Ori said as the cargomaster hovered at her shoulder.

Her hands moved across the display, directing the thrusters with discrete, precise bursts of power. Once lined up, thrusters on the pod slid it along the docking rail to lock into position, the walkway shuddering slightly with every impact. Lianna watched for a few dockings, comparing the cargo display with her own information. Satisfied, she stomped off down the walkway to Zarr, at the furthest end of the hold.

Ori waited until the woman was engaged in berating Zarr for some misdemeanor before reaching out to the cargo-docking console. Unlike the ship's AI, this station accepted her contact without question. Screens popped up into her vision, a 3D rendering of the hold and location of the port's shuttles. A mental nudge and the position of the next pod flashed on the screen. It was easy to lose herself in the simple task of placing each pod into its slot with the minimum of effort. Time melted away; between each delivery there was more than enough time to slide into the console's operating system and poke around. The back door to the navigation system was an unexpected gift. She may not need to bother about torturing the captain for the access codes after all.

She looked up to see Zarr, halfway down the walkway, waving to her. Cursing, she dropped the interface, closing the screens down. Immersed in her tasks, she hadn't seen the comms button blinking. "What?" she asked.

"Break time? We are allowed to eat, you know."

Zarr led her to a compartment off the cargo bay. It held a table and two benches, a water dispenser and garbage disposal. A battered portable cooler, labeled FOOD ONLY in Standard and Polini, sat on the table.

"How's it going?" the boy asked, heading straight to the cooler and pushing the lid open. He rummaged noisily around for a few minutes before retrieving two food packs.

"I can manage a few cargo pods," she said. Her sarcasm either went unnoticed or he ignored it.

"Yeah, well I was watching, you handled those pods like, amazingly. And this is the first time Lianna hasn't been down here yelling at me, so that's a win right there," he said, smiling.

"I am pleased to have met your expectations," she said acidly, settling herself on one of the benches, frowning when it wobbled under her.

"Yeah, Jen does her best, but things get forgotten," he said, following her gaze to the holes where bolts once used to secure the equipment to the deck.

Many things were forgotten, evidently. Ori noted the build-up of dirt in the corners, the scuffed, badly painted fixtures. A scratched and faded sign fixed crookedly to the bulkhead with a liberal use of industrial tape exhorted users of the compartment to clean up after themselves. Someone had scrawled an obscenity in one corner, giving detailed instructions on how best that could be achieved.

"This ship is not that large," Ori pointed out, accepting a meal pack from the boy, "and there is more than sufficient time between cargo drops." Slow didn't adequately describe the excruciating pace of the old ship. Her own ship, the one she lost, could have completed the entire run, cargo drops and all in five days. The thought of it, and all her lost crew, threatened to overwhelm her.

"Yeah, you're welcome to point that out to Jen, sure she'd appreciate the suggestion," he said, with another snort of amusement, "just, please don't say it around Lianna." He took a seat opposite her and tore open the packaging. "So, been to Ma'al before?"

"No," she said, while neuro-suppressors worked to reduce the levels of cortisol raging through her bloodstream, "this is my first run there."

If everything went to plan, the *Ava* would never drop into Ma'al space again, and all the crew would be dead. She took an experimental bite of the food. Cultured protein, she guessed, with some sort of spicy Orchetti-root-based filling, in a bread roll. Far from gourmet, but still significantly better than prison rations. She took a bite, chewing and swallowing without delay. Trainees learned at an early age to eat and drink whenever possible and to be quick about it. You never knew when the next meal would appear, or whether you would be in any condition to eat it.

"The domes are amazing. You'll love Main Dome; there a lake in the middle of it, and a spout that shoots water up into the air," Zarr rambled on, describing more of the highlights of Ma'al with a mouth full of food. "And there are shops, and the Polini silver quarter is— "

"I would like to eat my meal in peace, if possible."

"The first few days on a new ship are always hard. You'll settle in."

Ori saw his hand reaching for her in her peripheral vision. The half-eaten roll fell to the deck as she recoiled, jumping back from the table, her body shifting into attack mode, graphene mesh prickly and sharp. Fear coursed through her, icy shivers running up and down her back.

"Hey, whoa," Zarr said, holding his own hands up in a placatory gesture. "I didn't mean to frighten you." The boy rose, confusion and worry turning his awkward ears bright red. "It's OK, I'm not going to hurt you."

"Keep your hands off me, boy." Formless, irrational rage took hold of her. "I've spent most of my life in space," she snapped, "I don't need time to 'settle in'. And I don't need advice, either. Touch me again, and I swear— " The words died in her throat. Threatening the crew within hours of coming on board was hardly smart. "Leave me alone." She turned and stalked back to her post without another word.

"I'm sorry," Zarr called after her.

Her hands were still shaking when she reached the station. *You are damaged, voices whispered, like tiny feet on webs. Damaged, broken, weak. They will never take you back.*

"Shut up," she whispered to herself. More chemicals rushed through her, banishing the voices, and the anger. Warnings scrolled across the bottom of her left eye, the enhancements chiding her about the toll these constant stresses were taking. She ignored them, wiping them away with a thought and turned back to her tasks.

Three hours later, Lianna stalked back down the walkway, sheet clutched in one hand, scowl etched into her thin face. The cargomaster headed for the boy first, gesturing to the pods and her sheet with vehement intensity. In response, Zarr shook his head, pointing down to Ori's station. Now what was the boy telling her? Whatever it was, Lianna didn't come down to confront her, instead she stalked away again. The last pods were clicking into place when the woman appeared again, sweeping past Zarr without a word and heading straight for Ori.

The sub-dermal armor activated, sharp and prickly, but Lianna ignored her.

"Port, this is the *Avadora*, confirm all cargo delivered according to manifest," Lianna said, stabbing at her sheet as if angry with the information it held.

"*Avadora*, this is Port. All cargo delivered. Very smooth operation, much appreciated."

Lianna huffed derisively, and logged off the manifest with her ID chip.

"Right. Captain wants to see you on the bridge. Don't keep her waiting." She stalked off again without another word.

"No ma'am," Ori said to the retreating back.

All the way up to the bridge she worried over the summons. Had the boy complained about her behavior? They were close to their jump window, so she wouldn't be put off now, but perhaps some form of punishment would be enforced?

She still had weeks before they reached Tersen. She would have to keep her anger under control until then.

"You wished to see me, Captain?"

Compared to the bridge of a battleship, *Ava*'s command center looked like a maintenance cupboard. There were three consoles: the navigator's, the captain's, and the auxiliary station, if the ship ran to a second officer. A curve of syntheglass monitors relayed the sensor feeds, both internally and externally, although at least a quarter of them were either dark or malfunctioning. Every spare corner held a pile of miscellaneous items, netted and tied to the bulkhead, in case of loss of the artificial gravity. None of the piles looked like they had moved for years.

Jwali sat at his console, his back to her, studiously ignoring her, the nav panel live in front of him. The 3D representation of Six's system, full of ships, satellites, orbital platforms and moons, formed a tiny golden cloud as Jwali fiddled with the display, zooming around the system, unsuccessfully trying to look busy. At least two of the three drink containers arranged in a drunken line behind the console were days, if not weeks old.

"The cargomaster says you did an exemplary job on the cargo docking." Marisa had that look you got from too many stretches without anti-aging meds — patches of firm, young skin mixed in with wrinkled areas, and sagging jowls. Like all haulers she wore her dark hair cropped short; the single gold ring in her left ear a declaration of her married status.

Ori knew the only response should be a grateful *thank you, Captain*. In fact, she had made several small mistakes. Mistakes her trainers would have picked up immediately. Her back twitched at the memory. "Thank you. Captain," she managed, in the same voice she used when a guard needed placating. Marissa seemed not to notice, her gaze resting squarely on the back of the navigator's head, as Jwali continued to play with the resolution of the display, checking their position against all the other ships in orbit. Six Jump was a busy system.

"Zarr seems to like you, too. He could do with someone to give him a bit of direction. I'd be happy if he stopped going on about that damned feed of his." The gold ring, a small delicate thing, winked in the bridge lighting as the captain turned it through her ear.

He likes me? He was seconds away from being tossed down the cargo hold. Animals all of them. What did she care if one of them liked her?

"Yes, Captain," she replied, confused.

"I've read your file. You have your navigator's papers. Certified to S5 systems." The earring took another turn, smooth gold pressed between work-worn fingers.

Jwali's shoulders stiffened.

"Yes, ma'am." S5 systems were large, old ones like Central and Polinia, full of multiple occupied worlds, often terraformed millennia ago; orbital platforms, satellites, space-ports, moons and asteroid belts full of mining operations. And ships, lots of ships. Fleet battleships and cruisers, private vessels, civilian transports, freighters. Space was so huge the distances between objects were hard to grasp, however, fill up a system with enough things and plotting jumps in and out required pinpoint accuracy. No one wanted to be the navigator that dropped out too close to a Fleet battleship.

That the Directorate wouldn't give her a captain's rating still rankled. The certification, like her ID, was a forgery, but the agents knew that she had the ability to drop a ship into its exact position, even on in-system tactical jumps. The ability to plot a jump precisely and accurately into normal space was the basis of interstellar warfare. The cleansing of the galaxy was a sacred duty.

"I sincerely hope that taking a berth with us was not due to any undisclosed disciplinary issues with your previous berths. Or that you're another Ma'al obsessive. One on board is quite enough," said the captain, a quiet weariness in her voice.

"I wanted a short run, ma'am. I'm not interested in Ma'al." Reinnor's theories floated at the back of her mind, but Ori dismissed them. Who cared if the Republic languished under the covert rule of the Xi? In a few weeks, this crew would be dead, and she would be on her way to freedom.

"Good." Marissa switched her attention from her navigator to Ori and subjected her to a look of icy determination. "I want to make this very clear. I will have no hesitation in dumping you off my ship if you cause any problems. Dismissed. We're jumping in ninety-three minutes and Jwali has to make sure we land in the right system."

Three

O ri made her way back to the mess along the narrow corridors with their mosaic paintwork, overlaid with the scratches and chips of years of passing traffic. Introspection was not a trait encouraged by her people. Questions led to doubts. Doubts would lead you to an unpleasant and protracted death.

Despite this, Reinnor's words kept circling around at the back of her mind like noisy drones. She'd gone over the conversation, both in organic and digital replay, and concluded quite quickly that he was hiding something. Not an unexpected revelation — all these animals lied; the Xi most of all.

Tell us the truth and the pain will stop. Tell us where you come from and we'll let you go. We promise.

What had they lied about? The terrible thought came rushing up. Maybe the ship hadn't been destroyed, maybe there were others, other survivors.

No. Ori forced the images that provoked right back down. Down there was desperation and a deep, obsidian despair waiting to consume her. There had only ever been her. They'd escaped, most of them, she'd helped push them into the escape pods. The crew was safe. She kept repeating that, until the terror subsided, washed away on a tsunami of neuro-suppressors.

Her mind, however, would not leave Reinnor and his ideas alone. *They did not torture you for pleasure, they do not keep you prisoner for entertainment.* The animals could not be trusted, yet those words carried a weight Ori could not dismiss out of hand, as much as she wanted to.

If that were true, then what were these missions about? In all the years she had been in the Directorate's control, she had been taken from her prison nine times. First to Garrett's office, later Rossim's when he became Lord President, before transfer to a Fleet ship — always under the watchful eye of the Imperial Guard. A covert team would insert her into whatever the situation required, a team of handlers would monitor her every movement, with the ubiquitous AI oversight in case she caused any trouble, like trying to escape. In all that time, no one had ever explained what it was she was doing, or why. Nor had Ori ever been able to see a pattern or a motive, and the missions themselves made no sense. Five assassinations, although she had never been able to see any reason for them, unless they were political rivals. The other missions varied as well, three seductions, and one as a courier. What if the Republic didn't know either? Had Rossim and Garrett been blindly obeying the Xi all these years, without any answers?

Now, not only were the Xi offering freedom, but she was on a mission, unaccompanied, unmonitored, and seemingly left to her own devices. None of it made sense, but as Ori pushed open the mess hatch, she had to concede that perhaps it only needed to make sense to the Xi.

"Hey, Zarr, wait up," Davey called from the other end of the corridor. Zarr stopped, wincing inwardly. The older cargo hand was OK, but he had a big mouth, big opinions and used both too frequently. He also seemed to have made it his personal mission to torment Zarr any chance he got.

"Yeah, Davey." Zarr leaned against the bulkhead until the older man caught up, "What do you want?"

"Hey, that's no way to talk to a friend," Davey said, punching him on the upper arm, a playful gesture that had more weight behind it than it should. "Where's that choice piece of ass?"

Zarr felt himself go bright red. "I don't know. She went up to see the captain; not seen her since." He pushed himself off the wall and headed toward the mess. His hands, lodged in his pockets, clenched into fists. He wasn't going to give Davey the satisfaction of seeing him rub his arm. "You shouldn't talk about her like that."

"Oh, for fuck's sake, bo. You saw her, same as I did. No one like her takes a job on a heap of crap like this unless she's running from something. Or to someone. Either way, she's no hauler, no matter what she says. She's either someone's tremmie or some rich bitch pretending to rough it."

"Well, she's a damned competent one then," Zarr shot back. "Landed all her pods in record time, you should have seen it. Even Lianna couldn't find anything to complain about. Show me a whore that can do that. None of your feed girls could."

"Yeah?" He appeared to think about that. "Well, in that case, better keep an eye on her. When that cunt Jwali gets a sniff of her, she'll be his new pet."

"Me?"

"She's on your shift, bo." Davey whacked him between the shoulder blades, hard enough to rock Zarr forward. "Remember. *Sex. Power. Treachery.* Not my problem." He gave Zarr a wide grin and sauntered into the mess.

It's Wealth. Honor. Family, Zarr wanted to yell after him but instead he clenched his fists tighter and fought down his anger. There was no way he was getting into a fight with Davey; the captain was looking for any excuse to dump Zarr on the nearest rock. Once that happened, the chances of getting another berth plummeted to near zero. He just wished Davey would stop using the *Hearts* tag line as a long running and irritating joke.

Zarr sighed and rubbed at his arm. He was about to follow Davey into the mess when he caught sight of the new cargo hand sitting at the far table, her back hard against the bulkhead. Davey swaggered up and said something to her. She nodded warily, and answered, her face a mask of studied indifference; he backed away, deflated.

Once Davey left, though, the indifference drained away, leaving behind something Zarr recognized. Pain. He saw it every day in his own reflection, as much as he denied it to anyone else. Not physical pain, although he could see the shadow of that on her; this was the pain of a thousand humiliations and abuses. The transition from the boring mediocrity of his safe, middle-class existence to the perceived excitement of an inter-system hauler had been swift, brutal, and terrifying. You had to be either quick on your feet, or quick with your fists to survive. He was neither, so he'd plummeted to the bottom of the heap quickly. A position he had never escaped from.

She ran her hands through her hair in a gesture of utter exhaustion, picked up her mug, her eyes almost closed, on the edge of sleep. The sight of her, so alone and helpless, struck Zarr like a blow, something inside of him shattered into countless hot shards of anger and understanding, and he had to stifle the impulse to rush over and comfort her.

Four

O ri took another sip of rakosh and closed her eyes. Exhaustion tugged at her, icons pulsed in the corners of her eyes, demanding attention. The ship had jumped thirty-five minutes ago, with the tell-tale microsecond of gravity distortion. She needed sleep. Something rocked the table, startling her awake. The boy, Zarr, pushed a meal over toward her, followed by a handful of mismatched utensils.

"You look exhausted. I got dinner." He ripped the lid off his meal and dug around in it. "These are gold. The best ones always go first."

She stared at the packet. Jeraka stew with Orchetti noodles, according to the label. Her stomach growled with hunger.

"Why?" she asked, ignoring the food. Kindness always came with a price.

"Why what?" He didn't look up, instead he kept digging around in the gravy until he found the bits he wanted before popping the morsels into his mouth.

"Why did you bring me dinner?" she asked, the edge of anger seeping into her voice. What did the boy want? What favor would she be expected to give in return?

Zarr looked up, surprised. "Because I wanted to?" He tilted his head inquiringly. "Aren't you hungry?" he asked, the first hints of uncertainty in his voice.

The boy appeared genuine, probably too young and inexperienced to use food as a bargaining point. "Yes." She peeled back the foil lid and surveyed the contents with suspicion. After years of rations, she'd almost forgotten what real food tasted like.

Zarr chuckled at her. "You're lookin' at that like it's an Eidress lawyer. It isn't goin' to sue you." He laughed again, overtaken by his own joke.

She shoveled a forkful into her mouth, ignoring the boy's grin as he pushed a mug of water over to her.

"Have you ever met one?" she asked, abruptly curious. Hundreds of portraits of Eidress trained legal luminaries hung on the walls of the palace and Rossim's office. High court judges, prosecutors, defense attorneys. An Eidress lawyer was an anomaly, a lawyer who did not work for money. Why should they, when every single Ma'al adult was a shareholder in a commercial enterprise that could buy the entire Republic twice over, and still have enough left over to buy something small like the Orchetti Combine?

"An Eidress?" He shook his head. "Not one with any rank. You might meet an intern. Lots of them down in the entertainment dome. You can tell the second years, they wear the dark green che'b'ni, but without any gold." He brandished his fork in a circular motion. "The wriggly bits they put on. Embroidery, I think it is. I mean— " The boy stuffed a spoonful of stew in his mouth and proceeded to use the cutlery to emphasize his point. "Not all the hanjiles are so snobby. You often see Saliri of some of the other hanjiles down there." Zarr's face flushed bright scarlet, right up to the tips of those stupid ears. "Ah, is, um, that what you're looking for?" he stammered with embarrassment. "'Cause, you know, they're, like, strict about letting outsiders in. Though I can't see you as anybody's tremmie—"

Her mug hit the adjoining table with a resounding crash, a rooster-tail of water describing its arc. "Call me a whore again, boy," she said, her voice quiet and even, "and I'll make sure they never find your body."

Both Lart and D'vai leaped to their feet, concern pouring from them, as her fists clenched and the sub-dermal armor ran hard and prickly under her skin.

"Hey, I didn't mean it like that," the boy protested, half rising from his seat. The entire mess went silent. "I'm sorry."

"I do not need your pity, or your apologies." The rage pressed against her skull, threatening to explode, but while the rational part of her brain screamed for her to back down, to retreat, the all-consuming anger blotted out anything except the urge to strike, to take out her humiliation and pain on this stupid eijen. With an effort she re-established control, forcing neuro-suppressors through her bloodstream, dismissing the mesh. Pushing D'vai to one side, she stormed out of the mess, as the boy called out to her.

"Tey stop, please."

You will get thrown off long before you reach Tersen. Control, regain control.

"Leave me alone," she ground out, before striding off, leaving the boy standing by the mess hatch.

The lower reaches of the cargo holds were gloomy, liminal spaces, full of the creaking, groaning sounds of metal flexing in the strange world of hyperspace. Ori sank down onto the metal step and stared out sightlessly to the twilight world, replaying the scene in her mind, cringing at her complete inability to control her emotions. Whereas before her anger had been directed at the eijen, now it was turned inward to herself. This could be her last opportunity to escape, and she'd allowed one stupid boy to drive her to actions that could jeopardize all her plans. The boy, or Lart, probably, would be complaining to the captain by now, and Marissa had made her position clear; Ori could expect nothing more than to be put off at Corelli and Reinnor would have no choice but to send the Guard after her, unless he too wanted to experience the full force of the Xi's wrath.

Would they drag her back to Xia, as punishment? The cold metal of the stairs disappeared and once again she found herself trapped in the memories of previous encounters, the tightening webs at her wrists and ankles, the deep gloom of the Nest, the scuttling whisper of thousands of feet on silken strands. The relentless agony.

How could she fix this? Would the boy be open to bribery? Or would Lart? The idea of having to pleasure either of them nauseated her, but she had done worse. Above her a hatch clanged shut, and booted feet clumped across the walkway two levels up. Lart, or the boy come to tell her to pack her bags, they were doubling back to Six to dump her.

"Hey, you down there?" the boy's voice floated down between the restless containers. "I came to apologize. It was my fault." There was a long pause, and Ori could imagine him, hands jammed into his overalls, awkward ears burning red. "Lart says I'm an idiot, and to tell you, it's OK. No one's going to report you."

They hadn't gone to the captain? Her hands, clenched hard around the metal railing, tightened further. What would they want in return? Whatever it was, she could endure it. She should answer him, best to find out what the price would be now. Get it over with. "And what will it cost me, this magnanimous gesture?" The anger came out, even as Ori struggled to sound disinterested, unconcerned.

A long silence spread out through the hold, even the containers seemed to hold their breath. The boots clumped closer, the stairs vibrating as the boy descended a few steps, stopping above her.

"Cost you? By the Blessed Mother, it was my fault. It was unforgivable calling you a tremmie, even in fun. You don't owe me anything."

Her fingers finally relinquished their grip, albeit reluctantly. The boy sounded sincere, maybe he was too young to understand the leverage he had, or too naive. Whichever it was, Ori knew she had to both take advantage of it, and let it serve as a warning. No matter what the provocation, she had to maintain control, and not give the captain a reason to throw her off the ship. Once the *Ava* reached Tersen, then, and only then, could Ori strike back.

She rose to face the boy, and found herself at eye level with him. As she'd expected, the pockets of his overalls strained with the force of his clenched fists, and the awkward ears glowed red in the muted lighting. Also glowing was the rising bruise on the boy's left cheekbone. The leading hand was very free with his fists, it seemed, and although Zarr had scrubbed his face, damp lashes and red-rimmed eyes telegraphed the extent of Lart's punishment.

"I see that Lart has already punished you sufficiently. Perhaps that might teach you to keep your opinions to yourself in future," she said, sweeping past the miserable boy and up the stairs to the walkway.

By the time Ori reached the ablutions block, the inevitable exhaustion made every step an effort. As a Command Line, her body could handle injuries and stress that would kill an unengineered animal, but even she couldn't remain unscathed after so many years of abuse. It took far too long now for the chemicals in her bloodstream to return her systems to anything near normal, and the consequences of continually relying on artificial stimulants and suppressants to manage her emotional regulation was taking a toll.

It would take the *Ava* thirteen days to reach the agricultural world of Corelli. Thirteen days. She had commanded ships that could cross half the galaxy in that time, and here she was, imprisoned once again, with this filth. And she still had to get a look at the drives. She might have to seduce the engineer, though her skin crawled at the idea. This is what she had been reduced to — contemplating sex with animals. Distracted by disgust, Ori pushed open the hatch to the ablutions block, almost hitting the plump little maintenance officer.

"Water's hot. May the Mother send you peaceful sleep." Sukin smiled, and patted her on the arm as she went by, oblivious to how Ori flinched away from the touch.

I'll need more than your infantile beliefs for that to happen.

Ori closed the hatch behind her, grateful for the silence of the empty compartment. The isolation of the last ten years had left her unprepared for the rigors of social inter-actions, and the constant abuse, starvation and nightmares took their toll physically. The reward of a hot shower, free of surveillance, seemed especially welcome. She slipped out of her clothes and hit the button for the shower cycle. The water cascaded over her, warm and soapy, smelling of cheap fragrance. She leaned her head against the bulkhead and relaxed. No guards, no restraints, no AI recording her every move, only the familiar vibration of the drives and the almost-not-there tickle of hyperspace. The hatch opened behind, and Jwali entered, ignoring her and taking the shower furthest from her. The heat reached into her bones, as she closed her eyes and tried to pretend she was back on her own ship, among her family, safe.

Something hit her, sending her skull slamming into the bulkhead.

"So, you think you can ignore me, cunt." Jwali slammed her again, his naked body hard against her, one hand tightening on the back of her neck, the other crawling over her skin, across her hip. His fingers dug into her flesh, pulling her body back against his.

She should have been more alert, she'd let the lure of a hot shower, of privacy, of free-dom, overrun her usual caution. Now she couldn't retaliate. Any action, no matter how justified, coming so soon after the incident in the mess, would condemn her immediately. The captain wouldn't hesitate to throw her off, especially if Ori injured one of her family.

"Go on," Jwali whispered, "attack me. And I'll make damned sure the captain dumps your ass on Corelli. And you'll never get a berth off that mud ball. I'll make sure of that."

It took all her will to control the urge to retaliate. If she killed him, that would end any chance of freedom instantly. She forced her body to relax.

"Let me go, Jwali, I'm not interested," she said quietly, although she allowed a small amount of menace into her voice.

"Oh, you think I'm after a scrawny little cunt like you?" His hand moved between her thighs. "I hear you're some hotshot navigator." His breath scoured the side of her face. "Looking for a navigator's berth. Take this as a warning. There isn't one open here." His fingers dug harder, the nails biting into her skin. The clean scent of the shower couldn't mask the sweet/sour reek of floess. The Republic's only illegal drug, floess increased the sensations of sexual activity to a mind-altering intensity. Cheap, and easily available, its use was rife among the freighter crews, despite a long list of side effects like paranoia, irreversible brain damage and coma.

Her skull hit the bulkhead again, hard enough that her vision went dark at the edges.

She imagined him on his knees, pleading for mercy, his blood painting the walls, running across the floor. His screams. Although it made her skin crawl, she forced herself into acquiescence, something that years of imprisonment had imposed.

"I don't want to take your place, I only wanted work."

"Listen, cunt. Give me any trouble and I'll make sure you never work anywhere in this sector again. Do you understand?" His fingers jabbed inside her; she gritted her teeth against the pain. She would not give him the satisfaction of hearing her scream.

"Yes, I understand," she spat.

After he left, she remained unmoving, the water pouring over her until it ran cold. When the time came, he would be the first to die.

Five

Zarr pretended to be asleep when Ori came into the crew quarters. His entire face ached, the bruise rising darkly purple under his eye, the throbbing keeping him from sleep. Lart had a heavy hand, and used it freely. Not that he blamed Ori. Lart was right, he couldn't go around calling people whores. Except that wasn't what Zarr had meant at all. He'd been trying to warn her. Ma'al attracted all sorts of people: some good, some very bad. Every hauler had a story about being ripped off, or suckered into scams and other bad shit. Schemes for finding the source of silk, or how to snag a rich Ma'ali were the most popular. Once again, he'd opened his big mouth and said something stupid, upsetting people.

Now she probably thinks I'm a total loser, or a creep like Davey.

The hatch closed with a dull thud and the sounds of the ship faded away. For a moment there was silence as if she stood unmoving, then he swore he heard the tiniest of sighs. Her footsteps moved toward the lockers and the night light cast a pool of clear white in the darkness of the cabin. A door squeaked open, and he risked a peek through almost closed eyelids. Her back was toward him, the short strands of hair still damp on the ends, random wet patches on her overalls. So, she'd been in the shower, he guessed. The long line of her naked back appeared as she shrugged out of her clothes. A sinuous, perfect curve from the nape of her neck to the swell of her buttocks. Creamy gold skin, lighter than his own, but darker than anyone of Cimmili or Polini ancestry, covered a physique any professional athlete would kill for. His body responded immediately and he had to fight down the impulse to move his hand, only a little way. He shouldn't be spying on her like this. No looking, no touching was the first rule you learned on the freighters. She bent over to remove her overalls, the light catching the curve of her hip. The bruises spread across her skin, each one a black and purple violation, with the dark points of bloody nail marks harsh in the light. She touched one gingerly, hissing under her breath. Then her hand moved to her face, turned away from him, but Zarr had seen enough to know she was probing at another injury.

Zarr closed his eyes, unwilling to see any more, opening them again when she made a small sound of anger and pain. Ori stood under the light, facing him now, but still unaware of his spying. Smears of blood painted the insides of her thighs. Nausea rolled through Zarr.

Fucking Jwali.

Since the incident on the last run, the navigator had been keeping a low profile, but Davey had been maddeningly correct. The only surprise was how soon Jwali had acted. Zarr had hoped it might take him a few days, giving him enough time to warn her. Clearly, the appearance of a new, desirable target for his perversions had proved too much of a temptation. Zarr's arousal fled, replaced with anger. Jwali didn't care who he picked on, only that they were vulnerable. Van and Jen, being of almost equivalent ranks to navigator, were off-limits, of course, and Lart interested no one. D'vai was older than Zarr by a few years, bigger, and handy with his fists. One broken nose and Jwali had left him alone. That left him: small, young, alone. Zarr had tried other ships, but his obsession with Ma'al went before him, and he was marked as trouble. Freighter captains did not like trouble. Captain Marissa had taken him on, despite his youth, only because she struggled to get crew.

The light snapped off, he heard Ori's feet pad across the compartment, and the bunk opposite creaked a little. He'd failed. On his first day, he had failed her. He should have told her, in that first moment, what the danger was, warned her never to be alone with the navigator. This was his fault. Zarr closed his eyes, careful to make no sound as tears rolled down his cheeks and disappeared into his pillow.

Ori lay in the dark, trying not to hear the boy's pain. Caught up in her own misery, it had never occurred to her that the boy was awake until it was too late.

In the darkness, the boy gave out a tiny mewl of distress, and somewhere inside, her own grief answered him. Had her family mourned her? Had they believed she died in battle, with honor? That was the last time she had seen any of her siblings. Turning back from the escape pods, she'd propelled herself through the dying ship, with no gravity, no life support, only her battle armor between herself and hard vacuum as she searched desperately for survivors; corpses and wreckage filling the once-familiar corridors and compartments. The hatch to the escape pod appeared out of the chaos; a few meters, and she would have made it. Then the leading edge of the enemy's weapon caught the stricken vessel, tearing it apart around her. When she came to, all that remained of the enormous battleship was the tiny section holding her. Thousands of light years gone in an instant, and the start of ten years of pain and humiliation. Better, perhaps, if she had died in the explosion, or if the Hubnae had never found her.

No, she would not give in to despair. A few more weeks and she would be free. Ori pulled the blanket up around her ears, curling herself into a tight ball. While the boy slept, she called the memory to her and wrapped herself in the warmth of that long-ago moment. As the ship sighed and grumbled around her, she once again felt Tszcienna's arms around her.

```
[REM sleep achieved.
Subroutines initiated.
Data processing from nanite incursion underway.
Comparing to programmed parameters.
Mission unsuccessful. Parameters not achieved.
Information shunted to secure storage.
Accessible memory erased.]
```

Six

"The Senate is not going to be happy about this," Beten Casar protested, as he scurried along beside Rossim, struggling to keep up.

Rossim ignored his companion's distress. Served him right for being a fat, useless fuck. On either side of the corridors, palace staff flattened themselves against the walls to make way for the two men and their entourage of administrators, assistants, and various flunkies.

"I don't care," snapped Rossim, incrementally lengthening his stride. Maybe the old idiot would have a heart attack. That would be amusing. "We are not taking any actions that further weakens Fleet capabilities. I don't care that we've had three hundred years of peace. Leaving ourselves unprotected is madness."

"I agree but the Senate panics easily," said Casar, huffing loudly. "They think you're feeding them conspiracy theories and fear tactics; they think you're hiding something."

Needlessly aggravating someone as powerful as Betan wasn't wise; Rossim slowed his pace enough so the man could catch up.

Hiding something? The extent of the conspiracy was so egregious they'd have to execute him twice if he was caught.

Rossim stopped and turned to Casar, causing both entourages to abruptly descend into chaos. "You are supposed to keep them in line," he hissed, aware of all the eyes and ears around them. "And this investigation, you can't truly think they will go through with it?"

Casar flicked one fleshy hand in the general direction of his people and they scattered down the hallway out of earshot. Rossim's staff, better trained and more attuned to their boss's moods, were already withdrawing to a discreet distance.

"They are calling it the Freedom Square Massacre, and yes, there are factions in the Senate, Tel, although you might find it hard to believe, who don't like you." Beten folded his hands across his ample stomach, swathed in dark gray silk, and sighed. "I've tried to placate some of the less aggrieved Senators." His dark button eyes, embedded in pillows of ever-youthful skin, peered at him. "And that's going to cost you, by the way. They weren't cheap."

"So, I just add another handful of government contracts to you? Or would you like to be made Imperial Consort this time?" Rossim did not bother hiding his contempt. No matter what happened, he could not be deposed unless the Xi withdrew their support, and at that point, he would probably be dead and all his strategies would be for nothing.

Casar chuckled. "My dear Rossim, I would never presume to tell you how to handle these things." He looked down the hall, where his staff were beginning to show signs of impatience. "Looks like I need to get the children home." He patted Rossim with all the condescension of an elderly uncle. "I'll send you the list of senatorial 'appointments', for your approval."

"What about the more aggrieved Senators," asked Rossim, disengaging himself from the other man's paw. "What will it cost me for them?"

The button eyes narrowed. "Do not make the mistake of thinking me one of the idiots that infest the Senate. I understand you have resources even I do not have access to. I suggest you deploy them." Casar clicked his fingers and his staff coalesce into an obedient line, trailing behind their silk-clad master, looking, as Rossim realized, exactly like children following their teacher.

Imsu Pesek, First Secretary of the Directorate of Protection, followed the obligatory, but largely ceremonial, escort through the halls of the palace, ignoring the frescoes and the portraits and the countless works of art decorating the walls, and the ceilings, and every available surface, concerned solely with his meeting with Lord President Rossim. After a while he found the endless clutter of the palace receded into the background, and privately thought the collections neatly summed up the Republic's attitude to the past: a schizophrenic jumble of genuine memories interspersed with poor quality delusions.

Lost in thought, he barely avoided colliding with the leading palace guard as the retinue came to a sudden stop. Trolleys of artworks and assorted objet d'art blocked the entire corridor as palace maintenance milled around, dragging anti-grav platforms and enormous toolboxes from one side to the other, in no discernible pattern. Two maintenance staff elevated halfway up to the ceiling on an anti-grav platform were trying to wrangle an extremely large painting into position, while their colleagues below gave less than helpful directions. Palace security, Pesek noted, made no attempt to hurry the workers along, or to try and clear a path. They knew where the real power lay.

Helpless in the face of palace bureaucracy, and unwilling to devote any more mental energy to Rossim's insane scheme, Imsu Pesek sought distraction in the struggles with mounting the painting. It wasn't only the size of the canvas — Pesek had lived in apartments with smaller footprints — the frame alone, a gilded monstrosity of elaborately curling leaves and out-sized floral excrescences, must have weighed half a ton at least. The subject matter was on par with everything else in the Republic these days, Pesek observed to himself. A glorification of a long-forgotten war, in pursuit of some long-discarded goal. Except the goals remained the same, didn't they, even after hundreds of years. Power, and wealth, and still more power— that hadn't changed. The high-minded values of the Great War — equality and freedom— had slowly decayed until, as far as Pesek could see, there was little to distinguish the elite who ruled now, and the elite they'd replaced.

Depressed by this train of thought, and still unable to get past the maintenance crew, Pesek wandered over to one of the laden trolleys, examining the objects with varying degrees of interest. His own selection of pre-war collectibles were pitiable toys next to some of these pieces. He rummaged through treasures and rubbish until he found, tucked at the back of the trolley's contents, a small painting. Unlike the rest of the portraits of long-dead nobility that more resembled slugs than humans, whoever had painted this possessed real talent. The family portrait, of a tall man, a beautiful, elegantly dressed woman and two children was executed in the hyper-realism school popular in the later years of the Imperium. The details were so exact, Pesek almost expected the figures to move. The boy looked to be about eight, sitting at his father's feet, playing with a toy battleship. A girl stood beside her mother, one small hand on her mother's arm, the other holding a flower in an intense shade of blue. Imsu guessed she was about fourteen; the artist had captured beautifully the fine bone structure and the silk-like texture of her pale blonde hair. The girl's storm-gray eyes held Pesek's gaze as though staring into his soul.

"Do you know who painted this?" Pesek directed his question to one of the maintenance staff nearby, who, after giving the painting a quick look, shrugged.

"We're rotating stuff out of the lower storage units. This one hasn't been out in a while, could be a couple of hundred years old," the man replied, without much interest. "Not a lot of information on some of these pieces. I can look, sir, if you wish," he added, as if abruptly aware that someone in this area of the palace, and with this many guards, might be important.

"No, don't trouble yourself," Pesek replied distractedly, aware that his escort were becoming impatient. "I have a meeting with the Lord President, any chance you could let us through?"

Once the maintenance team cleared the route, Pesek and his retinue made their way to the Lord President's office unhindered. The door to Rossim's office slid open, the guards making anxious motions, whether because Rossim was eager to see him, or to get him inside and out of sight as quickly as possible, Pesek could not be certain. Probably a bit of both.

"Ah, Imsu, good to see you."

Rossim, noted Pesek, made no attempt to leave his position at the windows to greet him, merely waving him to one of the chairs flanking the desk. What was it with the Lord President and those damned windows?

"Lord President." Imsu bowed his head in the merest acknowledgment of rank. "It is always an honor." If this lack of groveling annoyed Rossim, the man gave no sign of it. The seat, at least, was comfortable, the type that encouraged you to lean back and relax. An unwise decision when dealing with Rossim.

"Drink?" asked Rossim, holding his glass in Pesek's direction.

"Thank you," replied Pesek. Although it was far too early in the day for him, sometimes you had to make sacrifices to get anywhere, and drinking with the Lord President of the Republic was hardly the worst thing he had done. The glass of hand-cut Nax'tl crystal Rossim slid across the desk at least held decent liquor. Ex-President Garrett, may the Blessed Mother cast his soul into everlasting flames, couldn't tell a good vintage from engine coolant.

"So, Imsu. How are operations in the Directorate progressing?" Rossim said, sliding into his seat, its resemblance to a throne quite deliberate, in Pesek's estimation. "Everything under control?" The movement was subtle, a finger crooked ever so slightly toward the painted ceiling.

Pesek molded his face into polite indifference, taking the glass in his outstretched hand. The AI monitoring bracelet circling his wrist flashed red once, twice, before going dark.

"We are secure, Lord President," he pronounced, probably a little too pompously —Rossim's lips thinned in disapproval.

"Good. So, give me an update. Are we on schedule?"

An update. Rossim made it sound like a marketing campaign. This covert operation was funneling armaments and trained personnel into a member system of the Republic to destabilize their government, so they could get their hands on the system's biggest monopoly. It was treason at the very least.

"As of this morning, Karis Samara, head of Hanjile Samara-Ketti, has nearly a thousand off-world mercenaries under his command, all of them classified as 'security personnel'. Most are ex-Fleet, or semi-professionals from the Orchetti Combine or our allies. With our assistance, he has managed to gather a surprisingly large amount of compromising material on members of the Ma'al Council, and masters of various hanjiles." Imsu took a large swallow of his drink, the alcohol flowing warm and spicy down his throat. "And he is using it to cement his position on the council."

Rossim gave a small grunt of satisfaction and downed the last of his own drink. "So, what's the next step?"

The next step would be inciting acts of terror against a civilian population. "We've supplied Karis with some...ideas." Pesek finished the last drops, wishing, despite the time of day, that he was a great deal drunker for this conversation. "Small incidents designed to throw the council off balance and give Karis the excuse to impose tighter security on both the off-worlders and the Ma'al population." It was a classic strategy. Create chaos, make sure the general population is edgy and frightened, undermine any opposition, before stepping in as the savior. Civilizations had been using it with varying degrees of success since mankind first formed into tribes. Pesek had warned Karis not to get carried away; these were to be small incidents, designed to minimize casualties.

"And Cimmili?"

Yes, Cimmili. Who had never forgiven Piali Eidress and her little band of cultists for swindling them (in Cimmili's view) out of limitless wealth and power, and who read the same texts on strategy and were aware they were being played, but were so enmeshed in their hatred and paranoia concerning Ma'al, that they were willing to take any chance to see their erstwhile colony brought to its knees. "Cimmili is happy to assist. So long as they get Ma'al back, they'd sell their own children into slavery. They're just wary of being caught in a conspiracy. They need some assurances."

In fact, the Cimmili Representative had been quite explicit about that last point. His system would not be the fall guy for the Republic if this plan fell through, and they wanted assurances to that effect. As insurance, Pesek had been told. Nothing personal. Pesek's view on Cimmili was that perhaps if they'd conducted the original planetary survey properly, they wouldn't have missed the source of the silk. An opinion he kept to himself.

Rossim sneered and poured himself another drink, pushing the bottle toward Imsu in invitation to join him. "Fuck Cimmili and their assurances. Tell them they're either in or out. There are plenty of other systems that would happily take over Ma'al should that be needed."

"But only Cimmili has the legal authority for that, Lord President," Imsu reminded Rossim carefully, deciding another drink wouldn't be advisable. "What other basis could we have for handing over a sovereign system to another?"

"I'm sure we can find a reason." Rossim settled back into his throne-like seat and regarded Pesek over the rim of his glass. "Peacekeeping mission, humanitarian crisis requiring an emergency act of the Senate. We'll think of something."

The creeping disquiet that had plagued Imsu ever since this madness was conceived began to grow. Rossim was far too cavalier for someone plotting treason on this scale. The alcohol sat in his stomach, cold and undigested, the warm flush replaced by nausea.

He found himself on his feet, abruptly done with this conversation. Rossim, caught off guard, jumped a little in surprise.

"My apologies, Lord President, I regret I have another meeting to attend." Pesek bowed, a little more deeply than he intended. "I will keep you updated on our progress."

Rossim stared at Pesek, his eyes narrowing with suspicion. "Don't start developing a conscience, Imsu. It's a liability for someone in your position."

Seven

The hatch crashed open, propelling Zarr from asleep to awake in a second, and almost into the bulkhead in surprise.

"Hey, Zarr. *Sex. Food. Laundry.*"

"Fuck off," he yelled, seeing it was D'vai. "I'll wake you up like that next shift, see how you like it." Fucking Davey, always pulling stunts like this, and always with himself the target.

"You can try," D'vai sneered, and laughed. "Anyway, your shift is starting, and I want some time to myself before Lart comes in and starts complaining. Hey, where's your girlfriend?" He jerked his head at Ori's bunk, empty and made up to military precision.

Damn, I hope she hasn't gone after Jwali or done something equally career-ending.

"Probably in the mess," he shot back, scrambling out of his bunk and grabbing clothes out of his locker.

Davey threw himself on his bunk and waved a hand dismissively. "Nah, just been there. The old man is finishing dinner."

Zarr pulled on his overalls and activated the tab; the seam closed silently. "I'm sure she's doing something useful." He took a parting shot from the hatch, "And it's *Wealth. Honor. Family,*" slamming the hatch behind him with a resounding crash.

Ori made certain she'd left her bunk before the boy awoke and well before the two idiots, Lart and D'vai, came back from the mess. The isolation of the cargo hold gave her the solitude she needed. Her fingers probed at her bruises, but the nanites were working diligently and in a few hours, there would be no sign of Jwali's attack. The other injuries would take longer. Nothing would heal the anger, the shame that burned inside her. How much longer would she have to submit, compromise, surrender to this filth? How much more humiliation could she endure?

She slumped between the bulkheads, frowning at yet more examples of the lack of housekeeping. Did no one clean on this ship? She had weeks to endure this. Her hand brushed her forehead and she winced at the throb of pain. Whatever the provocation, however, she would have to swallow whatever pride she had left and wait until Tersen.

Then she would see who was humiliated.

From above came the crash of the hatch slamming shut and the clatter of boots on the walkway. It seemed the boy had found her.

The corridors of the *Ava* were empty. This shift change, Lianna would be on the bridge, while the captain slept; Van would be down in engineering, no doubt love-talking to his drives; Jen would be trying to keep the *Ava* running; and only the Blessed Mother herself knew where Jwali was. Dead in his bunk, Zarr hoped, or better still, sucked out an airlock. The prick.

"Hey, Ava," he asked, looking up to the overhead bulkhead, a dirtside habit he should have lost months ago. "Where's Ori?"

"Port cargo bay," the ship's AI responded from the speaker in the comms panel.

OK, fine, working, not throwing Jwali out the airlock. Pity. He would be on board for that job. Zarr hurried off to the cargo bay, in search of his new crewmate.

He made sure to shut the hatch with a bang, so she knew he was in the bay; Jwali liked sneaking up on people, and Zarr figured if she was still feeling upset after last night — and who wouldn't be— it would give her time to compose herself. "Hey, you down here?" he called.

"Yes, Zarr, I'm here," came her voice from the other end of the bay. She didn't sound upset, which was a start. Her head appeared at the access ladder as Zarr, his boots clattering on the metal surface, reached her. Her hair, worn longer than most haulers, still didn't disguise the ugly black lump over her left eye. The mask of absolute indifference was in place though, as though she cared about nothing.

"Hey," he said, trying to keep his voice uninterested, "told you to mind that hatch down on D deck. Only us short people can fit through there." Silence greeted him. OK, maybe he should have pretended nothing happened, as her hand went to the injury, and the mask relaxed a little.

"Yes, I hit it on the hatch," she said slowly.

"So, what are you up to?" he said, although inside he was smiling at this unexpected relaxation in her guard.

"I was checking the cargo hold," she said, in the tone of someone used to giving orders, "and according to the logs"—she pointed to her sheet for emphasis—"you missed over half the containers on the last trip."

For fuck's sake, give me a break.

Zarr tried his most amiable smile. "Yeah, well, this isn't a heavy cargo vessel. Things are a bit slower on the *Ava*. I mean, we check the cargo, take a break, and hope Jen or Lianna don't find us anything to do", he replied, holding the grin. "Did you grab something to eat?"

The change was immediate, like a storm appearing out of nowhere. "I do not need a nursemaid," she retorted, her voice hard.

Dammit, keep your mouth shut. Add it to the list, don't touch, don't offer food. Check. Of course, his mouth, oblivious to the previous decision, kept on talking.

"OK, but Davey keeps some snacks hidden in the maintenance locker on C deck aft," he said, "if you're hungry."

"Keep your suggestions to yourself, I do not need your help." She pointed down the walkway. "Do aft, I'll do forward, and don't miss any," she said, in a voice of absolute command and stalked off, shoulders and back stiff and unyielding.

Zarr grabbed a sheet, watching her retreating figure. "Yes, Commander," he mumbled.

Ori finished the last sweep of the cargo bay, tired and empty, all the anger seeping away under the steady, monotonous work. She had been grateful! Grateful for the boy's sympathy, for his offered friendship. This was what her imprisonment had reduced her to, an object of pity by an eijen, an animal, a worthless thing. She had stood there and allowed the boy to feel sorry for her when what she should have done was rip out Jwali's intestines, and damn the consequences.

You are weak, said the voices, like the whisper of tiny feet on webs. *Damaged. They will never take you back.*

No doubt she would now have to deal with the boy, and his anger. Something tightened inside when she thought of him; those awkward ears and the dusting of freckles. She might need to find the words to placate him, distasteful though the idea was. Sometimes the situation required a different strategy to violence when the odds were too overwhelming, or the injuries too severe, or she couldn't fight back anymore. Each incident, though, deepened her shame, her fear that her control was slipping away, that she was becoming less.

The long climb up to the central walkway seemed to take forever and her head ached. She probed at the lump with tentative fingers, wincing when her explorations set off another series of throbs. Jwali would pay, as would everyone else who had heaped humiliations on her.

The comms panel beeped as she went past.

"Yes," she answered, trying to keep the irritation out of her voice, "Tey here."

"Oh, Ori," the maintenance officer's voice bubbled out of the speaker. "It's Jen here. Van needs a hand down in engineering, something to do with the auxiliary drive."

Her fatigue vanished. This was the opportunity she'd been hoping for. Now she could examine the drives in detail, and finalize her plans for taking over the ship and escaping.

Eight

Van only half-heartedly protested when Jen suggested sending the new crew member down to help. The plump little maintenance officer pointed out, with some justification, that Van needed a hand stripping out the auxiliary drive, and Tey seemed the competent sort.

Too competent was Van's opinion, but it was true. Working on a drive, even the auxiliary one, while in hyperspace wasn't a task you took on lightly. But dock fees at Six were high — too high for a captain buying spare parts against a future cargo — and there were few options left for him. Berths were hard to come by, even for engineers. For engineers with a "history" they were almost non-existent. At least the implant had stopped itching. Maybe this one would work, and maybe, finally, he could get himself sober, get a better berth, and make a new start somewhere far away from Six Jump.

Van looked up at a noise. The new hand, Tey, stood at the drive compartment hatch, her head brushing the top seal, with a noticeable lump over her left eye. Had she got into trouble already?

"What happened?" he asked, pointing at her head, "that's a nasty bump."

"Hit it on the hatch on D deck, Engineer," she replied, without any expression, or further explanation.

Interesting.

What was she doing down there, on a deck containing nothing except power relays and control boards? Jen might go down there to check on something, but she wouldn't send a crew hand, especially not one that had only been on board a day or two.

"Yeah, it's caught me a few times too," he said, lying. Van placed the wrench back on the tool caddie and wiped his hands. "You don't have to call me Engineer down here. I left Fleet a long time ago." Despite what he said, the use of his lost rank pleased him.

"Very well." She shrugged. "Van. What did you want?"

That is a very good question. Who are you, and why are you on my ship?

Something about her nagged at him. The way she moved, the way she spoke, didn't quite line up with her story. Of course, haulers were notorious for editing, or manufacturing, an entire back story; people wanted to escape any amount of bad shit, and running off to the freighters had always been popular among the more romantically inclined. Zarr was a perfect example. Left school at fifteen to become a freighter captain. See where that dream had ended up. Stupid boy.

"I need a hand with the auxiliary drive, thought you might want to help. Makes a change from counting containers and sweeping decks." An excuse sadly lacking creativity, and one she would be well within her rights to refuse. She was a crew hand, not an engineer's mate.

"I haven't stripped a drive out since training," she said, in a tone of not quite refusal, and Van got the distinct impression she didn't exactly object to the task.

"If you can follow instructions, you're already ahead of Zarr. He never shuts up." Van had never understood Zarr. The boy was smart enough; he could have gotten a job at the port — his father and a sister both worked there, so he said. He'd given it all up to spend a few days on Ma'al every month or so. All in service to an e-feed.

As the Ma'al government had become increasingly insular, and the tourist visas had dried up, Ma'al obsessives became a growing problem among the freighter crews. Some wanted to catch themselves a Ma'al citizen, others were convinced they had discovered the source of the silk, and a small but annoying group, like Zarr, obsessed over a stupid feed. *Hearts of Maal* had started out as a thinly veiled parody of Ma'al society, with its hanjiles and distinctive dress changed to grand Houses and elaborate costumes. The plots ranged from the insightful to the outrageously ridiculous, but quickly gathered a following across the Republic. The changed spelling was an acknowledgment that Ma'al had an entire planet of lawyers just waiting to sue.

"Yes." She nodded, and Van noticed how her hands, clasped firmly before her, relaxed, how she examined everything, assessing every detail in the drive room as if memorizing for a test. "The boy is irritating." Her attention turned full force on Van. "Where do we start?"

"We need to take the drive housing off. Think you can start on that side?" Once again, she gave him a look as if she was weighing possibilities. Van didn't think she was looking to score on Ma'al or had any interest in an entertainment feed.

"Fine. I'll need an induction socket though."

He gestured toward the workbench. "Take whatever you want." As he suspected, she selected the correct tool without hesitation, weighing it in her palm as if assessing its fitness.

The auxiliary drive was nowhere near the same dimensions as the main one, but they still had to stretch to pass tools across to each other. Time to do some digging.

"So, who did you serve under?" he asked, taking a part from her, and placing it on the trolley beside him. May as well start with the expected questions.

"Haruichi, mainly," she answered, without a visible reaction. A bead of sweat ran down her cheek and dropped into the bowels of the drive; she swiped at her face with a sleeve, grimacing as she hit the contusion.

Even with the climate control dialed right down, the drive rooms were always too hot. Van wore his overalls in the manner common to engineers; the top half knotted around his waist, with a short-sleeved top underneath, already sweat-stained, and slightly rank. She placed the tool on the caddy beside her and shrugged out of her overall top, securing the sleeves with a firm, efficient knot. The loose, sleeveless top she wore might have been white, once, now it was more a dirty gray, the cloth worn in places and tattered around the edges. A hauler's pay, while not fantastic, ran to decent clothes and sufficient food.

D'vai had regaled him with a detailed and lurid description of the new cargo hand's ... attributes. The older cargo hand had been too impressed with other things to note how her collarbones stood out starkly sharp, without the usual layer of cushioning flesh. So, she had spent a significant amount of time without enough food, and couldn't afford the most basic of new clothing. It was possible she'd fallen on hard times, struggled to find a berth, but her story had too many inconsistencies for him to accept. Few systems in the Republic would allow a citizen to starve, or go homeless. Some were more generous than others, but to reach this level of poverty meant you either came from outside the Republic, which was possible, or you had chosen to live without the Republic's support network. Such individuals existed; removal of your ID chip, although illegal, could be arranged, if you knew the right people. Without it, you became a ghost, untraceable, reduced to living on your wits, and whatever sale-able talents you possessed.

"On the *Markarii*?" he asked, probing.

"Garren had the *Markarii*. Still did, last I heard." She removed the last retainer bolt with a precise twist of the wrench and handed the secondary drive controller to him.

Navigator my ass.

Van placed the part on the trolley. "Yeah, Haruichi had another ship. Can't remember her name."

"The *Senglis Ji*," she returned, evenly. This proved nothing, all this information was freely available to anyone with the time to dig around the public databases.

To reach the induction drive, you had to almost climb into the drive assembly. She leaned forward, reaching down into the depths of the drive. Her top, shapeless and loose, dropped away from her body, affording Van an uninterrupted view of her breasts. They were as Davey had described them, firm, round, a good handful each, the nipples blushed rose. He hardened immediately, arousal hitting him like a bolt of electricity. He dragged his eyes away, struggling to retain control. When he looked back up, she was watching him warily, the wrench held ready.

"Sorry," he said, "I meant no offense."

For a long moment, she said nothing, her fingers flexing on the wrench. Then she grunted a tiny sound of acceptance and relaxed.

"I had a mate who served under Haruichi. This is years ago though," he said, as casually as he could, although his heart was pounding. Davey had also omitted the information that the new crew member also had the body of an elite athlete — or a combat soldier.

"Really." She handed him the wrench, without looking at him, and took a diagnostic pad from the work trolley beside her, applying each sensor pad to the drive component with precise, controlled moves. The light caught her hair, illuminating the pale strands into a glowing nimbus. A memory floated up from the dim past, although he didn't understand the connection. Three days' leave on a shitty little rock out on the far edge near the border with the Orchetti Combine. There were a group of them, two days into a marathon drinking session that had been his only way of socializing back then. One of them had been the Chief Security Officer, on one of the big warships, Van couldn't remember which one. A dour woman, taciturn to the point of silence on almost any subject — until she started the serious drinking. It wasn't long before the stories came out, of officers with questionable proclivities, and scandals involving high-ranking officials hushed up. This night, he remembered, Captain Hauirchi's name had been mentioned, and the woman had launched into this story, of the captain's first command, the *Senglis Ji*, ordered to the system containing Nianah Four, a hot, humid planet of countless tropical islands and warm, shallow seas.

Tey picked up another tool and applied herself to the internal housings. Van didn't doubt for a moment that if he left her to it, the entire drive would be rebuilt by the end of the shift. The memory itched again, demanded to be scratched. Why had he thought of that after so many years? It had been the drinking that had finally ruined his career. No matter how many times they sent him for treatment, it never seemed to stick.

"When was the last time she had the linings replaced?" she asked, interrupting his thoughts.

The question caught Van by surprise. Why did she ask that particular question? The distances between the *Ava's* stops were small, relative to the rest of the galaxy. Lining conditions only became a factor if you had to do a long jump, one that would push a ship's capabilities, not potter from one system to another. Navigators didn't ask those sorts of questions. Commanding officers asked, usually just before they needed to pull off a high-risk maneuver.

"It would be almost a year now, at our last refit. But they're good for at least another year. Why? Thinking of taking her for a spin?" Those clever hands stopped for a second, before resuming their task. That must have hit a nerve. Let's see what else he might shake loose.

"Have you been to Nianah Four?" he asked, on a hunch.

"Why?" She didn't look up from her task, but Van saw how her shoulders tensed.

"No reason, only you said you served with Haruichi. I used to hang with someone on the *SJ*, he met his first wife on Nianah."

"Hot, humid, boring. The water is too warm. Is that the place?"

Hot, humid. Yes. Boring? Nianah Four had a reputation as a party world. Clothes optional, sexual preferences as fluid as the warm sea.

Van wished he could remember the rest of the story; he knew it had something to do with a run-in between Haruichi and the Directorate of Protection over a prisoner. The Imperial Guard got a mention too, though what they were doing on a Fleet battleship, in the middle of nowhere, he couldn't recall. Too many drinks. All he remembered of the rest of that night was waking up outside his room in a pool of congealed vomit. One of many nights that ended like that.

"Haruichi is a good commander, I hear," he ventured.

That finally elicited a response. Van found himself caught in hard, storm-gray eyes.

"If you ever wish to give up engineering," she said, her voice as flat and hard as her eyes, "I'm sure the Directorate would take you on. They are short on good interrogators."

He wished he could be sure she was joking. Van had no idea why the Directorate of Protection would put an agent on his ship, but it would explain a great many things. No one who looked like her needed a job on a clapped-out freighter. Anyone with half her skills would be on the payroll of one of the big private security firms or pulling in obscene sums of money as a sole operator.

Unless you needed to get into Ma'al.

Ma'al had suspended tourist visas two years ago, and the big freight lines, the ones that carried the silk, demanded verification of who your great grandparents were before they even looked at your application. That meant whoever she was working for didn't want, or couldn't produce, the extensive background checks that would get her in that way. So, what was she after? The silk, probably. Or the Polini silver and gold smithing guilds. They had a significant presence in the off-worlder area known as the Enclave. Whichever it was, he suspected the target wouldn't stand a chance.

"Need to take the power packs out now," he said instead, trying to ignore the trickle of cold sweat running down his back.

"Yes, I know," she said, after a long silence. The tool she held weighed at least a couple of k's, and would make an excellent weapon. Van felt measured and judged by those eyes, as cold as the sea in winter. Once again, she seemed to come to a decision, placing the tool down with precision. When she turned back to him, all expression had gone. She pulled her overalls back up, did the tab up high enough to cover herself and leaned down into the drive. Her hands took hold of the access points and lifted.

"Careful, it's heavy," he warned. He got his own hands under the pack as well. It came out of its housing like it weighed nothing. How much of it was she lifting?

"I saw one dropped once," she said, with no apparent effort. "Everyone scattered thinking it would explode."

"I hope the chief engineer flogged their hides off."

"Oh, she did. After she finished laughing at them. Trainees. The whole pack of them forgot what the safety protocols were for."

Van grunted in agreement. "There are idiots, though, who try and bypass the safeties. Always ends badly."

"Who would be so stupid as to do that?" She seemed genuinely surprised.

"My mum had a saying: the mother of morons is always pregnant."

Van could swear, that for the briefest moment, she had smiled.

Nine

Jak Reinnor, Xi Liaison, slumped back into his chair, and was debating whether to order some food in, or call it a day and head home, when the palace AI informed him he had a call from Xia. Fear was his first reaction, followed by absolute terror as the monstrous image snapped into existence, towering above him.

"Great One, I am honored," Reinnor said, jumping out of his seat and bowing, his eyes fixed firmly on the soft woolen carpet at his feet. No gore and viscera today.

"We have a task for you. A small task," the alien said, without preamble or greeting. The Matriarch was supposedly over two thousand years old, and although silver now replaced her once-black hair, a fierce, sharp intelligence still burned in every one of her eyes.

"We are always happy to assist the Nest." Reinnor bowed again, his terror unabated.

"Excellent. I have our orders for the Brightstar. They are being sent now, in a secure message. You will see that she obeys."

"I will, of course, Great One." Jak took a deep breath and gathered his courage. Who knew when he would have another opportunity like this? "May I ask a question?"

For a long moment there was silence; Jak thought the Xi wasn't going to acknowledge him. Then that triangular head, with the two translucent palps, turned and looked directly down at him, the row of primary eyes almost surprised.

"Yes."

That was it? Just "Yes"?

"What do you want with Ori? Why can't you let her go?"

"That is two questions, Xi Liaison."

His heart hammering so hard, they should be able to hear it on the next floor, Jak forced himself to meet the Matriarch's gaze. "It is. Perhaps the first question. Why do you need Ori?"

The Xi moved lower, the palps writhing. Jak took an involuntary step back, his skin too tight as if it had suddenly shrunk, his clenched fists slick with fear.

"You do not trust us."

It wasn't a question.

He was going to be sick.

"No."

Did she recognize his distress? Or had she tormented him enough? Either way, the Xi pulled back. Jak sucked in a huge breath, trying to keep his stomach under control.

"We are a very old race, Reinnor. Older than you can conceive of. We have seen much. Endured much. The Brightstar is important. That is all you need to know."

"So, we just do as we're told. Like children."

The Matriarch shook her head, in a gesture Jak recognized as regret. "You are not a parent, Reinnor. I have thousands of offspring. I have had to make decisions, hard decisions, for the good of the Nest, yet I remember every one of my children."

And then the hologram winked out. Jak collapsed to the floor, bile burning his throat, heart almost bursting from his chest. He stared at the tufts of dyed wool millimeters from his nose and decided he would stay down here for a minute or two more and really admire the craftsmanship. After a few more deep breaths he finally unclenched his fingers, buried deep in the pile, and pulled his arms back under his prone body, grateful when the shaking died away. His legs might take a bit longer, he decided. Jak closed his eyes as tight as possible and tried to concentrate on his breathing.

"It was just a hologram," he whispered, "it can't hurt you." Which was a lie, and he knew it. If anything happened to their prisoner, heads would, literally, roll — followed by any number of other body parts. The Xi Matriarch had made her position regarding the prisoner and her future treatment very clear, and Reinnor was left in no doubt that he would be replaced if another screw-up occurred. "Replacement" being the euphemism for dead.

"You have to get up," he told himself. "You can't stay down here all day. What if one of the staff come in?"

That thought finally drove him to his feet, unsteady and lightheaded, but at least he was standing. Although it was far too early, Jak stumbled to the sideboard and poured himself a stiff drink, swearing under his breath when it took two attempts to return the stopper to the decanter neck.

His sheet pinged, loud in the silence of his office. The message from Xia, with the instructions. Perhaps now he might be able to see some pattern or clue to the Xi's motives.

Jak thumbed the sheet to active and initiated the decryption protocols. In less than a second the message appeared. He read it twice, to be absolutely sure.

Contact the Directorate of Protection operative as detailed in the attached profile. Take up the position of security officer for the designated guild. Infiltrate by any means the four major hanjiles — Eidress, Ansissi-Kai, Mathani, Demanchi. Obtain whatever information available on Ma'al silk. Continue until advised otherwise.

So, whatever the Xi were looking for, they were in those four hanjiles. Reinnor didn't believe for one moment the Xi were interested in the silk. So that left the lawyers, the scientists and the engineers. Interesting. Now all he had to do was get Oryelle to Ma'al before Rossim decided to do something to stop her, because one thing was inevitable: the Lord President would go ballistic over this.

Ten

Lianna leaned against the bulkhead, rubbing her back until the spasm passed. The mess was down this corridor, she'd get a mug of messil and then swing past the infirmary, pick up a pain patch. Although they were running low on first-aid supplies; the returns on the Corelli stop would barely cover running costs, let alone extras like pain patches. Tersen should be better, so long as they got in on time. Ma'al was the big unknown. Who knew what rules those xenophobic assholes might have dreamed up while the *Ava* was in hyperspace? The *Ava* could get there and find Ma'al wasn't taking any cargo at all.

Lianna straightened, wincing as the pain hit again. No money for regular anti-aging meds, either, and without them, neither Marissa nor she could run this ship properly, and the *Ava* needed a full cargo hold to make ends meet. But that meant four cargo hands, with all the expenses and issues that came with it. Lianna's face twisted in anger at the thought of their recently arrived crew member. There was something wrong about her; not merely the long legs and the beautiful face that had all the crew twitchy. No, this was something else. Something deeper, and darker. Everyone else got too carried away by how Tey looked, not what she did. And what she did was to treat everyone around her like dirt.

From down the corridor came the ping of the reheater, repeated after a few seconds. Who was in the mess? Not Lart and Davey, they were cleaning C deck. Marissa and Jwali should be in their bunks. Van or Jen, maybe. She needed to talk to Van about the maintenance schedule anyway.

Lianna halted at the hatchway. The new crew member occupied one table, her head cradled on folded arms, the mess lighting turning her hair into a soft halo of gold. The reheater pinged again, and Tey dragged herself up from the table as if sleepwalking.

"So, no wonder nothing gets done on your shift, if you're in here stuffing yourself instead of in your bunk," Lianna said, sudden irrational anger overtaking her. "I thought you were supposed to be setting that stupid Zarr an example."

All signs of fatigue vanished as the woman turned to face her. Lianna was familiar with security; every hauler ran up against port authority at least once in their career. Ma'al now teems with off-worlders, ex-Fleet for the most part, wearing the gray and black uniforms of the security forces under Hanjile Samara-Ketti. This was what Tey reminded her of. Military. Not the soft career officers with their pretty uniforms, or the nostalgia junkies trying to hold on to past Imperial glory. No. Tey was different.

A handful of times, Lianna had been unlucky enough to encounter real soldiers. Hard men and women. Mercs and private security for the most part. Dangerous and unpredictable. Tey was exactly the same.

"I wasn't aware the food was rationed, Cargomaster," the younger woman answered, "I couldn't sleep." Even in rumpled, worn-out sleep pants and a ragged top, Tey looked like she'd just stepped out of one of D'vai's fantasy sex feeds. Sickening jealousy hit Lianna like a punch to the guts. Jwali had confided that Marissa had made more than one comment on her beauty, and that knowledge now cut into Lianna's soul like a glass shard.

"I pay for this food, Tey," Lianna snarled, advancing toward her, fists balled tightly. "Remember that. I pay for the air you breathe, the water you use. I pay your wages. So don't give me any of your fucking whore attitude."

Something passed across her new crew member's face. A visceral anger and hatred that for a second became visible. Instinctively, Lianna took a half step back, some primitive part of her brain recognizing the shift in stance, the tightening of Tey's shoulders, as an imminent attack.

"Go on, bitch, say what's on your mind, throw something, attack me. I've been running freighters my entire life. I'm not afraid of you." Lianna forced herself to step forward, to ignore the fear coiling in the pit of her stomach, despite the fact Tey was half a meter taller than her. "You fucking open that pretty mouth of yours and I'll have you off this ship and blacklisted in every port in the Republic. You won't be able to get a job scrubbing shit by the time I'm finished with you."

Again, there was that fleeting emotion, a clenching of her jaw as if Tey wrestled with some inner turmoil.

"My apologies, Cargomaster," she said with grudging acquiescence.

"I should fucking hope so. Get back to your bunk, and next shift you and that useless boy can clean out the storage lockers on C deck."

Tey left without another word, and Lianna collapsed onto a stool, shaking. That woman was dangerous. The sooner the *Ava* got to Ma'al the better.

"Let me get this straight. You woke up, went to the mess in the middle of our off-shift, and now suddenly Lianna hates us so much that we're cleaning out storage lockers?" Zarr said, kicking a storage bin resentfully across the walkway, where only her intervening boot stopped it from careening over the edge. "Did you have to annoy her? Couldn't you have been nice. For once?"

Ori glared at the boy. Her irritation with Zarr was edging dangerously close to annoyance this shift. Exhaustion ate at her, weighing her down, every system glowed red. Ten years of imprisonment had left her unprepared for thirteen-hour shifts and broken sleep. The endless warnings were a distraction and no level of neuro-enhancers worked. It wasn't her fault Lianna had taken an instant dislike to her.

"Lianna wants this done now." Ori turned back to the current object of her attention, a storage locker containing a collection of rubbish and unidentifiable parts. "If it is not finished, you know she will give us something worse to do the next shift." Clearly the cargomaster took a perverse delight in sending them both off to do the most menial and dirty jobs on the ship.

Zarr threw his hands up in evident frustration. "Yeah, but couldn't you have apologized or—"

"Stop asking questions," she snapped. "Either help or go somewhere else." Would this boy never leave her alone? Nothing she said or did had any impact on his endless optimism. Or the fact that he appeared to be welded to her side. The first few times, when he had turned up in the showers minutes after she had arrived, Ori had put it down as coincidence. So long as it deterred Jwali's predations, she could tolerate it. Now she understood Zarr took care to be within sight deliberately, but why? The boy kept his hands to himself, didn't even glance at her, beyond the normal conventions of ship life. She had turned over the idea that he might be protecting her, but the idea was so preposterous she'd dismissed it immediately. She didn't need protecting. Nothing Jwali could do would come close to what the guards or the spiders had inflicted. She could put up with his pawing at her until they reached Tersen; plenty of time for revenge once she took the ship.

"Sorry, Commander."

"Stop calling me that." Dizziness swooped in, and her breath caught in her lungs, peripherals incandescent in response to her distress. *I earned that rank, and now it is a perverse joke for your enjoyment.*

"Sorry," he mumbled, as he turned away from her, shoulders hunched, fists firmly pressed into his overall pockets. Neuro-suppressors washed through her, instilling the artificial calm she knew she relied on far too much, but nothing assuaged the constant aggravation the boy caused. She sent the hapless storage bin spinning along the walkway, accompanied by a crash as she slammed open the locker door and began throwing the assorted miscellanea into the bin imagining Lianna's face with every impact.

Zarr worked silently for over an hour, an eternity for him, pulling lockers open randomly, tossing their contents to the deck in a sorting process comprehensible only to him.

"Hey, did you bring an extra bag for the rubbish? I'm full over here," he yelled. He was behind a door, so she could not see his expression, but the notes of injured feelings were easy to detect.

She could order Zarr, send him up the ladder to the next level ten meters above their heads. "No. I will go and find some more." Zarr remained sulking behind the locker door as Ori climbed the ladder to the walkway. The door on the storage locker stuck, the metal squealing in protest as Ori wrenched it open, only to jump back as an avalanche of bags, boxes and rubbish tumbled out.

"You OK?" yelled Zarr.

"Yes. Are all the lockers on this ship full of junk?" Ori called back.

"Davey thinks Lianna fills them up between runs so we have something to do."

From what she had observed of the Cargomaster, Ori would not be surprised. The one thing Lianna hated above all else were idle crew.

Her foot moved to the ladder; her hands full of bags. A vaguely musical noise drifted up; Zarr hummed as he worked, a habit she swore he did to annoy her personally. This tune was familiar, though.

"What is that?" she called down, pausing a few rungs down, the deck meters below her feet.

His voice floated up from behind the locker door. "The theme from *Hearts*. I didn't think you'd mind," he added, still defensive.

Organic memory, treacherous and uncontrollable, replayed the scene with perfect clarity; the sound as he approached down the hallway, stopping at her cell door. The click as the lock disengaged. The shame came flooding to the surface, remembered pain, unforgettable humiliation. Dizziness struck, peripherals flashing to red as stress overloaded her systems and the steps seemed to disappear from under her feet, only her grip on the rail preventing her from plummeting the long meters to the deck below.

She heard the boy yell her name, felt the vibration of his feet pounding up the ladder, his hands on her. *No, don't touch me!*

"For fuck's sake, Ori, you almost fell. Hold on, give me the damned bags." He attempted to wrench them from her grasp, but survival protocols had kicked in and her hands were locked to the rails.

"No, I can do this. I don't need help," she protested, all the while struggling to make her body obey her.

"Yeah, right, 'cause you nearly dropped six meters for the fun of it. By the Blessed Mother, I won't let you fall." Her hands unlocked, and only the boy, with both arms around her, struggling to stay on the ladder himself, saved her from falling.

Somehow, she made it back down to the deck, legs, hands, everything shaking, but still managed to pull herself away from him, to lean against the bulkhead, her breath coming in ragged gasps.

Zarr slid down the rail opposite, breathing heavily. "When was the last time you slept?"

She waved away his concerns. "I'm fine. I slipped, I don't need help," she said, while every system icon screamed silently in strobing red alarm.

"Yeah, and that's why you look like shit." He pulled his knees up, wrapping his arms around them in an unconscious defensive position. "Don't give me that 'I don't want your pity' crap, either. It's not pity to care about someone. Even a koré like you."

Koré. Idiot, the quantum computer embedded in her brain supplied. A D'jeblan word. *From whore to idiot.* She should view that as an improvement.

"You are from D'Jebli Prime?" That system had been one of Da Chet's original colony worlds before the war. Before the engineered side expelled all those who disagreed with their idea of how a civilization should be run, before that suicidal maneuver that reduced Da Chet to radioactive slag, and gave the unengineered victory.

Zarr shrugged. "Originally. The family were displaced and ended up on Six. When the war finished, my grandfather's dad tried to go back, but the family business, the estates, the house, everything had gone, taken over by others. Him and Grandfather spent years in various legal battles trying to get it back, without any luck." He shrugged again, a rueful, deprecating gesture. "Dad wouldn't have anything to do with it, said the only ones profiting from it were lawyers and politicians."

"Your family would have no love for the engineered then," she said, trying to sound as neutral as possible.

The boy's face changed, darkening. An angry scowl replaced his usual cheerful expression. "My grandfather spent every spare credit on legal fees and petitions and lobbying fat, useless politicians. Him and Dad argued all the time about it. The last few years, before he died, Dad stopped talking to him. Fucking Abominations destroyed my family, and millions more like us."

His vehemence didn't surprise her, she'd been on the receiving end of such anger since her capture. What was inexplicable was the pain his words caused her. Why should she care what an eijen thought of her?

"Come on," said Zarr, rising and offering his hand, "let's get these lockers finished and go get some food."

Ori could get up by herself, she didn't need assistance from anyone, let alone an eijen who had every reason to hate her. This small concession meant nothing, she told herself, as his hand tightened gently around her wrist, the fragile, delicate bones of his fingers barely brushing her skin.

"Yes, very well, but this time I get to pick, I'm sick of farei."

It was fifteen kilometers from one side of the port cargo bay to the other, if you traversed the hull in one sweeping arc. A perfect place to run, to escape, from the crew, from herself, from the boy. Fifteen kilometers of deep gloom, with the vast curve of the hull under her feet and the columns of containers on their racks rising above her, the lights set high up in the bulkheads unable to penetrate down here. A dark world, but not silent. Although not apparent, the old ship flexed and jerked in the strange world of hyperspace; the hull groaned and squeaked, transmitting the movement to the rails with their huge, rectangular pods, which in turn swayed, sighing in sympathy, the sounds echoing and rebounding through the cavernous space; it was like being in the belly of some gigantic, hungry beast.

In this twilight world, with her thermal imaging enabled, the details of the ship's structure morphed into a landscape of gray-green. Immense jutting ribs of the superstructure rose, curving away above her head; on the deck, piles of detritus, the flotsam of hundreds of voyages accumulated like skeletons on a sea floor. Islands of control modules jutted out of the debris, cloaked in dirt, almost invisible in the darkness.

Seven kilometers in, she had settled into a good pace, the obstacles reduced to calculations running down the right side of her interface; distance, height, approach vectors. She did not need to think, only give herself to the run, into the discipline, and it became easy to slip back into memory, to remember the security of the encasing battle armor, synced to her systems via the neural port, the heft of the weapons array. The constant reassurance that she was part of a great and sacred duty.

Now she was reduced to this. Running in filth. Hours after the incident, her skin still crawled at the remembrance of the boy's hands on her, the helplessness as she fell. Except she had not fallen, because he had caught her, saved her. An unquantifiable frisson of emotion hit her, as she approached a looming control module. The roughly cubical structure stuck up from the hull, almost invisible in normal light, the once-gray paintwork now covered in a thick layer of dirt. Her foot slipped in the muck, forcing her to adjust, so instead of hitting the ridge halfway up the module's side, she ended up in an awkward half tumble that only carbon-fiber reinforced muscles and enhanced functions saved from becoming a head-first crash into the deck. Ori climbed to her feet, dirt and debris sticking to her sweaty skin, stinking of grease, and old coolant and rusting metal. Her foot snagged on an indefinable mass of wiring and piping and she cursed, dragging herself away from the tangle.

What was wrong with her? The boy meant nothing, the crew meant nothing; all that mattered was getting to Tersen and escape, yet even now she could feel his hand on her skin, the reassuring tone of his voice. He had saved her.

Because he does not know what you are, said the voices. *He would have let you fall and spat on your broken body if he knew.* Once again that spasm of pain hit her, at the idea of Zarr's rejection and this time the rage would not come to wash it away. There was only this cold, heavy lump sitting in her chest, and feelings she couldn't — would not — process.

Around her the ship complained, and the containers grumbled, in sympathy or derision Ori couldn't tell, but she could not stay here in the gloom forever, although that seemed like the perfect place for her. Pushing all the turmoil back down, Ori set off again into the darkness, but the perfection she sought would not come and her hand hit the ladder a full thirteen minutes outside of her target time.

The climb up through level after level of containers — dark red, bright blue, rusty yellow, their sides painted with the names of the various freight companies in angular

Standard or flowing Polini — seemed to take forever, and Ori emerged onto the walkway stinking and unsettled. For a long moment she stood motionless, trapped in a malaise of uncertainty. Her plans now seemed pointless, futile; escape from the Xi, from Rossim, an impossibility.

Eleven

The door slid silently closed. There were days, like today, where Rossim wished for one of those ancient, solid doors, one he could slam shut and make a point. Instead, he had to content himself with ordering his staff to give him a few moments of peace, poured himself a large drink and took up his usual position at the window overlooking the square. Rossim decided he hated the new landscaping and he especially loathed the flowers and mementos that continued to appear, tied to the railings or laid out along the paving, despite the efforts of the palace staff, in front of a makeshift shrine decorated with tiny holo-lights.

A news drone flittered up and down the square, hovering over the display, sucking up a few more images for yet another segment on the disaster. Rossim poured a second drink, larger than the first, and rubbed the back of his neck to ease the unrelenting tension, to no avail. As each day went by, he found it harder and harder to remember why he'd wanted this job in the first place. Was redeeming his family's reputation and status worth all this grief?

And now Pesek was developing a conscience. And raising objections. What Rossim needed to work out was if this was a ploy to extract more concessions, or the start of a genuine crisis. The Lord President couldn't sweep the First Secretary of the Directorate aside like some lowly administrator. Pesek was a Senate appointment — only they could dismiss him.

The AI chimed.

"What?" he snapped.

"Lord President, Xi Liaison Reinnor is here to see you."

For fuck's sake, would he never get a break?

"Fine. Send him in."

Jak Reinnor pretended to admire a portrait of some long-dead nobody while he waited for the Lord President to see him. The original had once hung in the hall of the Imperial Palace on Da Chet. Now all the paintings, the artworks, the palace, and twelve billion people were radioactive slag. Jak checked the date; this obscure noble had been dead for over five hundred years, too late now for him to complain that this copy made him look like a Nian slug.

The enormous canvas occupying a vast expanse of wall further down was a different matter altogether. Palace maintenance had finally put up something new to look at.

Jak stepped back until he could take in the entire masterpiece. The frame was unfortunate; an eyesore of overwrought gilt excess, but he recognized the artist immediately. Jala ve Damiran Se. His mother had at least two of her works, and Grandfather had one particularly fine example at the summer house. Not as large a piece as this one, obviously, but in Reinnor's opinion, a much more accomplished work.

If he remembered correctly, this piece had been commissioned to celebrate the Imperium's victory over what would later become the Orchetti Combine. Of course, no one would have been so crass as to document the occasion literally. Anyway, a battle in interstellar space, no matter how decisive, rarely makes decent art. Instead, Jala mined the rich vein of Polini mythology, converting ten years of protracted and bloody space warfare into Qiana, goddess of Prosperity, accepting the surrender of War, Disease, and Ignorance.

Did maintenance not comprehend who was portrayed as Qiana? Empress Minassio D'e had accepted the surrender of the six systems on an orbital above Orchetti Prime, not on a field of battle, and none of the leaders of the rebellion were chained and half-naked. Although from what he knew of the D'e family, it wouldn't have been out of the question.

There were, as far as he knew, no publicly exhibited images of any of the D'e Imperial families. Not since the war ended. None of Empress Michinati D'e, whose insane attempts to replace all five thousand members of the Imperial Guard with clones of her current lover had started the public discontent. Or Emperor Ferrin D'e, her son, whose ruthless and unrestrained cruelty in response to the widespread unrest at the directions genetic engineering were heading only served to harden opposition.

And there were certainly absolutely none, public or private, of Emperor Serrios D'e, his grandson. Or Serrios's sister Carillon, her husband, Zema and their two fully engineered children. All of them died on Da Chet, incinerated in an orbital bombardment led by Admiral Danizitia that left twelve billion people dead and a planet destroyed for millennia.

Lost in thought, Jak nearly missed the door to Rossim's office sliding open; his invitation to enter. As usual, Rossim stood at the window, glass in hand, staring down at the square. Now there was a mess Jak was glad he wasn't involved in. The Senate was in full attack mode; at last count, three separate inquiries were scheduled, dozens of civil suits, and a good handful of criminal cases were before the courts. Hanjile Eidress must be wetting themselves with joy at the thought.

"Excellency, it is a pleasure to see you again," Rossim said, in that politician's voice that put Jak's teeth on edge. "Take a seat," he continued, waving to one of the imposing, padded chairs set before the presidential desk.

"I've been honored with a holo-stream from Xia," Jak began, settling into his seat, and taking care his new jacket wasn't accidentally rumpled. The watered silk, in the most exquisite pale violet, gleamed under the light from the Nax'tl crystal chandelier. Rossim eased himself into his imitation throne (he wasn't fooling anyone) and glowered at Jak.

"Ah, and what do our fucking masters want this time?"

Wasn't Rossim going to offer him a drink? Did Tel do this deliberately, or was he simply an uncouth bully? "I have the orders. For her," Jak said, aware of how much it annoyed Rossim that he wouldn't refer to Oryelle as an it.

Rossim put his glass down and sat up slowly. "Tell me."

Jak took a deep breath and launched into his speech. "She is to contact a Directorate agent, a member of a family in the Polini silversmith guilds." He paused, before calmly continuing. "She is to take up a pre-arranged position as a security officer for the guild. The guilds are concerned about the rising anti-Republic sentiment on Ma'al. From there, she is to infiltrate, by any means available, any of the hanjiles, prioritizing Eidress, Ansissi-Kai, Demanchi and Mathani. Ostensibly to gather information on silk. For an unspecified length of time."

The glass shattered against the wall, accompanied by a curse so blasphemous that Jak, despite anticipating Rossim's anger, gasped in genuine shock. Alcohol soaked into the expensive carpet, shards of priceless crystal glinting in the wreckage.

"This is fucking unbelievable. That thing, that Abomination, should have been up against a wall and shot the moment it appeared in our space. Are you telling me"—Rossim took a deep breath and Jak thought he might explode with rage—" its orders are to have a paid holiday, on Ma'al, the one world we cannot monitor, cannot take a fucking scout ship into, and fuck its way through those wealthy pricks?"

Jak winced. "That's about the gist of it, yes," he conceded, although the orders hadn't specified the method of approach. Jak vehemently disagreed with many of the decisions made about Oryelle, but antagonizing Rossim wouldn't help her or advance his ambitions.

"They cannot be serious. This is some sort of joke."

"I did query the Xi. I received the same reply I get whenever I ask: obey."

"No, Reinnor, this cannot stand. We cannot allow this to happen. The Xi have overstepped themselves this time."

Has Rossim lost his mind? How does he think we are going to countermand the Xi's orders?

"I'm sorry, but you know I can't do anything about it. I came to tell you personally, as a courtesy."

Rossim snarled, pushed back from the desk, and strode to the antique cabinet holding an impressive array of flasks, bottles and glasses. He poured himself another drink, hesitated and then filled a second glass.

"So, where is it now?" he asked, returning to the desk and pushing the second drink toward Jak.

Jak took the glass with a nod of thanks. "According to our operatives, she's taken a berth on the *Avadora*. It's an old ship. It will take her at least six weeks to get to Ma'al. Fortunately, the exchange at the Corelli and Tersen systems is cargo only, so there is no chance of her escaping before she reaches Ma'al."

Jak continued to hope Oryelle would see the strategic benefits of discovering the Xi motives, but he was pragmatic enough to know that if he were in her position, escape would be the top priority. To that end, he'd used his considerable powers to have the *Avadora* closely monitored.

"No chance? You haven't been here long enough to know what it's like. What if it hijacks the ship?"

"We believe the only viable option is at Tersen. Corelli is still too far from the border, the *Avadora*'s engines couldn't cover that distance in one jump." Oryelle was probably aware by now that the *Avadora*'s fuel tanks had been replaced with ones of much smaller capacity, meaning the old freighter would struggle to make the jump from Tersen to the nearest border colony. She certainly didn't know Jak had ensured the *Avadora* became her only available option. The Directorate wasn't the only department that could bribe and coerce labor reps.

"She would have to overpower the crew after they refuel at Tersen. The Port Authority will expect the navigator and Captain to log in. She can't kill them before their IDs are confirmed." The covert scout ship tracking the *Avadora* would alert him if the freighter deviated from its course, giving Jak plenty of time to intervene.

Rossim snorted derisively. "How many times did the Directorate need the Imperial Guard or the Fleet to retrieve it after a mission? How many times did I and that fool Babima, your predecessor, drag it back here, beaten and bloody, but still spitting defiance? That thing is perfectly capable of killing everyone and making for the border."

Jak decided Rossim didn't need to know about the scout ship and assumed a look of patient affableness. "I don't think so, Tel. I'll ask Fleet to send the *Kenthu Zen-ii* to Tersen, as a precaution, but I'm confident there won't be any issues this time," he replied, taking care not to sound too smug. Rossim had little patience for anyone who thought themselves smarter than him. That had been Fared Babima's downfall, so the rumors went. That and her total incompetence. Sometimes, recruiting from the best families didn't guarantee success. The stupid woman at least had the decency to retire to her estate and remove herself from society.

"Can Haruichi be trusted to do what is necessary?"

It had been one act of compassion, something any decent person would have done, yet Rossim made it sound like the captain committed treason. Another opinion Jak needed to keep to himself.

"Captain Haruichi is an exemplary officer who acted out of a misguided sense of honor. Nevertheless, we have suggested Fleet utilize her many sterling qualities somewhere else for a few months. They have her teaching an advanced strategy course at the Academy. Her replacement has been fully briefed on our expectations."

Of course, Jak also failed to mention his meeting with Oryelle on Six.

"It had better be. And the operatives on Ma'al? They'll be in place? I don't want it escaping at the last moment."

"I have a meeting with Imsu Pesek tomorrow. I'll need to be vague, but he'll provide a couple of agents without asking too many questions." Jak tugged a line of lace on his sleeve into a more aesthetically pleasing line.

Now comes the tricky part.

"Although, Tel, I have to say I'm concerned. If we intervene too early, she will not have time to complete her mission and the risk is that this will antagonize the Xi."

"I don't care what the Xi have promised it, that thing is not leaving Ma'al alive. I'm not suicidal enough to intervene before it has done whatever it is they want, but after that, I want it dead."

"Tel," Jak began, as delicately as he could, "with all respect. She is a valuable asset. If she had been treated a little more carefully—"

"Carefully!" Rossim slammed his fist down, making all the curios on his desk jump. "Do you know how many people it has killed? Including, I might add, the previous Lord President. In this very office. That Abomination smashed his head into the floor until his brains were spread across most of the room."

"President Garret's death was unfortunate—"

"Even if I agreed with you, which I don't, the damage was done long before it was handed over to us. The Xi had it for what? Two years? No amount of 'careful' handling is going to erase two years of torture by them."

"We didn't have to make it worse. All those years, all that pain we inflicted on her." With difficulty, Jak resisted yelling the truth at his president: *you and Garrett did that as revenge.* "You can't see past what she is," he said, instead.

"It's a fucking Abomination. It is everything this Republic fought against. Eight billion people on our side alone. And you want to make friends with it."

Blessed Mother, it was three hundred years ago.

"And we both know the twelve billion that died on Da Chet were only the beginning. Can we not put the war behind us and have a sensible conversation about this? Especially since now is surely the time to pull the Republic together."

"Oh, yes, pull the Republic together. It's one provocation after another. Ma'al holds us to ransom. Give us what we want, or no silk. The demonstration was only a symptom. Thirty-four dead." Rossim jabbed at the window. "Out there in that square. I've got systems threatening to secede over this. Some of them are talking about arming themselves. They think the Senate has betrayed them."

And they wouldn't be incorrect in that assessment. For decades now, the wealth generated by the outer systems poured into Central and Polinia; the reverse flow was less and less every year. Jak would have to start making a list of thoughts he had to keep to himself.

"I know. I have seen the analysis."

"You know the issues. The Republic is fraying at the edges. Systems can't see the value of remaining, and our only deterrent, the Fleet, is down to a third of its strength. Could you imagine the panic if anyone ever knew what we have done? We'd all end up in front of the same firing squad. It should have been executed the moment it entered Republic space."

Jak allowed himself a small show of anger. "Except the Xi want her alive, Tel. They have always been quite explicit on that point. You must agree that they have their own agenda, which they refuse to share with us."

"I suppose you've asked them?"

"Repeatedly."

"And?"

"I was informed that all decisions concerning the Brightstar are a matter for the Xi."

Imsu Pesek ordered the AI to set his office to "Private," waiting until the curve of syntheglass had completely opaqued, before sinking back into his chair with an expletive that could melt steel. Fucking Rossim. When he had agreed to this plan — no, scratch that. When *ordered to develop* a plan to illegally subvert the Ma'al government and put a Cimmili puppet in charge, he'd squashed his reservations and obeyed. He knew Rossim's reputation, though; he shouldn't have been surprised that the president seemed more interested in profiting from the silk trade than reopening freight routes and safeguarding citizens' rights.

Pesek swore again, though less blasphemously, and thumbed his sheet to active. The file image stared back at him. Why was this woman so important? Rossim's orders were clear—delay her getting to Ma'al, do everything to make her life difficult, short of serious injury or death.

Such activities were not unknown to the Directorate. Pesek had run several operations designed to cripple the rise of a political figure or facilitate the ascension of a preferred candidate. With the assistance of the ubiquitous AI network, personal sabotage was relatively straightforward.

Her applications for berths were quietly blocked, never reaching their intended destination. The unexpected death of the *Havali's Hope* navigator had caused some issues, but luck must have favored him, for even as that opportunity abruptly disappeared, along came the *Avadora*, a slow, old freighter. And as a bonus it came with this prize: Jwali.

By the Blessed Mother, this one was a piece of work. Imsu flicked through the information. Jwali ve Dev, navigator — though he'd barely scraped through training, and couldn't seem to get a berth with anyone other than a relative. You'd think that someone who'd just done six months of rehab would be more cautious. He hadn't been hard to bribe; half a brick of floess, a handful of credits, and he was willing to do anything. Pesek wouldn't know, of course, if he'd achieved anything until the ship dropped into Corelli space. He'd alerted the authorities there, in case intervention proved necessary, but the real opportunity would come at Tersen. A small piece of sabotage, only enough to get the ship held for a day or two, then a surprise search for drugs. Whoever she was, it would take her days to get out of that problem. She may not reach Ma'al for another month, maybe more. And if she got mouthy or aggressive, well, with any luck it could be a year or more before she saw the outside.

It should be straightforward, yet as Pesek examined the image before him, that sense of unease began crawling up his spine. Something about her seemed familiar, but Pesek was certain he'd never met her. He was sure he'd remember someone like her. The whole mess didn't sit right, and he hadn't risen to this position by ignoring his instincts. The Directorate had agents on Tersen; perhaps it might be prudent to have them keep an eye on the *Avadora*. It might be worthwhile trying to extract the woman, find out why Rossim wanted her intercepted. Leverage on anyone was useful, leverage on the Lord President, well, that was a gift beyond price.

Twelve

*S*he is running, her mother's hand gripping hers so tightly she has lost all feeling in
her fingers. The baby, her brother, is crying. A thin, hopeless wail that doesn't stop
except to draw breath. Beside her, the old man who'd kept up with them all the way from
the city swears loudly, then drops, the scarlet spreading across his chest, now a mangled,
bloody mess. The monsters, the invaders, in their black armor like the carapaces of
monstrous insects, are right behind them, herding the crowd with precision. Two more
people drop —the young woman, only just swelling with new life, and her husband
perhaps, or brother. It makes no difference. No one has any breath left for screams,
only strangled sobs, or curses.

The baby has stopped crying, flopping exhausted on her mother's shoulder, his big,
dark eyes without expression. The mass of fleeing people slows, begins to coalesce into
discrete groups. Murmurs rise. She looks around and they are surrounded by walls.
Walls that were not here last month when this was a park. They are trapped. Her
mother is crying now, a wail more hopeless than the baby's. The black line of armor
moves forward, implacable, pushing everyone closer and closer together, until she cannot
move. Rain begins to fall in a soft mist, except it is red, and the man beside her falls,
his head almost gone. There is this weird sound, and her mother's hand lets go.

The scream died in her throat as she snapped awake, her clothes glued to her body,
the rank sweat soaking the bedclothes, her heartbeat hammering in her chest.

Zarr's bunk light clicked on, a pool of light in the darkness of their quarters.
"Fuck, Ori, are you OK?"

Nothing worked. The interface wouldn't respond, warnings populated across her
vision screaming of rising stress hormones, rocketing blood pressure. The sub-dermal
mesh activated, prickly as it swelled. Her hands moved in a futile gesture to wave him
away, but his hand touched her leg and the response was instantaneous. The blow drove
the boy across the narrow space between the bunks, the sickening crunch as his skull hit

the metal frame horrifyingly loud. Zarr dropped to the floor, his body limp, blood already pooling under him.

No, no, no.

She threw herself from the bunk, landing beside his still body. For a long, terrifying second she feared she had killed him, as her fingers frantically searched for a pulse. The relief when she felt the steady beat could not be categorized, so she pushed it down with all the other uncomfortable feelings and turned to cataloging his injuries. Her hands moved methodically over his body, probing the depression along the cheekbone, already swelling purple, the spongy area at the back of his skull where the blood was already clotting in the fine brown hair. His pupils were nonreactive. He needed treatment, he needed the med bay, now.

Yet she hesitated. Questions would be asked, an investigation launched — perhaps something official at Tersen. Her entire plan hinged on being as inconspicuous as possible, not arousing suspicions. This injury would be reported, a matter of public record, and she would be beyond foolish if she thought the Directorate wasn't monitoring her every movement. Rossim did not need much of an excuse. He would send the Directorate of Protection, and the Guard, to drag her back to Central. Or worse, to Xia and the Nest.

There were a few options, none of them ideal. A fall in the cargo bay would do it, but that would entail carrying the boy through the ship, undetected. She dismissed it without any further thought, and chose not to ask why that was so. Anyway, even if she made it look like an accident, it would still invite investigation, and she couldn't afford that.

Any decision Ori might have made became redundant as Zarr's leg abruptly stiffened, hitting the bunk frame, tremors running up and down his limbs in waves. He was seizing.

The nanites swarmed to her fingertips as Ori desperately searched through screen after screen, searching for the correct program. The tiny machines could carry out simple tasks in bodies other than hers, but reprogramming them to heal someone so genetically different to herself was not something she had any training in. Not for the first time, she cursed that she had not been designed as a Technical. Hoping for the best, Ori slid her hand under the boy's head, releasing the microscopic machines to slide through the epidermis and sub-dermal layers and into Zarr's spinal cord.

The connection established, Ori brought up the data from the nanites. Heart rate, respiration, blood pressure, body temperature and lines of physiological information she had no hope of decoding. Some had warning icons beside them, but lacking nearly all medical skills, they would have to remain unresolved. She knew the basics, though. Interrogations required at least some understanding of your subject's physiology. It was a common ploy to provoke an overreaction from your interrogator, thereby hastening death, or at the very least, prolonged unconsciousness. Blood pressure, heart rate, respiration began to drop at her command and Zarr's body relaxed as she induced the coma that would save him, while the machines went after the damage. He would still have some bruising and a sore head, but those would heal faster than normal.

All she could do now was monitor the boy's condition as the nanites did their work; repairing the fractures, reducing the swelling, rebuilding damaged cells. Around her the ship carried on its endless protests in the way all ships did in hyperspace. In the compartment, the only sounds were Zarr's breathing and the hum of the life support. Lart and D'vai wouldn't be back for hours; Lianna had this watch and she wouldn't allow either of them out of her sight until the shift ended.

Zarr's head lay cradled in her lap — to protect the injury, she told herself. Nothing else to do but monitor the boy's condition. She could not remember a time before the interface, superimposed on normal vision, with its line of icons down each side, a constant stream of data scrolling across the bottom. Diagnostics, environment, target acquisition, weapons. Memory storage. Its icon nestled right down the bottom, the plain silver a contrast to the other bright symbols. Digital memory. It held everything she had experienced since the technicians had implanted the enhancements decades ago. It held the memories of her siblings, it held battles fought and won, and enemies conquered. It also held years of brutal training, and ten years of imprisonment. And it held the detailed memories of the battlefield, the pens full of the eijen, the culling — genocide on a scale never seen in the galaxy. No, to open that was to let it all out, all the horror. The nightmares were bad enough.

In the silence, her mind wandered. To Tszcienna. She couldn't pinpoint exactly when she became aware of Tszcienna as an individual, rather than simply another one of her carers, but she was probably three when she realized he came to see her alone, ignoring the other children. She had hundreds of siblings; all of them formed out of the same soup of amino acids, built base pair on base pair, genes spliced and shifted, epigenetic switches turned on or off, depending on the design requirements.

Tszcienna had been Technical. Frighteningly intelligent, Technical ran the vast breeding centers, designed weapons, ships and intelligent machines. Command Lines such as herself were superior military organisms, tasked with removing the eijen filth from the galaxy. There were other lines, designed for various administrative roles, and lastly the leaders, who oversaw the vast military machine, and ensured the sacred duty continued relentlessly. Every other task fell on the enslaved.

Zarr shifted uneasily, moaning in pain, and she felt a moment of helplessness. The programs that controlled her pain relief were severely damaged, the Hubnae had told her, their deep, rumbling voices filled with regret. We don't have the technology to repair them, they went on mournfully, as the jewels embedded in their carbuncled hides glinted in the bright lights of the Hubnae medical center. Very convenient, especially when you are about to turn over your patient (our apologies) to your ally for prolonged torture. Of course, if she hadn't killed so many of them trying to steal a ship, they might have been more forgiving. Ten years gives one a lot of time for regret.

Zarr's hand moved toward his face and she caught his wrist to forestall him. Her fingers easily encircled the still-childlike structure of his bones, frail and delicate, his skin brown against her gold, as soft as a child's. As she laid his arm down, the sleeve slid back to reveal a line of bruises tracking up his forearm, the half-moons of nails still visible. With something close to anger, she pushed up the other sleeve, revealing matching injuries. She released him, unexpectedly conflicted. Jwali seemed the most likely suspect, given his attack on her, so what else had he done to the boy? Diagnostics came back up as she trawled through the data, looking for clues. The nanites, following their basic programming, tackled the fractures and brain damage first. The wounds were closing, the blood disappearing from his hair and the surrounding deck as the tiny machines broke down anything not needed to continue the replication process. Now she knew what she was looking for, the signs were simple enough to find. So Jwali preyed on those he thought were vulnerable. He would soon understand he'd made a terrible miscalculation with her.

The nanites disengaged, their tasks complete. She laid Zarr back on the deck, watching for any signs of seizures as consciousness returned. His eyes opened, tracking across the bulkhead until they rested on her. Pleasure, then confusion washed across his face.

"What the—" Zarr rubbed the back of his head, wincing as he felt the lump. "Ow. What happened?"

She helped him sit up, her hands sliding around his ribs, feeling how slight he was under the camouflaging overall.

"You startled me, and I pushed you away. You slipped and hit your head." It didn't sound convincing, even as she said it.

"Yeah." Zarr struggled to his feet, a little unsteady. "Sorry, I heard you scream, I think. How long was I out?"

Good, if his recollection of the seconds leading up to the concussion remained blurry, she might be able to persuade him nothing much happened. "It was an accident, and you were only unconscious for a minute or two." Too late, she understood what was required — an apology. Contrition. In her world, you might apologize to a sibling or another Line of equal rank for a misplaced strike while training, or some other innocuous event. Apologies to those above you were pointless. Whatever the transgression, pleading would only make it worse. So, you stayed silent, and endured. "I didn't mean to hit you," she tried. "I'm sorry." She must have done it well enough to pass, as the boy smiled ruefully, and rubbed the back of his head again.

"Nah, I'm sorry. I shouldn't have touched you."

"Perhaps you should get it checked out?" Why was she doing this? The boy was fine, the worst of the injuries were healing, he should be grateful he was alive.

Zarr shook his head. "No, those things go into the log, 'cause the captain has to report those things — they get fined if they don't. Or the captain might decide you're too much trouble, and you get dumped on your ass at the next stop. Worse bit is if you get injured and you're on watch. You don't report an injury, you can lose your license. And if you get bounced too often from berths, the reps start demanding 'finders fees' to get you a gig. Or worse. Everyone knows what happens to the pretty ones, boys or girls."

She already knew what happened. Three reps had waved away her generous bribes for access to her body.

"Honestly, I'm fine," said Zarr. "Go back to sleep." He climbed back into his bunk; darkness filled the compartment as the light went out. She heard him roll over with a muffled curse.

Ori pulled the thin blanket up over her head. The nanites would continue to work, and by the start of the shift tomorrow, he would be healed. She pressed her fingers against the bulkhead, feeling the vibration of the drives. The metal was cold and unyielding. Not like skin at all.

```
[REM sleep achieved.
Subroutines initiated.
Data processing from nanite incursion underway.
Comparing to programmed parameters.
Mission unsuccessful. Parameters not achieved.
Information shunted to secure storage.
Accessible memory erased.]
```

Ori, uncomfortable at the prospect of facing Zarr, although she couldn't articulate to herself why, left the crew quarters early. Running into Lart and Davey, on their way back to the mess, was doubly irritating. It continually baffled her that on a ship of this size, she couldn't escape any of the crew. The fact that most of the ship consisted of cargo space might have something to do with it, she conceded.

"Hey, where's your shadow?" Davey grinned and elbowed Lart, who looked irritated and tired at the end of his shift. Lianna must have them cleaning as well —— both men were filthy and unaccountably wet, their overalls clinging to them in damp patches.

"In his bunk," Ori answered. She'd checked on the boy while he slept; the nanites, having completed their work, were dissolving into his bloodstream. "I couldn't sleep, I'm on my way to starboard hold for a cargo check." *And some peace and quiet away from all of you.* "Why are you wet?"

"Just came from there, Lianna says to call in on Jen, she needs a hand with some ducting she said. And the recycling pump on B deck broke down, main seal went halfway through the shift. You and Zarr will have to finish cleaning up down there."

"I thought she repaired that recently?"

"Yeah, so did she." Lart shrugged. "I don't know, she was real upset about it. Anyway, go find her, she'll tell you all about it. Me and Davey want a meal and a shower."

Davey followed the old man, turning once to give her a half gesture of goodbye, or something close. Ori filed that under more things eijen did, and headed off to find the maintenance officer. The small workshop was empty of Sukin, but full of piles of junk and tools and maybe spare parts, although it was hard to tell the difference between them and the rubbish. Every flat surface was covered in more piles, or boxes. In one corner a mug that might once have held rakosh now grew an impressive mound of some greenish muck. *Animals, all of them.*

Ava, where is Maintenance Officer Sukin?

Prayer room. Deck B compartment Four.

A prayer room. No wonder nothing got done around here.

Deck B was yet another mess. Patches of water and muddy boot marks covered most of the deck. A pile of sodden rags dripped into a storage container, a haphazard pile of tools and rubbish leaning against it. Compartment Four's hatch bore "Prayer Room" in angular informal Standard. Ori pushed open the hatch and stopped on the threshold, surprised. Everything was white. Bulkheads, deck, overhead, all white. And clean. This one compartment was the cleanest part of the ship Ori had seen. Four low white benches curved around a central bowl, in which a weak holographic flame flickered in the dim light. Sukin sat on the bench opposite the hatch, eyes closed.

Ori hesitated, unsure of how to proceed. Eijen had faith — her people had no need of such primitive superstitions, but the enslaved ones clung stubbornly to their religions, long after their worlds and civilizations were dust. As she stood, caught between interrupting and leaving, Sukin opened her eyes, the corners crinkling into a tired smile.

"Tey, you're up early," the round little woman said, rising slowly from the bench. "Thanks, I could do with some competent help."

"What happened with the pump? I thought you fixed it four days ago."

Sukin flushed, the smile disappearing instantly. "I did. I replaced all the seals. Suddenly the main seal goes again. I don't understand how."

Perhaps you installed it incorrectly was what Ori wanted to say, but some hitherto unknown part of her advised against it.

"Lart said you had some ducting that needed fixing. I will make sure the boy is down here soon to clean up the mess outside."

"I don't understand," the woman continued, ignoring Ori. "I fixed the pump, and the filters on the living quarters, and yet they're broken again. I've never had such a bad run of equipment breakdowns, it's like the *Ava* is falling apart." The woman slumped back down onto the bench, dirty fingers clutching at her little pendant. "I thought, if I could make this work for another year or two, that would give me enough experience to get a job back home. Steady hours, decent pay. See the boys more often."

Ori's first impulse, to leave the stupid woman and find something useful to do, seemed … the emotion that provoked made her uncomfortable in a way she struggled to quantify, so at a loss, she sat on an adjoining bench, deciding to give the maintenance officer a chance to gather herself, before setting about the repairs.

The silence caught her first. The little compartment must be insulated from the rest of the ship — she couldn't even feel the drive vibrations. And it was clean. No filth in corners, no piles of rubbish. The sullen pulses of amber in her peripheral vision ebbed away.

"You are not a person of faith," asked Sukin, her voice soft and low.

"No, I am not," replied Ori, but without the anger that question usually provoked.

"That's all right. The Blessed Mother cares for all of us."

An emotion that Ori did understand swept over her. Grief, followed by anger again. Where had this Mother been when Ori was being tortured? Where was she when they dragged Tszcienna into the hall that morning? Rage drove her to her feet, startling the other woman.

"I do not want to hear about your pathetic beliefs. I am going to find some actual work to do, instead of sitting around here wallowing in self-pity."

The hatch slammed shut behind her. Stupid eijen. Animals and their faith. She would be glad when they were all dead.

She wasn't in the mess, or the showers. Zarr paced through the ship, trying to look unconcerned and busy at the same time. All he needed was Lianna asking him where she was, and they'd both be in trouble. Engineering? Could be. He wasn't stupid, anyone could see that Van's interest was in more than getting help with the drives. Which was another thing. According to Davey, Ori was like an expert engineer. Or so he reckoned. Said he overheard Van and Jen talking. Even allowing for the other cargo hand's exaggeration, it still threw up more questions than he had answers for. Zarr was still pondering all these disparate facts, when he rounded the corridor, and ran, literally, into Jen.

"Argh, sorry, Jen," he said, bouncing off the plump little woman. "Wasn't watching where I was going."

Jen gave him that motherly smile, and patted him on the shoulder. "Blessed Mother, Zarr, you'll walk off into the cargo bay one day, not paying attention." She leaned back and looked him up and down. Zarr tried not to squirm under the attention. "She's down on B Deck, cleaning up. I think." Jen gave him another hard stare. "We were talking and she just stormed out. Something I said made her angry."

Hadn't you noticed she's always angry about something? And frightened. I hear her scream in terror every night, but if I try and help it's like the worst thing ever.

"She didn't sleep well, that's all," he said, instead. Ori wouldn't appreciate him spreading rumors.

Jen beamed again. "Well, off you go and give her a hand. I'm sure it will all blow over." And with another pat to his shoulder, Jen headed back toward the bridge.

B Deck. More cleaning duties. He could have stayed at home and got a janitorial job, and work less for more pay. Well, next stop Tersen, then a straight run to Ma'al. Zarr turned down the corridor, heading for the cargo bay. Maybe he could offer to show her around? Take her down to the Enclave, do some shopping. The Polini had some nice shops down there. Nothing either of them could afford, but it didn't cost anything to look. He stopped at a hatch marked MAINTENANCE ONLY. Who had time to go the long way when you could duck down through the maintenance shafts? Zarr pushed open the hatch, making certain to close it properly behind him. No point in annoying Jen unnecessarily. Wish she'd stop patting him like he was one of her kids.

It took a moment for his eyes to adjust once the hatch closed. The only illumination down here was the strip of yellow emergency lighting that ran along the top of the bulkhead. There wasn't a great deal of room; Zarr had to turn sideways to fit between two feeder stacks and scoot alongside the bulkhead before he could wriggle into the maintenance shaft proper. Headroom was an issue, you couldn't run along here, but for someone short, it wasn't a problem. Ori would have to walk half crouched over to get through some of these areas.

Ori. Ma'al. Surely it wouldn't hurt to ask her? It wasn't like a date or anything. Maybe—

"Well, look who's scurrying around like a little rat in the dark."

No, not here, where he couldn't run, couldn't hide. No one would hear him. *No, Blessed Mother, no.*

Zarr jammed his hands deep in his pockets and turned around. Jwali was lounging on a power conduit box, a portable light hanging above him from a makeshift hook. A scrap of white cloth lay beside him. The tiny pile of bright purple crystals sparkled incongruously among the utilitarian surroundings.

Floess. Jwali is down here, using, and I've seen it. Oh, this won't be good.

"Navigator," he said, trying to stay calm, be cool, though he could feel the sweat break out down his back and palms, and his heartbeat thundered in his ears. Nausea rolled and swelled in his stomach. "I was on my way to the cargo hold. Checking cargo." A wave of ice-cold terror ran through him.

"Ah, helping out your pretty whore, no doubt. I hope she's taught you some new tricks. I was getting bored with the same old routines." Jwali didn't move, except for his hand. He wet one finger and touched it lightly, delicately, to the shimmering purple, before just as delicately licking off the fragile crystals with the tip of his tongue.

Zarr took an involuntary step back, his back hitting the wiring array that ran the length of the shaft. In the dim light, he could see Jwali's pupils blow out as the drug hit him.

"I have to go." He searched desperately for some excuse, some leverage that would get him out of this. "The cargomaster will be expecting me."

Jwali, shook his head, slowly, and stood up. "Oh, Zarr, you know how much I hate it when you lie." His hand stretched out again, and another tiny dot of glitter danced on the end of his finger. "Now come here, like a good boy, and have some fun." He waggled the finger back and forth languidly.

"No, please, Jwali, I don't want to." The first tear slid down his cheek, and he swept it away angrily. He slid a fraction along the array, hard metal biting into his back through his thin overalls. Jwali's arm slammed down, blocking Zarr's escape. The finger, with its bright, poisonous load, came closer.

"Now, we've gone through this before, boy." Jwali pressed closer, his breath hot and sour. "You do as I tell you, and you get to stay on my ship."

"No," Zarr said again, weaker this time.

"Your little whore can't save you."

Zarr was trapped, held between the biting metal, and the all too obvious hardness of the navigator's arousal.

"I tell you what, you be a good boy, and I promise I'll leave her alone. It'll be you and me like always." The tiny purple crystals wavered in Zarr's sight.

"Please," he whispered, as the first sweet flake touched his lips. "You have to promise. You'll leave her alone." There would be no shopping trips, or catching a mug of rakosh in that little café down near the Enclave. No window shopping in the Polini quarter, but she would be safe. "Please, don't hurt me."

Thirteen

First Sister roused her from her contemplation of the new hatchlings. "We have a problem," she said, her palps signaling concern. "The Meians are here."

The Matriarch rose, fighting back the fatigue that every day became more irritating, and relinquished the infants to the care of their nurses.

"Do you know what they want?" she asked. As they moved down the webbed tunnels, subservient females prostrated themselves and pods of males paused their games to watch; she administered a soothing caress or chitter of encouragement as she passed.

"To complain about something, I suspect," said First Sister, acidly.

When they reached the center, a lone Meian stood in the circle of light, while three more Meians stood corralled off to one side, under the watchful eyes of the Nest soldiers.

"Welcome to Xia—" the Matriarch began.

"Consider this an official protest," the Meian representative interrupted, its wings rasping with anger. "We have tried to be patient but these repeated violations of the pact must cease." Rainbow splinters of light glanced off its iridescent armor, painting the ghostly webs with fugitive splashes of color that danced across the strands as the emissary stalked across the floor. "We have tried to discuss this with you and the Hubnae, but our concerns have been ignored."

The light caught in the Meian's multifaceted eyes, sending shards of rainbows across the deep gold chitin. Unlike the Xi, the insectoid race either lost (or had excised from their genome) the other pairs of vestigial limbs, so that they stood upright and bipedal like the humanoid races. They'd kept the wings, though, large diaphanous appendages, which they used to convey strong emotions. Or to make a point.

The Matriarch made no reply. She knew the Meians well; no one would get a word in until it finished delivering its message.

"You have assured us that the alien is imprisoned because of terrible acts it committed against yourself and the Hubnae, but now we discover it is free? And on its way to Ma'al, without supervision? What treachery is this?"

Behind the emissary, a pod of hatchlings chased the shifting colors up and down the web. On any other day, it would be amusing. A delegation from the Meian Autocracy was unexpected and unwelcome and now the Matriarch needed to ally its suspicions. Quickly.

"We needed a task completed." The Matriarch spread her palps in a placatory gesture. "A small mission, nothing important. And it is being supervised."

"A small mission?" The angry rasping increased in volume. "Do you mock us? Or do you think us stupid? We warned you, when the war started, not to interfere. You ignored us, and continue to do so, despite our protests. You select their president, control their internal security forces, influence their elections. All these actions are in violation of the pact we made. Have we not suffered enough in this futile crusade? We lost entire systems to the last race we tried to help. And now, as a last insult, you force the Republic to keep an engineered, enhanced and augmented soldier, of unknown origins, as a prisoner. It is an outrage."

There were times when the Matriarch truly regretted her species' involvement in this pact, despite the valid and cogent reasons for its existence. Both the Xi and the Hubnae, and later the Meians, strived repeatedly to raise numerous races out of barbarism. They tried benevolent god scenarios, ruthless dictatorships, and benign partnerships. Nothing held, nothing endured. Civilization after civilization crumbled and fell, or turned on their overlords, before turning on each other. After hundreds and thousands of years, it became too depressing. The Hubnae refused to engage anymore, pulling back to a handful of systems, ignoring those they once tried to help.

"We dispute whether it is a violation of the pact. We merely suggest; they are free to ignore us." That wasn't entirely true, and they both knew it. The only reason the alliance hadn't fallen apart over this was the continued Hubnae support. If they ever decided to withdraw that support, though, the pact would fall apart. Who knew what would happen after that? Hostilities, of a limited sort, broke out all the time, mostly out of boredom. A serious conflict would be a disaster. "We simply wanted her off Central for a while. Once this task is completed, we assure you, she will be eliminated, and all records of her existence erased."

Lying to the Meians didn't trouble her. The Xi philosophy was always that the ends justified the means. And in this case, the stakes were high enough to justify almost all deceptions.

The Meian ambassador halted in the pool of light, its arms folded in the universal gesture of disbelief. "Of course," it said, the insect's tone heavy with sarcasm, "you'll tell us what this small task is?"

This was getting out of hand. She should rip its head off and feed the remains to the hatchlings and be done with it. The Hubnae would intervene before the conflict went too far, and the young ones could do with the entertainment. Behind the annoying insect, First Sister made an astonishingly obscene gesture, forcing the Matriarch to use all her willpower not to burst into laughter. "We lost something. Or, more accurately, a possession of ours was stolen. We believe it is on Ma'al. The Brightstar is to retrieve it." Another lie. What they hoped the Brightstar would find had never been theirs.

"We know you. If any other creature had done what it had, you would have flayed it alive and fed the still writhing corpse to your males. This one must be important and we will discover why. You would do well to remember our military strength matches yours."

The air congealed as silence enveloped the chamber like a dark cloud. Even the young ones froze, as all in the chamber held their breath.

She'd never thought the Meian would be bold enough to call her on this. The Xi had built a galactic empire, no, two, before this stupid insect's race had evolved from creeping filth. On the other side of the chamber, her sister made another gesture, one of agreement.

Enough.

The barest shift in her stance signaled her sister, a wet, crackling sound filled the chamber, and the Meian's armored head rolled across the floor to land at the Matriarch's feet. The body toppled slowly, wings rasping in death throes as the young ones swarmed down from the webs in a wave of chitinous, scuttling hunger and leaped on the still-living flesh. In seconds all that could be seen was the heaving mass of bodies, fighting for morsels.

"How unfortunate," the Matriarch said, as her sister wiped the blade clean with exquisite care, "if the stupid insect had recognized how close it was to death, perhaps it might have moderated its manners a little more. Now we will need to deal with them before the Hubnae intervene. Again."

One of the young ones staggered out of the heaving mass, missing legs, mewling in distress. In the feeding frenzy, Nest mates were sometimes mistaken for food. The Xi dispatched it with a flick of her blade, and the pieces of the infant disappeared as quickly as the Meian ambassador's body. This could only be a delaying tactic; the Hubnae would not allow the conflict to drag on. All she needed was a month, maybe two. If the Brightstar hadn't found the stolen material in that time, the whole enterprise would be for nothing.

"Shall I mobilize our troops?" her sister asked, one set of eyes monitoring the children as she handed the blade back to the waiting soldier. The remaining Meians were herded out by their guards, no doubt carrying reports of this latest Xi outrage to all who would listen. Which meant the Hubnae would be here soon.

See what I do in the name of friendship, Carillon.

Nothing much remained of the Meian ambassador's body, apart from a few golden scales. The Matriarch kicked one across the floor to the juniors on clean up duties. "Yes, why not. Let's have a bit of excitement before our allies become too tedious and start whining about peace talks."

Fourteen

Ori pushed against the seat's frame, concentrating on getting the last bolt into position. The hole, warped by years of wear, refused to cooperate. *Look at you*, the voices nagged at her, *on your knees scrubbing floors like one of the animals. You should be ashamed to be undertaking such menial tasks.*

Behind her she could hear Zarr angrily jabbing at the compacted dirt in the far corner of the compartment. The boy had warned her more than once about annoying the cargomaster, now they were both down here in the cargo break room with explicit instructions not to leave until, as Lianna put it, "every square millimeter meets our new cargo hand's exacting requirements."

The whole debacle had started innocently enough. After weeks of enduring the wobbly seating and accumulating grime, Ori had taken the opportunity at a meal break to ask when the maintenance officer would be down to begin repairs. It seemed, at the time, a perfectly reasonable request. The maintenance crew on her ship, on any of her people's ships, would expect to be informed of any issues. None of them would take it as a personal insult. The warning jab from Zarr came a second too late.

The motherly little woman flushed with anger. "I've got an entire ship to keep running and you want me to fix a seat?" The entire mess acquired an atmosphere approaching absolute zero. "You must think I have nothing else to do?"

D'vai sniggered, ignoring Lart's warning look.

"Maybe we all joined Fleet while I wasn't looking," came Lianna's voice from the mess hatchway, "the *Ava* would make a fine battleship, once we get the old girl cleaned up."

No one laughed. Beside her, Zarr groaned, dropping his head into his hands. Only Van's absence saved the entire situation from being a total humiliation.

"I meant no disrespect," Ori said. "Cargomaster," she added, belatedly. It hadn't helped. Lianna didn't even bother disguising her pleasure at her humiliation, even less so that the rest of the crew evidently agreed with her. Once again Ori had seriously misjudged a social position.

She checked on the boy's position, and exerted her strength, pulling the metal back into position. The bolt dropped neatly into the hole, a few turns of the wrench tightening it. She gave the seat an exploratory shake, pleased, beyond any expectations, that the seat was firm and unmoving. That was the seating and the table completed. Over the last six hours neither of them had moved from the break room. The bulkhead now sported a new coat of military-gray paintwork, and the sign hung straight, affixed soundly to the wall, its obscenities cleaned off. For the last hour, while Ori worked on the seats and table, Zarr had attacked the built-up grime where deck met bulkhead. In total silence.

In fact, the boy hadn't said a word in hours. Thinking back, Ori now realised he had been withdrawn and unusually quiet for days.

"Fuck."

Ori spun around. Zarr nursed his hand, a mess of torn skin, blood and smashed knuckles.

"The tool slipped," he said, motioning with his head toward the corner. "I hit the edge of the support beam."

The medical kit sat open, its contents spilling out across the table. Both of them bore cuts and abrasions; the tools were worn and barely up to the job. "Come here," she ordered. The gash extended across the back of his hand, the blood already drying in a serpentine path across his skin and gluing his fingers together.

He held out his hand, flinching when she touched him. "Does it hurt anywhere else?" she asked. He hadn't complained of any lingering after-effects of her throwing him across the compartment and nearly killing him.

He shook his head, eyes fixed firmly on the deck.

"You are angry with me," she said, groping for an explanation, as she wiped the wound clean, applied the necessary topical anesthetic and sealed the torn skin with a battered regen unit, its off-pitch hum irritatingly loud in the silence.

"No." His gaze lifted a little, but he was still avoiding eye contact. "Yes."

Something was wrong, Ori could see that.

"I've served all my life on well-run, well-maintained ships. How is it a flaw to expect some degree of professionalism?" It seemed like a rational question.

"Because this is the *Ava*," Zarr yelled, pulling his hand away. Ori jerked back in surprise at the boy's sudden rage. "We're all just trying to keep going, one day at a time. There's no money, the runs are getting harder, fucking Ma'al is getting crazier every day. It must be so good to work on nice new ships. If it's so fucking nice, how come you're here then? Slumming with us?" His voice rose in volume as the anger poured out of him. The scarlet flooded across his face, and up to the tips of the ears that seemed not quite so awkward now. His accusations stung her, as they had never done before, digging into her, provoking her.

"Because I had no choice, the same way I've never had—" She stopped herself in time. *Never had a choice? Where did that come from?* Choice was a ridiculous concept. No one had choices; the animals only thought they did, delusions perpetrated by culture and belief. She had been designed, trained, bred for a purpose, as a part of her people's sacred quest to wipe out all forms of primitive, unengineered humanity. Eijen. Animals. Fit only to be enslaved or slaughtered.

"No choice?" Zarr leaped up, backing away until he pressed against the bulkhead. "Don't tell me you had to come with us. Was that why you're out here, because you kept pissing off your crewmates?"

What was wrong with the boy? His fury was out of all proportion to this situation. She was on him in two steps, her hand shooting out to drag him closer. He didn't struggle, hanging compliant in her grasp, a prey animal response.

"Tell me what happened," she demanded, pushing him down onto the seat.

He just shook his head, tears sliding down his cheeks to splash onto his overalls.

"Did Jwali hurt you?"

A long silence, then he gave a miniscule shrug.

She had no idea what to do, or say. Her first instinct, to hunt Jwali through the ship before slowly and methodically breaking every bone then slowly eviscerating him, was not possible. Yet.

Zarr wiped his face with his sleeve.

"He's been after you too, hasn't he?" he whispered. "I'm sorry."

"I wasn't seeking pity," she said, sharply. Zarr flinched in response. Some part of her knew she should say something, but the words stuck in her throat. Why was she feeling this? Why did it matter?

In one corner of her peripheral vision, an icon pulsed orange, distracting her from her inadvertent cruelty. Environmental sensors. Why were they suddenly activating?

Ori searched the overhead for the air vents, holding her hand up, fingers feeling for the flow of air.

"Something's wrong," she said to Zarr. "There is no air coming out of the vents. I can't hear the induction fans." How long had it been off, while air quality fell enough to trigger her systems?

"What? They're probably just off-line. I'm sure it's OK—"

"Sukin, are you there? Airflow in the cargo hold has ceased. Van, are you there? Drive room, can you hear me. *Ikaluos*. Ava, what's happened?"

"Life support is reporting critical errors. All life support systems are currently off-line," intoned the ship's AI.

Zarr tugged frantically at her. "Ori, we're still six days out from Corelli. We need life support."

"All hands report to the mess. Now." The captain's voice almost cracked with strain. "We have an emergency."

Fifteen

Ori hung back at the mess hatch, telling herself that Van and Sukin would be trying to fix whatever was wrong, and her urge to help the engineer was merely concern at the delay to the voyage, nothing else. Yet she continued to linger, until Zarr gave her another one of his nudges, accompanied by a raised eyebrow.

D'vai and Lart turned up, confused and half asleep. This was every crew's nightmare, right up there with becoming stranded in normal space or a decompression event. Without life support, they would all die, choking on their own waste. Even though the *Ava* was on a scheduled run, there was no such thing as long-range tugs, not for freighters like this. If they couldn't get the systems going again, or something else went wrong, the crew would have to send out a distress call and wait for someone to stop and pick them up. The ship could drift, alone, with only the captain, maybe Lianna on board, until a repair crew could be brought back. That could take weeks. If Marissa didn't have the credits, the *Ava* could be lost, prey for salvage teams. Getting the insurance companies to pay up could take months.

Lianna and Jwali stepped through the hatch, the cargomaster's face tight with fear, Jwali looking seemingly unconcerned. For a second she indulged herself in the luxury of imagining his slow and painful death, hoping he would look her way. He remained on the other side of the mess, studiously avoiding eye contact with anyone.

Ori surmised that Marissa was down in engineering, assessing the damage and working out how to tell the crew. She steered the boy to a seat and slid in beside him. "It will be all right," she said, the words falling out without any conscious thought on her part. She had to stop doing that.

Zarr shot her a look of surprise. "Yeah, I know."

Lart slumped down in the seat opposite, deep lines etched into his gray, sagging flesh. D'vai joined him, dropping into his seat and pushing a steaming mug of rakosh in the old man's direction. "Anyone know what happened?" the younger man asked. His voice was level, but Ori could see the fear in D'vai's face.

Captain Marissa stepped through the hatch, followed by Sukin, clutching her pendant and Van, wiping his hands on a rag, his face expressionless, which didn't bode well. The crew all stood, Ori catching up a second behind, and managing to join them without looking flustered. The crew had never displayed this level of formality before, an indication of how troubled everyone was.

"Please sit," the captain said, waving them all to a seat with a nervous gesture. "As you know life support systems are off-line, and have been for at least six hours. Seems we've burned out a cylinder in the main pump assembly." Van remained expressionless, the rag twisting in his hands. The maintenance officer stared fixedly at the deck, the little pendant enveloped in hands white with strain.

"Is that bad?" whispered Zarr.

"Only if we don't have a spare," Ori answered softly.

"Unfortunately, we don't have a spare on board," continued Marissa, "so we will have to ration what air we do have until we reach Corelli."

"We are six days out from Corelli," Ori pointed out. "That's nearly sixty thousand liters of air." Zarr jammed her hard in the ribs. This time she took the hint. "My apologies ma'am."

"Yes, thank you for pointing that out, Tey, but you are correct, without the air recycling systems, there is a danger..." Marissa paused. "A very slight danger that we could run out of air before we reach Corelli."

This time Ori stayed silent as the calculations flowed across her screens. The systems had been off-line for six hours, and nobody had noticed. Air quality in the cargo holds had already begun to degrade as the lack of circulation allowed waste gases to accumulate, from the bottom decks up.

"How slight?" asked Zarr his fists jammed so hard into his pockets the seams strained.

"We will make it. If everything goes well. If nothing else goes wrong," Ori answered, keeping her voice low as Marissa tried to be reassuring, but did a bad job of it. Van stepped forward, Ori felt his gaze fall on her, like a physical blow. Something was wrong.

"Look, it just means we'll need to be careful until we get to Corelli. We'll get the parts we need, and it will be a novelty, we haven't hit dirtside there in a few trips. It will take—" Van glanced at the captain, seeking confirmation. Marissa's tight, hard nod wasn't exactly reassuring, but Van soldiered on regardless, "It will take a day or two to get the part in, run a few tests and we'll be on our way."

Why wasn't Sukin saying anything? This was her area of responsibility: life support, waste recycling, equipment maintenance. How had the stupid woman not stocked enough spare parts?

"Does this mean we'll lose leave time at Ma'al?" asked Zarr. Ori reigned in her exasperation. Of course, that was all the boy was concerned about.

"Yes, Zarr," said D'vai sharply, "you'll have to cut short your little fan orgy. What a—" Whatever he was going to say morphed into a yelp as Lart landed a sharp smack to the younger man's ear. D'vai subsided into sullen silence, rubbing at his throbbing face without further comment.

"Shut up. All of us want our leave, not just Zarr."

Lianna stood. "Listen, we'll get there, but if we miss our slots none of us will get paid, and you'll spend your entire leave sitting on your asses doing nothing."

"We don't get paid, we'll be back to signing up for state assistance," Lart said, turning his attention away from disciplining D'vai, "or we'll have to find another berth somewhere."

Sukin clutched her pendant tighter, and murmured under her breath, no doubt an entreaty to her deity to save them. Ori's own path was less clear. If the crew were forced to wait on Corelli for any length of time, how would that affect her mission? How long would the Xi wait until they either intervened, or ended the operation completely? She couldn't take that risk. If the *Ava* became stranded, her only choice was to find another ship — either steal one, or get taken on as crew and head for the border. That was the logical, rational plan. So why did she feel ill at the thought of leaving the *Ava*? Ori shut down those thoughts before the voices came back to denounce her.

Marissa addressed the crew again.

"We're going to drop out, and send a message to Corelli. As a precaution. Then we'll jump again. Van is setting up some emergency pumps to keep what air we have circulating. Everyone will confine themselves to crew quarters and the mess, unless necessary. Cargo checks will still be carried out, but only in the top rails, and only for a few hours at a time. Report any signs of respiratory distress immediately. We will get to Corelli. No one is going to lose their berth — we might be a bit late, but we'll still get paid. I guarantee it."

"Can we do it?" asked Zarr, almost whispering. Lart and D'vai tried to look as though they weren't eavesdropping.

"We can, so long as we are careful, and nothing else happens. Van will make sure we get there."

"Ori, wait up," called Van.

Ignoring Zarr's knowing grin, Ori waited until the engineer reached them. The meeting had dissolved a few minutes ago into stunned, fearful silences and whispered conversations. The captain left with Lianna, both women looking like they'd aged twenty years in moments. Jwali followed them without speaking or acknowledging any of his crewmates. Sukin disappeared, probably off to her prayer room. That should annoy her, but Ori felt a creeping sympathy for the woman. Lart and D'vai went by, the old man's hand on the younger man's shoulder, his aged skin gray and sunken. Despite the boy's optimism, the possibility of running out of air, no matter how slight, or becoming stranded on Corelli, was affecting everyone, including herself.

"I'll leave you two to discuss drives or something," said Zarr, still grinning. Van made a half-hearted swipe at the boy, who ducked away. Ori shooed him off down the corridor before rounding on Van.

"No spare cylinders? What is wrong with that stupid woman? Why don't we have any spares?" and instantly regretted it as his face convulsed in anger.

His hand closed around her arm, dragging her down a side corridor. "We had two when we left Six," he spat at her. "Two. One's gone missing, and the other one is damaged. Someone's taken a hammer to the filament housing. You wouldn't know anything about that, would you?"

"Me? Why would I want to destroy life support?" Ori asked, pulling her arm away. "It was sabotage? And you think I did it?" The maintenance officer's complaints about all the repairs now seemed less a reflection of her abilities, and something more sinister. Sabotage on a spaceship was tantamount to murder and treated as such. "Did you tell the captain?"

"No, of course not. Tell her we've got a saboteur on board? She'll know exactly who to blame, won't she."

Someone on board was trying to stop her from getting to Ma'al.

"So, you pretended we never had them, or that you lost them? Why would you do something like that?"

"Jen has a family to support; you didn't think I'd let her take the blame for something that wasn't her fault? You, on the other hand, have a watertight cover story, I'll give you that," Van continued, shoving his face closer to her. "Which would be fine if you were far less attractive and a damned sight less competent. Your superiors must think we're all too stupid to work it out."

"I didn't do it. I don't know who you think I am—"

"You're fucking Directorate, that's what I think you are." Van's finger stabbed into her chest, punctuating every word. She had killed for less provocation than this, yet she allowed him to drive her back against the cold metal bulkhead as he crowded into her, stinking of coolant, grease and sweat. "If you wanted to get off at Corelli, why didn't you get on a ship that was stopping there, instead of ours?"

Directorate? All this time she'd thought her story was accepted, her cover intact, yet Van hadn't bought any of it. If she denied it, then what? What alternative story could she come up with that would be more convincing? More importantly, who was the saboteur?

"Listen, saying that out loud could have extremely bad consequences. For you. I didn't cause the sabotage, but it's directed at me. I don't want to stop at Corelli, trust me. Someone doesn't want me going to Ma'al." Rossim, it had to be. He obviously saw her as a threat, but why? Surely, he didn't believe that the Xi would let her go? She certainly did not believe them. Now she might have to pretend to be Directorate.

"No one on this ship would do such a thing."

"Do not be naive. People will do anything for money or power." She still had to get to Tersen, she still had to escape. *They did not torture you for pleasure, they do not keep you prisoner for entertainment.* If she had learned anything in the last ten years, it was that the Xi did nothing on a whim, and never allowed emotions to rule them.

All this was theoretical anyway. If they didn't get to Corelli, any options disappeared. They now had a common enemy. Rossim. "You cannot breathe a word about this, Van. I will find out who the saboteur is. You need to get the *Ava* to Corelli, as quickly as possible."

She should go, before anyone saw them. Since those few hours in the drive room, Ori hadn't seen much of the *Avadora*'s engineer, apart from a polite nod as they passed in the mess.

"I should go," he said, quietly, his hands moving onto her hips.

"Yes," she agreed, uncomfortable at this intimacy.

"Ori," Van began.

"Hey, guys." They sprang apart as Zarr rounded the corner, hands as always, stuffed into his pockets, eyes firmly on the deck. "Lianna's on her way."

"You brought this danger here, to us," Van whispered, as he passed her.

"And I will fix it. It's not as if we have a huge crew."

I know who I suspect. Proving it will be difficult. Getting anyone to believe it might be impossible.

[Subroutines initiated.

Data processing from nanite incursion underway. Insufficient contact

Mission unsuccessful. Parameters not achieved.

Information shunted to secure storage.

Accessible memory erased.]

Sixteen

Shantis sol Chiml's "Final Symphony" was reaching its climax when the AI interrupt-ed. "Imsu," said the AI, almost apologetically. Imsu Pesek replaced the tiny statue onto the shelf, adjusting the position precisely as the last frenetic notes faded.

"Yes?"

"Maridel Eidress is at reception. He is asking to see you. He does not have an appoint-ment. Shall I refuse access?"

His hand stopped a hair's breadth from the next item in his collection, a carved wooden box inlaid with a stone that no longer existed in its natural form. "An Eidress? Did he say what he wanted?"

There was a brief silence as the AI interrogated the human manning the reception desk.

"He says he wishes to discuss a Keren Ha'haru with you."

Maridel Eidress was short, for a Ma'ali, which meant he was about average height for any other race in the Republic. Pesek wouldn't have described him as thin. More like … slender, delicate, would be the appropriate word. The First Secretary of the Directorate gestured to a seat and the Eidress lawyer settled with the care of a feather alighting on water. Imsu took his own seat, feeling almost awkward.

"How may the Directorate assist you, Saliri Eidress?" inquired Pesek, steepling his fingers and adopting his most professional demeanor. In the few minutes it had taken for the lawyer to reach his office, Pesek had refreshed his memory of this "Keren Ha'haru." Another one of Rossim's "little favors." Why the Directorate had to silence a medic, he had no idea, but the president's use of the bureau as his own private problem-solving factory was beginning to wear on Pesek. The question was, how had the Eidress lawyer tracked the case to him?

"You are mistaken, sir," the lawyer said, his lilting accent giving the Formal Standard a musical tone. "I am not a master of my hanjile. One day, perhaps, when Lord Eidress wills it." His smile was professionally courteous, but never reached anywhere near his grass-green eyes, set in a face as delicate as the rest of him. His cheekbones could probably cut glass. Like all the Ma'ali, the man could be any age from mid-twenties to over a hundred. The enormous wealth generated by the silk gave every Ma'al citizen access to the latest and most sophisticated anti-aging meds. His hair, dark as midnight, was dressed in a series of complex braids that coalesced into the standard simple plait bound in three places along its length by rings of chased and engraved Polini silver. So not only was Maridel wealthy, he had two partners.

More than I've managed to acquire.

Lord Shizuri Eidress. Head of Hanjile Eidress, and renowned throughout the Republic for his legal expertise. The one person, in Pesek's estimation, who could prove to be the insurmountable obstacle to Rossim's coup. Imsu could still recall the thrill of reading Shizuri's judicial opinion on the infamous Li'ssi Gernl case.

Li'ssi Gernl had been a young man with too much money, and far too little interest in fulfilling his duties as the scion of one of Polinia's wealthier families. To maximize his fun times, he commissioned the creation of two clones, and accelerated their growth, before proceeding to school them in every nuance of his life. They were then dispatched to deal with the boring parts, and Li'ssi was free to pursue the fun bits. Sex, drugs, more sex. The usual. That was until an unfortunate racing accident wiped out the two clones. Or were they both clones? The cousins in line for an enormous inheritance argued the remaining Li'ssi was merely a copy. He maintained he was the original. No one could tell.

After years of protracted legal wrangling, the Supreme Court of the Imperium ruled that it didn't matter. In the absence of proof, this Li'ssi was as likely to be the original as not. The vast estates went to him. The cousins were furious, everyone else was ecstatically happy as this Li'ssi applied himself to his duties with admirable enthusiasm.

You'd think a four-hundred-year-old inheritance law wouldn't have caused such a stir, given there hadn't been any form of cloning permitted since the end of the war. However, Shizuri's ruling that the law still stood, that clones had individual person-hood, and therefore full inheritance rights, had managed to upset more than a few people. But that was conservatives for you — always getting fired up about something.

"My apologies, Eidress." The first rule, call them all Saliri, was superseded by the second rule—call them by their hanjile name unless you are friend, or family. Since Imsu Pesek was neither, it was Eidress from now on.

Maridel Eidress waved one delicate hand in gentle dismissal. "No insult was intended." The other equally delicate hand smoothed out the dark green silk of his che'b'ni with its swirling, informative thread work. "I am here to discuss the Medic Ha'haru case."

"As far as I am aware, Eidress, the trial was held weeks ago. The individual in question pleaded guilty."

It would have been polite, now that the courtesies were observed, for Maridel Eidress to drop back into the informal form of Standard. "Medic Ha'haru claims he was coerced into making a confession. By threats, and actual physical violence," the lawyer continued, in musical Formal.

"I'm sure the good medic is now regretting not mounting a better defense, but I cannot see how engaging you—"

"My apologies, sir," the lawyer said, with another wave of his hand. "You misunderstand. I was not engaged by Medic Ha'haru, but by his mother."

The image flashed into Pesek's mind of a plump suburban woman, probably in a lowly administrative position somewhere, or a teacher. Harmless, powerless. "Well, I'm sure she's an honorable woman, concerned for her sons." Hanjile Eidress did take on "charity" cases; most people somewhat cynically viewing such activities as a way for the lawyers to soften their image.

The Eidress tilted his head and regarded Pesek quizzically. "Of course, you wouldn't have met her." Pesek suddenly grasped how the other man surveyed the room, cataloging everything; the generic, state-issued furnishings, Pesek's tiny collection of pre-war artifacts, the faux wool carpet. "Understandable, Sylvie Casar rarely leaves her estates these days."

Pesek felt his stomach fall through the floor. Sylvie Casar. The medic's mother was a Casar. Not a teacher, not harmless, and certainly not powerless. He felt his face go tight as the head of the Directorate of Protection struggled to hide his shock.

"It wasn't in the report."

"No," said the lawyer, his voice quiet derision, "that information was suppressed at the trial. Madam Casar doesn't like unnecessary attention, especially where it concerns her sons."

He was enjoying this. The fucking Ma'ali was enjoying tormenting him. Pesek knew it was his own fault. He hadn't read the file, simply flicked the job to a junior administrator to deal with. Too caught up with managing Rossim's little coup.

"But his brother, Seilis, my understanding is that the case was watertight," he said, trying to claw back some supremacy.

The Eidress smiled again, the corners of his eyes crinkling. A smile of condescension. "Seilis Casar is a troubled young man. He has already been transferred to a private and secure facility off-world. To recover, and receive the best treatment. Her other son, Keren Casar, is a different matter. Madam Casar is concerned that his pride may have driven him to accept punishment for crimes he clearly did not commit, rather than reach out to his family."

No, Pesek thought bitterly. The fucking medic rolled over knowing that his status as a Casar would get him out, but how did that concern the Directorate? He couldn't have known who fabricated the case against him.

"I am still somewhat confused, Eidress. Why are you here, in my office? Surely this is a matter for the civil authorities, and the Law Courts?"

Maridel Eidress leaned back in his chair, one delicate hand smoothing the swathe of viridian and gold fabric that would buy a city block, and smiled. "Because the good medic maintains that he was in the employ of the Directorate of Protection at the time of the arrest."

Of all the things Imsu Pesek expected the lawyer to say, that wasn't anywhere on the list. "You jest, surely. Why would the Directorate need a medic?" Pesek furiously racked his brain; as far as he knew, the fucking medic wasn't employed by his department, but it wasn't out of the question. "I would need to check our records, of course. This is a large organization." He should have read the file. Always read the file, or get someone you trust to do it. He'd done neither and now look where he was, in the grip of the Galaxy's most ruthless predator, an Eidress lawyer.

"Of course, sir. The official request has been lodged."

An official request? The fucking Eidress obtained a court order? He was representing a Casar, of course he had an order. Veiled as an official request for information, but it amounted to the same thing. Once someone started digging, the Blessed Mother alone knew what they might find. If anyone discovered what they were doing on Ma'al, they'd be lucky to avoid execution. Pesek knew when it was time to concede defeat.

"Perhaps it might be simpler if you told me exactly what you want me to do," Pesek ground out, dropping back into the informal forms, politeness be damned.

"Release Madam Casar's son. Erase the conviction." The lawyer smiled one last time, an expression of utter contempt. "We will then advise Medic Ha'haru that a small holiday, off-world, would be advisable. And as a courtesy, we will not be pursuing compensation."

Keren knew the exact moment his mother decided he'd learned his lesson. The prison population did not like people who assaulted children, and the medical unit became quite familiar to Keren over the weeks, as his various injuries were treated. This latest one, a fractured cheekbone, was nearly repaired when a pair of prison guards appeared in the doorway, startling the trainee medic so much she dropped the regen unit.

Both guards executed clumsy bows; the medic stopped, hand halfway to the dropped tool, frozen in astonishment.

"Our apologies, sir," the older guard said, bowing again. "We are to escort you to the release area, where you can collect your belongings." There was no hint of irony. He hadn't been nearly so helpful two weeks ago when he'd slammed Keren into a railing. The poorly trained medic had struggled so much trying to fix his ribs, that Keren angrily snatched the unit from her hands and carried out the procedure himself.

"A vehicle is waiting for you," the other guard interjected, anxious to please. "Can we get you anything?" Both men were clearly terrified that he would exact revenge for their mistreatment of him.

For a moment or two, Keren gave serious consideration to doing exactly that, before shame overtook him. This was his own fault. His impetuousness had got him into this situation — he should have grasped that reporting Ori's treatment would bring consequences — and his pride had kept him here for weeks, when one call to his mother would have released him in seconds.

The release procedure played out as Keren expected, right down to the package of new clothes, hand-delivered. As Keren unfolded the suit of indigo silk, the assembled guards and the prison warden watched with astonishment and envy. Sylvie's taste was always exquisite. His mother's contracted Eidress, Maridel, also made an appearance, ensuring the documentation met his exacting requirements.

The vehicle sent to collect him was one of the estate fleet, AI-controlled, silent and swift. Keren moved through the streets of the capital effortlessly, the heavily tinted windows protecting him from the stares of the populous. To be fair, he corrected himself, the inhabitants of the capital were used to the sight of similar luxury vehicles, often marked with a family crest or company logo, and considered themselves far too well bred to gawk. It was easy to pick the tourists, who did gawk, and sometimes even pointed. His mother thought crests and logos immensely gauche; a Casar didn't need to remind the people who they were.

As the car swept closer to the gates, his nervousness grew, his heart beating faster as they turned into the drive, until the vista opened out and his family's estate appeared before him, the spires and turrets of the house reaching into the sky. The vehicle glided to a stop, the door opened with the barest whisper of sound, the scent of flowers and cut grass assailing him. Home. One of the house servants appeared, seemingly out of nowhere, to take his bag and disappear toward the rear of the building. Keren climbed the stairs to the double doors, noting the changed plantings on either side of the sweep of semicircular stairs. His mother had a planting scheme for each season; this year the winter scheme featured tubs of gold and purple dwarf evergreens, clipped into precise cones.

"There you are." Sylvie Casar's melodious voice flowed down the steps to envelop him. "I thought perhaps you'd decided to go back to that little apartment of yours."

It shouldn't bother him that his mother remained unchanged, forever a young woman thanks to access to the Republic's best medical care and an abundance of the latest anti-aging treatments.

The gown of turquoise silk flowed from fine-boned shoulders to a tiny waist, before ending up brushing the tops of a pair of immaculate heels in matte silver.

His "little apartment," overlooking one of Central's most beautiful parks, was larger than most houses, however, Sylvie thought residing anywhere other than the ancestral estates was the equivalent to living on the streets. She included the palace in that category, which told you everything about his mother.

"How could I do that, after everything you've done?" he said, leaning in to kiss her on each cheek. "You didn't need to buy me new clothes though."

"Oh, it was nothing." Sylvie took his arm and guided him through the doorway and into the entrance hall. Half his little apartment could fit in the space. "I couldn't have you wearing those horrible clothes. I really don't know why you'd want to walk around in rags."

The "rags" had cost the equivalent of a mid-level bureaucrat's monthly salary, but many years of experience had taught him to simply agree; Sylvie would accept nothing less than total acquiescence. Her heels made sharp clicking sounds on the ivory marble floor, the sinuous veins of real gold winding across the massive slabs glittering in the light from the chandelier of hand-cut Nax'tl crystal occupying three stories of the stairwell. Twin staircases with marble steps and ornate gold newel posts swept up either side. A fireplace— a real one — crackled and flared at the sudden inrush of cold air, the mantle of pale pink granite almost dwarfed by a floral arrangement of exotic blooms and two enormous baroque candlesticks. In winter, the house AI kept the indoor temperature of the public spaces cold enough to have natural fires. Sylvie insisted it imbued a homely feeling to the house.

Keren followed his mother across to the entrance to her sitting room. "Thank you, Mother. And thank you for sending Maridel, although I could have handled the paper-work by myself." Maridel had also made it clear that Sylvie did not wish to discuss Seilis, or the circumstances of his arrest. Keren's brush with the law would be put down to youthful exuberance and bureaucratic mismanagement. In other words, everyone would pretend none of this ever happened, and it would never be referred to again. Keren remembered Seilis as a solemn, quiet boy, with straight brown hair and brown eyes, who rarely smiled. Sylvie had many children, the offspring of her twenty husbands and countless lovers, the embryos all grown in the uteri of women grateful for the privilege of carrying a Casar. Keren was certain that if she could have got around the Article Thirty-Four laws, Sylvie would have an entire incubation facility set up.

"Nonsense, he loves doing these little jobs," said Sylvie with an airy wave of her hand that set the multitudes of silver bracelets tinkling like bells.

Keren would bet a year's salary that Maridel Eidress, the latest in a line of lawyers contracted to the Casar family, despised doing these "little jobs." Keren would also bet that Maridel himself had almost no say in where his services were offered. Families such as his did not employ Maridel; they were selected to receive the honor of having an Eidress lawyer at their command. The prestige conferred by this arrangement was so great that it could advance or destroy one's social standing. Ma'al had no need of money, but the leverage this tactic produced was beyond measure, as the elite of a dozen worlds fought and maneuvered to be worthy of a Ma'ali trained lawyer.

"And where is Maridel?" Keren asked, trying to sound uninterested. He should have known better. Sylvie rounded on him immediately, artificially dyed and brightened green eyes narrowing in suspicion. Decades of navigating the socio-political landscape of Central's elite had honed her instincts to the sharpness of a medi-scalpel.

"Why? What else have you gotten yourself into?"

"Nothing, I just wanted to be certain how long he thinks this little off-world holiday I'm taking should last." Lying to their mother was a survival skill all of Sylvie's children developed early, if they wanted any sort of private life. The experience of having a childish folly, or even worse, a heartfelt ambition or desire, dissected and mocked at length over the dinner table, was something to be avoided at all costs. Once had been enough for Keren. Of all of them, Seilis had seemed oblivious to Sylvie's relentless cruelty. How wrong they were. His brother was unlikely to see the outside of the private, expensive, and exceedingly secure facility for a very long time. If ever.

Keren held his breath, waiting for the inevitable interrogation, but his mother simply turned away, leading him to the sitting room where afternoon tea sat on a small table between two well upholstered chairs — the ones with the monstrous carved feet, that had always terrified him as a child.

Keren took his seat as Sylvie enthroned herself. "Oh, well, he's gone into the city, but he'll be back for dinner. You can ask him then," she said, pouring him messil, even though he hated the stuff. The pile of draci cakes was an obvious trap; showing the slightest interest laid him open to one of Sylvie's acidic lectures about his weight, which would lead to the inevitable argument over Keren's refusal to use the Casar name to further his career. Of course, there was the little detail that if the Directorate had known who he was, Keren would never have been approached in the first place, or been dragged from his bed at gunpoint, beaten, tried and convicted of crimes against children. He would never have met Ori.

Keren accepted the bowl of pale green liquid without comment or complaint, and hoped he could survive his mother until dinner. Getting the lawyer alone for a few minutes would be difficult, but not impossible. Sylvie always had a crowd for dinner. Children, lovers, hangers-on. The only unknown was whether Maridel would be amenable to Keren's request. Of all the tasks Maridel was asked to do, finding an illegally imprisoned engineered super soldier wasn't exactly in his job description.

Seventeen

"Shouldn't you be in your bunk?" Lart slumped into the seat opposite, and slid/slopped a mug of rakosh across the mess table. "The captain's given orders. If you're not working, stay still to conserve the air."

Zarr shrugged and pulled the mug and its attendant puddle toward him, mopping the spill with his sleeve. "Not tired," he said, despite exhaustion tugging at him. The old man was right, he should be in his bunk. So should Ori. Where was she? Their shift finished two hours ago, with an entire deck of storage lockers cleaned and sorted, a testimony to Lianna's determination to fill in every extra second the *Ava*'s race toward Corelli afforded, regardless of the air quality, or the risk to her crew.

"Where's Davey?" Zarr asked, more to fill the silence than any interest in the other cargo hand. "If he's jerking off somewhere, Lianna will shove him out an airlock." Tensions were running beyond critical on the *Ava*.

Lart gave one of his derisory grunts, as if the idea of Davey suffocating in hard vacuum was entertaining. "Nah, Jen has him down in life support. Says she needs someone there to alert her if anything needs attention." Lart took a loud slurp. "Dozy cow, that's what the AI is for."

Zarr caught himself just in time. Anyone with half a brain could tell something was going on, but contradicting Lart had painful consequences. He'd asked Ori, in some vain hope she'd give him a straight answer. Instead, he'd got a lecture about missing a row of containers. By the time he'd come back, all containers checked and marked off, his crewmate was gone. He just hoped she didn't run into Jwali. A shudder ran through him at the thought.

Of course, Ori could be down in engineering "helping" Van. After the crew meeting, he'd crept back to where Ori and Van were huddled in the alcove of a hatchway. He couldn't hear what they were saying, but both of them were really angry. Though, Zarr conceded, that didn't mean they weren't together. He'd seen enough relationships to know people did weird shit sometimes. His parents, for example.

Lart leaned back and took another long gulp from his mug. "So, you're waiting for her?" he asked, interrupting Zarr's worries. Errant drips from the old man's mug soaked into his worn and dirty overalls. "Wasting your time, boy," he pronounced.

Zarr felt his ears flame in embarrassment. "I've no idea what you're talking about. I'm not tired." Great, here comes another lecture. *Stupid boy. Why don't you get a decent job, settle down. Come home, your mother misses you. Stop wasting your talents chasing some dream of Ma'al. Grow up.*

"I don't need another parent telling me what to do. My dad—"

Lart leaned across the table, stale rakosh breath washing across Zarr's face. "She's dangerous." Lart's hand clamped down on Zarr's arm. "She's either running from trouble or heading straight to it, and if you get caught up in it, you'll end up in trouble too." Zarr tried to pull away but the old man held him tight. "I've seen her type before. Far too comfortable in givin' orders, and expecting them obeyed. Mark my words, she'll leave a trail of bodies behind her, and if you're not careful, you'll be one of them."

What was the old man going on about? Ori wasn't dangerous. Sure, yeah, she liked giving orders, and after a while you ended up doing what she said. Most times she was right. But Lart'd never heard her crying at night or had to pretend to be asleep when she woke up screaming.

Zarr gently disengaged his arm from the old man's grip. "She's OK, really. I'll be fine. I know what I'm doing." Couldn't he have one day without people telling him how he'd fucked up, yet again? The anger grew in the pit of his stomach. The family curse, Granddad called it. As if that excused his father's rages.

"You think I'm an old fool." Lart shook his head. "But I served nearly forty years in Fleet, before they dumped me. Whatever she says she is, it's a lie. She's an officer, or was one. And officers have to do something really fucked up to be chucked out of Fleet." He upended the mug, sucking noisily at the dregs, before slamming his mug down. "Ask Van, he'll tell you. Except I think she's got him by the balls."

"Blessed Mother, Lart. How can you talk about people like that?" Zarr pushed away from the table, unable to stop his voice rising, feeling his ears burn with anger. "Ori's never done anything to you, she does her work — better than anyone I've ever met. Just because she reminds you of some asshole in Fleet doesn't make her bad."

"Who is bad?" came Ori's voice.

Zarr froze, his hands instinctively burrowing into his overall pockets. "Lart and me were talking," he began, turning slowly, caught between truth and deflection. His crewmate stood in the hatchway in ragged sleepwear, her hair, now far too long for a hauler, clinging damply to her neck.

At that moment, Zarr's imagination supplied the vision of her in a full officer's uniform of dark blue and gold, and his breath caught, somewhere deep inside his chest. "I was thinking of hitting my bunk," he added, trying furiously to control his wayward body.

She ignored him, her gaze going straight past him to skewer Lart. "Who is bad?" she asked again. Technically, Lart outranked her, but you'd never have guessed that from her tone. The old man shifted uneasily, bony hands clutching his empty mug, all his bravado of a few minutes ago drained away.

"No one," he said, not meeting her gaze. "We was just talking about the old days. When I was in Fleet."

The silence dragged out, until Zarr wanted to scream to cut the tension.

"Zarr should be in his bunk," she said finally. "We are supposed to be conserving oxygen, not sitting around wasting it. Do not delay him again."

There was an unspoken threat under there, Zarr could almost feel it. Lart said nothing in response, only giving a tiny nod of acceptance, his eyes still firmly fixed on the scratched tabletop, his skin ashen under the harsh lighting. Ori let him sit there, head bowed, for another excruciating moment before turning and leaving without another word.

"Night, Lart," Zarr said, scrambling after Ori, although she had not told him to or even acknowledged his existence.

They were both halfway down the corridor when he stopped. "I don't think you're bad," he said.

She didn't turn, merely coming to a halt, although he saw the way her shoulders tensed under the tatty cloth.

She set off again, her stride lengthening until he had to scurry to keep up. "You have no idea what I am."

Eighteen

"Have you settled on a destination for your holiday, Keren?" one of his sisters asked from across the table. Ferinia, her name was, Keren remembered. The girl, with curled and color-tipped blonde hair, a copy of their mother, tilted her head in inquiry. At least her eyes were still their natural brown. Keren suppressed the shiver of distaste.

"Yes, Keren, where are you going?" Sylvie's question shot down the crowded dinner table, past the floral displays and the crystal glasses and the shining silver, with the accuracy of an AI-guided missile. All conversation ceased. Everyone — siblings, half siblings, two of his mother's latest lovers, one husband, and an estate manager, pretended to concentrate on their meals. Except Maridel, who continued to politely ignore the blatant flirting from one of the boys, whose name escaped Keren, and turned his attention to Sylvie.

"I'm not sure, Mother," Keren replied, his voice calm, while his hands knotted themselves under the napkin. "It depends on how long I decide to take off from work."

Please don't answer, Maridel, otherwise I will have no excuse to talk to you later.

The lawyer obligingly said nothing, continuing to watch Sylvie as though her words were the wisdom of the ages.

How does he do that? Continually pretend to be fascinated?

"Well," Sylvie pronounced, "it's hardly important, is it?" She raised her glass and took a minute sip of wine, the pale-yellow liquid barely touching her lips. "It's not as if you're doing anything lifesaving is it, at your little clinic."

Keren's fists clenched in anger. His "little clinic" was one of Central's major medical centers. Even with advanced technology, people still got sick, still hurt themselves, still needed medics. Sylvie kept an entire team on-call to cater for her every real and imagined medical emergency. However, he would never get a chance to talk to Maridel if he annoyed his mother.

"No, Mother, you are correct. Nothing I do is important."

Blessed Mother, he shouldn't have said that. Sylvie's expression hardened; her perfect lips twisted into a scowl. *Here it comes, I'm going to be eviscerated at dinner. Again.*

"If you will permit me, madam," interrupted Maridel, in his musical Formal Standard, "I did have some pressing business with Medic Ha'haru, if you would excuse us?"

Siblings, half siblings, the two lovers, the one husband, and the estate manager all stopped pretending to eat and sat, open-mouthed at this. Interrupting Sylvie Casar, especially when she was about to cut someone down, was suicidal. Maridel appeared not to notice.

"I know how important it is to maintain my services to your satisfaction," the lawyer continued. "It would be disappointing if my contract was withdrawn due to any perceived inadequacies. On either side."

Blessed Mother, did he just threaten her? To have a contract withdrawn was political and social death. Even three seats away, Keren could see the rage behind his mother's bright green eyes. Everyone held their breath. The multitudes of silver bracelets jingled loudly in the silence as Sylvie gave an imperious wave of her hand.

"Of course, Maridel, your duty to our family is beyond reproach." The hand waved again. "Keren, you are excused."

"Thank you, Maridel," Keren said, once they were both far enough away from the dining room not to be overheard. "I was about to be torn apart there."

Maridel ignored him, opening the door to a smallish room, one of many whose sole function was for decoration, or so Keren assumed, because he'd never seen anyone use it. The house AI adjusted the lighting to the pre-set evening ambiance, the soft light gliding across the lawyer's elaborate braids and touching each of the silver jile rings encircling the main plait. Keren realized he knew nothing about Maridel's life, not even the names of the two husbands or wives that each of the rings represented. Did the lawyer have children? Or siblings? How did it affect him, having to serve Sylvie for perhaps years at a time?

Maridel made an annoyed huff. "Your mother is cruel, self-centered, and shallow. No thanks are necessary."

Keren stopped in shock. No one spoke about a Casar like that, not in public.

Maridel clasped his hands, his face impassive. "I am Eidress. I serve my hanjile, and obey the Saliri and Lord Shizuri. It does not mean I have to tolerate such behavior from anyone. Especially a contracted client."

Maybe Sylvie had overstepped with all her "little jobs". Maridel obviously took pride in his work, and dealing with his mother every day would stretch the patience of the Blessed Mother herself. This didn't mean the lawyer would help him.

"So, Maridel," Keren began.

"You do know it wasn't the Directorate that employed you?" interrupted Maridel, shifting into informal Standard. "I haven't found out yet who it was."

Keren's carefully rehearsed speech died on his tongue. "What do you mean, it wasn't the Directorate?" he said, trying to keep his voice calm. He nearly succeeded.

Maridel gave an impatient sweep of his hand. "The Directorate would have worked out who you were in a matter of hours, but when I spoke to Imsu Pesek, he had no idea who you were. Even your family's resources couldn't hide you from the Directorate's AIs. Whoever blackmailed you knew enough to pretend to be Directorate, but didn't have all their resources, or competence."

Keren was about to say "But why?" when the realization sunk in. It wasn't the Directorate imprisoning Ori, but someone else. Someone who had the resources to employ guards and set up a secure house away from Central's network. There weren't many people or organizations who could do that.

"They were holding someone prisoner there. A woman. I want to find her."

Maridel didn't even raise an eyebrow at this, merely gave that annoyed huff again. "It's always a pretty face. Either way, it won't be easy. They may not be Directorate, but they know how to cover their tracks. You will need to tell me everything that happened in order for me to find her."

Keren was certainly not going to tell the Eidress everything: that way led to a very long prison sentence, maybe even execution. In any case, Maridel didn't need to know those details, only what she looked like, and her name. That should be enough. What did concern him was what would he do if the lawyer found her.

Three days later and it still rankled. Imsu Pesek, First Secretary of the Directorate of Protection, outwitted by an empty-headed socialite and a lawyer.

No. He'd been outwitted by Sylvie Casar and an Eidress. There were few more powerful combinations to be found anywhere on Central. Even Rossim would struggle against that.

Imsu placed his sheet back with extraordinary care; the impulse to smash it against the edge of his desk was overwhelming, but he had not risen to the head of the Republic's security bureau by giving in to emotions. The file he had neglected to read, the one he had dismissed as unimportant, lay open on the sheet interface. He had read it through twice, especially the confession taken down by Central's law enforcement, clearly less interested in Keren's fantastical story than the mountain of evidence helpfully provided by the Directorate.

Pesek had hoped the lawyer had made a mistake, missed some vital clue that would allow him to claw back the advantage. A vain, stupid hope. Hanjile Eidress trained the best and most ruthless legal minds in the Republic; Maridel would not have overlooked even a misplaced comma.

The door pinged, and at an impatient wave of Pesek's hand, the AI opened it to admit one of his staff with his morning messil. Pesek waited until the door slid closed again before immersing himself in the tiny rituals of preparation — setting the pot to boil, dropping in two compressed balls of leaves. Waiting for the brew to acquire the exact shade of pale green. Finally, to slowly pour the steaming liquid into his favorite bowl of almost translucent white syntheglass.

He cradled the warm glass between his hands, inhaling the herbal scent. He would find a way to turn this disaster to his advantage. At his command the AI de-opaqued his office window, a floor-to-ceiling expanse of syntheglass overlooking the plaza. As Pesek sipped on his messil, his mind turned over the conundrum; Keren Ha'haru's testimony laid out in detail how he was approached and recruited by someone purporting to be Directorate. The medic had multiple meetings with an agent who blackmailed him to work as a medic in return for releasing Seilis Casar. The only other information was that Keren had been taken to a remote house, where he was confined to an infirmary and a set of rooms and spent nearly two months treating the minor injuries and complaints of what sounded like a security team. Why an abandoned house needed a security force wasn't stated, although Pesek noted that Keren had been "vigorously interrogated" over this point. No doubt the source of his complaint about being assaulted.

The last warm drops swallowed, the empty bowl still cradled in his hands, Imsu stood looking out at the busy plaza below. The flashes of dark-green silk only served to deepen his sense of dread; this was all slipping away from him. *Enough. I'm getting like Rossim, spending hours—*

Rossim. How had he missed such an obvious connection?

It was the Lord President who wanted the medic silenced. Did it follow that Rossim knew about the house and what went on there, whatever that was? Why would the Lord President need a covert military team and a blackmailed medic when he had the entire Directorate at his disposal? Were they connected to Ma'al? Pesek returned the bowl to the tray and paced the length of his office.

Any attempt to contact Ha'haru would be blocked now; Maridel Eidress would make certain of that. Rossim certainly wouldn't answer any questions and would not take kindly to anyone bringing unwanted attention to any Directorate activities right now, just as his covert undermining of a sovereign system was ramping up.

Whoever Rossim had employed for this enterprise knew enough to behave like a Directorate agent, yet not enough to do a proper background check. Granted, being a Casar meant the medic had the resources to hide his identity from most scrutiny; the Directorate AI had to do a lot of digging before it uncovered the truth. A fact that hadn't saved the incompetent agent Pesek initially flicked the task to.

Optimism scoured away his previous depression. If he found out what the Lord President was up to, that might give him a priceless advantage. Governments had toppled over lesser scandals, Rossim would give him anything to keep quiet. It might even be enough to regain some control over the coup project. Pesek picked up the sheet and scrolled through the medic's confession. While the AI searched for anyone matching the description of the fake agent, he would start looking for the house.

Nineteen

Jwali's footsteps, hurried and unsteady, echoed across the cargo bay, bouncing off the rows of containers hanging in the gloom with their endless squeaks and groans. Ori followed; her feet silent on the metal walkway. In the right corner of her interface, Jwali was a blue dot overlaid on a schematic of the *Ava* as he stumbled down into the belly of the ship. A strange destination for a navigator, especially as the cargo bays were supposed to be off-limits; the lack of air circulation made the holds, especially the lower reaches, too risky.

Ahead in the darkness, Jwali stopped, cursing at some unseen obstacle, and Ori flattened herself against the bulkhead in case he turned and saw her. The seconds dragged on, with nothing but the complaining containers all around as Jwali hurled incoherent insults, while the cold metal seeped through her overalls and into her body. He was the saboteur, Ori was certain, but what she'd said to Van was also correct — anyone would betray them for sufficient incentives. Except Zarr. She would not believe the boy was that duplicitous. Or Van. Or Sukin. Yet, if it meant a comfortable job back on her homeworld, extra pay, would that be enough for the maintenance officer to betray them? And Van? Did he secretly mourn the loss of his career? Davey would sell his own mother for sex, but was too stupid to do anything as complicated as destroy a pump cylinder. He wouldn't even know where to start looking.

Unless he was one of Rossim's spies. They could all be spies, even the boy. That thought got pushed back down. Not the boy. Not Van. Not Sukin.

Whatever had drawn Jwali's wrath sailed over the railing and bounced and clattered its way down four levels to disappear with a crash in the darkness below. The footsteps started up again, clattering down another level, along a walkway, followed by the grate of a locker door opening somewhere much further along. The schematics showed no critical systems down here, except power conduits, and the idea of Jwali trying to damage those was ludicrous. He'd fry himself first, solving several problems.

The interface flicked vision to infrared; the traces of his body — a handprint on a railing, the brush of a leg against a bulkhead — led her to the stairs above the walkway. The navigator lay sprawled against the locker door, legs outstretched, a square of once-white cloth spread across his recumbent chest, the minuscule pile of iridescent flakes glowing purple in the dim light.

He was getting high. She had tracked him through the entire ship only to discover this filth indulging himself while on watch. This was why her people had taken up the sacred duty of cleansing the galaxy of worthless, untrustworthy eijen. No race deserved to survive that allowed such dereliction. If she threw him over the railings right now, watched his body break and smash on the hull below, it would be an improvement.

Jwali's moan interrupted her. Head thrown back, eyes closed, his hand moved inside his clothing as the drug took effect. Disgusted, Ori turned and made her way back to the upper levels of the hold. If Jwali was here pleasuring himself, it was entirely possible another one of the crew was the saboteur.

But not the boy.

Zarr pressed back into his hiding place, letting the shadows envelop him. Ori passed him, unknowing, so intent on following Jwali, she hadn't seen him shadowing her every move. So, Ori thought Jwali was behind all the unexplained breakdowns. He could have told her that, if she'd asked. No one else on board would jeopardize their crewmates by sabotaging life support. Van's story about having lost the spares was ridiculous, almost as ridiculous as taking the blame for it. Anyone who spent any time with the big engineer knew he could find every spare part, down to the last bolt, in his sleep if he needed to. And Jen may be disorganized, but she wouldn't have let the *Ava* leave Six Jump without back-up parts for critical systems. Something serious was going on. And he wanted to know what it was.

Jwali's moans reached their inevitable climax; Zarr fervently wished one of the container stacks would inexplicably give way at the crucial moment. The Blessed Mother would forgive him for such a thought. No one deserved it more than that prick. They'd be at Corelli tomorrow, at least he'd get a few days off the ship. Everyone could do with a little peaceful shore leave.

"Van says everything's quiet in engineering," Zarr informed her, dropping onto the bench.

"Good," she replied, not looking up from her sheet. It was tedious using the slow and primitive device, but she couldn't risk anyone seeing her using her interface.

"You going to tell me what's going on?"

Ori laid down her sheet. "Nothing is going on."

Across the scratched gray tabletop, those ordinary brown eyes bored into her, laser-focused. "Come, on, I'm not stupid. Something's going on. Why is Van taking the blame for the cylinders going missing? Why don't we have spares? Why is everything suddenly breaking down?"

"The *Ava* is old, and you told me that Sukin—"

"Jen," he interjected. "Everyone calls her Jen. It sounds weird when you call her Sukin."

Ori took a deep breath and tried again. "Very well. Jen. She struggles to keep the ship going. That is obvious."

"Which you've pointed out. No wonder she doesn't come out of her compartment anymore."

That the maintenance officer was hiding never occurred to Ori. The revelation that Sukin — no, Jen — was hiding because of Ori's criticism made her uncomfortable in some indefinable way. A brief surge of neuro-suppressors took care of that.

"Tell me about Ma'al," she asked, to divert him.

"So, we're not going to talk about the cylinders? Or the other breakdowns, or why Jen has Davey down in life support watching the displays rather than leaving it to the *Ava* to monitor?"

"No, we are not. The *Ava* will reach Corelli tomorrow. Air quality in the crew quarters and bridge is still acceptable. There is nothing for you to be concerned about."

She thought he might argue or ask further questions, instead he threw his arms up and in a tone of complete exasperation said, "All right, what do you want to know? Politics, social structure, economics, sex?"

"I would be astounded if you knew anything about sex. Ma'ali or otherwise." The blush spread across his face, right to the tips of those awkward ears.

"I know," he mumbled. "A bit."

"I'm not interested in sex, tell me about the silk." The source of everything Ma'al.

"Everyone knows about the silk," he said. "I saw some once. A Saliri, in the entertainment precinct. Some incident and she came down to sort it out. From one of the minor hanjiles, but you should have seen it. Pale green. The usual description is like moonbeams across water or some shit like that. Still doesn't come close. I sometimes wonder what it would be like to touch it."

"It is only cloth. Surely the industrial uses are more important?" Combined with carbon molecules, the composite materials were stronger, lighter, more resistant to both tensile and compression forces than anything else ever discovered.

"Yeah, you'd only be interested in composite armor, or other military uses," said Zarr, upending his mug and slurping the last of his rakosh.

"Meaning?"

"Meaning I can't see you getting all excited over a pretty dress. You don't seem the type."

"There's a type?" she asked, realizing she was repeating the medic's words. Where was he now, the little round man with the unruly curls? Back at his pleasant clinic, his obligations met? Ori hoped his brother was suitably grateful.

"Yeah, you know." Zarr wriggled with embarrassment, acutely aware that maybe he had fallen into a trap. "Pretty stuff. Dresses, hair, jewelry. That sort of thing."

"So now you're an expert on what I'm interested in?" she asked, watching with some amusement as the scarlet flooded across his face and up to his ears.

"No, sorry." He sighed. "No, not an expert. Obviously, you could be interested in anything you wanted," he said in the manner of someone parroting a lesson.

Why did everyone think that because she was a soldier, she didn't like beautiful things?

"I have read," she said, deciding to avoid the issue, "that their entire economy is dependent on it."

"Yeah. The first person to discover how it's made, or find an acceptable substitute will not only destroy Ma'al, but Six, Tersen, Corelli, and most of the freight companies. People like us. Gone."

"That explains the xenophobia. Their entire existence is at stake." She picked up both mugs and refilled them, pushing Zarr's over to him before she was aware of what she had done. What was wrong with her? "I don't understand, though; why not diversify, invest in other industries? This reliance on one source is insane." She'd be tucking him into his bunk next.

"Yeah, well." Zarr sipped at his drink. "The hanjiles are like that. They've been suspicious of everyone for so long, they won't even consider anything that means greater contact with the Republic."

"And Cimmili?"

Zarr pushed back from the table and wandered over to the vending unit, returning with two snack bars. "Cimmili fucking hate them with a passion. You won't find a single person in that system that doesn't believe Piali Eidress swindled them out of Ma'al." He checked both bars before sliding one across the table to her. "The Senate representatives refuse to speak to each other."

"I can see their point of view, though. Her foundation purchases what appears to be a worthless Marginal as a utopia project, and forty years later money is pouring in. From an unknown source. Cimmili would be right in suspecting something vital was missed in the surveys." She unwrapped the bar and took a nibble out of the end. Ah, she liked this one. It had pieces of dried dracina fruit in it.

"Oh, it gets better. Right before the silk appeared, the entire colony was on the verge of collapse. The original contract said if Cimmili had to rescue them, the system would revert to them. Only the Great War stopped them. Everyone was too busy burning worlds and hunting Abominations to care about Ma'al."

Hunting Abominations. Images from the feeds flashed in front of her. Not a great leap from burning Da Chet to burning people. Nausea roiled through her stomach.

He took another bite, scratching at the back of his head at the same time, crumbs raining down onto the tabletop.

"Does your head still hurt?" She could still remember the sound of his head hitting the bunk, the feel of that fine brown hair between her fingers. The line of bruises up each arm, the unmistakable signs of abuse.

"What? No. I've got a hard head, my dad says," he replied, grinning.

"Sometimes," she said, remembering his distress in the break room, and her cruelty, "it is better to fight back, despite the odds."

She saw the moment understanding replaced confusion. The red spread to the tips of those ears in seconds.

"Yeah, well. Maybe."

Twenty

P esek steered the vehicle up the winding road to the house, cursing under his breath
every time a wheel hit a bump or pothole. He was seriously out of practice driving
manual, but allowing the AI network to navigate was too great a risk. The journey would
be logged in the system, and he wanted to keep this secret until he knew what he was
dealing with.

What remained of once-extensive gardens spread out on either side of the treacherous
road, the grass yellow and dry, punctuated by overgrown hedges and patches of dead
shrubbery. A magnificent atoria tree, bare now that winter had arrived in earnest, stood
guard on what must have been the front lawn. A line of tall evergreens, dark and menacing
in the late afternoon gloom, marched along the fence line, disappearing behind the house.

The medic had described a house about a two-hour drive from the city in a remote,
rural setting, with enough detail of the interiors to allow Pesek to draw up quite a short
list. This address was number three; the property once part of a larger estate, now owned
by a company with offices registered on Orchetti Prime. It had immediately set off Pesek's
instincts.

The house looked abandoned, at least from the outside; its distinctive architecture,
plain and symmetrical with faux quoins on each corner, placed it squarely in the first fifty
years after the Great War. Five evenly spaced windows — now boarded up — were set
either side of a central door.

Pesek brought the car to a stop and stepped out, weapon drawn. The front door
was locked and wouldn't open even with a Directorate access code. To his right, a path
disappeared into the overgrown shrubbery. After a moment's hesitation he followed it,
the aging stonework snagging at his clothes, the overgrown lawn encroaching across the
gravel brushing against him as he crept along the wall.

The remains of a patio spread out from the back of the house, ornamental stone railings
toppled into the dying garden, paving buckled and mossy. Three utilitarian chairs, their

paintwork green and unmarred, sat in a group looking out over the yard to the line of evergreens.

What was left of the heavily armored rear door hung by one hinge, charred and twisted from an enthusiastic use of explosives; boot marks and splatters of blood marring the threshold.

Although Pesek was certain the house was empty, he entered with every sense on alert, stepping slowly down a short hall still redolent with the stink of burned wood and urine. Pockmarks of bullets traced a line across fading, peeling frescoes, now repainted in abstract streaks and splatters of dried blood.

He eased open the first door, every nerve end tingling in anticipation and fear. It had been years since Pesek had been in the field; chasing floess runners and smugglers surrounded by an armed, trained team was an entire league away from prowling alone through what appeared to be a covert military camp. This room held nothing but line after line of bunks, enough for about twenty men, some still made up to military precision, others looking like their inhabitants had been pulled forcibly from the blankets. More splatters of blood, more bullet holes.

Another door opened onto the mess, food rotten and congealed on plates, the storeroom and cooler empty, doors flung wide open, the floor scuffed and filthy with muddy boot prints. Pesek found another hallway, the frescoes replaced with military green, leading to a training room of some sort, with an area surrounded by heavy metal bars, the mat worn and stained, faintly smelling of piss and sweat. In one corner a battered training bot lay abandoned, the metal casing scratched and dented.

The infirmary was further along the hallway, exactly as Keren had described it. Next door was the medic's quarters, the blankets tumbled on the floor from when Keren was dragged out in the middle of the night. The drawers and closet stood open and empty; all evidence of occupation removed.

The last door opened onto a short hall; a single heavy metal door set in its end. Pesek tightened his grip on his weapon, unsure of how to proceed. If there was still danger in this house, it may well be hiding behind that final door, although he wouldn't be surprised if it was a body. Pesek crept toward it, back flat against the cold wall and opened it slowly, to reveal a cell of featureless gray walls, and a rotting, malodorous piece of foam that might have been a mattress, years ago. The medic said there were guards. Whoever they had been guarding, he or she was long gone.

Back in the house, Pesek found the room where the house AI had been. Now the room was empty, bare wires sprouting from the walls.

He searched again, every room, every cupboard, every storage unit. He was about to give up when some gut instinct took him back to the infirmary. Again, Pesek went through every locker and drawer, finally pulling the cover off the scanner bed. Something hit the floor with a familiar clatter. His triumph swiftly turned to disappointment; the dark, inactive sheet was a spiderweb of cracks. It was possible he could still retrieve some information from it.

This was one of those rare occasions when he fervently wished they were operating under the old Imperium laws. He could have had a forensics team out here in hours, a full sweep for material completed and a comprehensive genome sequence done in a few minutes. Every single person who had ever spent any time in this house would be identified, their genetic profile already logged on a central database. Now citizens had the right to genetic privacy and guarded that right fiercely. Even convicted felons could petition to have the databases scrubbed of their profiles. The war had left a deep and lingering suspicion of the power genetics gave authorities. He could try for a court order for such a controversial test, but that would raise too many questions, and he had no answers.

After taking one more look around the grounds, Pesek headed back to the vehicle. He tossed the broken sheet into the charging slot and headed back to the city, picking his way down the laneway in the gathering dusk, so involved in navigating that he failed to see the drone rise from its hiding place and head away in the opposite direction and disappear behind the dark line of trees.

Twenty-One

Zarr squashed down the last item into his bag and turned to Ori, leaning against the bulkhead, and pretending to be uninterested. "I don't know why you don't want to come. Everyone likes shore leave. Corelli isn't that bad. For a giant farm."

Until Marissa could find the credits for two new pump cylinders, the *Ava* would remain in the orbital docks, and all unnecessary crew were on leave. Davey and Lart were already at the airlock waiting for the shuttle, eagerly anticipating clean air, fresh food, and getting uproariously drunk. "Unless, you know." He could feel his entire head going bright red. "Van wants you to stay."

Her expression went from annoyed to positively thunderous. "I am staying," she said, rigidly upright now and enunciating every word as though speaking to an imbecile, "to help with life support, so that we can get to Ma'al and get paid."

Zarr dropped his bag on the deck with a loud thump. Blessed Mother she made him so mad.

"Yes, but first we have to get two cylinders," he yelled back, mimicking her patronizing tone. "And last time I checked, they don't give them away. The money has to come from somewhere. And since when are you an engineer or a maintenance officer?" Why couldn't she admit she wanted to stay behind to play hide the shaft with Van and be done with it, instead of this constant battle to prove she was more disciplined, more professional than anyone else?

"Whatever," he said, grabbing his bag and pushing past Ori before she could start arguing again. "Go and ask Lianna, but don't be surprised if she bounces your ass straight onto the shuttle."

"Cargomaster, if I may have a word?" *Pretend she's a higher-ranking Line, be respectful, not groveling.* As expected, Lianna was down in the drive room with Van, taking stock and deciding what extra parts they absolutely needed to install the new cylinders. Sukin – no, Jen — must be off somewhere else. Since that tense first meeting, the woman had kept to maintenance and the deck containing the life support systems. Lart had made one or two pointed remarks about competence and "fuck-ups" until Van overheard him. After that, Lart kept his opinions on Jen's abilities to himself.

That Marissa was also there shouldn't be a problem. The captain was a reasonable, intelligent woman; it was Lianna she had to convince. The three of them were clustered around one of Van's work benches, a line of spare parts neatly lined up, a toolbox spilling its contents everywhere.

Van's joyful expression when Ori stepped through the hatch nearly had her give up on the spot. Since their encounter after the meeting, it felt like she couldn't move without Van suddenly being there as well. Surely the engineer couldn't believe Ori wanted to stay on board so they could spend more time together? It was unthinkable. You did not couple with eijen; it was like having sex with animals. There were rumors, of course, of those who indulged in such perversions. They tended to fall into two types: the ones who used it to terrorize and torture the enslaved, and those who formed unwise attachments. Both paths were dangerous and often led to the same end — a public and protracted death, if one of your own Line didn't kill you first as a matter of honor.

Lianna looked up from her sheet, her permanent scowl deepening at the sight of her cargo hand. "What is it, Tey? We're busy and you're supposed to be waiting for the shuttle."

Marissa looked up, frowning before returning her focus to her sheet, clearly leaving crew matters to her second-in-command.

"I wanted to request permission to stay on board. I have skills—"

Lianna's sheet slammed down on the bench. "What fucking part of *get on the shuttle* did you not understand? We do not need your skills."

Ori, her face burning, the neuro-suppressors too slow to counteract the tight knot of rage and shame, waited vainly for Van to intervene. *I thought he wanted me to stay?*

Marissa stood silently by, still ignoring her. Van didn't meet her eyes, suddenly finding something more important to do on his own sheet. The silence stretched out, ominous.

"My apologies, Cargomaster," Ori finally managed to grind out, although there was no tone of contrition. "I will return to the waiting area with the rest of the crew." She turned on her heel and left, sending a last, venomous glare at Van, only the late arrival of icy chemical calm prevented her from embedding the hatch in the bulkhead.

Zarr took one look at Ori and decided to say absolutely nothing as his crewmate dropped her bag on the deck and took a seat on an upturned storage crate. Davey, stupid to the last, opened his mouth, but a vicious jab from Lart had him closing it again with an audible snap.

Dammit, she storms into these situations, expecting total obedience from everyone, and then gets all twisted up when it doesn't work.

If it had been anyone else, Zarr would have made some attempt to console her. With Ori, he'd found it was safer to simply let her be. She could be as scathing and dismissive as Lianna when sufficiently annoyed, and by the look on Ori's face, the cargomaster had managed to really provoke her. The problem was, he realized with flash of insight, that they both wanted to be in charge, and neither woman was the type to back down.

CORELLI

One

The Six Jump, Corelli, Tersen, Ma'al run didn't attract the luxury passenger lines that frequented the richer, inner systems. Before Ma'al became completely xenophobic, a steady trade of mid-level passengers out of Six Jump kept a small fleet of passenger ships busy, but once that dried up, there were few options for a non-Ma'ali, regardless of how much money one had.

Of course, Keren could have taken one of the family yachts, if he'd wanted to draw unnecessary attention to himself. He could imagine the scenario. The moment he dropped into Corelli space his ship's ident would be flagged by the port AI and you'd be able to hear the collective raising of eyebrows across the systems. He'd never get anywhere near Ori after that.

Therefore, Maridel — helpful, efficient Maridel — had arranged passage for him on one of the bigger freighters that carried a few passengers as a side gig.

Used to the mild climate of Central, Keren's shirt stuck to his body in clinging wet patches and made the sweat drip off his nose the moment he stepped out of the terminal.

My hair is going to frizz into a mess.

The shabby little vehicle waiting for him was at least climate-controlled, although the AI set it to subzero temperatures that turned his clammy skin icy and had him digging through his bag for a jacket.

At least Neuvo Dacilo provided a reasonable hotel — if reasonable included one lumpy bed, a screen with dead patches on the display, and a stunning view of the neighboring building's wall. Keren was simply grateful it was clean and climate control worked; he didn't fancy trying to prize open the single window. The trip from the shuttle terminal had taken far longer than he'd expected, crowds of people on the streets slowing down the traffic. The city AI helpfully explained there was an annual commemorative festival; Keren winced. Hadn't these sorts of celebrations fallen out of favor? It seemed obscene to gloat over the deaths of twelve billion people. *You're biased. It's easier to be sympathetic now you've met an engineered person.*

That brought him to his present dilemma — finding Ori. Maridel had set up a meeting with a contact in the local Eidress office. Corelli's trade in Orchetti root spawned a labyrinthine network of commercial contracts that were Hanjile Eidress's core work. Maridel had been able to discover Ori left Six on a freighter, but he couldn't discover which one. Keren hoped that the local Corelli office would be able to help him locate her.

Keren unpacked his bag, laying out his belongings on the misshapen bed. The one set of decent business attire would be the obvious choice — on Central. Here, it might be obvious for all the wrong reasons. No, the safest option was an off-white shirt in a subtle silk mix, and a pair of black pants, the cheapest and most unobtrusive clothing he owned. Corelli was unlikely to be across the latest fashions, so he could get away with a looser style of pants without his trendier friends judging him; he hated the clinging, revealing cut that was all the rage this season. Still, regarding his reflection in the room's lone mirror, he didn't look too bad. Weeks of prison food had shaved off all the excess weight he'd piled on at the house, and he'd gotten back into a bit of exercise, so the clothes fit well. A rigorous application of hair products tamed his errant curls back into something approaching respectable, though he worried how they would react to the Corelli weather once outside.

Stepping out of the hotel lobby into the street was like moving from a cooler into a sauna. With the local time past midday, the afternoon sun had a real bite to it, sweat sticking his shirt back to his skin before he'd gone half a block. At least his hair was still behaving itself. The city seethed with people, half of whom were visibly drunk and the other half well on their way. Bars opened onto the street, the potent local brew and frigid air pouring out in equal measure. The city colors of blue and white were omnipresent — clothes, banners, holo-projected birds and weird flying insect things, signs proclaiming LIBERATION in bold fonts.

The Neuvo Dacilo offices of Hanjile Eidress occupied a four-story building in a quiet side street lined with spreading atoria trees, their dense shade a welcome relief from the heat. A plain metal plaque set into the gray stone of the facade simply read *Hanjile Eidress*. It needed nothing else. This building represented the wealthiest, arguably the most powerful, group of people in the entire Republic.

The door of frosted syntheglass slid open silently at his approach and a blast of cold air, subtly perfumed, enveloped him.

Inside, a floor of the finest marble in a shade of gray only marginally paler than the facade, flowed across the foyer space. A conversation area consisting of a cream sofa and two comfortable looking matching chairs, flanking a low glass table, sat to one side. Keren suddenly felt under-dressed.

"May I assist?" asked someone in flawless Formal Standard. Keren turned and had to look up. Maridel was considered on the short side for a Ma'ali, and was still half a head taller than Keren. The woman in front of him was taller still. Not quite as tall as Ori, though. The soft lighting slid across the dark-green silk and picked out the lines of gold that covered nearly half of her knee-length che'b'ni. A discreet line of lace peeked up along the edges of the high collar and the ends of the long, tapered sleeves. Keren had gone through a phase where he'd studied the iconography of Ma'ali embroidery; he could still pick out the odd symbol here and there.

Keren remembered his manners. "Eidress, I am honored," he said, bowing from the waist, right hand to his chest, "I have an appointment with Saliri Irinis."

The woman returned the bow. "I am Saliri Irinis, Keren Casar." She gestured across the marble expanse. "Please, let us discuss this in my office."

Saliri Irinis's office wouldn't have looked out of place in the Palace, or anywhere on the Casar estates. Although the ceilings were not quite as high, the quality of the frescoes eclipsed those of most public buildings on Central. Perhaps the Great Chapel, in the capital, might be finer, but it would be a small difference.

She waved Keren to another comfortable chair and took her own behind a desk of pale gold wood inlaid with dark roundels of some semi-precious stone. "My cousin Maridel speaks highly of you," she began. "He rarely bestows such praise."

You mean he rarely bestows such praise on off-worlders.

"Maridel has served our family with great distinction. He is an honor to his hanjile," he said, smoothly.

Irinis nodded, clearly pleased that Keren knew the Ma'ali blessing. "How can I assist you, Keren Casar? Beyond that of your family's extensive capabilities, of course."

Unlike Maridel, who styled his hair in a series of convoluted braids and twists before they met into the single plait, Irinis opted for a simple pulled-back look, her braid of midnight black snaking across her shoulder to pool in her lap, adorned with only one silver ring, proclaiming her single status.

How intriguing, noted the part of his brain that obsessed about beautiful women. And she was beautiful, with the high, sharp cheekbones and fine bone structure all Ma'ali had inherited from their Cimmili ancestors. Instead of Maridel's grass-green eyes, hers were a bright blue, fringed with long lashes. Keren hastily pulled his body back into line.

"I'm not sure how much Maridel has told you," Keren said, feeling his way. Maridel was far from stupid; he would have made his own assumptions from what Keren didn't tell him. "I'm looking for a friend, who I think is here in Neuvo Dacilo. All I know is that she is on a freighter, currently in the orbital docks. I just don't know if she is on the docks still, or is here, on Corelli."

Irinis leaned back in her chair and regarded him. "Maridel said very little, which is his way. But he did inform me you were looking for a woman. I must ask, does this woman wish you to find her?"

Blessed Mother, it's like something out of a romance feed. The rich man takes a fancy to someone and when she leaves, spends his life trying to find her again. Or does Irinis think this is some sort of creepy stalking thing? Fuck.

Keren opted for semi-honesty. "I'm concerned for her. I treated her in my professional role as her medic. I was ..." How to describe being dragged out of bed at gunpoint, and ending up in prison? "I was called away, before I had a chance to follow up."

"And she requires your assistance? To the exclusion of every other medic between Central and here?" One hand performed a graceful arc, encompassing all of Corelli.

Time to pull rank. "Her medical condition is confidential. It requires specialist knowledge to treat." As an Eidress, Irinis would be an expert on privacy laws; Ma'al invoked them often enough to protect themselves. He could see, though, that she remained unconvinced.

"Normally I would not assist you, but Maridel has spoken for you and requested that I help. Regardless of my feelings, I trust his judgment."

So, a Saliri of Hanjile Eidress trusted Maridel enough to override her own instincts. *Interesting.*

"Thank you. I assure you, I mean her no harm. If she does not want my help, I will respect her wishes. I need to know she has recovered."

In response, he was subjected to another long, assessing look. "Eidress," she said finally, addressing the omnipresent AI, "I need a search of all freighter crews currently on Corelli." She tilted her head in inquiry. "Her name?"

"Oryelle Tey," he supplied.

The last syllable had barely left his lips before the AI responded. "Oryelle Tey, cargo hand, *Avadora* out of Six Jump. En route to Tersen, then Ma'al. The ship is in the docks awaiting repairs. The individual is currently in Neuvo Dacilo. Do you wish me to ping her ID?"

Irinis frowned for a microsecond before resuming her impassive demeanor. So Hanjile Eidress had AI capabilities on par with the Directorate. They could locate anyone, without their knowledge. Even his family couldn't do that. Well, not legally.

"I swear I am discreet. Nothing that occurs here will ever be spoken of," Keren assured her. Irinis continued to look skeptical.

"I am risking a great deal on Maridel's word, Keren Casar." The struggle between Maridel's trust and her own instincts was palpable. Keren held his breath.

"Yes, Eidress, locate the individual," she said finally.

"The individual is two blocks from here, on the corner of Main and Dacilo. Do you require directions?"

Blessed Mother that was just down from the hotel. He could have walked right past her.

"No, thank you." He rose and bowed. "Thank you, Saliri Irinis. You have my gratitude and that of my family."

Irinis rose too, looking a little surprised. It was rare that off-worlders invoked the centuries-old traditions of obligation. They were only words, though. No one took these things seriously anymore. If they did, from now on if Irinis asked, any Casar was duty-bound to assist her. Imagine explaining that one to Mother, or Uncle Betan.

"Maridel was correct. You have great honor, Keren Casar. Should you require help, ask; invoke my name, and it will be given."

Yes, that's simply being polite, isn't it? Otherwise, I've got myself into a mutual obligation pact. Until the debt is cleared, I've tied Hanjile Eidress and my family together. No, it's only manners, that's all. Only words.

Maybe he should say goodbye now and get out of here before he had to marry someone. "Thank you, Saliri Irinis," he said again, placing his right hand on his left breast and bowing. "I will leave you now, I'm sure you have more pressing duties."

Once outside, Keren headed for the shade and leaned his head against the smooth trunk of the sheltering tree. That had been simple politeness, hadn't it? Traditions from hundreds of years ago that meant nothing? He was tired, and hot and anxious, that was all. Ori was only a few blocks from here; he couldn't believe finding her had been so easy. At least she would be glad to see him. He hoped.

TWO

Ori leaned on the railing of the tiny verandah and stared out at the surrounding fields, conceding that Zarr's comment was accurate. Corelli was a giant farm. As far as the horizon, all she could see was an endless expanse of deep green where centuries of terraforming had erased an unremarkable mountain range, diverted numerous rivers, and drained countless wetlands, to replace them with the single most useful crop in the Republic — Orchetti root. A high protein vegetable, it could be processed into an almost limitless array of foodstuffs, from breads, to her favorite snack — thinly sliced roots, deep fried and salted. A wave of silver danced across the fields as the air movement revealed the leaf undersides for a second. A faultless bowl of deep blue sky stretched overhead to the horizon, where distant storm clouds drew a thin, dark line.

Reinnor's message still sat, visible on the interface.

The Xi want you to infiltrate the Ma'ali hanjiles. What they are looking for is there. I am almost certain it isn't the silk. Rossim has tasked the Directorate with stopping you. Be careful.

Her first instinct was to dismiss Reinnor, his theories, and the message completely. Tersen was only a few weeks away. Escape remained her goal. The information regarding Rossim was redundant. Clearly the Lord President was behind the sabotage, somehow. Her suspicions fell almost completely onto Jwali, but she was uncomfortably aware that any of the crew could be Rossim's or the Directorate's agents.

The breeze moved through the port camp, ruffling a lone shrub and scattering dying leaves across the gravel path, relieving the mid-summer heat a little. A line of identical beige demountables stretched either side of her small cabin, with more spreading out behind and in front of her. None of the crew could afford accommodation closer to the city center, so Zarr, Davey and Lart were all here in these little metal boxes, barely larger than her cell back in the old house, waiting for the *Ava* to be repaired.

Yet as Ori watched the dancing leaves, she couldn't dismiss a growing curiosity. What were the Xi after? Reinnor's assertion that it wasn't the silk seemed accurate. The trade in silk went back hundreds of years; if the Xi wanted it, they could have ordered the Republic to annex Ma'al at any time and simply taken it. What were the hanjiles hiding?

"Hey, we going?" yelled Zarr from his verandah, distracting her. "I'm hungry."

"You're always hungry," she replied, but without anger. Davey and Lart had disappeared not long after sunrise, with a vague story about meeting up with another crew, but it was just as likely they were hunting new berths. Despite Van's best efforts, after three days, the ship still lay in the docks. All of them, including Ori, were beginning to fear that Marissa couldn't come up with the money for the repairs.

She'd spent more than a few hours last night, poring over parts sites, but cylinders didn't just drop out of the sky and the meager amount in her account wouldn't buy a quarter of one, let alone the two needed.

All spaceports had a town like Neuvo Dacilo, often the original landing site of a colony, where the collection of port buildings grew like an organism across the ground. There was no discernible pattern, although you could see where successive governments had tried to impose order. As the vehicle — Zarr called it a "bus" — meandered through the patchwork of suburbs, industrial areas and tracts of office buildings, the boy kept nudging her to point out yet another example of agricultural abundance, or an especially large piece of machinery, until she threatened to sit somewhere else and he slumped back in his seat, quietly mutinous.

At every interminable stop the number of passengers increased, until all the hard syntheplaz seats were full, and the narrow aisle stuffed to standing room only. Nearly everyone wore almost identical clothing; the women in wide-legged blue trousers with stiffly starched blouses adorned in an excess of ruffles and dangling ribbons, the men in pleated skirts (blue again) with white, high-collared jackets. The outfits seemed impractical for agricultural work.

"It's busy today," Ori said, attempting to coax the boy out of his sulk. An obsessive checking of her account hadn't revealed any undetected funds and she needed a distraction from the crowd. Despite all the passengers, climate control still had the air at near freezing; she pulled her jacket, a cheap print-run, closer. It helped disguise the threadbare state of the rest of her clothes.

The man standing in the aisle, so close as to be almost pressing against her, leaned down. "It is festival day, ma'am," he said, in a flat, nasal Standard. "Everyone is going to the city."

Festival? Ori looked at Zarr, who shrugged with insolent indifference and she had to stifle the impulse to smack him. Though a festival might explain the costumes. The planetary AI offered a wealth of information, but she ignored it, having no interest in the goings on of eijen. The biggest problem was what to do now. The *Ava* may never leave Corelli, not if Marissa couldn't raise the credits. Here, dirtside, she was far too vulnerable; her skin crawled at the press of bodies all around her. It didn't require much imagination to conjure an assassin lurking in the crowd. She did not need Reinnor's warning; she knew Rossim's capacity for ruthless treachery. Only his fear of the Xi had kept her alive all these years. Perhaps she should emulate Lart and D'vai and start looking for another berth.

The bus finally lumbered into the main terminus, disgorging the blue and white crowd who headed en masse through the exits. Ori and Zarr followed, emerging into a wide boulevard festooned with streamers, banners, and an overabundance of holo-projectors, filling the air overhead with garish and competing images of swooping birds, iridescent insects with impossible wings, and exhortations to patronize this or that establishment. The humid atmosphere was thick with a mélange of cooking food, perfume and sweat. Overhead, tiny drones dropped glitter bombs onto the crowd, emitting snatches of music before flitting off to find more targets. In the distance, thunder rumbled, barely discernible under the noise.

"Oh, it's the Liberation Festival," said Zarr, pointing excitedly at the decorations. "I didn't know Corelli held them at a different time of the year. I'm starving, let's go get some food." He proceeded to push his way through the crowd to the line of food vendors set up along the street. Ori followed, keeping one eye on the boy while checking the local interface for "festival".

By the time she reached him, Zarr had procured two paper-wrapped skewers of cultured meat protein dripping with sauce, and Ori now knew that this festival celebrated the liberation of this sector, three months after the destruction of Da Chet. The local network had also issued a storm warning for the entire region. None of the locals seemed concerned, so Ori dismissed it without another thought.

Zarr waved his meal at the masses. "There's a parade and a Freedom Play as well. Who knew Corelli were such traditionalists? This is going to be fun, come on." He disappeared again, forcing her to follow him into the crowd. Bodies in blue and white pressed against her amid swirls of glitter raining down from the darting drones; laughter and shouts and blasts of music assailing her senses. A trio of port workers in orange overalls, reeking of alcohol, stumbled past, shoving people into each other. Shouts of outrage and disapproval followed them, largely ignored, except for a few obscene gestures. Ori made it to the other side of the street and finally spied Zarr.

A tall tree, reminiscent of the one outside the house, rose out of the pavement, spreading both welcome shade and a sprinkling of white petals across the crowd. The boy stood with a group of young Corelli, all dressed in the blue and white outfits, laughing and pointing at the dive-bombing drones. Drifts of rainbow glitter sparkled in their hair and caught in the ribbons and ruffles of their clothes, the ephemeral sparkles subliming away to nothingness in seconds. Beside Zarr, a girl, dressed in her festival costume, a multitude of fine white ribbons reaching to her small waist, her brown hair twisted up under a little white cap, leaned in to speak to Zarr and he smiled, playfully catching at one of the ribbons.

A hot, bitter anger engulfed Ori, as sharp as acid. The snack Zarr bought her crushed in her clenched fist, her stomach twisting in rage. A flood of neuro-suppressors swept through her bloodstream in response as she fought the impulse to march over and drag him bodily away.

One of the boys, his dark curly hair flopping across his eyes, threw his arm over Zarr's shoulder, offering a drink from a flask. Treacherous organic memory erupted and dragged her in.

She removes her helmet; the breeze cool across her hairless skull and thick with the reek of smoke and death. One of her siblings hands her a water bottle, his smile lighting up in pleasure.

Where were her people, her Line? She would never see them again, Ori realized with absolute certainty. She would never fight for her Line again; the sacred duty of cleansing the galaxy would go on without her. Her vision blurred and she scrubbed away the tears with her sleeve.

Then Zarr's hand rested on her arm, "Are you OK? You look ill. Is it the heat? Come over here." He guided her into the dense shade, where someone — the girl with brown hair — pushed a cold drink into her hands.

"I'm all right, Zarr, it was just the heat," she said, falling into the lie. The drink proved to be a freezing concoction of fruit and too much sugar, but it helped distract her. "No, I'm fine," she said, pulling herself upright. "I'm better now."

Zarr looked doubtful, but didn't pursue it, for which she was inexplicably grateful. Any more lies were abruptly curtailed by a wave of movement in the surrounding crowd. The center of the street cleared, everyone pressing back along the pavements, climbing up to sit on walls or perch in the limbs of the street trees.

"What's happening?" she asked, pulling the boy back into the relative safety of the massive tree trunk.

"Oh, it's the parade, ma'am," answered the girl, executing a bobbing curtsy. "We always have a parade, and then it's the play. Doesn't your homeworld have one?" Her pretty face scrunched up in doubt and confusion.

"My crewmate is from Orchetti; they have different festivals, don't they?" said Zarr, adding a gentle nudge of encouragement. "This is Alise," he added, going bright red.

As far as Ori knew, the Orchetti Combine had been part of the Imperium until the end of the war, and no doubt had their own way of celebrating the incineration of twelve billion people. "Yes," she said, still fighting for emotional control, "we do celebrate liberation." This must have been enough because Alise smiled, and dropped another bow. Ori could swear she could smell the hormones pouring off Zarr.

Further conversations were interrupted by a blast of martial music and the appearance of a troop of local youths, dressed in a semi-military style uniform, in the ubiquitous blue and white. Behind them followed a cargo flatbed, anti-grav fields disguised under swathes of fabric, pulled by an agricultural tractor of mammoth proportions. The crowd edged back, compressing all those behind them, including herself, Zarr and the group of Corelli youngsters. A tableau of a holo-projected lumpy white vegetable and an improbably huge insect took up all the flat bed. After a second, Ori recognized the vegetable as being an Orchetti root; presumably the insect was some sort of pest. The crowd began booing loudly and throwing glitter bombs at the insect.

"Wait till I get back home and tell my mum about this," yelled Zarr, "she'll piss herself laughing." He shook his head. "Farmers."

Three more pieces of machinery followed, all carrying promotional signage for local businesses; then a marching band, playing almost in tune. The crowd clapped enthusiastically, children hoisted onto their parents' shoulders waved madly, the machines emitting ear blasting horns in response. The group of port workers from earlier — drunker, louder and more obnoxious — shoved their way through the crowd, hurling insults and obscene gestures in equal measure. Lightning strobed briefly behind the buildings, throwing everything into sharp relief.

"What about this storm?" Ori yelled to the girl, who dragged a sheet out of her pocket and poked at it for a few seconds.

"Weather control says they have it contained," she yelled back, "it'll cool things down."

Another flatbed appeared, this time hauled by teams of men and women in matching outfits.

"This is the best bit," Zarr yelled over the noise and pointed down the street. Ori ignored him as the flatbed drew level with their section, the crowd screaming in appreciation. In one corner, a peripheral flashed red, and without a conscious thought from her, a new interface popped up, long-forgotten. The one used to analyze crowds — specifically the mass movement of eijen. A useful tool for the forced relocation of entire planetary populations.

The new flatbed held six figures: three men, three women, all naked, except for a thick layer of dull silver body paint, and long chains linking metal collars at throat and wrist, the skin showing red and inflamed at the intersection of flesh and metal. As one, the crowd began to chant.

ABOMINATION!

ABOMINATION!

Beside her, Zarr and the girl joined in with enthusiasm. Her skin tightened and the sub-dermal armor activated, prickly and sharp. An object launched out of the mass of spectators; something rotten smashed against one of the mock Abominations, red juices mingling with the silver paint. The target, an older woman, staggered slightly. The interface scanned the crowd, pulsing icons highlighting disturbance foci. The crowd, all unknowing, was splitting, coalescing into patterns of drunken excitement and bloodlust.

Zarr fell silent, looking to Ori in confusion. Evidently Six Jump did not incorporate this into their festivals.

"I thought this was supposed to be an entertainment?" Ori half shouted to the girl, who jumped up and down with excitement as another missile found its mark. She had to repeat herself, the noise was overwhelming. The warnings were becoming more strident; not for the first time, Ori fervently wished she had her troops, the warrior clones designed and bred to follow the orders of their imprinted Command Line.

The girl shook her head. "No, these six have been selected by the city council as part of their community service. You know, for minor crimes." The delicate white ribbons danced and fluttered; Zarr moved closer, almost pressed against Ori's side in sudden apprehension. Nausea roiled through Ori's stomach, the waves of hot and cold spreading across her skin, the mesh rigid as the crowd howled obscenities and rained garbage down on their fellow citizens. All six of the people on the flatbed were now coated in rotten vegetable matter as the machine edged slowly through the crowd. Close by, the group of drunken port workers were shoving and yelling at the surrounding participants, whether in objection or alcohol-fueled aggression, Ori couldn't tell. The next object was neither vegetable nor rotten. The rock, taken from a nearby garden, hit one of the women, blood spraying across the group. The woman collapsed, crumpling into a bloody heap. The chanting faded a little, and the girl stopped her wild jumping. Under his freckles Zarr went a pasty green color.

"I think we should go," Ori said, searching for a way through the mass of people. An official climbed up onto the vehicle to examine the fallen prisoner, the other five huddled now at one end, their terror obvious even at this distance. Too late, warned the interface, crowd reactions were at critical. Ori scanned the crowd again, desperate for an escape route as the first drops of rain began to fall.

The fighting between the port workers and the crowd escalated, obscenities and pushing devolving into random fist fights. As the violence swirled and spread, the youngest one, his orange overalls a glaring point against the blue and white, climbed nimbly to the top of a nearby stone wall. He raised one fist into the air and bellowed. "Long live Emperor D'e!"

Emperor Serrios D'e, Supreme Ruler of the Imperium, leader of the Engineered side of the Great War. Dead. Incinerated with his family, and the entire population of Da Chet. They paid the price for being too lenient, too concerned with persuasion. Her people, the True People, had learned millennia ago — there could be no compromise. The sacred duty of cleansing the galaxy of the eijen, the sub-humans, did not permit sentiment or concessions.

The silence fell across the crowd like someone had pressed mute. Was this man insane or just so drunk he didn't realize he'd just signed his own death warrant?

A shock wave of outrage roared through the crowd as the silence shattered with the united howls of the drunken, angry mob. The port workers tried to rescue their reckless and foolish colleague, but the crowd outnumbered them and he was dragged down from his pedestal. Local law enforcement in severe black uniforms appeared, swinging stun sticks with ruthless abandonment.

Lightning strobed across the sky, the faultless blue replaced with dark, heavy clouds, followed by a crack of thunder that rattled the nearby shop windows. Rain pattered down onto the canopy of leaves.

The terrified mass of revelers turned to flee the violence, a wave of bodies heaved and roiled across the street, crushing Ori against the tree. She struck out, driving her fists into bodies, finally clearing a space around her.

When she turned around, the children, the girl, and Zarr were gone.

Three

Keren pushed his way through the crowds, wishing that he'd gone back to the hotel with its lumpy bed and climate-controlled comfort. Sweat sprang from every pore and his painstakingly tamed curls were now a frizzy mess, the industrial strength hair products abandoning the fight the moment he left the cool elegance of Hanjile Eidress's offices and stepped into the thick, oppressive air with its stink of bodies, alcohol and greasy food.

The corner of Main and Dacilo might as well have been on the other side of the continent as far as ease of travel was concerned. No one seemed inclined to move at more than a leisurely stroll, and knots of drunken, noisy revelers coalesced outside every bar and food vendor.

"No thanks, I've had enough," he told every single drunk who grabbed him and pressed an overflowing glass or flask into his hand. Despite his best efforts though, Keren was swaying ever so slightly by the time he finally reached the intersection. The holographic animals screeched and darted at him, dumping glitter across the sea of blue-and-white-clad bodies, all deep into party mode — dancing, singing, embracing strangers or throwing mistimed punches, depending on mood and depth of inebriation. The patrolling law enforcement, in incongruously stark black uniforms, seemed content to let the chaos reign unfettered, although their hands never left their stun sticks.

His stomach churned with a combination of too much alcohol and not enough food on top of the heat. A wide awning overhanging a shop front offered welcome shade; Keren leaned his forehead against the cool syntheglass, conceding he had no hope of finding Ori in this melee. He should head back to the hotel, get cleaned up, and clear his head.

A piercing blast of music roused him from his misery. The crowd surged, pressing him back until the door's access panel dug painfully into his back. The marching bands and the giant holo-insect were amusing, but his blood ran cold when the crowd started chanting. These sorts of celebrations had grown out of the purges in the terrible aftermath of Da Chet's fall. Hundreds of men, women, and even children had been hauled through the streets to similar chants, to meet horrific, inhumane deaths. Over the decades, the inner worlds had allowed or encouraged such celebrations to fall away, with entire systems developing collective amnesia whenever the purges were mentioned. Squashed into the shop doorway, Keren had no idea what precipitated the shouts of outrage that went up around him, but he heard all too clearly the battle cry of the old Imperium.

"Long live Emperor D'e."

The silence following was so profound, he flinched. Someone nearby screamed, not in fear, or pain, but in rage, the sound taken up by the surrounding throng, an animalistic, primeval outpouring of bloodlust.

Chaos erupted. Parents rushed past clutching screaming children, a man staggered out of the melee, blood streaming from his head. Keren rushed forward, with no other intention than to assist the injured, but was driven back by the black-clad law officers swinging crackling stun sticks, uncaring who they struck. Over the sounds of the riot, thunder rumbled.

The crowd became a human wave, dragging Keren along the street away from the intersection, only a fortuitous collision with a lamp post arresting his progress. Intent now only on finding shelter, Keren searched frantically for a gap in the street-turned-battleground. Lightning arced, illuminating the landscape in blinding light, and threw into sharp relief a pale blonde head, taller than most, on the other side of the street. Thunder rumbled, and the first fat drops of rain plummeted down.

"Ori," he screamed, and cursed himself for his stupidity. The ebb and flow of humanity shifted as he pushed and shoved his way through the crowds, trying desperately to keep that blonde head in sight. The rain began to fall harder now, the bright afternoon sunlight swallowed up by dark clouds, the brief flashes of lightning followed closely by thunder.

The crowd slowed, caught in the entrance to a narrow laneway. Another flash, far too close, split the sky; the thunderclap that followed rattled every window in the buildings lining each side. He could see Ori ahead, further down the road. Bodies pressed in on every side, the panic contagious. Children screamed or cried, adults alternately cursed, or prayed. A young man stumbled, and would have been crushed if Keren hadn't grabbed him in time. He stammered thanks before disappearing back into the crowd.

The next strike was so close the entire area lit up in a flash of intense white light. The sound that followed, less than a second later, was so loud that Keren feared he had gone deaf. He thought his eyesight was going too, until he realized all the streetlights were out;

it was as dark as evening now, the storm clouds blocking the afternoon sun. Somewhere ahead, a bottleneck must have cleared as the crowd surged forward, anxious for escape from the torrential rain. Keren pushed forward, but when he got to the point where he'd last seen Ori, she was gone.

Zarr clutched Alise tightly as the tide of people swept them down the road. He'd given up trying to see where Ori was, the footing underneath was treacherous, wet and muddy and littered with rubbish waiting to trip you up. Twice someone near them slipped over, to disappear with barely a cry into the panicked mob. Bodies pressed in all around them, elbows and feet leaving bruises, voices full of confusion and fear and anger filling his ears; he almost fell a dozen times on the sodden, muddy road. A fist, or foot maybe, slammed into his ribs, and he couldn't stop the cry of pain. Alise clung to him, sobbing. The mass of people began to slow, squashing together tighter and tighter, in response to an obstacle ahead, that Zarr couldn't see, but could almost feel through the bodies.

"We have to get out of here," he yelled, "before we get crushed."

"Over there." Alise pointed urgently to a dim passage between two shops. As the crowd pressed tighter, Zarr and Alise wormed their way through the massed bodies, until they could slip into the tiny gap between two buildings.

A twilight darkness replaced the afternoon sunlight. All the streetlights were out, the buildings lining each side of the street loomed black and menacing, their windows briefly lit with each strobe of lightning. They were both soaked to the skin. The rain thundered down, falling off the overhanging roof of the passageway in a continuous curtain of water, making any conversation almost impossible, but at least they were in less danger of drowning.

"What is happening?" she yelled over the noise, her cheek pressed against his chest, the little white cap plastered to her wet hair.

Zarr shook his head. "I don't know, they've all gone mad."

How had it gone so wrong so quickly? One minute everyone was happy, Alise smiling and laughing at his jokes, the next people were dying, crushed underfoot. He could still hear the crackle of the stun sticks, the screams of the injured. And the fake Abominations — what in the name of the Blessed Mother possessed Corelli to keep such obscenities? Six Jump and Tersen had outlawed such things decades ago.

From down the street came the crash of breaking glass, and a roar went up from the crowd. More crashes, followed by screams. People ran past, their arms laden with goods, clothes, electronics; a man with his arms full of boxes, a woman clutching jewelry, the chains gleaming in the rain.

"Where are the Betarazta, the law?" Alise asked, "They should be here, protecting us."

"I don't know. Probably still trying to control the rioting. I'll bet they never expected this."

"It was the drunken off-worlders' fault," Alise said vehemently. "We have never had this trouble before."

I suppose throwing rocks at old women had nothing to do with it.

Zarr wisely didn't say this out loud. "I'm sure he's regretting it now." An uncomfortable thought surfaced. Had his father or grandfather watched such parades? Had they thrown garbage at pretend Abominations? Zarr vowed that was one question he wouldn't be asking next time he was home.

"Hey, maybe there's a door down here," came a voice from the street. Zarr pulled Alise back against the wall, where they both froze, hardly daring to breathe. A figure stood outlined against the light.

"Oh, Great Xi, please protect us," Alise whispered.

Fucking great, just wonderful. She's a spider worshipper. Trust me to fall for a heretic.

"Nah," replied another voice, "these shops back onto the ones on the next street. Let's go around, might find a few more goodies to liberate."

The footsteps faded away.

Zarr looked down the narrow passage, where a gate stood outlined against the gray. "We need to find Ori," he said.

"Zarr!" Ori scanned across the maelstrom of heads for the boy. "Zarr, where are you?" she yelled again, with no response. The mild anxiety his disappearance caused began to morph into something approaching fear as Ori surveyed the chaos all around her. Knots of fighting were still breaking out between the blue-and-white-clad natives and any off-worlders. Fists and blood and whatever weapons came to hand swirled among the terrified bystanders, who ran helplessly in circles clutching screaming children, or stumbled away nursing injuries.

The stifling afternoon heat had fled with the arrival of the storm. Now the rain hammered down, the thin stuff of her clothes clinging to her skin, rivulets running off her. Despite the cold, her skin felt hot and tight; the sub-dermal armor pulsed and twitched in response to an inexplicable anxiety.

He's fine. He's here somewhere. I'll find him.

She tried calling for him again, climbing onto a large planter, the flowers all crushed, to get a better view. A hand clutched at her leg, perhaps attempting to drag her down, perhaps seeking help. It didn't matter. Her foot lashed out and the eijen, a large ponderous oaf, screamed and stumbled away, blood streaming from his crushed face.

This was the boy's fault. He should never have left her side. She should have dragged him away from the Corelli youths, she should have got him out before all this erupted. Anxiety crawled like insects burying into her skin as every peripheral glowed red, her interface struggling to cope with the mass of systems warnings. Twice she thought she saw the boy, and shoved and fought through the packed bodies to reach him, only to be racked with frustration and anger when it wasn't him.

Ori was sure Zarr and the girl had been swept further along, but the double line of black-clad officers, most now in rain-slick body armor and carrying riot shields all emblazoned with CBF — Corelli Betarazta Force — now blocked the street, intent on regaining control through the unrestrained use of stun sticks and brute force.

Prevented from going any further, the crowd began to thicken, lining up in opposition to the Betarazta. The fights died away as people turned their anger to the line opposing them, heedless of the storm's rising intensity. Insults flew, which the law ignored, then the first missiles hit — pavers dug up from the roadside or rocks plundered from walls and gardens. Patience on both sides evaporated as the line of black-clad men and women began forcing the crowd back up the street, jabbing at them with stun sticks on full charge, the air reeking with the smell of charred fabric and burned flesh.

Lightning illuminated the entire area, followed by thunder that rattled windows up and down the street, provoking more loud screams from the crowd. The next strike was so close, Ori heard the sizzle of electrons as the bolt struck something, perhaps a tree, across the road, with a blinding flash and an ear-splitting crack that triggered her sound protection protocols.

Flaming debris flew silently across the crowd as her systems shut down hearing for a full second. As one, the entire mass of people panicked, their screams shocking after the silence. The line of black held for perhaps a second or two; Ori glimpsed the terrified face of a woman law officer, then she, and all her comrades were gone, trampled or swept away, along with anyone unlucky to not move fast enough. The sub-dermal armor hardened to maximum, providing some protection as she slammed into obstacles in the crowd's path. Hands tore at her as the desperate eijen struggled for any support. The synthecrete roadway was treacherously slippery, though not always from the rain; some of the objects she was forced to tread on gave way underfoot.

Then suddenly the pressure vanished as the street opened into a large, open space, trees and grass spreading away into the distance. Ori moved away as quickly as she dared, dragging her ripped clothing about her, but no one paid her any heed. With a last rumble of thunder, the rain petered out and a wan ray of sunlight struggled through the clouds. The crowd resolved itself into individual figures, bloodstained, bruised, their clothes torn and filthy. Girls carried in the arms of strangers or family, the dancing ribbons and white caps now dark with blood and filth; men dragging bodies out onto the grass, to the cries and screams of loved ones. Sirens began to wail across the city.

Everything became too loud, too bright, despite the slowly dissipating storm. Once again, Ori found herself sucked back down into that long-ago memory.

Another successful mission, another world cleansed of the eijen filth. Overhead, a V of aircraft screams past, on their way to obliterating the remaining cities. The long line of the enslaved trudges onto the transports while in the distance, around the holding pens, the warrior clones work ceaselessly, tossing the bodies of the culled into neat piles. There is already a line of sooty fires blazing.

A young man, little older than Zarr, stumbled past, one arm hanging at an unnatural angle, the bone protruding from the purpling, swelling flesh. His eyes stared at nothing, or perhaps everything. Was Zarr laying somewhere, trampled to unrecognizable flesh and broken bones?

Blood clotting everywhere in thick, dark pools. The screams, the stench of death. The wails from the pens as the eijen realized their fate.

Surrounded by death and terror and pain, Ori came to a sudden and terrifying realization.

Zarr was eijen.

They were all eijen. Zarr, Van, Jen, even Lart and annoying Davey.

If her people's ships dropped into Corelli space at this instant, every single one of them would be either culled — the elderly, the sick, the injured, women too close to term, children too small to care for themselves — or enslaved, torn from their homes and taken across the galaxy to spend their short lives in brutal slavery. All of them.

In that instant her mind filled with the images, in graphic detail: the boy's face on the piles of dead, Jen in the lines of slaves. Her siblings would slaughter them all. She had slaughtered them all.

The world, the park, spun, her skin was tight and hot then icy cold, peripherals screamed in silent red, strobing in response to dangerous levels of cortisol and adrenaline. They were not *eijen*. They were *people*. She had murdered millions of people.

Hold on, the neuro-suppressors will kick in soon. The seconds passed and still the artificial calm did not come. In vain Ori activated the systems again and again, but nothing happened. She swayed, the muddy ground swimming in her vision. Concerned faces ringed her, strange voices rose and fell, but all she could hear were the screams of the dying.

What was wrong with her? Why was nothing working? Had too many years of abuse and torture permanently damaged her? *See,* said the voices. *We told you. Damaged and weak and imperfect. Only fit to be culled, like the eijen.*

The world swam again, just as it had on the ladder on the *Ava*, the air thick and cloying, pressing on her. Ori had a brief impression of a body, thickset and male, hard against her, his hand on her shoulder as if to steady her. The knife struck from behind, an expert blow aimed between her third and fourth ribs that would have been a killing thrust save for the sub-dermal armor. The knife point stuck briefly before skittering across the mesh, gouging a long, deep wound parallel with her rib cage, then gone.

Four

Zarr gripped Alise's hand as they crept along the passageway, the sounds of looting still loud behind them. The rickety gate was locked but Zarr had no problems ripping off a few panels, enough for himself and Alise to slide through. Alise wasn't impressed at this latest example of lawlessness, but conceded that given everything going on around them, a few pieces of real wood hardly counted.

The rain began to ease, from a thunderous roar to a quiet pattering. The thin, high wails of emergency vehicles were the first noise Zarr heard, then the whirr of drones. Alise looked at him, her face white, eyes round with fear. They crept along the twin of the adjoining lane, this one full of malodorous bins and muddy puddles, to emerge into a smaller, narrower street, lined with a mix of shops and two- to three-story office space.

"Do you know where we are?" Zarr whispered, although the entire street was empty.

Alise pointed to the right. "Liberation Park is down there," she said, equally quietly.

Another posse of drones zoomed past, all emblazoned with the Betarazta insignia, all heading in the direction of the park. The sirens grew louder.

"We have to find Ori," Zarr said, although he had no idea where she might be. Not at the park, though, not where the sirens were rising in a cacophony of telegraphed disaster. He wished he could convince himself of that, as an icy knot of fear grew in his stomach with every passing moment.

"The Betarazta will be searching out wrong-doers, Yaol. We will be safer if we go to them."

Zarr wasn't sure that line of reasoning held up when you were talking about law enforcement, but he followed Alise along the street, her hand warm and slightly sweaty in his, past the closed shops and the empty cafes, trying to stay under cover. The clouds were clearing, and the late afternoon sun still had a bite to it. His clothes clung to his skin, damp and unpleasantly clammy.

The closer they got to the end of the road, the louder the signals of disaster became. The sirens were now a wall of high-pitched, ear-shattering noise. Blue and white lights strobed off the store fronts, so bright that Zarr had to shield his eyes.

At first, all Zarr could see were a sea of black and white Betarazta vehicles. Beyond them stretched green grass and tall trees, a little battered from the rain, but nothing that would justify this response.

Alise tugged on his sleeve. "Yaol, look."

His brain refused at first to comprehend the scene stretched out in front of them. The lines of black-uniformed law caught his attention, military tactical armor gleaming in the returning sunlight. The crowd they held back was not the angry, seething mob that had swept him and Alise away. They stood silently, almost unmoving.

The bodies were everywhere. Men, women, and — *Blessed Mother* — children. Civilians and law enforcement moved among the silent forms, covering them with whatever came to hand. Not quickly enough, though, because Zarr could see the broken limbs. He could see bones. He could see...

Bizarrely, as Zarr emptied his stomach onto the rain-wet path, all he could think of was his mother's disapproval. *Fancy throwing up in public, in a park.* He staggered away and collapsed on the ground, wiping his mouth on his sleeve. *Blessed Mother, the world has gone mad.* Vaguely he was aware of Alise sobbing loudly, and some part of him knew he should be comforting her, but then who would comfort him?

"Zarr." Alise shook him. "Zarr, isn't that your friend?"

Friend? I don't have friends. I have crewmates. I have...

"Ori?"

Among all the different shades of brown and black, her pale hair stood out like a beacon.

"Ori!" he screamed again, and tore across the sodden grass to where she sat, leaning against an ornamental sculpture of some sort. Overcome with joy, he flung his arms around her, forgetting for a moment her dislike of being touched, and was overwhelmed when instead of pulling away, she clung tightly to him.

"I was so worried," he babbled, aware that he probably sounded like an idiot, and waited for the inevitable reprimand.

Alise's mouth formed a perfect O of shock, Zarr followed her gaze, his hands were thick with blood.

"You're bleeding," he said, reaching for her again. "We have to get you help."

Ori slumped back against the stone, her wet skin gray and sick-looking. She shook her head, waving him away. "No, I can't," she whispered, "They'll kill me."

The lane opened onto a wide boulevard, lined with office blocks and expensive-look-ing boutiques. Keren helped a woman in torn and dirty orange overalls to a bench under a wide tree.

"Thanks," she said, in a thick Orchetti accent, the rising tone at the end of nearly every word. "I thought there for a minute, I was a goner."

"Wait here," he said, "I'll find some help."

A crash further up the street made them both jump. The crowd spilling out of the laneway were not in the mood to return peaceably to their homes. A well-aimed chair from a café exploded a shop window, to whoops and cries of approval. Seconds later the shop contents were hauled away in great armfuls of merchandise, swathes of fabric dragging in the dirt as the looters ran up the street.

The next shop must have installed break-resistant syntheglass; the chair, a table and even a substantial planter box rebounded to a rising chorus of anger.

"This isn't good," the woman said, brandishing a sheet at him. "There's a city-wide curfew in effect immediately. There's rioting across the city. And they're advising all non-Corelli citizens to get off the streets."

Keren pulled out his own sheet, the alert from the Corelli network pinging immediately he thumbed it into active. A rising sense of unease began somewhere down in his stomach as he read the increasingly frantic alerts. Across the city, angry crowds were looting businesses and attacking off-worlders indiscriminately. The Corelli First Minister had issued mobilization orders for the planetary-wide militia, Corelli's quasi- military force. What if Ori somehow became caught up in this? He had to find her.

The looters, abandoning the unbreakable glass front, moved further along, searching for easier targets.

"Go," said the woman, pulling herself up with a wince of pain. "I've got friends not far from here. I can look after myself. You should get off the streets now." She limped away without another word.

He should head back to the security of the hotel, or perhaps the Hanjile Eidress offices, they were closer. It was too dangerous out on the streets, but he had to find Ori. The logical course was simply to follow the increasing drone traffic and the rising wail of sirens.

After the noise and chaos of the riot and the fury of the storm, the still, silent crowd, all dressed in their blue-and-white festival finery, was unnerving. A line of law enforcement, in shiny new silk and graphene tactical armor and clutching military-grade weaponry, faced them behind a high metal barricade. That was a worrying development.

The increasing militarization of the outer systems was becoming a source of concern even among his family's societal strata. Like most citizens, Keren rarely gave much thought to the status of the Fleet. Three hundred years of peace and no perceived threats in the known galactic neighborhood had cast an air of complacency over the Republic. Many believed that the Xi, or one of the other non-humanoid races, would come to their defense if needed. Keren had serious doubts about the altruism of the Xi, and even less faith in the Hubnae or Meians, for surely, if they had any interest in helping, one of them would have intervened in the war.

"I'm a medic," Keren announced, as he approached the crowd, "I'm here to help." No one said anything, but the crowd parted silently to let him pass through. "I'm a medic," he repeated, feeling stupid, reaching the barricade with no response from the armor-clad figures.

One of the figures detached themselves; he bore an uncanny resemblance to Captain Twari, and Keren had to suppress a shiver of revulsion.

"And you are?" the man said, barely glancing up from his sheet.

"Keren Ha'haru," he said, "from Central." He swallowed a flash of sudden fear — what if his brief stint in prison was still on his records? No, Maridel was nothing if not thorough. No one would ever see that information again.

"Medic Ha'haru? Of Admiral Danizitia Medical Center?" The man, clearly an officer, looked up, suspicion and disbelief etched into the worn planes of his face. Keren tracked how the other man's expression changed as he took in the silk shirt and pants, their value still evident under the mud.

"Come through, come through." He gestured impatiently, almost pushing his troops out of the way and opening a gate in the barricade. "We're waiting on activation of the emergency response. In the meantime, make yourself useful."

Keren bore the man's abruptness with equanimity: emergency services were probably struggling to respond. The officer slammed the gate shut behind Keren as if expecting the silent crowd to stampede through it.

"I am happy to help," Keren began, "now what—" His words died in his throat. Keren had never experienced battlefield conditions, or even the aftermath of a disaster. The former was three hundred years ago, the latter happened only on distant worlds, out on the border. Now he was looking at a synthesis of both tragedies.

"What happened?" he whispered.

The wide, green park, with its tall trees and garden beds packed with color, was subsumed by death. Line after line of bodies made neat rows on the pathways as teams of Betarazta and civilians covered the mangled and bloody corpses with makeshift shrouds. The injured lay, or sat, on the sodden lawn, now churned into mud, some silent, others weeping, without help or attention.

"There was a riot, specifically a number of riots. It started in the city center but spread with frightening speed," the Corelli officer said, coming up behind him, his tone devoid of emotion. "We have countless crush injuries, other injuries consistent with assault, also cuts from broken glass and thrown objects. Quite a number have been injured in altercations with our personnel." Keren recognized the deliberate suppression of grief in the man's voice. "The death toll is in the hundreds; thousands more are injured."

Overhead, e-feed drones jockeyed for space with law enforcement. From beyond the trees a solitary drone appeared, the green and white stripes of its cargo signaling its status as medical equipment.

"Start wherever you like. We don't have any equipment or shelter. All we have are a frightened populous and an unprepared force." The man pointed to the descending drone and its cargo. "I guarantee that will be absolutely useless."

"Why aren't you taking them to medical centers?"

"We've commandeered every vehicle possible, but every facility within a reasonable distance is full."

Keren headed across the grass, feeling the eyes of that silent crowd boring into his back as he revised the triage protocols for mass disasters. First step would be to identify those who were bleeding, unable to walk or had obvious external injuries. Perhaps he could utilize some of the crowd, or law enforcement. Surely not all of them had to man the barricade?

In the clearing sky, the afternoon sun was still unpleasantly warm, gluing his wet clothes to his skin. What he wouldn't give for a set of clean, dry clothes, or scrubs, preferably.

Shouting from behind him distracted Keren from his ruminations. Two of the black-clad law officers were chasing a boy across the swathe of muddy lawn. The boy ran clumsily, his arms waving in the air, his words lost in the noise of drones and shouts and vehicles; why he picked Keren out of the hundreds of people wasn't clear, but the moment he saw him he tore across toward him, the two officers hard on his heels.

"I need a medic," the boy was screaming. "Please, she's dying. I need help." Keren tried to yell a warning but the boy, intent on evading the pursuing Betarazta, didn't see the area of churned earth. His feet slid out from under him, his momentum propelling him head-first into Keren. The two of them sprawled back onto the ground, the boy on top of him, arms and legs still flailing.

Then the weight was gone as both officers reached Keren, yanking the boy off and holding him, his feet kicking helplessly in the air, between them.

"Please," he sobbed, "she's dying. She needs a medic."

"Go on citizen," one of the Betarazta said, in a flat, nasal Standard, "we'll send someone to find his friend. He's probably passed out somewhere."

Across the park, just behind him, were row after row of dead and injured. Keren knew he should leave the boy to law enforcement. He had to prioritize his efforts, help those still capable of surviving.

"These officers won't hurt you," Keren said, trying to be reassuring, "they'll find your friend. He'll be fine."

"Why won't you pricks listen to me?" the boy screamed, in obvious frustration. "Ori's dying."

Ori?

The boy was covered in blood.

"Put him down. Now," Keren commanded, with the same snap of power his mother used. "You." He pointed at the boy, unceremoniously dumped onto the ground by the startled officers. "Take me to her immediately."

She was dying. Ori was dimly aware of Alise's voice, full of concern and fear. The girl's hands were on her, laying her down on the wet grass, pressing against the wound. It didn't matter, she was dying. It was fitting.

Abomination, they had chanted. Is that what she really was? No different from those incinerated on Da Chet, or executed during the purges? Or was she worse? The engineered had wanted to remake the Imperium. She had been responsible for galactic wide genocide.

"You have to hold on, ma'am," Alise pleaded with her. "Yaol has gone for help, someone will be here soon." The girl knelt beside her, her hands bloody, long strands of brown hair straggling down from her rain-soaked bun.

"I don't deserve to live," Ori whispered. Or thought. Hard to tell now. No interface at all. No peripheral icons, no constant stream of information. No neuro-suppressors.

"Don't say that, ma'am," Alise said, pressing something against the wound. Her little cap, the fine white cloth sodden and dark, the ribbons training bloody streams in the mud. "The blessed Xi will send a miracle, I'm sure."

Ori grabbed the girl's arm, pulling her close, seeing the small, upturned nose and fine cheekbones, the smear of blood across her pointed chin, her skin white with fear. "The Xi will not help me. I killed them, too, all their little ones screaming as the fire took hold. I didn't know it was a nursery, I didn't know it would spread so fast."

The cool, dim tunnels, lined with silk, the vague, omnipresent stink of decay. The torture — relentless, brutal, methodical — went on for months, yet she had not given in.

She had not known it was a nursery. All she'd wanted to do was escape.

Her fingers dug deep into the girl's flesh as Alise pulled back, terror and confusion replacing concern. "I didn't know. I swear." The girl gasped, and Ori dropped her hand, her strength ebbing away.

It was very cold. Despite the late afternoon sun forcing its way through the fleeing clouds, driving the remaining moisture off in wispy vapor, a deep chill settled in her. Not the cold of hard vacuum, a part of her mind reminded her. There were no words to describe that in any language Ori knew. Maybe in Xial; she should ask them next time they tortured her. No. There would be no next time.

"Ori, I'm here. I'm back. I've brought help."

Zarr, a functioning remnant of her mind told her. *Not eijen.*

More hands on her. Not Zarr, not Alise. But familiar. She remembered how to open her eyes. Keren knelt beside her in filthy, torn clothes, the mop of unruly curls flattened and dripping with rain.

"Medic. What are you doing here?" she managed.

"Saving you. Again."

Five

He'd expected to find her unchanged, as she had been back in the house. Beaten, bloody but still defiant, still stubbornly raging against those she thought beneath her. Instead, Keren found her semi-conscious and blood-soaked, in the lap of a hysterical young girl.

The girl let out a wail of absolute terror on seeing Zarr, babbling incoherently about trying to save Ori, and the Xi, for some inexplicable reason. The two Betarazta officers at least had the decency to look ashamed at their previous indifference.

Keren fell to his knees beside her before pulling the ruined shirt over his head and tearing the delicate silk into useful pieces. "Lay still." An unnecessary command — she had lapsed back into unconsciousness, her skin pale and cold. "Help me turn her," he ordered, expecting one of the guards to assist, but it was the boy who threw himself down beside Ori, his jaw set resolutely.

"Hey, medic," one of the officers said, "we need to get back to our posts. There's a lot of injured people out there."

As if he didn't know that. As if he couldn't hear the sirens, or the screams. He should be down there, coordinating the medical teams, saving as many people as possible. There were children down there.

"Please," whispered the boy, "don't leave us."

Keren half turned to the Betarazta, addressing them over his shoulder, "Go. I'll come down as soon as she's stable. I'm sure more assistance is on the way. Find some more volunteers, start prioritizing those who can't move, are having trouble breathing, or are in danger of bleeding out."

As he spoke, an entire fleet of drones bearing green and white striped cargo swept overhead, heading further down the park. "Go on, they'll need every hand to unload and help."

"They'll need medics, too," one of the officers said acidly, before motioning to his companion and heading back toward the chaos, shaking his head in disgust.

"Here," Keren said, trying to push down the overwhelming guilt and placing the boy's hands into position on Ori's unresponsive body, the remains of her clothing muddy and blood-soaked, feeling him flinch away at the contact.

"She doesn't like to be touched."

I know. But how do you know that?

It spoke to some level of intimacy; that, and the obvious concern the boy had for Ori's welfare.

"It will be OK; you're helping to save her. What's your name?"

"Zarr. Ori's my crewmate," he added, "and this is Alise." He indicated the young girl. She looked terrified, tears tracking down her face, the blue and white clothes covered in blood and mud, clotting blood clinging to her hands in thick lumps.

"Zarr, we're going to roll her toward you. Alise, if you can support her head?"

Zarr still looked uncertain, but followed Keren's instructions, gently rotating Ori's body until she lay face-down as Alise guided Ori's head until she was cradled in her lap.

Keren could see now where the initial strike began near the spine, extending out in a long curving slash parallel to her ribs. She ought to be dead.

"Hold her still," he said, probing the wound, searching for the source of the bleeding. His fingertip grazed something that writhed at his touch, and he nearly jumped with fright.

The sub-dermal armor. Probably the only thing that saved her.

"Is she going to be all right?" Zarr asked, looking at him strangely.

"Yes, of course she is," Keren replied, as he began packing wad after wad of material into the wound, all the while entreating the Blessed Mother to intervene. He didn't understand why Ori was still unconscious. The injuries she'd sustained at the house were far more extensive. Was there some other cause he was missing?

"All right, I'm going to put this pad over the wound and press down to stop the bleeding."

"Will it hurt?" Zarr asked.

"A bit. But it's the only way."

Zarr nodded, looking unconvinced.

Keren spread the last scrap of silk over the wound and pressed down.

"It's all right, Ori," Zarr said softly, as Ori moaned and shifted in pain. The girl burst into tears, hiding her face in bloodstained hands.

Blessed Mother, help me.

"Alise, calm down. She's going to be all right."

Ori made another unintelligible sound, one hand clutching at the boy. Zarr twined his fingers in hers and Keren felt her entire body relax but was mortified as a sudden rush of jealousy overtook him.

"I think the bleeding has stopped," he said. "If I can have your shirt, Zarr, I can make a bandage." That came out a bit harsher than he intended, but the boy shrugged out of his shirt without comment.

By the time Keren tied off the makeshift dressing, Ori's color had improved.

"OK, let's get her comfortable until we can move her."

The grass was unpleasantly damp, hardly a fit place for recovery, but it was all they had.

"They're setting up tent things," Zarr said, pointing down the park. "Can we take her there?"

Keren didn't turn around, making sure Ori was in a comfortable position, the wound away from the mud.

"Yes, soon. Once they have the emergency wards up and you can see them taking in equipment. Otherwise, we'll just be moving her from one muddy patch to another."

By then, he hoped, Ori would be conscious.

Keren wiped his hands and pulled the cover up a little higher on his patient. Outside, the park lay silent and empty, the last of the wounded moved to the emergency wards dotting the park, and all the dead moved to the city's overflowing morgues.

The last nine hours had been the most exhausting of his entire professional career. Ever since the first cargo drones dropped their loads, it was clear to Keren that the Corelli government was floundering. From their position on the slight rise, he, Zarr and Alise had watched the chaos unfold — emergency medical facilities not deploying correctly, drones caught in tree branches, newly arrived troops clashing with the Betarazta and civilian volunteers.

And all the while Ori remained semi-conscious, although Keren was sure the bleeding had stopped. Without equipment or supplies, all he could do was hope that her systems would eventually heal her.

It was the boy, Zarr, who must have finally seen he'd had enough.

"Hey, Keren? Why don't you go and help? They look like they could use it."

He'd been torn between staying there with Ori and mitigating the rolling crisis in front of him.

"Are you sure?" he'd said, but he was already rising and brushing off the worst of the mud.

"We'll look after her," Alise assured him.

So he had left her in the care of the children and run down the slope. Five hours later he was overseeing three functioning emergency wards and over twenty medical staff and volunteers. Ori was brought down soon after, still unconscious, and placed in a quiet alcove, away from unwanted attention.

Zarr, exhausted and frightened, hadn't objected when Keren offered him a light sedative. Now he slept soundly in the next bed.

Keren twitched the privacy curtain further over, and then slumped down onto the hard syntheplaz seat beside an empty bed, a deep and overwhelming fatigue filling him. Just a small nap, he told himself, pillowing his head on his folded arms.

Her hands reached out to him as he fell, disappearing into nothingness.

"Zarr!" she cried, the last shreds of the dream clinging to her, terror and dread. The fog of sedatives threatened to pull her down as she struggled back to consciousness.

Where was she? White walls, the smell of cleaning chemicals. For one moment of absolute terror, she thought she was back in the infirmary. Back in the house. No. Somewhere else. She went instinctively to the interface, to find it gone. No icons pulsed sullenly; no systems screens fed her information. Nothing. Ori pulled herself upright, flinching when someone pulled aside the dividing curtain.

"Ori, hush, it's me. You're safe."

It was the medic. Keren. Once again trying to reassure her as if she were a lost child.

"Where is Zarr?" she demanded, trying to force her thumping heartbeat back down to something close to normal, her fingers clutching the covers, as if she was about to be thrown off.

He didn't fall, you didn't lose him.

"Keep your voice down, it's close to dawn. He's here, he's safe." Keren moved back the curtain to reveal the boy, on a hospital bed, curled under a blanket, sleeping soundly. "Frightened, obviously, a few bruises and lacerations, but nothing serious. I gave him a light sedative."

The cold knot of fear loosened a little. He was safe. It was just a dream. A wave of dizziness swept over her, and she collapsed back on the bed. Keren was there in an instant.

"You're in a temporary medical ward in Liberation Park," he said, almost whispering. "Do you remember what happened?" He moved to help her sit up, his face all creased with concern, but she waved him away.

"I was stabbed." Ori remembered that much. The hand on her shoulder, the bright sting of the knife. Pain. Blood soaking into clothes. The girl.

"Alise?" she asked, looking around.

"Zarr said her family came looking for her. She's safely home by now."

She nodded. Things were becoming clearer. So long as she didn't think about what had happened.

The boy's face on the piles of dead, Jen in the lines of slaves. Death, so much death.

No interface. No systems. No control.

She began to sob uncontrollably, tears pouring out of her, splattering onto the green striped hospital cover. Keren held her, and this time she did not pull away, did not dismiss him.

What was wrong with her?

"It's all right. You're safe now."

She wanted to laugh, to tell this little medic with his mass of rain-flattened curls that she would never be safe anywhere. And that no one was safe from her. Instead, she rested her head on his shoulder as, gradually, the fear eased, and she was able to sit back and wipe the tears away.

"There, better?" he said, handing her a cloth to wipe her face, a tentative smile tugging at his mouth.

Ori nodded. The feelings could be pushed down if she concentrated. Not as good as the interface, but it would have to do.

"How long was I unconscious?"

"About eight hours. Dawn is about an hour away. Are you hungry? I can go and find something?"

"No. You have not explained how you are here. Again."

"I'm on holiday; thought I'd see what was happening out on the border. I didn't expect to rescue you from a riot," he said wryly. "Can I check the dressing?"

On holiday? Ori found that difficult to believe. Why would someone who spoke and dressed like Rossim come out here to a giant farm?

"Tell me first, did you complain about my treatment as you promised?"

The gentle humor fled. "I don't lie, Ori," he said, scowling. "Yes, I complained. I hope it did some good."

I've managed to insult one of the few people prepared to help me.

The emotion that threatened to overwhelm her this time was shame. Ori felt herself go as red as Zarr. "It did. Thank you. I didn't mean to offend you."

Keren smiled and nodded. "Come on, let's see how that wound is healing."

She lay back down and let him pull back the cover without protest, scowling when she saw the hospital gown. Far too short, covered in bright pink and blue flowers. She stared suspiciously at Keren, daring him to laugh, but his expression remained impassive.

"Can you roll over?" Ori moved to her left side, flinching instinctively as Keren moved the ridiculous gown aside.

His fingers moved across her skin, feeling along the length of the wound. "You're fortunate the sub-dermal armor activated, otherwise you'd be dead. I think I touched it. Gave me a fright when it moved."

"The armor reacts to stimuli. It is not alive." At some level, her defense systems must be still working, otherwise, yes, she would be dead.

"How long will it take the nanites to heal you?" He stripped off one of the pain patches above the wound and applied a new one.

How to articulate her fear that the nanites were dead too? How would she survive without them? Her shoulders lifted in a minuscule shrug of resignation.

"My systems are damaged; I don't know if the nanites are working anymore," she said in the tone of someone describing the weather.

Keren couldn't see her face but he must be able to see her distress in the rigid lines of her body. His hand rested for a second on her shoulder; this time she did not flinch away.

"When did this start?" he asked, smoothing the pain patches into position, his voice calm and neutral.

"After the stampede. Before I was attacked. I tried accessing the neuro-suppressor menu and nothing happened." Although her voice remained expressionless, her hands tightened on the covers, knuckles white, fingers digging into the cloth.

"What happened that you needed neuro-suppressors for?"

"Emotions. It has been difficult, on the ship." She paused, struggling. "I find people difficult."

People. Not eijen. They weren't eijen. She had killed people. The guards, Garrett, Rossim were all correct. *Murderer.*

"So, they failed before you were stabbed? During the riot?" Keren refastened the gown and stood back so she could make herself comfortable.

Anger began to replace fear. "The reason is unimportant," Ori snapped, pulling herself back up to a seated position and tugging the covers over the offending gown. "The systems refuse to respond; diagnostics tell me nothing is wrong. Clearly there is a malfunction. One I am unable to fix. Tell me when I can take the boy — take Zarr — and leave."

"There isn't any rush, surely? In a few hours, when he's awake. He's had quite a shock."

"Good."

"I'm going to get some food," he said, his stomach grumbling loudly enough that she heard it. Hers responded in sympathy.

"Rest. I won't be long; we'll talk about it when I get back."

She made no response, merely nodding tightly, her gaze fixed firmly on the wall behind Keren's head, her arms tightly crossed.

Keren slid open the curtain and stepped quietly past the sleeping Zarr.

Zarr froze as the curtain slid back, the medic's shadow looming on the wall behind him, before the curtain closed again, leaving only a tiny sliver of light. Footsteps padded quietly past Zarr's bed and down the almost empty ward.

He hadn't meant to eavesdrop, but the voices had dragged him out of sleep. Ori's first, calling for him. The sedatives made the period between sleep and waking a nebulous place, and he wasn't sure if he'd dreamed it. Then the medic, Keren, hurried past, and Zarr heard him shush her. She'd asked about him. Zarr. It had been like her first question. And she used his name, not "the boy".

Zarr lay in the hospital bed and straining to catch the conversation. Keren whispered, barely audible, even this close. Yet as he listened to their back and forth, what he was hearing became apparent. He should have realized before, back when the medic was saving her. He knew her. Not quite as friends, Zarr could hear the wariness in Ori's voice, but more than a random meeting of medic and patient. OK, coincidences happened, maybe they'd met once at a clinic or something. Sure, that was it.

Then she began to cry, and he wanted to leap from his bed to comfort her, but Keren was there. And then the moment was gone.

"You're fortunate the sub-dermal armor activated, otherwise you'd be dead."

What in the name of the Blessed Mother was sub-dermal armor? There was a long silence, the type Ori would pull when you asked her something stupid. Or personal.

"How long will it take the nanites to heal you?" The medic then asked, like he wanted to know what she had for dinner. Zarr's blood ran as cold as the ice on Ma'al. Nanites. A technology so forbidden that just thinking about it was illegal. He couldn't have heard it right, Ori didn't have nanites. And then she was talking about her systems, and neuro-suppressors and the armor being alive, until Zarr buried his head under the pillow and wanted to scream in absolute terror. This was what Alise had tried to tell him. Ori had killed Xi, she had said, sobbing so hard one of the other medics had had to slip a sedative patch onto her.

No, this was a dream, he told himself, a side effect of the painkillers and whatever else they'd pumped into him. Any minute now he'd wake up and realize it. Ori couldn't be that. Them. The enemy. She just couldn't.

It would explain her uncanny ability with engines, and pod-docking and navigation, a voice sounding all too much like his dad's whispered in his head.

"But they were evil," he whispered back, pressing his face into the mattress so no one could hear him. "She's not evil. She's just clever." But even as he said it, Zarr knew it was more than that.

Now you'll have to report her, and they'll investigate you and all the crew. They'll investigate us. Your poor mother, to have a son that associates with Abominations.

The medic was coming back. Zarr froze again as the footsteps slowed at the foot of the bed.

Please, I'm asleep, please don't check.

There was a brief flash of light as the curtain was withdrawn, then Zarr was alone again. As quietly as possible he slid out of bed, grabbed his boots and the new clothes piled on the chair beside him and ran, out of the ward and into the Corelli dawn.

The moment Keren left, all her bravado fled, and Ori collapsed back into the pillows.

Emotions.

Her fingers dug into her scalp as another wave of anger and shame flooded over her. If only she could reach into her mind and yank out all these feelings. All the images. Of burning bodies, and lines of terrified, desperate people. People. Not eijen. Men and women and children, marched into the transports, never to see their homeworlds again. Never to see their families, or even another member of their species again. The Khatjarit made certain to disperse each conquered race across the thousands of worlds they controlled, minimizing possible unrest.

Please, come back. I can't deal with this.

Her systems remained inert, despite her pleas. She had to hide this from the boy, from the crew.

Footsteps. Keren was returning.

Ori wiped her face on the hem of the disgusting hospital gown and hid her clenched fists under the covers, fighting for control.

Keren navigated the dividing screen while carrying food packets and water flasks with ease, placing the tray on the bed and offering her a flask of water, and two sealed packets. Ori released her hands, pushing down the covers in a petty display of disdain and took the food.

The first packet yielded deep-fried Orchetti chips, heavily seasoned with farei.

"Do you want to talk about the neuro-suppressors?" asked Keren, who obviously thought that his pretended preoccupation with his food would fool her. The second packet held draci cakes. She should ask Zarr to get those tarts he kept going on about. She glanced toward the curtain, debating as to whether she should check for herself that he was uninjured. Better to let him sleep, put off any questions for as long as possible.

"No." Then after a moment, "It was the heat," she said, dismissively, before selecting a chip and methodically shaking off the seasoning.

"The heat caused your enhanced augmentation systems to, what? Overload?"

Hearing him say it out loud highlighted how stupid her excuse sounded. However, that was infinitely better than trying to explain what really happened. He knew what she was capable of — in a limited way, in a context of imprisonment — but his compassion was unlikely to survive the knowledge of what she had really done.

"It's possible it may come back online, reset itself. Relying on suppressors to handle unpleasant emotions isn't sustainable. Even for us eijen," he continued, laying his food to one side, oblivious to her struggles.

Did he see her flinch at the use of that word? Ori waited for the inevitable mockery, but Keren simply sat there, his gentle, competent fingers clasped in his lap, no hint of scorn anywhere in his expression. He seemed content to wait like that all day, it seemed, until she felt able to speak.

"It was like that. Before," she said finally, although she addressed this to the bag, unable to look at him. She had never discussed her life before her capture with anyone before. "I always had more." She stopped, reaching for the right words. "I always struggled to control my emotional responses. More so than my Line siblings."

"Under those circumstances I would recommend a good psych tech and a neural realignment." He shrugged. "Not an option for you, I know. But I do believe it is possible to learn to cope."

Ori wished she shared his optimism.

"I will have to. Until the systems come back online. I have learned to tolerate Zarr, so perhaps it is possible. Now, please tell me I have something other than this floral nightmare to wear. Rossim's assassin will have reported on my probable death by now, and I'd like to be back on the *Ava* before they realize they were mistaken."

"I know your ship is on the Ma'al run, but you still haven't told me what you expect to do there," Keren said, rummaging under the bed and handing her two bags. Ori took them a little warily, then tried unsuccessfully to conceal her pleasure with the new clothes, laying out and examining each piece. These were much higher quality than the cheap print runs Reinnor's agents had allowed her. The cloth was soft and smooth, in a deep blue.

"I have no idea. That is what the Xi want, so we are all forced to obey. Me, Rossim, and that fool, Reinnor."

"Jak Reinnor? The newly appointed Xi Liaison?" said Keren in surprise. "Xi Liaison is a diplomatic post, a dead-end for the assholes and idiots, according to my uncle."

"No, this must be another one," she replied absently, the flowery gown hitting the floor as she pulled on the new clothes. Plain dark work wear, utilitarian and comfortable, the most popular garment of choice across the Republic. "This one is Directorate."

"About the same height as me, long auburn hair, always immaculately curled, over-dressed and a little too obsessed with the Xi?"

Her head came up slowly, fingers arrested in their task of wrangling the sleeve closure. "You know him?"

"Yes. Well, I met him at a charity gala, once. It was on the feeds, he's the latest Xi Liaison. Not Directorate."

"He asked me to trust him," Ori said, each word heavy with anger. "He said he regretted my treatment."

"He's only recently appointed. It could be he didn't really know. He might have been genuine."

"Why do you defend him?" She pulled him closer, examining him. "Why are you really here? You still haven't explained how you found me or why I'm here, with new clothes and food."

"After you left, the house was raided. In the middle of the night. I think they killed all the guards. They dragged me out, fabricated some charges and threw me in prison."

She let his arm drop; he rubbed it, grimacing. "I warned them that one day they would all be disposed of. You are fortunate you survived. You have still not told me how you found me, or why."

Keren flexed his arm. "The rest of the guards kept making jokes about you being executed. I had to know if you were still alive. And as for finding you – I have a friend in Central Port Authority; they owed me a favor."

Six

Jak Reinnor tossed his sheet back on the desk in disgust. Nothing. After weeks of scrutinizing page after page of reports, notes, and records covering the last ten years, the only conclusion he could reach was that all the previous Xi Liaison were either idiots, or psychopaths. If any of them had any insight into the Xi's plans or Ori's part in them, they'd failed to make any mention of it.

He was beginning to believe that many of the previous incumbents were specifically selected for their incompetence, so Rossim and Garrett's sickening abuses would go unreported.

Jak poured himself a drink, vowing he'd cut back soon, and slumped back into the overstuffed chair. Above him, the dancing youths were obviously having a better time than him.

"Central," he asked, out of patience and at a loss on how to proceed, "where does the name Oryelle come from? Is it Xi?" Perhaps that might give him a clue as to Ori's origins.

"The name is unknown in any Republic database. There is a word, *or-e-el*, which means highly visible, or luminous, in three dialects of Xial."

"Hmm. It isn't a regional variation of a more common name? What about e-feed characters?" It was common in some strata of the population for parents to name their children after the AI-generated characters in popular stories.

"The search was thorough, Excellency. That name is not recorded anywhere in the Republic, or the Orchetti Combine."

It actually sounds peeved.

"My apologies, Central. What about Tey? Is that family name recorded?"

"Tey is the Xial word for star."

That wasn't what I asked.

"So let me guess. Ore-ell tey means a brightstar. Like a super nova?"

"You are correct."

"That makes no sense. Her name means Brightstar, which is what the Matriarch calls her. Why does she have a Xi name?"

"I am sorry, Excellency, I did not understand the question."

He had to stop talking to himself, it was getting embarrassing. "Never mind, just thinking out loud." It was a legitimate question, though. Why give her a Xi designation? Didn't she have a name of her own? An hour later, after once more going through the transcripts of the Xi, he had to admit defeat. Whatever Ori's real name was, it wasn't recorded. Reinnor, who had a reasonably good idea of the extent of Xi interrogation methods, seriously doubted the Xi hadn't been able to extract that information. Had it been redacted from the records? He had too many questions and almost no answers.

"Are there any references to the word Brightstar in any of the databases?"

Silence.

"Central, are you there?"

"My apologies, Excellency, I thought you were thinking aloud again."

Blessed Mother, another one that thinks it's a comedian.

"Please answer the query."

"There are one million, fifty-nine thousand three hundred and nineteen lawful entries for Brightstar. Five unlawful entries."

Jak sat up; his drink forgotten. Unlawful entries were forbidden topics, usually on genetic engineering and associated technology, or anything to do with the engineered side of the war. Technically, it wasn't illegal to access the information, but doing so would flag you in the system; too many flags and the Directorate would be alerted. Most citizens tried to avoid that sort of attention.

"Can you give me the top entry?"

"Of course, Excellency, you may access all databases."

It took Jak a second to process the AI's response. Where was the obligatory warning every citizen received?

"What? All of them?" This was ridiculous. No one was allowed unlimited access to information regarding the engineered, or their technologies.

"The office of Xi Liaison, and the office of the Lord President of the Republic, have full access to all databases. This was contained in your induction package, Excellency."

Jak could swear the damned AI sounded indignant. Although it had a point; he had skimmed over the mountains of information provided as part of his induction, and if he hadn't asked this specific question, might have remained unaware of the vast power at his fingertips.

He poured another drink, and glass in hand, paced slowly back and forth across his office, as he absorbed this new information. He wanted to be Lord President, he wanted to get the Republic out of Xi control.

But what if he didn't need to? What if being Xi Liaison was enough – more than enough? What if none of the other incumbents had realized? Or cared?

"All right, Central. Go."

"The Brightstar Laboratories, owned by Dr Zema Esen ve Naaro and Her Imperial Highness Dr Carillon D'e, was the pre-eminent genetics facility in the Imperium. Under the leadership of the Chief Geneticist, Her Imperial Highness Dr Carillon D'e, hundreds and thousands of engineered organisms, ranging from plants to force-grown humans were created. Controversy erupted in 4503 IE when it was revealed that her two children were fully engineered and enhanced organisms. Widespread rioting broke out across—"

"Stop," Jak commanded.

Blessed Mother protect us. Why would the Xi call an engineered soldier after a facility owned by the two most notorious scientists in the Imperium? Wasn't that facility on Da Chet?

"Do you require any more information?"

Jak hesitated. It wasn't impossible that Jak's activities were being monitored, either on Rossim's orders, or on Imsu Pesek's initiative. Tel would be alert to any threat. Jak decided to proceed extremely carefully until he had a better grasp of the situation.

Fortified by the warm pool of liquor in his stomach, Jak thought hard on the least dangerous approach. No point in asking about the laboratory's research, that was a matter of public record and long-standing propaganda.

Jak's interest in the war and its reverberations down the centuries could be described as minimal, at best. Understandable, then, that he hadn't known the name of the facility.

He should have asked Kellia. If their mother despaired of Jak's obsession with the Xi, his sister Kellia's interest in the Great War and the defeated engineered bordered on the pathological. Their mother lived in constant terror that they were all about to be arrested as traitors.

To this day, Jak didn't think his mother had ever forgiven her.

Carillon D'e was the first scientist to build a fully engineered organism from the base proteins. If she'd confined her talents to producing pretty and unusual blue flowers, her first commercial success, no one would have objected. Then the rumors started — that her own children were the first two of a vast store of genetically engineered embryos, bred to take over the Imperium.

It was a step too far. Although the Imperial family and a majority of the aristocracy supported most aspects of genetic engineering, the idea of possible heirs to the Imperial throne being *created* was anathema. Violent protesting broke out across the Imperium, facilities were bombed, prominent scientists murdered in the street.

Even then, her money and her position as the sister of the reigning Emperor, Serrios D'e, would have shielded Carillon from most consequences. But she continued to inflame the situation with ever more enthusiastic and strident calls for the Imperium to make itself over as an engineered utopia. The consequent widespread opposition then erupted into full-scale civil war.

"Central," Jak said, picking his way through the minefield of possible traps, "is there any record of Carillon or Zema having contact with the Xi?"

For a moment Jak thought it wasn't going to answer.

"Her Imperial Highness Dr Carillon D'e was Xi Liaison at the time of her death."

The empty glass fell from his grasp, rolling across the priceless carpet and coming to rest against a table leg. The Xi knew her. The Matriarch was alive then; she'd actually met her and made the most notorious war criminal in history a member of the Nest. It was unbelievable.

The Brightstar. Oryelle Tey was somehow linked to Carillon D'e. Did Rossim know? Unlikely. If he'd ever suspected such a connection, Ori would have been dead years ago, regardless of possible consequences.

The AI chimed. "My apologies, Excellency, but Agent Finn is here. He says he needs to see you urgently."

Now what?

"Send him in."

Seven

Compared to its daytime temperatures, the pre-dawn Corelli air was distinctly chilly. Zarr pulled his clothes and boots on hurriedly, wishing he'd taken the hospital blanket with him, although the growing brightening beyond the trees pointed to another hot and steamy day.

Despite the early hour, the park and its temporary hospital was busy. Medical personnel moved from building to building, and three vehicles silently came to a stop at a makeshift parking area and disgorged teams of yawning men and women in hi-vis overalls

He had no idea what to do. If he went to the authorities, would they believe him? And what if they arrested Ori, and there was some totally innocent explanation for all this?

What if it is true?

A wave of nausea and dizziness hit him and he stumbled away from the doorway to the shelter of a grove of trees before collapsing onto the ground.

He had to do something. Ori would come looking for him sooner rather than later and then what? He couldn't just go running out into the park screaming that there were Abominations on Corelli. It would start another riot. More deaths, more injuries. And Alise, they would know she was there with him, they'd drag her in for questioning too. Zarr leaned back against a trunk, wrapped his arms around his knees, and tried to think logically.

If Ori was one of Them, the medic knew too, and had known for a while, and hadn't reported it. Ori hadn't hurt him, or Alise, or Van. She worked hard. She cried in her sleep. Ma'al was only a few weeks away. If he said nothing, did nothing, what then?

The alternative was terrifying. The laws might be three hundred years old, but that didn't mean they weren't still enforceable. The very festival here on Corelli was a celebration of exactly that. Mass arrests. Mass executions. Twelve billion people incinerated. Men, women, children. More deaths in the purges that followed. What if they didn't believe Zarr didn't know what she was? What if they arrested his family as well? And Jen, and Van and Lart. They'd arrest them, too.

Although the authorities did all they could to suppress them, few in the Republic hadn't seen at least some of the illegal feeds recorded in the aftermath of Da Chet. Now Zarr imagined his family, his crewmates, facing that horror.

No. He would not tell. He would hold on until they got to Ma'al and hope that Ori disappeared into the domes and he never saw her again.

"So, this mission, on Ma'al. You really have no idea what you're supposed to be doing there?" Keren gathered up the last piece of trash and checked the cubicle one last time. Ori stood by the window, hands behind her back, shoulders square, the very image of a soldier on watch. Outside, the noise of the construction crew disassembling the temporary hospital blended with the voices of medical staff and local law enforcement. At her feet sat the remaining bag of clothes; Keren would bet one of Sylvie's silver bracelets that every item was meticulously folded.

"No," she said, turning away from her survey of the park, the early morning light gilding her features in soft gold, "but I am beginning to believe that it is important. Rossim would not attempt murder in broad daylight unless there was a very good reason. The Xi would act swiftly if they thought for a second he was betraying them."

"Any idea what that reason was? Surely if he wanted you dead, he could have done it while you were in prison?"

She shook her head, clearly confused. "No. The Xi would hold him responsible anyway. And ..." She paused. "He took enjoyment from my imprisonment. From my torture. The guards would not have touched me otherwise. Something has provoked him. He was angry that the Xi offered me my freedom, but I do not believe they intend to keep their word." Ori relaxed her stance, leaning back against the cubicle wall, arms crossed. "Annoying though it is, I believe that fool Reinnor is correct. The Xi did not keep me prisoner, did not torture me for some idle entertainment. It is something to do with Ma'al. I don't know what. He does not believe it has to do with the silk, but what else does Ma'al have? But if I can find out what it is, then I will have an advantage. Then we will see what the Xi are willing to offer."

She spoke of torture as if it meant nothing. Was there a point in anyone's life where such abuse became routine? Or was she simply refusing to let her pain show? "You think you can bargain with the Xi?" he asked, trying to conceal his own skepticism. The Xi were worshipped in some backwater worlds, raised to the level of household gods. No one, as far as Keren knew, had ever asked the Xi what they thought of this. Maybe next time he ran into Reinnor at one of Sylvie's events, he would speak to the man instead of avoiding him.

"That is the least of my problems, I must get to Ma'al first. The *Ava* lies in the docks, minus two pump cylinders mysteriously damaged. More of Rossim's work, I think."

"I don't know anything about ships. How long will it take to repair?"

"That is not the issue. The issue is money. Our captain does not have the credits. I do not have the credits. Even if the entire crew emptied their accounts, I doubt that would be enough for one cylinder, let alone two."

Our captain. So, they have gone from being eijen, less than animals, to crewmates.

"Perhaps I can help?"

"You have already saved my life, bought me clothes, fed the boy. I'm not sure you understand how much ship parts cost."

Years of concealing his family's wealth from judgment and opportunism made Keren wary of revealing all his resources. "I have enough, I'm sure. I think your assessment is correct, the answers are on Ma'al. You never know, it might be enough to bring down Rossim."

"They are five thousand credits. Each."

His ruined shirt, now a pile of blood-soaked rags, cost twice that. "Don't worry. I can find that sort of money."

Eight

In the early morning light, the streets were silent, broken only by the occasional distant siren and the crunch of broken glass under their boots. The stink of smoke from the burned-out shops hung in the already-too-warm air, although it was only a few hours after sunrise. Ori found Zarr outside, watching the teams pull down the last of the emergency buildings, the air thrumming with the flights of cargo drones.

"Have you heard from Alise?" she asked as they skirted around the remains of a torched delivery van, the lettering all scorched and bubbled, and the back access door ripped open. Ori thought of the girl, offering the sodden scrap of white as a bandage while the dark puddle grew beneath her.

In her peripheral vision, the boy's ear burned deep scarlet. "Yeah. She got home OK."

She shrugged, as if it was of no consequence, although she didn't understand why Zarr had barely spoken a word since leaving the park and wouldn't look at her.

The streets were largely empty of humans but they teemed with a fleet of cleaning bots scurrying up and down the roads and pavements, sucking up the discarded bunting, rubbish, and lost possessions. Whole stretches of pavement were gone, the fist-sized missiles now lay inside looted shops, or scattered across the roadway, some dark with blood — a constant source of annoyance to the machines.

Beside an overturned table, one of the tiny machines bumped and whirred impotently; the ragged, muddy lace wrapped around its pincers snagged on an abandoned paving stone. Back and forth it went, seeking escape from its restraints.

Zarr stopped as its frantic movements brought it to his feet. For a second he regarded its futile attempts at freedom, then his boot sent the little bot flying to rebound off the table leg, one pincer bent and twisted. He continued down the street without a backward glance, leaving Ori behind, stunned and confused.

The machine lay on its side, its tiny tracks turning slowly. If she left it, eventually the power cell would give out, and if no one came to its aid, the machine would die, trapped in the web of lace.

Ori took the knife from her boot and cut away the imprisoning material. Still the machine didn't move. She picked it up and it sat quiescent on her palm, its lone functioning pincer opening and closing. Did it sense the machines in her? The nanites, the sub-dermal mesh, the hundreds of enhancements placed inside of her? Zarr was not eijen, but she was closer to this machine than any of these humans. Ori looked for Zarr, but he was already in the next block, evidently not waiting for her.

She took the bent pincer between finger and thumb, slowly forcing the metal back into something close to normal. The bot gave a beep and seemed to test the function of its repaired appendage. Ori placed it back onto the ground, where there were no obstacles to trap it.

"Be careful," she whispered, "don't get caught again."

The bot, released, whirred and then sped after its team. Ori turned and followed Zarr.

"What are you two doing on the streets? The government's declared a curfew." Apart from the bots, the only other activity on the streets were the constant patrols; this was the third one in as many blocks. The officer's stun stick tracked unwaveringly to Ori, the woman's thumb hovering over the trigger, while her two companions clutched their shiny new military-grade weapons possessively. The militarization of law enforcement, enacted swiftly in the wake of the unrest, added another layer of uncertainty to every encounter.

"We were injured, and getting treatment at a medical center down there," Zarr replied, pointing down the street. "We were just released, officer, sorry, ma'am." Despite Ori's advice, the boy still sounded defensive, but at least he kept his hands open and in view.

"We have accommodation at the port crew camp, officers," Ori added. "We have a note from the medical center as proof." She made no attempt to reach for her sheet, it was always prudent to wait for instructions.

Permission was granted with a jerk of the stun stick, the three officers scanned the four lines as if expecting a confession of treason, but finally handed the sheet back. At this rate they wouldn't make it back to the camp by nightfall.

As before, the stun stick waved them on, the threat overt. "Get back to camp," the officer ordered.

Although the boy said nothing, Ori was sure he was as relieved as her to reach the sanctuary of the camp and their tiny cabins.

"Do you want to eat in my cabin?" she asked, suddenly feeling lost. Zarr stood there, his hands buried deep in his pockets, staring at the ground.

After a moment, he shook his head. "Tired, think I'll just go and rest."

"Well, at least take some of the food with you," she protested, handing him one of the bags Keren had given her. "There are still some cakes left. Keren did not eat all of them."

"No, I'm not hungry," he said, turning away.

Zarr was refusing cakes? "I have not thanked you," she said, trying to keep him a little longer. "For the clothes, and helping."

He shrugged. "Yeah, well, he asked me to do it. The medic, I mean. Keren."

The silence stretched out between them, and Ori couldn't find the words to reach him. Had she done something wrong? Had she — and icy terror ran though her — had she said something? Something she should not have, and now the boy suspected her?

"I thought I was dying. I think I frightened Alise."

He still didn't say anything. Then. "She's a colonial. A Xi worshipper. She must have got confused. That's all."

And she knew. Alise had told him something. Because the Zarr she knew would never hurt a bot, nor speak so dismissively of anyone.

Jwali drained the last mouthful of the local brew and slammed his glass down on the counter. Outside, the streets were almost empty; anyone stupid enough to think they could wander around and gawk at the damage soon came to the attention of local law enforcement. Better to be inside, better still to not move from this bar, at least until he had to return to the *Ava*. Behind him, the giant screen over the bar played an endless loop of footage from the riots, continuing across the city, interspersed with earnest commentary from the AI-generated anchors and stern lectures from Corelli authority.

"Stupid fucking hicks," muttered Jwali.

"I couldn't agree more," said a voice, as a figure slipped onto the bar stool beside Jwali, pushing another glass, full of the dark, potent beer, toward him. "Got what they deserved."

Jwali looked from the proffered drink to the stranger, immediately suspicious. This was either a sting by the local cops or a pickup. *Ava*'s navigator wasn't in the mood for another night in a cell, or a quick fumble out in the back lane. He just wanted to get drunk and go back to the *Ava* where at least the air was the right temperature.

"Do I know you?" he asked. The man half turned, a smile crinkling youthful, plump skin, his clothes non-descript and bland. The face was anything but: strong jawed, clean shaven. Jwali felt a stir of interest. Maybe just this once he could indulge himself?

"Oh, I don't think names are important, do you, Jwali?"

Jwali's stomach turned over and cold fear ran up his spine. The man opposite was not looking for pleasure. His eyes, a uniform flat brown, were lifeless, devoid of any emotion. The beer sat heavily in Jwali's stomach, making him nauseous.

"What do you want?"

"Drink up," said the stranger, nudging the glass closer, "and we'll have a little chat."

The beer went down in three gulps, all the while the other man paid no attention, simply watching the passing traffic without comment. Behind them, the other customers murmured among themselves as the First Minister of Corelli expressed his anger and disappointment with the situation.

The empty glass slid unsteadily across the beer-sticky counter and Jwali waited, terror eating him alive.

"It's always disappointing," the man said, as if genuinely sad, "when someone lets you down. I mean, you give them a simple task, well within their capabilities, and they still fuck it up."

Any hope Jwali had that this might be a random stranger cruising for a bit of fun, vanished.

"I've tried, I mean the *Ava* is in dock now, we haven't got the money for parts, we could be here for weeks," he gabbled. "I did what you asked."

"I didn't ask for anything." The stranger's hand landed gently on Jwali's leg. A casual observer would see two people getting to know one another over a few beers. No one would raise the alarm. The blade, slender and razor-sharp, pricked Jwali's thigh. "My colleague, however, made it very plain what was required. Police involvement. Arrest. Removal of the woman off the *Avadora*." The pain increased, fire spreading up his leg as Jwali froze in place, terror rendering him immobile.

"Your case is still pending with the Six Jump authorities," the man continued. "One call and a warrant will be issued for your arrest. Imagine how disappointed your aunt would be. It might affect her getting another contract, you never know."

"All right," Jwali squeaked, "all right, I can do it. I can. The bitch is on the edge. One push and you'll need the fucking Imperial Guard to drag her off. She's fucking insane."

Why the Directorate agent (because who else could he be?) smiled at that, Jwali had no idea, but the knife withdrew, disappearing as if by magic, leaving behind a spreading dark patch and throbbing pain.

"One last chance, then. Because I am in a good mood." And he pushed his full glass along the counter. "Here, to help with the pain. We'll be waiting." The stranger stood and leaned in, planting a long kiss on Jwali's cheek. His warm breath, beery and sweet, ghosted over Jwali's skin as his thumb dug viciously into the wound. Then the stranger was gone, leaving the *Ava*'s navigator white with pain and shaking with fear.

"Blessed Mother," Zarr yelled, clutching his bag close to his chest. "Has everyone decided to leave at the same time?"

Ori grabbed at the boy to steer him against the protection of a wall as the crowd pushed and shoved in desperation, only to have him flinch away from her. The Neuvo Dacilo shuttle terminal reverberated with yelling, arguing, protesting, crying voices. Families huddled together, bewildered children clutching favorite toys, while their parents stared at the flashing holo-screens projected in the too-warm air above the crowd. Clearly the climate controls were struggling.

"I'm fine," he said, angrily, evading her attempts to prevent him being crushed. "I can take care of myself." All she could do was nod mutely. What had gone wrong? He would not look at her, had barely spoken more than a few words, and most distressing of all, avoided any physical contact. Unable to process the pain this caused her, Ori led him to the only safety she could find, a tiny space between a support column and an overflowing waste bin. Zarr screwed up his face in disgust.

"Gah, this place stinks. Couldn't we have found a better place to wait? I hope Davey and Lart get here soon, so I can get out of here."

Ori make a show of using her sheet, although she had sent their location to Lart minutes before via the Neuvo Dacilo Port AI. Zarr ignored her.

"They are on their way; movement through the terminal is nearly impossible," she said, deactivating the sheet and stowing it in her bag. "Let us hope that the shuttle to the dock is less chaotic."

Zarr shrugged, dismissing her concerns.

Despite the increased patrols and the harsh curfews, the Corelli government still struggled to calm the situation. Images of the riots filled every news feed, accompanied by increasingly inflammatory commentary. Ori had given up counting how many times she had seen the chained woman fall, blood spraying out across the crowd, or the heavily censored image of a body, the orange overalls dark with blood, swaying gently from the branch of one of the spreading street trees.

Long live Emperor D'e. Drunken stupidity or something else? Whether the dead man had been part of some underground movement as some of the feeds were implying, or merely a fool, the lesson was plain. If anyone found out what she was, lynching would be the best she could expect.

"Davey's here," Zarr called, without turning around.

Davey emerged from the crowd sweaty and red-faced. "Blessed fucking Mother," he cursed, loud enough to draw disapproving glares from a few bystanders. "It's fucking chaos. Is everyone leaving Corelli?" He dumped his bag at his feet, pushing Zarr's toward the waste bin and its noisome contents.

"Yeah, that's what I said." Zarr hastily retrieved his bag before Davey could kick it any further. "Have you seen the old man?"

Ori didn't bother removing her focus from her scanning of the holo-boards. "Davey, leave him alone," she commanded. Davey froze in the act of nudging Zarr into the column. "Why you pair cannot stand still and be quiet for a few minutes is beyond me," Ori said with a manufactured sigh, in an attempt to coax the boy out.

"Sorry, Ori," Davey muttered. Zarr crossed his arms and ignored her.

To one side, a well-dressed man berated a terminal employee in High Polini, punctuating the smooth, round language with increasingly hard jabs with his fingers at the unfortunate worker's chest.

"Poor bugger," Davey's voice slammed into her ear. "Doesn't he realize the man can't understand a word he's saying?" He gestured at the two in disgust.

"He's asking about his family, they were supposed to meet him here, but he can't find them. He's terrified they're lost," said Zarr.

"I didn't know you spoke Polini," she said.

"Six Jump Port Authority entrance exams," the boy said, flatly. "Standard, Formal, and Polini are taught out here, you know."

"Yeah," said Davey, once again nudging Zarr roughly, "but not much use on a freighter." Ori's upraised eyebrow was sufficient warning, Davey took a step back. "Hey, has anyone see Jwali?" Davey said, attempting to divert her anger. The cargo hand craned his neck, trying to see over the ocean of heads. Holo-screens flashed on and off above them, with lines of ships and boarding gates.

"Jwali's taken the earlier shuttle," Lart said, appearing out of the crowd and waving his sheet for emphasis, "he messaged me earlier."

"Probably couldn't bear to be seen with us," muttered Zarr, stretching. "Have to be grateful for small blessings."

Ori pointed across the concourse. "Our gate's this way."

The corridors leading to the space dock shuttles were almost silent; everyone they passed kept their heads down and conversed in whispers. Davey looked confused when Zarr maintained an excessive and obvious distance, but said nothing. Even the usually loud red head was quiet, affected by the tension.

Unlike the small and utilitarian craft used to move crews from planet side to their ships in orbit, the shuttles running between the enormous space docks and orbitals above Corelli and the planet's surface could carry up to two hundred passengers, in something closely resembling comfort. Their trip down had been noisy, with Davey and Zarr tormenting each other, and everyone else. Now they all filed on silently, the boy taking a seat as far away from her as possible. Everyone stowed their bags and took a seat.

"I'm telling you," Davey whispered savagely, "we're gonna hit Ma'al and suddenly there'll be only half pay, or no pay at all. Does she think we're stupid, that we — OW!"

The red-headed boy's diatribe was cut short by Lart's fist. "Don't talk like that about the captain." Lart raised his hand again, only to find his intended blow intercepted.

"Once is enough, Lart," Ori said, releasing the old man, who rubbed at his wrist, "and you are quick to criticize others when it suits you."

Lart hunched back in his seat, scowling. Next to him, Davey sent her a grateful smile. Ori ignored both men, her attention focused on Zarr, who continued to ignore everyone and everything around him. The shuttle continued its smooth climb out of Corelli's atmosphere to the orbiting space dock where the *Ava* lay.

By her calculations, the cylinders should have arrived by the time the shuttle docked. At first, Van was ecstatic at the news that she had "acquired" the vital parts, but became less enthusiastic as Ori laid out the somewhat convoluted story that accompanied it. Lying was not something that came easily to him, he said. Lying to Marissa was doubly problematic.

The captain had known him long enough to know he didn't have that sort of credit lying around.

"Why can't you tell her you bought them. You're an unknown. She'll accept that from you more easily than some convoluted story about a mate owing me a favor," he'd said, his image filling the entirety of the sheet. "And forget the cylinders for the moment; are you OK? Davey says Zarr told him you'd been injured in the riot. Davey said he wouldn't tell him anything else."

"He exaggerates," she'd told Van. "There was a minor disturbance, local law enforcement overreacted. We got caught in the crowd, and I was injured. Accidentally. That was all." She'd left the dressing on until the next day, just to be sure, but the nanites appeared to be working, and not a mark remained of the seven-centimeter-long knife wound that nearly killed her. The neuro-chemical systems were another issue altogether. Despite her constant prodding, they refused to work. Diagnostics insisted that everything was working as expected.

"You OK?" Davey whispered, looking between her and an isolated Zarr.

"I'm fine," Ori answered, relieved when the shuttle lurched slightly then connected with the docking port. There was the usual scuffle for bags and personal belongings as the hatch spiraled open. Corelli's main space dock stank, full of the reek of humanity with a hefty mix of engine coolant, the cheap fragrance of cleaning chemicals, and food. Everyone crowded into the airlock and waited for the hatch to open as it cycled through.

"Thank the Blessed Mother we're back in civilization," muttered Lart. "If I ever see Corelli dirtside again, it'll be too soon."

The hatch opened.

"Hey look," said Zarr, with a deadpan expression, "it's Van."

Van scratched absently at the implant, then stopped, and then couldn't decide what to do with his hands. Damned if he was going to squash them into his pockets like Zarr. As the slight shudder of the shuttle docking ran through the deck, he decided on crossing them in front of him. Too bad if it made him look cranky.

The airlock cycled open and the stream of passengers flowed through. Ori's pale hair, half a head above the tallest passengers, was one of the last to come through. What was wrong with Zarr? The boy pushed past everyone with a face like he'd eaten something rotten.

"I thought I'd come and check you all came back," he said, "thought you might like Corelli."

"Yeah, of course, they're only hanging off-worlders from trees. Lovely place." Lart hoisted his bag over his shoulder.

"It is good to be back," Ori answered, dropping her bag on the deck, her gaze fixed on Zarr. "Corelli was not pleasant, and I suspect the situation there will get steadily worse."

"Wait," Van called out, as Lart and Davey began to head off toward the *Ava*. "I. Well I have some bad news."

"The cylinders are not here?"

"Yes, they're here, arrived a few hours ago. It's not the cylinders." Each one of his crewmates looked at him with fear. "I heard from a mate of mine, it's not general knowledge yet."

"What? What isn't?"

"There's a rumor going about that Ma'al is shutting the border. No one is getting in. Or out."

Nine

Keren had a head full of questions and no plan when he turned up at the Hanjile Eidress offices, bags in hand, and wearing the indigo silk suit. The luxurious seating and cool, scented air of the foyer was a welcome balm after the violence and terror of the last two days. A young man, his dark green jacket adorned with a narrow strip of gold, brought him refreshments and informed him Saliri Irinis would see him soon.

"Thank you, Eidress," said Keren, using one of the few phrases of Formal Ma'ali he knew. The young man smiled and bowed.

"Have you been on Corelli long?" Keren switched back to Standard, having exhausted his repertoire. The Ma'ali language, like everything else, was a construct, a long-forgotten dialect studied only by a handful of academics before Piali Eidress decided to resurrect it. The Formal dialect had a much-deserved reputation for being difficult to learn and few bothered beyond a couple of stock phrases.

"Nearly six months, sir Casar," he replied, the distinctive Ma'ali accent imbuing the flat tones of Standard with a charming musical quality. "It is an honor to serve."

Irinis appeared, just as Keren was debating which of the superb pastries he would try next. *They probably have their own pastry chef.* He brushed the crumbs from the dark silk and followed the steady swing of midnight plait and its freight of Polini silver.

"I confess I am a little surprised to see you so soon, sir Casar. Did you not find your patient?" Irinis ushered him into her office, the door sliding closed behind him.

"Please, call me Keren." Keren slumped into the embrace of the well-padded chair and restrained a sigh. "Yes. I found her; thankfully in time. She'd been—" He was about to say *knifed in the back* but pulled back in time. "She was injured in the disturbance."

Irinis took her seat behind the beautiful desk. "The riots, you mean. I trust she will recover?"

Keren shrugged, a gesture of acknowledgment and despair. It had been more than a riot. For a few days Corelli had teetered on anarchy.

"It was a minor injury, thank you for your concern. Now, if I was given to pessimism, the incident outside of the palace, and now this, on an otherwise peaceful world, might lead me to think the Republic is falling apart." The levity he was reaching for fell flat.

"That is not pessimism, merely an acute awareness that perhaps it is not falling apart, but it is beginning to unravel." Irinis regarded him over steepled fingers, her blue eyes cool and appraising. "I believe you have found your patient; she is well it seems. So, what else can Hanjile Eidress do for a son of Sylvie Casar?"

"I need a visa. I want to go to Ma'al."

Jwali limped down the walkway to the unused maintenance locker. The *Ava* was strangely silent, locked in the docking cradle. The squeal of the door was unnaturally loud in the cavernous cargo hold, and Jwali peered around nervously, alert for any of the crew. When he was sure no spies lurked in the gloom, he moved the box of junk on the middle shelf, and pulled open the false compartment. The tiny flask, barely larger than his hand, unscrewed smoothly and he transferred the sliver of foil from the concealed pocket in his overalls.

That done, he replaced the flask into its hiding spot and positioned the box of junk. *There, now that's taken care of I can turn my attention to that whore.*

Firstly, though, he had to take care of his leg. He couldn't go to the infirmary, fucking Lianna or Marissa would want to know how he was injured, and Lianna would want to take it to the authorities or make a fuss, and Jwali didn't want that.

He shrugged out of his overalls and slowly peeled back the makeshift dressing. The bleeding had stopped, finally, but it looked inflamed, and when he touched it, pain shot up his leg. The ship's only medi-repair unit was kept in a locked cabinet, but Jwali had worked out the codes years ago; his aunt was so blasé about security if it didn't concern her. He'd also lifted a supply of pain patches and dressings.

Destruction of diseased cells and regeneration of new ones was not a painless exercise; even with two patches Jwali still cursed as the beam touched the wound. Designed to treat only minor injuries, it took several passes before the flesh sealed, leaving a thin line of red scar tissue.

The hard line of the railing pressed into his back as he collapsed, white and shaking with relief. Slowly the pain ebbed away, leaving him free to decide his next move. The bitch wasn't afraid of him, that was the problem. His usual methods wouldn't work. Oh, he might force her but Jwali knew the moment his back was turned she'd kill him, damn the consequences. No, the way to get to her was through someone else, someone she cared about. Van was a possibility, but the new implant seemed to be working, so the usual play of alcohol, then drugs, then blackmail, wouldn't work. Now the engineer had somehow produced the missing cylinders and couldn't be touched.

That left Zarr.

That should be easy. Get him back on the floess, rough him up a bit, have a little fun and watch him run whining to his protector. If he was really lucky, the stupid whore would put up a fight, and he could watch them beat the shit out of her, before dragging her off in chains.

As he shrugged back into his overalls, Jwali contemplated taking a small hit from his stash, just to take the edge off, then decided against it. He'd need all of it to thoroughly fuck up the boy.

Ten

Keren hadn't intended to return to the elegant offices of Hanjile Eidress, but once back in his room, with its lumpy mattress, he wondered what to do next. Ori was safe, at least, and if all went well, on her way to Ma'al. The sensible course was to return home. He had his career, his apartment. But the enigma surrounding Ori continued to haunt him. Why Ma'al?

He'd met Rossim a few times, the first at one of Sylvie's weddings. His mother married and divorced regularly. Seilis, on one of the handful of occasions when they had had a normal conversation, ventured the idea that Sylvie used her constant stream of weddings, parties and other manufactured events to keep herself in the public's imagination.

Uncle Betan had appeared out of nowhere and introduced Keren to Rossim as "one of Sylvie's more sensible children". Rossim had made some crude remark about one of the guests and Keren formed an immediate and deep loathing of the man, unsurprised to discover Rossim and Betan Casar were allies. Both were rapacious, self-centered and cruel, and by all accounts the long-dead and unlamented Lord President Garrett had been worse.

Rossim was plotting something, that much Keren was sure of, and knowing him, it could only be to the detriment of Ma'al and Ori. After only a few seconds of indecision, he'd packed his bag, checked out and found himself on the doorstep once more of the offices of Hanjile Eidress.

"Madam Sylvie wants you to return home. Immediately." To anyone who might be watching the feed on a twenty-hour delay from Central, Maridel appeared completely at ease and non-committal. Keren harbored no such illusions; the possibility was quite high that the Directorate was monitoring this conversation.

"However, she is aware that current conditions make this difficult," continued Maridel, "and your mother understands how much you need to return to your work."

Keren doubted that his mother had ever thought that, let alone expressed it out loud. As he leaned back in his chair, he caught Irinis's eye. One immaculate eyebrow arched in amusement, leaving Keren struggling to maintain his composure. Ask anyone in the Republic, and the general consensus was that Ma'al society was humorless and repressive, hardly surprising given the colony's founding principles of Duty, Honor and Obedience.

"I then informed her of the invitation. She is very proud that a Casar has been given such an honor," Maridel continued.

By the Blessed Mother he's a good actor. No wonder he can handle Sylvie.

That Maridel and Irinis were willing to organize the invitation at all was a miracle. It should have been impossible. For months the news feeds had been full of sorrowful stories of family and friends separated by Ma'al's tightening of its entry requirements. Even those living on Ma'al in the sprawling section known as the Enclave were reluctant to leave, afraid they might not be able to return. There had been demonstrations and outbreaks of violence. Yet here he was, granted a visa in under an hour.

"Therefore, Madam Sylvie is sending one of the yachts, something appropriate for such an honor. Of course, she will ensure it has everything you might need during your conference."

Keren swore Maridel's mouth crinkled slightly at that. Knowing Sylvie, she would send the most impressive of the Casar family ships, every state room overflowing with the most exquisite items. The ship would come with a full crew, but sadly, due to Ma'al's strict entry requirements, only Keren himself would be granted entry to the planet. Maridel looked suitably mournful as he conveyed this information to Keren and whoever might be eavesdropping. Maridel expressed his regret, but the Ma'al government was exceedingly clear on this point, however, he assured Keren he would be well looked after.

The call finished with non-committal pleasantries. Keren killed the feed and the screen slid soundlessly back into its recess. Master Irinis turned away from the window, for a second evoking a striking similarity to Ori that discomfited him for some reason.

"Thank you again, Saliri Irinis, for your assistance," Keren said, bowing formally. Irinis returned the gesture.

Irinis waited until the door slid shut before settling herself in her chair and activating the screen. A few seconds later it brightened, and Maridel's image appeared.

"Master Irinis, I am honored." He made the required genuflection, Irinis nodded in acknowledgment.

The link between the Hanjile Eidress offices on Corelli, and an identical office on Central was seamless and lag-free. Ma'al could not run a trading empire or conduct its legal activities with communication delays of over twenty hours. The technology, obtained from the Xi at an extraordinary price, was not available to anyone else in the Republic.

"He seems like an honorable man," she began without preamble.

Maridel frowned. "He is. Unlike the rest of his family."

"I have sent you Keren's message. There is no reason why you should have to wait sixteen hours to read it, just ensure the lag time is correct before replying." Irinis felt nothing but relief when Maridel showed no resentment at being reminded of such basic information. Some of the younger members of her hanjile could learn to emulate Maridel's equanimity. Then again, that quality was precisely why he'd been placed with Sylvie Casar.

Irinis rested her chin on her steepled fingers. "Lord Eidress is concerned. He believes Karis is deliberately inflaming tensions both in the Enclave and among ourselves, and using that as a pretext to bring in yet more off-world security personnel. Do not share this information, but I strongly suspect pressure is being applied to some hanjile heads to support Karis's ambitions. He isn't clever enough to pull off something of this magnitude; he's getting help from somewhere, and our suspicions lay firmly with Rossim and Betan Casar."

"And you think Keren is part of it?"

"I don't know. Whatever he is mixed up in could have nothing to do with this, but I am not convinced. Why does he suddenly want to go to Ma'al? And who is this woman? We have conducted a thorough analysis of her ID and she is not from Orchetti. All the information we have on her is constructed. So why was she a prisoner and who was Keren really working for? And why is he so keen to assist her?"

"The woman is attractive, I gather. It could simply be that. A pretty face has overturned more than one sensible man or woman before. Tylis Mathani being a case in point."

"The council made her Head of All because they feared ever more power concentrating in either our hanjile or Ansissi-Kai. Under normal circumstances her weakness would not be an issue, but now she has fallen into Karis's clutches, the danger grows increasingly greater. It is more serious than one woman's choice of bed mates."

Maridel took the reprimand in his stride. "My apologies, Master Irinis."

Irinis waved irritably. "No, I did not intend that to be so harsh. The situation is very concerning, and Lord Eidress requires all of us to serve to our utmost extent. Karis Samara is gaining too much power far too quickly, and these constant 'security' issues in the Enclave are making things worse. The latest edict is a case in point. The Republic resent us enough now, why inflame the situation further?"

"Then how can I assist?"

"We placed you with that bitch, Sylvie, for a reason. Although she has all the intelligence of a Nian slug, her social cachet opens doors everywhere. Doors that remain closed to us. Stay close to her, monitor events in the capital. Send me every piece of information you gather, no matter how trivial."

"It is an honor to serve."

"Take care, Maridel, if Rossim or the Directorate suspect you, you will be in great danger."

"I will, Master Irinis. Duty, Honor, Obedience."

"Duty, Honor, Obedience," echoed Irinis.

Eleven

The Hubnae representative rumbled across the floor of the Nest, the six stump-like legs imparting an undulating motion to its progress. In the light of the central shaft, the many gems set into the thick hide winked and glittered.

The Matriarch watched it approach with weary patience. The Hubnae could not be hurried or coerced, or chivvied into anything; from the most trivial decisions to the weightiest matters of state, they took their own sweet time about it.

Finally, it reached its intended destination and half curled into a sitting position. Its eyes, an unrelieved black, fixed on the Xi with unblinking intensity.

"Having fun?" it rumbled. The Hubnae were neither male nor female, or both, depending on how one defined such things, and where in the life cycle an individual was.

The Matriarch pushed down the impulse to reply with an obscenity, choosing rather to sigh almost theatrically. "We were provoked. You know how the Meians are. Annoying insects." She added an extravagant gesture with one foreleg, an action far more obscene than mere words.

A deep rumble, the Hubnae equivalent of laughter spread across the chamber startling a pod of youngsters. "They are young, they will grow out of such behavior in a few more millennia. And the report I heard, points to you being more than a little provocative yourself. Decapitation and then feeding the body to the children is a little extreme," said the Hubnae, but without rancor. The Xi and Hubnae ruled multiple galaxies while waiting for multicellular life to crawl out of the mud. The Meians were a recent addition to their alliance, with only a hundred thousand years of advanced civilization under their metallic carapaces.

The Xi gestured with her naked palps, the equivalent of a shrug in her culture, since she lacked shoulders. The Hubnae representative rumbled in a deep basso, its bulbous proboscis pulsating.

"Can we get to the nub of the matter," it asked, scratching its flank absently. "This game you are playing with the alien. We still cannot see the logic of it or indeed the need, but if you are determined, then we will not stop you. Nor," it interrupted as the Matriarch moved to speak, "will we assist. Your pet cost the lives of many of my fellows, friends, and clan too. So long as you do not annoy the Meians anymore, we will not interfere."

The Hubnae response wasn't surprising. The slug-like race put clan, kin and friendship above all, and could not be blamed for not wanting to have anything to do with the alien who had slaughtered indiscriminately in her attempts to escape. In truth, there were many Nest mates who held similar views; the incineration of an entire nursery could not simply be forgotten. Was the death of a thousand infants worth it to save three hundred trillion? Opinions for or against depended on whether the lives in question were Xi or human.

"We understand your feelings on this. We too suffered from her rage. We will make amends to the Meians, but we still maintain it is possible to save the humans. We just need the right circumstances, and a little luck. We survived, and rose above our base natures. The humanoid races can as well, if they are given time."

The Hubnae huffed mournfully. "You know our views on this. We should let events unfold. There will be other humans you can coddle in other sectors of the galaxy, after these are gone."

Coddle? Does it think we do this out of sentiment? Losing her temper would be unwise.

The Hubnae uncoiled itself, rising up on its hind legs, the entire bulk of the massive body supported without visible effort, to look the Matriarch directly in the face. "We remind you that although we have no issue with you amusing yourself with this creature, we will not tolerate further breaches of the pact. If you are planning any other activities, then we advise you, most strongly, to stop. Unless you wish to make us an enemy." It stayed there for a moment, silent, watching her reaction, before coiling itself back down.

The Matriarch did not experience the same physiological reactions to fear as the humans, but that did not mean she didn't feel it. Her two vestigial limbs quivered, a drumming of anxiety against her abdomen, and she had to fight the ancient desire to run. "The Nest understands," she said, forcing her palps into a gesture of acceptance. "We championed this pact. We will adhere to it." Could the Hubnae tell that she was lying? Its black eyes betrayed no emotion at all. "Very well. What do we have to do to end this current scuffle with our allies?"

Twelve

Imsu Pesek left the warmth of the little rental car, pulling his coat tighter against the cold. Mid-winter on Central was a miserable affair, a mix of snow, sleet and strong winds driving anyone who could leave out of the capital and onto warmer climes.

Those left behind did their best to stay indoors, only venturing out in heated garments, or if rich enough, in silk-blend clothes. Today Imsu was neither indoors nor blessed with silk undergarments to keep him warm. The heated coat helped a little, but the wind whipping around the old house threatened to bowl him over with every frigid gust.

He clutched the small case tighter and made his way through the undergrowth to the side path. Since his last visit rain and snow had beaten the dry grass down, drifts of yesterday's snowfall still lingered in shady areas, while windblown debris piled up along the fence line. Sadly, the old atoria tree hadn't survived the winter storms, its massive roots now exposed to the elements, the trunk half buried in the muddy ground. Pesek didn't consider himself sentimental, but the sight of the downed tree, the smashed limbs spread across the dead grass, seemed especially poignant, a metaphor for the current state of the Republic.

Rossim is spiraling into megalomania and he will take all of us, and the Republic down with him. We should be reaching out to Ma'al and all the disaffected, bringing them back to the common goal of solidarity.

The scenes coming out of Corelli were especially heartbreaking. Each day thousands of people were fleeing back to their homeworlds, stripping Corelli of a substantial section of its workforce. The Senate, in its inimitable way, made soothing pronouncements, but behind closed doors the fault lines were growing, between those wanting tougher rule and those suggesting a more peaceful approach. No prizes for guessing which view Rossim and that loathsome toad Betan Casar subscribed to. Perhaps it was time to push back against Rossim; the Lord President's plan was madness. It was treason. Career, advancement, privilege — were they worth this?

Among all this uncertainty Imsu had this puzzle to decipher — what had gone on at this isolated house? The damaged sheet yielded nothing more than half a message, a few lines detailing abuses of the guards against the prisoner. Those few lines left him nauseous.

To that end, he risked jail, the end of his career and disgrace for himself and his family, by breaking some of the Republic's most severe laws: the use of genetic profiling.

The case, no larger than his sheet, weighed in his hand as he slipped along the side wall. The rear remained untouched from his previous visit, except now one of the chairs lay on its side, no doubt a casualty of the wind. Although the door still hung forlornly, squeaking in the gusts, the hall was warmer than outside. Pesek set the case down and touched the lock, the case springing open. He retrieved the analysis tool, which lay cool and heavy in his hand.

A squall hit, sending freezing sprays of rainwater through the doorway; in the wind the door squealed louder. The spray of blood still painted the wall, the bullet holes punctuation points across the ancient plaster.

Was he really going to do this?

Despite all the laws surrounding genetic engineering, there were still loopholes. Fleet personnel had their genetic profiles recorded, in the event of death. As did all members of the Imperial Guard and many planetary law enforcement agencies; quasi-private security firms also kept such records. Everyone pretended it didn't happen, so long as no scandal erupted.

The average Republican citizen universally condemned the practice, at least publicly; the war still evoked strong emotions, the riots on Corelli were proof of that. Imsu would be beyond naive if he believed he could simply identify the individuals here and then bring them to justice.

He pressed the start button and a green light sprang out from the tool's end. The instructions said pass the ray slowly and evenly over the sample. He worked his way up and down the walls and along the floor, sweeping the light back and forth as steadily as his shaking hands would allow.

The door squealed again and Imsu froze, unsure. For a second he thought he'd heard something else, another sound under the tortured door and the wind. Slowly he slid his weapon from its holster and laid down the analyzer. Seconds passed. Icy tendrils of fear, colder than the storm outside coiled in his stomach. Another moment passed. Nothing.

"It's only the wind," he muttered to himself, picking up the analyzer again and holstering his weapon. He decided the mess had too much rotting food to bother testing, so he made his way down the hallway to the room with the dead bot. The green light played over the worn matting, across the battered machine and then the heavy ring of bars. Finally, it beeped, the signal that the analysis was completed. He drew out his sheet, thumbed it to active and tapped the analyzer onto the input node. His sheet emitted a rising crescendo of tones and the information downloaded.

A loud crash from inside the house startled him and he cursed, nearly dropping the sheet.

It's just the storm. A tree branch hit the roof, or a window.

Imsu laid the sheet down carefully and removed his weapon from its holster. He crept along the hallway to the empty, untouched bunk room where the blankets sprouted green mold. To the mess, where the discarded meals were reduced to unidentifiable lumps on plates thick with dust. The infirmary was empty, so too the medic's quarters.

That left the cell. His palms were slick on the weapon's grip, his fingers flexed, seized with sudden cramp. Now he was regretting not keeping up with his field training.

The green hallway, with the lone door at the end, was deserted. Whatever had caused the crash was not evident, and that began to worry Imsu. He knew, from his reconnoiter of the exterior, that all the windows were boarded up.

The cell door was closed. Had he left it like that?

At least his hands weren't shaking as he reached for the handle, grasping it firmly and flinging the cell door open. The cell was empty. His shoulders sagged in relief. It must have been the wind, blowing a branch or some other piece of storm-tossed debris onto the roof.

By the time he returned to where he'd left the analyzer, his heartbeat had returned to normal and the data transfer was complete. Imsu stared at the information in confusion. Twenty-three names scrolled across his sheet. All of them Imperial Guard. All of them recorded as either dead, or in prison. None of them were supposed to be on Central, let alone here, in this secret prison. And who were they guarding? The sheet began a loud, urgent beeping.

"Blessed Mother," he breathed, in shock. Now he had his answer, now he knew who, no — what, Rossim was hiding.

Warning. Engineered Organism Detected

His legs refused to hold him up and he slid down the pock-marked wall in a heap.

Warning. Engineered Organism Detected the sheet continued to inform him, the flashing, strident red burning itself into his mind. His shaking hands found the control node, and turned it off. He had to get out of here, he had to get to back to the capital and warn the Republic. Rossim was hiding an Abomination. It was beyond treason; this was a violation of the Republic's most sacred taboo. All this time, had he played them all for fools? Was Rossim's strident condemnation merely an elaborate charade while he hid the Republic's enemy in their midst? This would destroy the government.

Pesek pulled himself to his feet, swallowing his nausea. Using the wall as support, he staggered along the hallway. The ruined door squeaked in the rising wind, rain gusting through the open doorway in freezing sprays. He put his hand out to steady himself, the floor treacherously slippery under his feet.

The bullet smashed into the frame, showering Imsu with splinters. He flattened himself against the wall, his weapon drawn. Outside, the light was failing, a heavy gloom settling over the landscape, the dark line of trees merging into the lowering clouds. Silhouetted against the doorway, he would be an easy target. Another round whizzed past, embedding itself in the wall further down the hall. He should have brought more weapons. He could have brought a handful of proximity mines, scattered them across the ground. But he was a bureaucrat with a few months of weapons training, not a field agent. His expertise was political assassination, not actual killing.

The rain became heavier, pelting down with a ferocity that obscured everything. He had to get to the vehicle. But whoever was out there was probably a professional. They would know Imsu would go for the car. Staking it out, and waiting for him to make a run for it would be the logical action.

Imsu leaned back against the wall and thought through his options. There were no other exits from the house, and he had only one weapon. Running for the car was suicide. But it was dark, and getting darker; the rain reduced visibility even further and would mask most sounds. If he could reach the line of trees, lose his attacker there, and head for the main road, maybe he could get help? Or at least get to somewhere with people. Surely, they wouldn't shoot him in front of witnesses? Imsu dragged his coat higher to obscure his face and slowly edged around the door. No bullets came flying out of the rain, no assailant leaped on him. Hunkering over, to make as small a target as possible, Imsu muttered a small prayer to the Blessed Mother, and made a run for it.

He nearly tripped over the upturned chair in the dark, its leg catching and ripping his trousers. Cursing himself under his breath, Imsu kept going, jumping the two steps down to the overgrown and sodden lawn, his attention split between the line of trees in front of him and trying to see if anyone was behind him. Freezing rain sluiced off his head and down his neck, soaking him under the coat. His shoes weren't made for cross country running, especially not in a swamp. He lost track of how many times he stumbled and fell. Fear kept him going, anticipation of that one shot that would tear through coat and skin and lungs kept him running, half bent over, his breath catching in his chest. The trees were closer, much closer, a line of giants looming up out of the rain. The ground under him abruptly changed, going from wet grass to churned, muddy soil. Imsu staggered and fell, face-down into the mud, his weapon flying from his hand into oblivion.

"I'd stay down there," came a voice. "No need to run anymore."

Imsu pushed up and rolled over. No way was he dying shot in the back, like a coward. All he could see was an indistinct figure against a somber, rain-soaked background. But he knew that voice.

"I know you," he said, trying to feel around for something, anything he could use as a weapon, and encountering only mud, and freezing slush. His assassin stepped closer, resolving out of the rain as a medium height man, dressed for this weather and carrying a large, black handgun, one of the new silk/graphene composites.

"Finn. You're Hirio Finn. You used to work for the Directorate," Imsu said, incredulously. "I thought you went to work for Fared Babima."

Finn squatted down, until he was at eye level. His weapon never wavered though, remaining fixed on Imsu.

"Yes, I did. Now it is Jak Reinnor."

"But..." Imsu struggled up to a sitting position. "That's Xi Liaison. It's a ridiculous diplomatic post. What are you— You know, don't you?"

"I'm just here to do my job. Don't make it harder than it needs to be."

"How could you? How could you betray the Republic like this? We fought a war, billions died to wipe them out and you're here protecting one?"

Finn's expression shifted from impassive to annoyed. "Protecting what?"

"This." Imsu tore the sheet from his coat pocket, uncaring if Finn saw it as a threat, and tossed it across the mud to land at the other man's feet. "Turn it on. See what I found. I know what has been going on here."

Imsu watched as Finn thumbed the sheet to active, while never letting his attention drift from his quarry. In the gloom the flashing warning cast a surreal red glow over Finn's face.

"No," the man said, rising and dropping the sheet to the ground as it continued its endless cry of betrayal. **Warning. Engineered Organism Detected.** "This isn't right. This is some ploy, some trick."

"I took an analyzer from storage. I found twenty-three individuals who should be dead, or in prison, and that—" Imsu pointed at the sheet. "Whoever you're working for has betrayed the Republic, betrayed us all. What are you going to do about it?"

The shot was shockingly loud. Finn holstered his weapon, and picked up the sheet, thumbing it off. "My job," he said to the rain.

Thirteen

"This is your fucking fault, Zarr," Davey yelled, his face scarlet with rage. "What the fuck did you do to her down on fucking Corelli? Since we got back, she's been impossible to work with."

Zarr, trapped between Dave's anger and the starboard cargo bay bulkhead, had thought it would be a relief not to share a shift with her. It. Ori. But as usual everything had gone to shit, yet again.

"She fucking threatened to throw me over the railings! She's insane." After giving Zarr one more push, Davey spun away, his hands flinging out in frustration and rage. Zarr took the opportunity to get some clear space behind himself in case he had to make a run for it.

Zarr tried his most placatory tone. "Corelli was bad for everyone, Davey. At least you weren't in a riot." Davey and Lart had been in a bar over the other side of Neuvo Dacilo when the troubles started, and watched the entire disaster unfold on the bar's screens.

Davey marched straight up to him, and stabbed his finger into Zarr's chest. "This," Davey said, through clenched teeth, punctuating every word with another driving stab, "is your fault."

Zarr watched Davey stomp away, sending the walkway shuddering in sympathy. In the twisted logic that was the universe, it was indeed his fault. It had been a total fuck-up to give Ori the cold shoulder so publicly. Everyone had noticed; Lianna had made an acidic remark about playmates having a tiff. Only Van hadn't said a thing, but Zarr caught his glance; confused and then annoyed.

Davey's furious footsteps receded into the background noise of the bay. Zarr shoved his hands deep into his pockets, cursed, took them out and then tucked them under his arms. He had no idea what to do. Since returning to the Ava, the outraged certainty of Corelli had drained away minute by minute. Sometimes he thought he'd dreamed it all, that entire scene in the medical center. But then he remembered Ori and the medic discussing nanites, and sub-dermal armor and systems like they were chatting about the latest e-feed. He'd very carefully asked the AI about "sub-dermal armor"; the results had terrified him all over again. It seemed that prior to the war, heaps of people were working on this reactive mesh, modeled on some shit called "engineered graphene" that sat under the skin and would protect the wearer from things like — oh, I don't know — knife attacks.

But. And this is where it all fell apart. She was still Ori. Angrier, yes. But he would be too if his friend had suddenly started avoiding him.

Friend. She had never hurt him, or Van. Or Jen. And he'd felt like an absolute dick sitting at another table, leaving her all alone. All the stories he'd grown up on about the evil Abominations seemed like far-fetched fantasies against the reality of knowing one. She still cried in her sleep, and ate Orchetti chips without farei, and hated inefficiency and dirt ...

Zarr slid down to the deck, trying to hold back the tears.

"Well, look who's sniveling in the corner like a little bitch. Lost your little friend?"

Zarr wiped his nose on his sleeve and stood up slowly. At the end of the walkway Jwali lounged against the hatchway, an evil grin plastered across his narrow face.

"Don't worry. I'll play with you."

Ori slammed the hatch behind her with a crash that reverberated through the entire section, dislodging a shower of dust from the overhead.

"Stupid eijen," she screamed into the silent prayer room. "Stupid, lazy ..." She screamed again, incoherent with rage and fear and a good handful of other emotions she couldn't identify, and lashed out at one of the seats. Its support buckled under the impact.

Ori collapsed onto the deck, her entire body shaking under the emotional onslaught. Six days since the *Ava* jumped out of Corelli space, and there was no sign of her systems coming back online, no matter what she did. Diagnostics continuously looped through the menus and reported everything was operational. Except nothing was operational. Nearly a week of having to deal with normal, unenhanced vision, no neural computing power.

No neuro-suppressors.

Without them the dam that held back her emotions had disappeared and she spent every waking moment in a maelstrom of rage, fear, and despair. After only one shift with Davey, she wanted to ram his skull into the nearest bulkhead.

Sometimes it would catch her unawares, like a sudden attack, or an ambush. She'd be engrossed in some menial task when the glimmer of light on a bulkhead or the sound of a distant engine made her turn. And in that moment, she was paralyzed, overwhelmed by an emotion so profound that words couldn't begin to capture it. Pain was too small a word, grief too insignificant. The loss of her siblings, the purpose that once guided her, the home she had known — all gone. And there was no way for her to go back, to reclaim what was lost.

What if they never come back?

Overwhelmed, Ori curled herself tightly into a defensive ball, the deck's cold seeping through her thin overalls. It wasn't only the loss of her systems, she finally admitted to herself. It was Zarr. Six days and he'd barely said a word to her. Oh, he did his job — with a ruthless precision she had never seen in him before — but he sat at another table in the mess and never spoke to her unless necessary.

She missed him.

She missed Zarr.

His awkward ears, his tuneless whistling, his damned hands always stuffed into his damned pockets. Calling her commander. That infuriating grin.

How? How had this happened? She had never been close to anyone. Not since Tszcienna. Not any of her Line siblings, not any other Line, either. Pleasure yes, but not this. Not this terrible pain that wouldn't go away.

And now she had to face the truth. He knew. Somehow, he'd worked out what she was, that was the only explanation. How, she had no idea, but she had to face the real possibility that they would come for her at Tersen.

Slowly she dragged herself up and around, hugging her knees as she stared into the flickering holo-flames and tried to will the tremors to stop. No interface. No Zarr. She would never get to Ma'al, she would never find out the truth. That lying, duplicitous scum, Reinnor, would never get his answers. She would die, either on Xia or in front of a firing squad on Central.

Rossim had won.

She had failed. She had been mere weeks from escape and had allowed herself to think of these animals as human — worse, as companions, as equals.

The hatch swung open and she turned away, in case it was Zarr, or worse still, Jwali. Van lowered himself down beside her. "Are you OK?"

"I don't know what happened," she lied, wiping away the tears. "I felt dizzy."

It was a pathetic lie, and she braced herself for Van's derision, but the engineer shook his head, and slid his arm around her. It was so easy to let go and lean against him.

"It's Corelli," he said, as if that explained everything. "Nothing's been the same since then." His arm encircled her, the warmth of his body pressed against hers.

The air felt charged, full of suppressed emotions and hidden meanings.

"Ori," he said quietly.

Even if he was not eijen, she could not. She should not, but a long-suppressed fire raged in her, and her body leaped in response. His hands guided her body astride his, her fingertips tracing the angular lines across his skin.

Van's lips ghosted across her skin, leaving a trail of wanting in its wake. "You can trust me," he breathed, his hands touching, questing. Finding. She arched under his touch.

No.

Ori pulled away, the fear propelling her across the deck, until the bench dug into her back.

"No."

His hands reached for her, only for the movement to be abruptly aborted as confusion, frustration, and concern chased themselves across his face. Her stomach turned over. She had trusted Zarr, cared for Zarr. And look where that left her. In eight days, the *Ava* would drop into Tersen space, and not long after the Imperial Guard would drag her off the *Ava*. Van, Jen, Davey, and the rest would be witness to her arrest. Her humiliation.

"No," Ori said again, although Van hadn't said a word, or moved toward her. She had made a terrible mistake in trusting any of these — whatever they were. They may not be eijen, but they certainly were not Khatjarit, not the True People.

She levered herself up off the floor, caught in a mess of conflicting feelings. Want. Fear. Anger. Sorrow. "I made a mistake."

"Please. I don't know what to say, Ori." Van rose to his feet, but kept on his side of the circle formed by the benches. "I'm sorry, for whatever I've done to frighten you." He gestured at the seats. "Please, can we talk about this?"

She wanted to apologize, to explain, but she couldn't find the words. "I can't," she said, walking past, leaving Van behind.

She had no idea where she was going as the tears she had so much difficulty in controlling blinded her, so habit took her to the cavernous cargo bay and its rows of unquiet containers.

Her boots echoed through the space, along the metal walkway, until Ori stopped at the rail. Above her stretched the railings, below she could make out details as far as her normal, unassisted sight could see, the last rows coalescing into one dark whole.

It was a long way down. Her hands grasped the metal railing, squeezing until her knuckles turned white. It was a long way down.

She could still feel his arm around her, his scent, his touch.

No Van.

No Zarr.

No escape.

The darkness called her. A few seconds of falling and then nothing. An end to everything. Better than being dragged away in chains. Far better than the terror and agony of the Nest and its multi-legged torturers, or enduring Rossim's glee as he witnessed her execution. Even if the mesh activated, the impact would still be fatal. She placed one foot on the bottom railing.

A noise from much further up the cargo bay distracted her. Voices. Zarr most certainly, and the other? Jwali. Whatever the navigator was up to down here, it was unlikely to be a social call. Perhaps before they reached Tersen, Ori should make a point of ensuring the navigator ended up dead. They couldn't execute her twice.

Yet she remained on the railing, only a step away from oblivion. How would interfering in whatever perversions the navigator was indulging in help her? The boy was going to betray her the first chance he got. He'd already made his feelings obvious to everyone, so why should she rescue him?

Fourteen

J wali caught him before he made it to the next hatch, the navigator's fingers clamping onto Zarr's overalls like a vice.

"Now, now," Jwali scolded as Zarr attempted to run. "It's been ages since we've had some fun. You must be getting bored."

Who could save him? Not Van, or Lart, or Lianna. Maybe Davey was still in the bay? Ori. She was the only one likely to be close. The one person least likely to want to save him.

"No, please," he pleaded as Jwali dragged him down the walkway. He struggled again, nearly escaping, but Jwali snatched his arm with one hand and cuffed Zarr across the face with the other so hard he saw stars. Dazed and sobbing, Zarr made no more protests as the navigator pushed him roughly into the storage compartment, pulling the hatch firmly closed behind them.

Zarr stumbled away into the corner, desperately scanning the piles of rubbish for anything resembling a weapon while Jwali lounged against the bulkhead watching his futile attempts with enjoyment.

"Here," said Jwali, kicking a length of piping across the deck, "try this."

The syntheplaz rolled to a stop a few meters away. His head throbbed from Jwali's blow, making thinking too hard.

Should he pick it up? Was this another one of Jwali's games? *Please, Blessed Mother, save me.*

"What? Too fucking scared?" The navigator levered himself off the bulkhead and sauntered closer to Zarr. His boot kicked at the pipe again, so that it smacked sharply into Zarr's shins before rebounding back onto the deck.

Sometimes, the only option is to fight back, despite the odds.

Ori told him that. In the mess. And then she'd made him rakosh and he'd got them both an energy bar. Zarr bent down and slowly picked up the pipe.

"Oh, so now you think you're some sort of tough guy?" Jwali said, laughing.

The pipe was heavier than Zarr had expected, and it took both hands to hold it, the end wobbling as he raised it in front of him.

Jwali laughed again, rummaging around in his overalls. "Drop the pipe and tell me you're going to be a good little bitch and take your meds."

Zarr swung the length of syntheplaz with a strength driven by fear and shame and a bone-deep anger. The navigator, too concerned with searching for his drugs, never had a chance to dodge as the pipe cracked into his skull. His body crumpled to the deck like a dropped rag. Zarr stared at the unmoving navigator in shock.

The hatch crashed open.

"What have you done?"

"I killed him," the boy said, in shocked disbelief, dropping the length of industrial pipe, which rolled across the deck leaving a line of successively fading scarlet imprints in its wake.

Ori turned over the navigator's body, almost gagging as the reek of floess came off him. The pipe had hit Jwali squarely on the side of the head; blood matted his hair and was collecting in a small pool on the deck. This was the opportunity she had been waiting for. If she killed Jwali now, she could blame it on Zarr. No one would believe his story of Abominations; he'd be in prison, and she would be on her way to Ma'al. It wouldn't take much. Her hands moved over Jwali's skull, her fingers feeling out the slight depression where the end of the pipe had encountered the bone. A little more pressure, an infusion of nanites, and this piece of filth would be dead.

And then it would be Zarr they'd come for.

It would be him dragged away in front of his crew. His friends.

Imprisoned.

Abused.

She rose, leaving the unconscious navigator in the widening pool of blood. The boy hadn't moved, paralyzed with shock, his hands clenching and unclenching in unconscious stress.

"Zarr," she said, kneeling until she was at eye level. His entire body trembled. "Yaol, listen, he isn't dead. You didn't kill anyone." Her fingers traced the swelling down one side of the boy's face, the purpling bruise spreading out, obliterating the freckles. The rest of his skin was as gray as the omnipresent paintwork, even those ears. His eyes stared off into the distance, unfocused.

Moving slowly, Ori took Zarr's hands in hers. His fingers curled, clutching tightly at her in response.

No amount of theory or training truly prepares you for the first kill.

It was hot that day, a breeze stirring the dust of the training ground as her cohort lined up. They were too young yet for projectile or plasma weapons the trainers explained, as Ori took the short blade, holding it as instructed. Fear made her palms slick; her fingers gripped the handle tightly.

Their targets stood huddled together, not old enough yet to truly appreciate the danger. Her strike had been clean and fast and her trainers had praised her skill. By the end of the session, all the eijen had been dispatched, with varying degrees of proficiency. The blood-soaked dust refused to stir, even as the breeze picked up.

Zarr's eyes suddenly focused on her, wide with fear. "I know," he said, in a whisper.

He wasn't talking about Jwali. "Yes, I know you do," she said softly.

"Are you going to kill us?"

For a second, she couldn't see, or breathe for the pain. He thought she was going to kill him?

I was going to. That was the plan. Remember?

No, I changed the plan. Plans can change as circumstances dictate.

She shook her head. "No."

"Why?"

"Who would call me commander?"

Zarr nodded as though that answer made sense, then jerked his head to where Jwali still lay unmoving on the deck.

"What are we going to do?"

As much as Ori wanted to, killing Jwali was out of the question. The only strategic course was damage control. And for that she needed Van. Whether he would help was another question entirely.

"Ava, notify the engineer. There's been an accident."

The moment Van stepped through the hatchway, Ori announced, "I hit him." The words rang out in the cramped space of the compartment, echoing off the walls like they were trapped inside a bell. To his credit, the big engineer didn't ask too many questions, instead fixing his gaze on Ori and then the navigator. His dark eyes roamed over their faces as if trying to calculate how much damage could be wrought with just a word or two.

"Is he dead?" he finally asked, his voice oddly calm.

Ori noted that Van didn't seem particularly upset at the possibility of someone dying. "No, unfortunately," she replied.

"OK. What about Zarr? Who did that?" Van's attention shifted to Zarr.

"He did," Ori said, pointing at Jwali.

Van shrugged and checked Jwali much as she had, though he probably wasn't contemplating killing the navigator. "I think he's coming around." He eyed Ori and Zarr cautiously. "Best to stay well back."

Jwali stirred, cursing as he rubbed the side of his head with his fingers stained red from his own blood. "You two are going to pay for this," he snarled, levering himself unsteadily off the deck with a curse. "I swear you will never get a berth anywhere, no matter how many cocks you suck. It wasn't her, Van; it was her little bitch that did it. They ambushed me."

"He attacked Zarr. I meant to kill him, and I still do," Ori said icily.

"Fuck off, bitch, you can't touch me, you've already done enough to get your asses slung off. Go on, kill me, and see what happens then."

Fifteen

"I think I made it clear about rough behavior on my ship." The captain stood with her back to the nav panel, her patchwork face creased and sharpened with anger and exhaustion.

Lianna had greeted Jwali's injuries with screams of outrage you could hear across half the ship. Lart and Davey came to see what all the fuss was as Van dragged Jwali to the med bay. Neither of them expressed any concern as to their navigator's condition.

"You did, ma'am." One of the first things you learned during training was that no excuse would mitigate the coming punishment. Better to accept what was about to happen and put your energies into surviving it.

"I have my navigator in the med bay, with serious injuries. He says Zarr attacked him, that the pair of you ambushed him."

"Zarr is not capable of attacking anyone. I hit him because I caught him assaulting Zarr. And neither of us could have ambushed Jwali if he was at his post. He was on duty, yes?"

Marissa frowned. "Yes, your point is valid. I also struggle to believe Zarr would attack anyone. And I will investigate Navigator Jwali's absence from his post later."

"You can do whatever you wish. But Jwali is a predator and a pervert and you endanger— "

"That's enough, Tey," interrupted Marissa, with real anger. "I don't care about your accusations or your feelings. I need a navigator; I don't need crew members who can't control themselves. You'll be paid for your work until Tersen. After that I don't want to see either you or Zarr anywhere near my ship, or my crew again."

That Ori had sufficient leverage to make this all go away was not lost on her. The *Ava* was on its way to Tersen only because of the cylinders Ori had acquired. But she had sworn Van to silence, forbade him from telling anyone, let him take the credit. She would not undermine him, even to save herself.

"Since when has either of us not carried out our duties? And why is Zarr being punished?" she said. "Throw me off if you wish, but the boy has done nothing, apart from being the target of ongoing abuse by your navigator." No doubt Jwali would make another mistake, with someone with less self-control than her, and he would be dead.

Marissa's fingers worried at the small ring of gold. Ori could see doubt growing by the second.

"I can't," Marissa said, finally. "Lianna will never agree to anything other than you two being thrown off. She is the co-owner. I can't override her objections, and Jwali is family."

"Then at least give Zarr some sort of recommendation. He does not deserve this treatment."

"On one condition. You and Zarr keep well away from Jwali. From now on he will remain on the upper decks and you will confine yourself to the cargo and crew decks. Any repeats of this violence, any complaints at all, and I will make sure no ship ever gives either of you a berth. Is that clear?"

"Perfectly. Thank you, Captain. I will adhere to these conditions and ensure Zarr does too," she said, and this time the gratitude was genuine.

"Good, be ready to leave when the ship docks at the refueling station."

"Refueling? I thought we left Six Jump with full tanks?"

"Not that it's any of your business, Tey, but I made the decision to swap out the bigger tanks for more cargo space. Another one of those decisions captains must make these days."

The distance between Six Jump and Tersen was far less than the distance between Tersen and the border. The *Avadora* wouldn't make it. All this effort, all this pain. And all along, there had been no hope of escape.

Jwali kept his eyes firmly shut, hoping that if his aunt thought he was still asleep, she would leave him alone. He honestly didn't know what was worse, being hit by that little whining bitch, Zarr, or being fussed over by Lianna. Who would have guessed the boy had it in him? All Jwali wanted to do was go to his quarters and lie down. Instead, he was here, tucked up in the most uncomfortable bunk on the *Ava*, while Lianna went ballistic over first-aid supplies.

"I counted them, three days ago. There were ten patches left and two packs of dressings. Now they've gone." That last word was accented with the resounding crash of the supply locker door rebounding off its frame.

He couldn't pretend to sleep through that. "I don't know, Aunt. I'm not in charge of the supplies." *That would be your job, Cargomaster.* Of course, he couldn't tell her the remaining patches and dressings were hidden in a disused locker along with his stash of floess. At least he'd had enough sense to return the medi-repair unit to its locked cabinet. Lianna would literally tear the *Ava* apart to retrieve that.

Lianna whirled to face him, her thin face scarlet with rage. "I told Marissa that one was no good, not to employ her, but no. We had to have a fourth hand." Lianna paced up and down the tiny sick bay — three steps up, three steps back, her bony hands flying around in formations of frustration and anger. "Now do you know what she's going to do?"

Jwali knew better than to proffer an answer, merely shaking his head. He needed another pain patch. And another hit. His head ached, and not just from being hit with a length of pipe. It was a nasty surprise to find out the boy had balls after all.

"I said," his aunt yelled from two steps away, "do you know what Marissa is going to do?"

"No, Aunt," Jwali replied, "please tell me."

"She's going to give that useless Zarr a recommendation, so he'll get another berth. Just because you went for a walk while on duty. Have you ever heard such stupidity?"

"What?" Jwali levered himself up on one elbow, although his head swam with dizziness, and his already empty stomach threatened to disgorge its lining. "She's not going to throw them off?"

"That bitch goes all noble and Marissa falls for it. Tey nearly kills you, and next thing, my wife is making eyes at her and letting her get away with it."

There was no point in arguing with Lianna. Jwali seriously doubted that Tey was even remotely interested in the dried-up stick that was Marissa, but it had been entertaining, putting the idea into Lianna's brain and watching it eat her away. He slumped back on the hard pillow with a theatrical groan.

Lianna immediately started fussing again, patting at the covers and checking the sensors, even though he was certain she didn't understand half the information. "You lie still, I'll get you some food," Lianna said, prodding at her sheet as if she could poke the knowledge out of it. "Once you're up and about, you can eat with us."

Did he hear that correctly? Eat with Lianna and Marissa? "Why would I be eating with you? I eat in the mess."

Lianna looked up from torturing the sheet. "Oh, yes. Marissa said that you must stay on the upper decks — the bridge, your quarters and ours. Until we get to Tersen. That bitch and Zarr will stay down in the lower decks."

Jwali's stomach did another lurch. His stash was in the lowest part of the cargo hold. If he couldn't go down there, how was he going to get a hit? The only upside in all this was that bitch was getting thrown off. He'd done his bit.

The *Avadora* couldn't reach the border. It could never have reached the border. She would have killed everyone, tortured the captain, and found herself stranded out in deep space somewhere, waiting for life support to fail.

I have made a mistake.

How could she have been so stupid? Once again, she had underestimated an opponent, once again her lack of forethought had sabotaged her plans.

She should have jumped ship at Corelli, instead of letting her feelings dictate her actions. Everything had been a mistake. Tszcienna, her capture, the endless, futile escape attempts. Zarr. Van. One mistake after another.

Failure.

Reinnor had known. He had lied about being Directorate, he had lied about helping her, and now Ori was certain he had always known that she could not escape. The death of the *Havali's Hope* navigator had been for his benefit.

Now Zarr knew what she was, and they were both being put off at Tersen. Ori no longer feared Zarr denouncing her, but what if he was targeted by Rossim? Or slipped up and told the wrong person?

This was a nightmare.

She would send Zarr back to Six Jump. And she would find the first ship going to Ma'al. Before, she had no choice, but now Ori was determined. She would find out what the Xi were looking for. She would find it, and use that information to destroy Rossim, Reinnor and the entire Republic.

She would make them all pay.

Sixteen

After a few weeks of sporadic hostilities — a few ships lost on either side, a colony or two destroyed — the Hubnae became insistent and the inevitable peace talks began in an orbital high above the Hubnae homeworld.

The Matriarch scratched absently at her belly with one prehensile palp, and decided to become annoyed at the tardiness of the Meian delegation, although the Hubnae had made a real effort this time, she had to concede that. The loading bay now stood empty of ships and machinery; the only space large enough to accommodate the Xi. The Matriarch was familiar with Hubnae architecture, away from utilitarian spaces such as docks and recreational areas the spaces devolved into narrow, sinuous tunnels of smooth, ivory synthetics, dimly lit and far too warm. In other words, totally unnavigable for a fully grown Xi and claustrophobia-inducing for the young ones. Swags of greenery and bright fabrics hung overhead and soft carpets covered the hard metal deck. Her shuttle, the matte-black hull bristling with weapons, was an incongruous anomaly.

The junior beside her twitched nervously. The first time out of the Nest could be overwhelming and the Matriarch reached out a palp and gently stroked the thick black hair. The young one relaxed visibly, chirping in relief. It was a breach of protocol, and the Matriarch should discipline it for that, deciding instead to soothe the child in whispering chitters. She had been young once, though it was long before the founding of the current Republic. Extreme longevity gave one a perspective that shorter-lived races could never understand. The rise of the engineered humans had been inevitable, their attitude toward those who did not share their idea of a Utopian future of a fully engineered society designed and bred to order depressingly familiar, and the Matriarch and her sisters looked on in weary despair as yet another fledgling civilization tore itself apart. Intervention was forbidden under their agreement with the Meians and the Hubnae, yet in the end they had broken that agreement.

No.

She had broken the agreement for the sake of one human she called friend.

It was a decision she had ruminated over for nearly three hundred years, and she still wasn't sure it had been the right call. The arrival of the alien they designated as Brightstar had thrown them all into turmoil and reopened old disagreements.

A stir at the other end of the bay heralded the Hubnae representatives, undulating across the carpets in a wave of twinkling jewels. Behind them came the Meians, carapaces blinding in gold and rose. The Matriarch gave the junior one last reassuring pat, rose on her silver-gray legs and contained her impatience.

The delegation came to a halt, the Hubnae curling themselves, with much fussing and adjusting, while the Meians spread out in a fan formation beside them, wings rustling in barely suppressed anger.

So, it's going to be like that, is it?

"Thank you for coming, Great One," rumbled the Hubnae leader, its voice like stones tumbling in a tin. "Perhaps we can begin?" It waved one stumpy foreleg at the cluster of metallic carapaces.

"We demand reparations." The grating voice of one of the Meians cut across whatever the Hubnae were about to say, stepping forward, wings rustling menacingly. "We demand justice."

The Hubnae's eyes, unrelieved orbs of blackness, fastened onto the Matriarch. She couldn't tell from their expressions whether they expected her to break down in remorse, or exterminate the entire delegation there and then.

It certainly won't be the first option. But some degree of reconciliation is required. If only to keep them placated for a little longer.

"The Xi will do whatever is right. What do you seek in reparation?"

The rustling rose to a crescendo, then ceased at a gesture from their leader. "The two systems on the border," she demanded.

The young one sidled closer and whispered pertinent statistics. It would be a small loss, and there would be those in the Nest who would use it against her, but the plan outweighed all these considerations.

"Done, anything else?"

The entire dock filled with the rumble of Hubnae laughter, rocks tumbling down cliffs. "Let us move on to ending this incident and getting back to our lives."

"We will withdraw our fleet, and offer our apologies for the unfortunate misunderstanding that led to the death of your hive mate," the Matriarch said.

"You cut off his head and fed him to your children," protested one of the Meians, a smaller figure, the coloring less pronounced. One of the males.

"He did accuse us of lying," the Matriarch pointed out, staying reasonable, at least for the moment. "And the children are easily excited. They meant no disrespect."

"No disrespect?" the little male squeaked with indignation. One of the larger females took a foreleg and dragged him back and out of earshot. The Matriarch had to work to suppress bursting into laughter. Beside her, the junior had both palps folded across her abdomen, an expression of deep confusion.

"Do not worry, little one," the Matriarch chittered to her companion, "this is not like the human races that get all upset over lost dignity. We will resolve this quickly and then be back in the sanity of the Nest."

"Was that smaller one a male?"

"Yes, little one. Not all races have sexual dimorphism as pronounced as ours. It can seem strange at first, but we must be tolerant."

"Do you think the males talk during sex?" she whispered.

"I have been told they do, but it is expected. Do not concern yourself. See the Hubnae have them under control and we will finish soon."

Indeed, the Hubnae had the Meians handled. Everyone would return to their own systems, it was agreed, the two disputed systems would be turned over to the Meians, and from now on all sides would restrain themselves from feeding accredited ambassadors to children or pets.

"One thing more," demanded the Meian leader. "This thing you keep prisoner, the engineered one. We want your word, sworn here before all of us, that it will not be released. If you have no need of it, we want it executed."

"Well, of course," the Matriarch said, lying yet again, "that was our intention all along."

Seventeen

Ori's hand hovered over the hatch handle, then she pushed it open, stepping into the calm, white compartment. Zarr sat on the deck, knees drawn up to his chest, looking like he wanted to disappear. She crossed the space to the adjoining bench in two silent steps, then folded herself onto the deck, legs crossed, back straight.

As before, the silence caught her off guard. No vibrations from the ship's engines, no grumbling machinery or clanging hatches. No raised voices. The holographic flame flickered softly, casting dots and dashes of light across the clean bulkheads and the boy's hunched figure. The flame drew her, and the random play of light and movement stilled the churn of emotions.

Zarr shifted, a tiny movement in her peripheral vision. "Can I ask you something?" he asked, almost whispering.

Ori knew what was coming - the unpicking of information, the weighing of allegiances. "Some questions are best left unanswered," she said, gently. "But ask, and I will do my best to answer."

"Are there more?" Zarr asked, his eyes searching hers.

"More?" Ori frowned, not sure what he meant.

"Like, you know. You," Zarr said, gesturing at her. "In the Republic."

Ori understood now. Was he worried that there was an entire secret community of abominations living under the nose of the Republic?

"No," she said, shaking her head. "I am alone here."

"But. I mean." He leaned forward, his curiosity overwhelming any fear he might still harbor. "You have family? Somewhere?"

"Yes. Outside the Republic. A long way away." Too far. Too late. Ori now saw her siblings, her Line, the Kharijite, through the lens of Corelli, of broken bodies, and destroyed civilizations. *Murderer, the voices said.*

Zarr seemed to digest that, his face crumpling into sorrow. "I'm sorry I was horrible to you," he said, his ears turning red in the dim light.

"It's all right," Ori said, trying to put him at ease. "I understand that it was a shock. Marissa has promised me you will get a good reference. I will find another berth. This embargo Ma'al has enacted cannot last forever."

Zarr looked up at her, surprised. "But I thought you didn't want to go to Ma'al?"

"A good soldier must be able to adapt to changing circumstances," Ori said, repeating a phrase she had heard many times.

"And you're a good soldier?"

Once she could have answered that in a second, without thinking, her belief in her mission absolute. The feeling came back, the same one that hit her on Corelli. All the people in the street, the children in their blue and white clothes, the dancing ribbons, and she could see them again, herded onto the transports, or their bodies, stacked like rubbish, waiting to be burned. This time she concentrated on the flames until the feeling passed.

"I thought I was. I obeyed orders. I did not question. I think that was a mistake."

Zarr made a small noise of understanding, his legs stretched out, hands resting quietly in his lap. Ori leaned back against the bench and wrapped herself in the silence and the light.

"Is the captain going to confine us to quarters?"

"No," Ori replied. "Jwali will stay in his quarters and on the bridge, and we will stay on the lower decks until we reach Tersen."

Zarr grinned. "He's going to be pissed at that. His stash is down here."

"I know," Ori said. "I followed him once, but he has moved it since then."

"If we find it, that's proof."

Ori shook her head. "No. We cannot prove it is his. We must catch him with it, preferably with witnesses. He is not that stupid. He will be very careful."

"He sabotaged the pump, didn't he? And the fan assembly in life support, and took the cylinders? And you know why."

"Certain people want me taken out of whatever game I'm in," Ori said, her voice low. "I suspect they have pressured Jwali to achieve this."

"And the stabbing? That was them too?"

"Yes," Ori said, her jaw clenched.

"Must be a very important game then," Zarr said, his tone serious.

They did not torture you for pleasure, they do not keep you prisoner for entertainment. The Xi were looking for something. Something important. Something only she could find. What could she find that no one else could?

Ori turned to Zarr "You told me, more than once I think, that there were stories, about the engineered escaping Da Chet. Where did they go? And what was the story about a theft?"

"I thought you said it was rubbish."

"I am beginning to think I have been wrong about a great many things. Tell me about Da Chet."

TERSEN

One

Boots clattered on a walkway two levels up. Zarr. She knew all their footsteps now, and all their habits — Zarr's snuffles as he slept, Davey's laughter you could hear clear across the cargo bay. She'd seen images of Jen's partner, and their sons, and listened to stories about Lart's granddaughter. Van. She knew his scent, the itchy spot where the new implant kept him sober, his voice, the feel of his hands on her. The aching need of that moment had never left her.

Sometimes, like now, she thought perhaps she was imagining all this. That at any moment she would wake and be back in the house, in the cell, waiting for death.

She couldn't recognize herself anymore. Where was the soldier? Where was her belief in her sacred duty to remake the galaxy into engineered perfection?

And where did she go from here? Returning home was impossible, she saw that now. Would they let her stay here, on the *Ava*? If she found what the Xi wanted? No. Rossim would stop at nothing to see her dead.

The future stretched out before her, a dark, empty path. No home, no family. No friends.

"Hey," Zarr's voice floated down through the gloom, although it wasn't so dark that his normal, unenhanced vision wouldn't see her cowering in the darkness. "We'll be dropping out soon. I've left our stuff with Van." Was it relief or shame she felt when the boy remained where he was, giving her time to shove her trembling hands into her own pockets and climb up to the main walkway. By the time she reached Zarr, she'd regained control and felt a stir of pride at that achievement.

"We're seventeen minutes from exit," she said, pretending everything was normal as she retrieved the cargo sheet from its spot near the hatch, "we should be in position; Lianna will use every excuse possible to deny you a reference."

Ori headed off toward the hold, only stopping when Zarr didn't immediately follow.

"I'm not going back to Six," the boy said, shoulders set defiantly. "I'm going to Ma'al. With you." His ears fairly glowed, and each freckle stood out sharply on a face congealed into stubborn refusal.

"We had this discussion," she said, and turned on her heels and continued toward the end of the walkway lengthening her stride so that the boy was forced to almost run to keep up with her. "It is safer for you to return home, and anyway, we have no idea if we can get to Ma'al. We may be stuck at Tersen for weeks."

"You had this discussion; I'm just expected to do as I'm told. Hey." His hand grasped her arm, only to hastily pull back as she rounded on him.

The obvious terror in his face made her inexplicably angry. Unlike Lart, Ori rarely used physical force to discipline the boy, finding Zarr responded better to a mix of sharp-tongued reproof and precise instructions.

"You are going back to Six," she said, enunciating every word. "I do not need you hanging around me on Ma'al" She winced at this cruelty, but she told herself it was for the boy's protection.

"You can't tell me what to do." Zarr was nearly yelling at her in frustration. "I can help. Why do you always treat me like an idiot?"

It had been a mistake to open up to Zarr. She didn't know which was worse, his suffocating protectiveness, or his enthusiasm for an adventure. An even larger mistake to ask him about the engineered and the end of the war. The sheer number of theories, verging from the plausible to the ridiculous, was overwhelming and frustrating.

"Have you forgotten Corelli? When you nearly died?" Zarr said, making little stabbing motions at her with his fingers.

"Will you stop doing that," Ori said, swatting his hand away. "You have told me everything you know. Which amounted to absolutely nothing. Conjecture, hearsay, and outright paranoia, all based around a few sentences retrieved from a three-hundred-year-old device by someone widely regarded as insane. There is absolutely no proof that some sort of secret weapon is hidden on Ma'al or anywhere else." *Except the Xi think there is. And that alone is worth more than a thousand theories.*

"I never said it was a secret weapon. I told you it was a research facility. Da Chet was the center of genetics research, not a weapons facility. The only weapons they had were the orbital defense network. And if there is nothing there, why can't I go to Ma'al? You know there's something there, you just don't want me to come."

Of course she didn't want him to come. Unrest was spreading through the Republic, the last news feeds they'd accessed in the hour before they jumped, made that plain. He would be safer back home. Once Rossim knew she'd survived the attack on Corelli, he would try again. And anyone close to her would be in danger. She could make her way to Ma'al alone. On a new ship, with a new crew. If the border opened. What would Rossim do if she became stranded at Tersen?

"Look," Zarr said, his voice rising again, this time in anger. "We'll get another berth on Tersen. It's not the end of the world. It will be OK." Both ears burned scarlet, matching the flush spreading across his face. "I'll be with you. I'll make sure no one—"

Her patience, stretched too thin over too much pain, snapped.

"I don't need you," she screamed, her brief dominion over her emotional control gone. "I don't need you, or any of you. Leave me alone!"

"I will then," Zarr yelled, red-faced and furious. "I hope they find you, you ungrateful, selfish bitch." And with that, he stormed off down the walkway, slamming the hatch with such force that the entire walkway shuddered.

The compartment seemed too quiet without him. Ori stood alone and wondered what she should do. He hadn't meant it, had he? She should go after him; the *Ava* would be dropping out into normal space very soon.

The superstructure screamed as the entire ship lurched sideways, throwing Ori across the walkway and into the bulkhead, the impact driving all the air from her lungs, only the mesh, activated by the abrupt movement, saving her from serious injury. As it was, she fell to the deck, dazed and bleeding. Emergency alarms sounded, filling the hold with strobing red lights and ear-splitting sirens.

The ship squealed as if in agony, punctuated by crashes as some of the containers broke from the rails and plummeted down into the lower reaches of the hold. Ori dragged herself to her feet and limped across to the comms panel.

"Bridge, what is going on?"

There was no reply.

"Bridge?"

"Ship?"

"Ava here," replied the AI, in its emotionless voice.

Good, the AI was still online.

"Ship, patch through the feed from Tersen Port."

"...collision alert. I repeat, this is Tersen Port, *Avadora*, you are out of position. You are too close to T Five and on a direct intercept course with Refueling Station Alpha Four. You must alter your course now. Please respond. This is a collision alert."

"Ship, give me our position." The AI spat out a string of numbers. Somehow the *Ava* had dropped out deep inside the gravity well of the gas giant, a mistake of terrifying stupidity.

Another crash, this time closer, and Ori spun, realizing in that moment where the boy was.

"Zarr?" she called, but there was no answer. For a second she was torn between the two crises, Zarr lost in the cargo hold, and the ship crashing.

The comms system activated again. "*Avadora*, this is Tersen Port Authority." Whoever was on duty was working hard to keep the panic out of her voice. "You are on a direct collision course with Alpha Four. You are on a collision course with the HCV *Trailing Venture*."

What had Jwali done? She needed information, a navigation panel, to analyze the situation.

"Collision alert. Initiating safety measures," intoned the AI. Across the ship, hatches slammed shut, compartmentalizing ship sections in case of a hull breach.

"Bridge, can you hear me?" No reply. Where were Jwali and the captain? One of them surely would intervene. If they knew how. This wasn't the sort of scenario freighter captains would train for; only military personnel would know how to maneuver a ship in such tight quarters in such a short time frame.

She didn't have time to run to the bridge, or engineering, even if all the hatches were open. If only her interface worked.

Think!

The interface was active, the diagnostics menu still worked. The sub-dermal armor still responded, if only automatically. The nanites still healed her. It was an insane, last-ditch option, but the only one she had. If she did nothing, they would all be dead, and so would everyone on the station, and the freighter, and anyone caught in the blast radius. The nearest cargo control panel lay at the opposite end of the walkway; she sprinted to it, uncaring who saw her, and hit the activation panel. Nothing happened. She slammed her fist into the console side; the controls sputtered into life and then died. She spat an obscenity and grabbed the handle on the access panel, the hatch giving way with a loud squeal of tortured metal. She took the knife from her boot and selected one of the data cables, cutting it near one of the junctions. Now to open the input port.

The blade bit into her skin, the blood running warm and sticky down her spine. Somewhere, down the end of the walkway, Ori could hear the boy screaming; he must be trapped in one of the sections. She would rescue him later, if they survived. The blood made her fingers slippery and it took two attempts before the cable slid into the neural port.

The first time the Republic had tried to hack into her systems, she had resisted. Forcibly. Garrett had lifted one finger, almost negligently, and the guard fired, taking out her knee in an explosion of agony. Garrett pointed out that they knew she could survive the trauma of losing all four limbs, and then they would do the scan anyway. Cooperate, and you will receive medical attention. Refuse? President Garrett had shrugged his elegant shoulders and gestured toward the guards. She'd understood. She'd been trailing blood and bits of bone when they dragged her to the bed, restrained her, and plugged their machine into her. The scans were repeated, often, and Garrett had supervised every session. And every time they tortured her, she'd used the nanites to build a better, more stable connection, in the hope that at least it might reduce the pain, and perhaps, give her an opening into the Republic's network. Now wasn't the most ideal condition, but imminent death had a way of rearranging priorities.

The nanites swarmed to the neural port, seamlessly welding the data cable to her own neural network.

Please, if Jen's Blessed Mother exists, let this work.

A sledgehammer of pain exploded in her head as strobing color blinded her. Every nerve felt like it was on fire. She fell to the deck, clawing at the metal in a futile attempt to escape her own body, now spasming with agony.

She opened her eyes, and instantly regretted it; the brightness sent stabbing pain through her head to counterpoint the throbbing. She tried again, and inside her mind something shifted. Peripheral icons sprang into full view on either side of the interface, flashing red and amber, while a steady stream of warnings and system updates scrolled across her vision.

It worked!

She had no idea how, but was grateful beyond words that it had. She could always interrogate the system logs later. Right now, she needed to save the ship.

Initiate connection.

Rossim had always feared her ability to talk to the AIs; in reality, she could no more merge consciousness with the machines than he could, but it did make the interface easier, faster, more fluid.

Ship, give me navigational control.

The walkway dissolved, to be replaced by the navigation panel, the *Ava*, the *Trailing Venture*, the station, and every ship or object within the system, a tiny gold mote around the gravity wells of each of Tersen's planets.

By the void. What had that eijen filth done? He'd dropped them into the same orbit as the refueling station. The *Ava* was still carrying far too much momentum from the exit, she was headed right through the station, and into the planet. To make it worse, one of the big freighters, a heavy cargo vessel, was on approach to the station as well. The *Trailing Venture* would have too much mass to move quickly, especially in the tight lanes around the stations. Space might be vast, but at the speeds they were going, space could run out extremely quickly.

There was no move she could pull off that would save them from this. They could fire the thrusters, take the *Ava* down and under the *Trailing Venture*, but she'd still hit the station, and with any luck be destroyed immediately. The alternative was to plunge down into the gas giant's atmosphere and die there.

According to the numbers scrolling across her screens, they were eighty-nine seconds from impact. She could hear Zarr screaming for her from the other side of the walkway. All the emergency hatches were closed, so he couldn't see her violating every single line of Article Thirty-Four. All he would know was the *Ava* was in terrible danger and he was alone.

"Zarr, get to somewhere safe," she yelled, hoping he could hear her over the sirens.

Initiating jump drives.

The ship shuddered as both the main and auxiliary drives came online. She felt a momentary pang of regret; the *Ava* was deep into T5's gravity, to compensate meant precise calculations, and the inevitable destruction of the drive she had helped rebuild with Van. She wouldn't be able to escape, but at least they wouldn't die.

The calculations flowed across her vision, and she reached out, feeling the slippery interface between this reality and hyperspace. In the background the port controller's voice rose in panic.

Open jump point

In her mind she saw the point opening, a blue-white pinpoint blossoming out into a vast web of energy.

In three, two, one.

Jump.

Gravity disappeared. For a fraction of a second, she floated in the not-quite-there tickle of hyperspace, then the *Ava* crashed back into normal space. The entire ship slewed sideways, a hideous groan and squeal reverberating through the ship as the drives, stretched beyond tolerances, died under the load. The cargo bay filled with the sound of tortured metal, as more of the pods, suspended on their rails, swayed and twisted with the shock. The crash of dislodged pods reverberated through the walkway under her, seismic shocks of metal pushed past its limits.

Fire braking thrusters

The *Ava* shuddered again, the vibrations running through the superstructure as the thrusters came on, slowing the *Ava*'s trajectory.

Position?

Right on target, in the Lagrange point for T5's most distant moon. A stable orbit, empty, safe. They were safe.

The warning sirens fell silent, as she collapsed to the deck. Sight, both normal and enhanced, were gone again, she was essentially blind until those systems came back online, if they ever did. Her head pounded, burned, screamed in agony. The drying blood glued her overalls to her skin, stiff and tacky, while the slash in her neck stung from the sweat plastering her hair to her skull. Bile swirled in the back of her throat as she fought the terrible disorientation of disengaging from the AI. Nausea hit and she threw up in ragged, heaving spurts. The nanites disengaged and the bloody cable dropped to the deck.

Where was Zarr? She pulled herself up off the floor, finding her way along the walkway by organic memory alone.

"Zarr," she called, her voice catching in her throat. "Zarr, can you hear me?" Sight returned, blurry at first, and only normal vision, but better than blindness. Another bout of nausea hit her, and she fought not to throw up again. "Zarr," she called again, but only the subsiding noises of the containers settling replied.

She started down the ladder, her hands clamped to the rails, while she scrabbled, panic-stricken for a foothold. "I'm coming," she called, keeping her voice calm, as the blood soaked into her clothes and her vision came and went at random. "I'll find you."

Ori imagined him trapped under one of the containers. They weighed over a thousand tons each; if they fell, you would be crushed, beyond any medical help. Enhanced vision suddenly snapped on and she winced in the abrupt brightness. Wavelength flicked down to infrared as she stumbled along the walkway, searching for the orange form that would be Zarr.

An entire line of containers had collapsed. Two had burst under the pressure; a steady stream of powdered Orchetti root pouring into the darkness, generating a small cloud of dust. The penultimate container hung almost vertically, held by the twisted remains of the single clamp, one dented corner resting on the container below it, its ruined companions stacked like the discarded blocks of some giant race. The entire weight of the container now rested entirely on the integrity of the single clamp and those of its downstairs neighbors. Zarr lay on the bottom container, blood soaking into his brown hair, wedged between the inner hull and a thousand tons of metal and cargo.

To reach him, she would have to climb over the walkway railings, drop to the top container, make her way, somehow, down to where he lay, and get herself and Zarr back up to the walkway, all without disturbing the unstable pile. One wrong move and the clamps, or even the entire rail could give way, taking Zarr and her with it. At any other time, it would present few difficulties. Now, half blind and dizzy, rescuing Zarr was a monumental undertaking. That she could simply walk away and leave the boy never occurred to her.

Somewhere across the cargo hold, metal squealed, followed by a crash that shook the walkway and set all the containers rocking dangerously on their rails. The corner of the hanging container etched a gouge in the metal, deep enough to put her finger into, and the thin stream of dusty powder became a torrent, filling the hold with fine dust. It didn't matter that she could barely see or hold herself upright, she had to move, and quickly.

Her hands, slick with fear, slid on the railing and she swore, one of Rossim's more popular obscenities, and had to wipe them on her overalls twice before she had a firm grip. Every movement precipitated another trickle of blood down her neck; the nanites were working as fast as possible to repair the wound but their job was made more difficult by her constant exertions.

The topmost rail was at least four meters below the walkway. The metal dug into her fingers as she hung from the walkway deck, with at least another two meters to the rail. The cloud of Orchetti root dust engulfed her, clogging her lungs and eyes; she ordered her systems to cease breathing, relieved beyond words when they obeyed. She could survive without oxygen far longer than normal humans but she would have to breathe eventually. She couldn't wait any longer.

Her feet hit the rail as the cargo hold echoed with the squeaks and groans of tortured metal. Below her, the boy stirred slightly. Good, he was still alive, but in a confused state he could roll off the side and plummet to the deck below. The angled side of the container gave a barely navigable route down.

She stepped cautiously onto the container, feeling it shift uneasily under her weight. Zarr moaned, struggling toward consciousness. Another step, and the clamp above her head squealed, tortured metal protesting.

Two more steps. Vision, normal and enhanced disappeared.

Will you stop doing that.

Either her systems were listening, or it was just coincidence, but her sight snapped back, and her cautious steps to where Zarr lay didn't cause any more movement.

Ori knelt beside Zarr, her hands moving over his body, as they had mere weeks ago. It looked like another head wound. It was just as well the boy had a hard skull.

In the distance, a hatch slammed, accompanied by raised voices. Zarr moaned again, flailing slightly as Ori settled him over her shoulder. She took one tentative step onto the sideways container, only to retreat as it shifted alarmingly, metal grinding against metal. It would not take both their weight.

Meters above them, the walkway offered the only option. Ori took two steps back, grimacing as the container squealed and moved slightly, then she sprang forward and launched herself and Zarr up toward the walkway decking. Her fingers scrabbled for a secure grip, and for a few terrifying seconds they hung, held only by two fingers. By the time Ori regained the walkway and was able to lay the boy down, she was shaking, vision once again blurry, her stomach roiling with nausea. Below them metal squealed again as the containers shifted, then the entire stack gave way, crashing into the deck below, a releasing a cloud of powder that obliterated the walkway in a fog of choking dust.

The voices were closer now, Ori heard Van calling her name. She had to get back to the console before he arrived. Zarr was still unconscious, his body turned ghostlike by the powder. She turned him on his side, afraid he'd choke, brushing the powder off his face with brisk efficiency. Help was coming; she had to remove all evidence of her activities.

The console hatch lay discarded, its hinges torn and twisted. The mess she'd left behind shocked her. A bloody handprint on the bulkhead and a trail of dark splotches marked her attempt to stand. The most damning issue was the cut data cable, the dried blood flaking off the ends.

There was nothing she could do; Van was nearly there. The break room held cleaning supplies and a small maintenance cart and welder, but too far away to clean all this up before he got here. She didn't have near enough time to repair the data cables, so she settled for wedging the panel back into position. That would have to do. As soon as she got Zarr to the sick bay, she'd come back and fix all this. She slumped back against the console as the hatch crashed open and Van rushed in.

"Fuck, Ori, you look like shit," exclaimed Van. He hurried to her side and eased her back against the bulkhead.

"Forget me, I'm fine. Zarr is up there." Ori pointed along the walkway. "See to him first."

Van looked doubtful, but complied, his boots clattering along the walkway to the boy. A minute later he returned, Zarr cradled in his arms where he looked even more childlike than usual, covered in a thick dusting of Orchetti root.

Ori pulled herself to her feet. Another bout of dizziness hit, she promptly threw up and fainted.

Two

The dream this time was not of death, not of slaughter and enslavement. Not of genocide. She was six. In two months, she would leave her Line's compound for training. It would be years before she returned. If she survived. Even at this age she knew that failure meant death.

One of the other Lines had returned from a cleansing. They had brought back these animals, a trophy, a curiosity. Tszcienna somehow managed to get permission to see them.

Tszcienna. The too-clever, too-ambitious Technical who had designed her.

The animals were hairy, brown with yellow spots and long tails that flicked back and forth. They had the softest noses, like velvet. And big, brown eyes. And they were so gentle. In the memory she holds out her hand, her chubby fingers clutching a piece of fruit. She feels their lips, all soft and warm, nibbling at the treats, tongues chasing the sticky juice across her tiny palms. She remembers Tszcienna laughing. It was the only time she ever heard him laugh. He asked her what they smelled like, and she had struggled with the concept. "They smell...warm?" she'd said, and then was instantly afraid that this was another test and she had failed.

"Warm is a perfect description," he said gently, picking her up and holding her close.

She remembers. The feeling of being held, the connection she had always felt with this man. Slender, beautiful, with dark hair and eyes bluer than any sky she had ever seen, and she had seen many skies.

Safe. She had always felt safe with Tszcienna.

Distantly she became aware someone was calling her name. The name the Xi called her, laughing at their own joke. She didn't want to leave this dream, even as she knew where it ended. How all the dreams ended.

In death.

"Ori?" someone said, again, more insistently.

Consciousness returned with a surprising lack of pain and the comfort of cool sheets and a soft pillow.

"Keren?"

Van appeared, looming over her. "No, sorry, just me." It took her a moment to grasp he was kneeling. Ori pulled herself up on one elbow, though her head spun and her much-abused stomach threatened to eject itself. The mess tables loomed above her, the seats unbolted and pushed to one side as she rested on a mattress laid out on the mess floor.

She wasn't on Central. She was on the *Ava*. She was in orbit around Tersen. Her hand went to the port, probing at the dressing that covered most of her head.

"I feel better," she said, willing for that to be true.

"Yeah, I hit you with a couple of pain patches. I don't know what you collided with, but you were pretty banged up. And filthy." She had a moment of panic, imagining him running a scanner over her. No, you had to be qualified to operate a medi-scanner, and a freighter captain couldn't afford one anyway.

"I was down in the lower cargo bay, got thrown into the bottom. A couple of the containers have split, there is Orchetti powder everywhere," she lied, then remembered. "Where is Zarr?"

"Behind you." Van motioned over her shoulder. The boy lay on an identical mattress, a clean white dressing above his right temple. Someone, Van probably, had pulled a blanket up to his chin and tucked it firmly around his slight frame.

"He fell off the walkway, onto a container." She sat up, and everything spun around her.

"Hey," said Van, grabbing hold of her and easing her back onto the pillow, "you need to rest, the port will send a medic."

Just what she didn't need, an official port officer poking at her. "Why are we here, rather than in the sick bay?" she asked, using the nearby seat as a handy leverage point. The mess spun a bit, but her stomach stayed in position this time.

Van went very still, his brow crinkling in distress. "We put Lart in there. And Davey."

"They are both injured?"

Slowly the engineer shook his head. "Davey's dead. Crushed. We put him in there until the authorities get here, but Lart won't leave him."

Davey was an aggravating, lazy, sex-obsessed idiot but in that moment a wave of grief surged through her. "He did not deserve that," she said quietly, and meant every word.

Van squeezed her shoulder gently, and for a second Ori allowed her cheek to rest against his arm. "I will tell Zarr. I know they were always fighting, but they were crewmates. Now, where is Jwali?" Ori climbed to her feet. "I want a word with that useless lump of slime."

Van rose, offering a hand as support. "He's in his quarters, heavily sedated. He's had some sort of breakdown, I had to pull him out from under the nav console, the fuck-wit has lost it completely. You'd better watch yourself; he kept screaming that you were an escaped criminal, and that he had to stop you, and that the Directorate was after him, that they were going to kill him. The captain doesn't believe him of course, but Lianna is looking to blame everyone else except herself for all this."

"How long until the investigators get here?" Ori took a moment, as the compartment spun around her, Van's hand warm and steady.

"We're still waiting on a tug; you dropped us right out in the wastelands. That was one spectacular bit of navigation, by the way. Even if it did fry the drives. We'd be dead otherwise."

"That's what training will get you," she said, as she ran the calculations. At least twelve hours to get here, and then tow the *Ava* back, get her settled into the dock. No, the investigators would be on as soon as the last clamps engaged. So, one, maybe two days. Then what?

"Is that what you're going to tell them? The port investigators won't be put off by *training*," Van said, waving his hand in a vague circle. "Or do you—" He stopped, turning almost as red as Zarr. "Do you have some sort of..." His voice trailed away.

This situation was becoming ridiculous. Ori pulled herself upright, using the mess table as support. "Do I have what? Some sort of magic password? I told you before, I'm not who you think I am—"

"You're Directorate," hissed Van, looking around in case there was anyone within earshot. "Stop trying to deny it."

Van's absurd delusion might be useful. The investigation team would want to know how she saved the *Ava*. The engineer was correct, simply stating she was "trained" wouldn't convince them. But she would need Van's help.

Ori decided sitting still was an excellent idea at this stage, until her stomach decided to behave. "Van. I can't confirm who I am. It's too dangerous." That much was true. "But I can't use my—" What was the word? "My status, to get us out of this. I must remain under cover." Again, almost the truth. "I need your help. To come up with a story that will satisfy them."

Van grinned. "Sounds like a plan."

Zarr's footsteps echoed in the silent cargo hold. The last pod had come to rest against the outer hull, the jumble of destroyed pods an untidy pile on the hold deck, twisted metal and scattered contents mixed with broken rails. Getting that section's hatch open would be a nightmare. Starboard hold was worse. It would take them days to get this cleaned up. If anyone bothered. Maybe this was the *Ava*'s last run; with all the drives fried, the captain wouldn't have the credits to pay for repairs. The whole crew might find themselves dumped on Tersen.

The whole crew except Davey. Zarr had known from the moment he came to that something was wrong. Ori sat beside the makeshift bed, looking like she'd rather be anywhere else than right there.

"Who?" he'd asked, dragging himself up to a sitting position.

"Davey."

He hadn't expected it to hurt so much. Davey had made Zarr's life miserable at times, with his pranks and stupid jokes, and his endless fantasy girls. But he'd also distracted old Lart on more than one occasion, sparing Zarr the full force of his anger.

Sex. Laundry. Money.

Zarr scrubbed at his face with his sleeve. He wasn't going to start crying again; it was time he started behaving like an adult.

He wandered along the walkway to the aft cargo console. The maintenance hatch looked like someone had ripped it off the hinges, and wedged it back in with a sledgehammer. It took two attempts before he could force it open.

Wasn't this where Ori had logged into the AI? Fear gripped him, cold and dark. No one could see this. Racing off to the break room he came back with cleaning supplies and the maintenance kit. He went over the entire console and the walkway, cleaning the blood collected in grooves and ridges. He cut and re-patched every cable. Finally, he removed a hatch from a redundant console three levels down and welded it carefully into position.

The hatch opened further down, and Ori stepped through. Zarr pushed everything away around the bulkhead strut, and hoped she wouldn't notice.

"Zarr?" she called, then saw him. "What are you doing?"

Zarr pushed his hands down into his pockets and shrugged. "Cleaning up. There was a bit of a mess," he said, "and I came to see the damage, Jen is talking to Van. They didn't want me there." Zarr suspected the engineer and the maintenance officer were trying to find the best way to tell everyone the *Ava* was unsalvageable. Not that it mattered. They were still going to get their asses dumped on Tersen. The captain might be grateful for Ori's help, but Marissa wasn't one for changing her mind.

"Come then." Ori gestured toward the hatch. "Hanging around here is of no value. We will find Jen and see what can be done. The port investigators are due soon. No doubt they will want to interview us."

No doubt they will. And how are you going to explain your miraculous talent for piloting and navigation? From a clapped-out secondary console?

Zarr followed Ori silently, his fists balled hard. Although she'd hidden it, Zarr had seen her gaze flick to the console. Was this going to be another thing they didn't mention?

"They were here." Zarr gestured with a wave of both arms, up and down the empty main axis of the ship as if trying to conjure their crewmates out of thin air.

"Van will be in the drive room. Perhaps Jen is in the prayer room. Given everything that has happened. What?" Ori asked, catching Zarr's look.

"You missed an opportunity there, to rag on Jen's faith. You're getting soft."

Ori chose to ignore that. "I'll go and find Jen. Go to the drive room, see if Van is there, get an update on when the tug will be here."

The prayer room was empty. Ori stood at the hatchway and stared into the white serenity, perplexed. Where else would Jen be? In her quarters? That meant going back up to the upper decks and running into Lianna. Not a strategic choice now. She headed instead for the maintenance compartment. The hatch opened with a squeal. The level of mess hadn't reduced in the weeks of the voyage, although the mug and its fetid growth was gone.

Jen sat curled in one corner, hands clasped tightly around her knees amid a pile of spare parts and coils of wire.

"I expected to find you in the prayer room," Ori said, pulling the hatch closed with another loud squeal.

Jen didn't look up. "I tried. But I'm too damned angry."

The grease gun lay half buried under a ragged shirt that still held the dead-fish smell of drive coolant. "Anger, I understand," Ori said, applying the tool to the hinges. "Jwali should pay for Davey's death."

"That won't bring him back. 'Forgive our anger, for we are lost and in need of comfort,' is one of the lines from the Prayer for the Dead. The Blessed Mother knows our hearts."

"You intend to forgive someone who killed our crewmate and nearly killed all of us?" As soon as she said it, Ori regretted the harshness.

Jen began to sob. The greasing tool turned fitfully in Ori's hands as she fought the instinct to run, instead folding herself down to sit beside the distraught woman. Tszcienna had been dead for two days when the trainers came for her and her siblings. The children had formed a neat line in the hall while the records were checked once again. Ori had tried not to look at the spot where he'd fallen, and the memory of the blood pooling under him in spreading scarlet.

She had been well aware the nursery staff were watching her, alert for any signs of emotional dysfunction, so the anger, the grief was pushed down, hidden, unacknowledged.

"Is it wrong to want revenge?" She had wanted someone to pay for Tszcienna's death, but the competing desires of revenge and obedience were too much for her six-year-old mind. The result had been years of nightmares, ruthlessly suppressed after the first few nights brought her to the attention of the monitors. She hadn't been the first child to sob noiselessly into her pillow, too terrified to make a sound. Her only comfort was the memory of his arms holding her.

Ori placed the grease gun down beside her on the deck, and slowly encircled Jen's shoulders with one arm, every muscle tense with apprehension.

"You're not very good at this," Jen said, in a half sob, half laugh. "I don't imagine you've had to do much comforting in your life."

"No," Ori replied. Jen's warm body rested against her own, soft and pillowy flesh pressed against the harder planes of Ori's frame. "I came to see what your assessment of the damage is, and how long it will take to repair."

"Repair?" Jen pulled away. "We will be lucky if the insurance pays out. The *Ava* is dead, Marissa can't afford two drives, and the cost of salvaging all the damaged containers. We're all getting let off at Tersen."

Three

"What the fuck are you up to, Jak?"

The fury of Rossim's question stopped Jak midway across the expanse of carpet. Rossim stood behind his desk as though it were a fortress wall, his face suffused with ruddy anger. The cold winter light gilded Rossim's suit of pale silk with bluish highlights and touched the uncharacteristically mussed strands of his hair. "A near collision with a refueling station, almost taking out a heavy freighter? Was this retaliation?"

Retaliation? It took a minute for Jak's mind to follow the Lord President's paranoia. "No, of course—"

Rossim's fist came down on the golden wood of the presidential desk, making everything jump. An exquisite glass orb, jolted out of its wooden mount, rolled away to smash in a cascade of diamond splinters on the floor. "You're in charge of it. And this is what happens?"

"What are you talking about? No, of course it wasn't an act of retaliation." Jak felt a pang of remorse at the orb's demise. It had been a beautiful object. "She saved everyone, according to the reports I'm receiving." Rossim's hatred of the woman was becoming ridiculous. Of course, his family had lost nearly everything, due to some very poor decisions, but the war ended nearly three hundred years ago with the obliteration of Da Chet, and the subsequent elimination of any surviving engineered and their supporters. This alien, from outside the Republic, had never been a threat. If the Hubnae hadn't found her, she would have died alone in the utter oblivion of deep space, with no one in the Republic any the wiser. Only the Xi wanted her kept a prisoner, and only the Xi knew why. "The maneuver, by all accounts, was spectacular," he added.

"Spectacular?" Rossim pushed his chair away in a gesture of absolute fury; it too crashed to the ground, but being of sturdier material than the globe, cracked the marble tiles. "It isn't a thing to admire, it's a fucking Abomination," screamed Rossim. Jak took a half step back, and wondered if the AI would open the door if he had to make a run for it. Rossim looked like a man on the edge, which made some sense — the inquiry into the Freedom Square Massacre would begin soon. That didn't fully explain this display of rabid fury, however. Rossim had faced down the Senate on numerous occasions and walked away unscathed and outwardly unruffled. Was the disgrace and poverty of his ancestors really driving this insanity?

Jak paused, picking his words with care. "Really, Tel, this is beneath you. She is one person, not a ravening horde of Abominations bent on revenge. I do think you're taking this far too personally."

Rossim froze, his face a mask of icy fury.

"Personally? Do you know what my family suffered, how long it's taken to rebuild our place in society?"

It probably wasn't the best time to point out that choosing the wrong side in a war had consequences. Rossim's great, great, great, whatever, grandfather, Lo'oal Rossim, had staked his future, and that of his family's, on the engineered side winning. The purges had been brutal. By the end, the non-engineered side were executing people who emptied the trash, or cleaned the labs, or lived on the same street as an engineered sympathizer.

"No one condones what happened to Sanel Rossim and her children." Now, nearly three hundred years later, the purges were universally condemned. Then, in the blood-bath following the fall of Da Chet, no one had raised the smallest protest at the public execution of a woman and two small children. "But Ori doesn't deserve to be judged with Abominations."

"No? Perhaps we should judge it on the entire nursery of Xi she incinerated in one of her escape attempts? Or the many fine officers and men she has murdered since?"

Jak fell silent, momentarily shocked. She'd burned Xi infants and was still alive? He refrained from pointing out that those fine officers and men were likely responsible for assaulting, raping and generally brutalizing their prisoner.

"We have no idea, not a clue, why she must be kept a prisoner. The Xi refuse to discuss any details at all. If what you say is true, that she has caused the deaths of many Xi, surely you see that this makes her far more important. There must be a reason for it. The Xi never do anything without a reason." That was the telling indicator. That the Xi would put aside the murder of their children and persuade their allies to take no action.

From somewhere out in the square a drone whined past, loud in the deep silence filling the office.

"You are insane," said Rossim finally. "You can't believe that." He moved like a man drugged or half asleep, righting the chair with visible effort. "I won't believe that thing is of any use to the Republic." The light shifted, catching in the shards of multicolored glass, sending fugitive rainbows across the painted walls.

"I'm not saying she is, or isn't. Merely suggesting you accept the idea that the Xi have a plan that we are not privy to." Jak collapsed into one of the facing chairs, sighing. "I have operatives on Tersen and at the docks to make sure she doesn't escape." Jak decided that Rossim didn't need to know that the Ava was limping into Tersen docks, and may not be going anywhere. "Once the *Avadora* jumps, she has no choice but to go to Ma'al. Then, maybe, we might discover some answers." His ship, *The Sleeping Princess,* was being prepped for departure at this very moment. He would get Ori onto another ship, one less likely to fall apart mid jump.

Rossim lowered himself into the chair and glared at Reinnor. "Answers? You really think the Xi can be bargained with?" he said, the rage replaced with contempt. "It makes no difference. They have assured me that the Abomination will never go free. Don't think you can hide your ambition from me, I know you're trying to leverage its mission to your advantage. Too late. Right now, that thing you admire so much is sitting in a cell and I've made certain that it will never leave Tersen alive."

Four

The slight shudder through the superstructure signaled the engagement of the docking clamps. It had taken nearly two days for the tug to arrive, secure the *Ava* and tow her to the docks in high orbit around the gas giant, T5. More than enough time for anxiety to spread through the crew like a disease.

"It will be the port incident investigation team," Van said, his hand warm on her shoulder, "full of questions, but you have your story straight so it won't be too bad."

"I've been on the receiving end of questions before. I'm sure I'll survive." The crew had cleaned up the damage as best they could, except for Jwali, who remained in his cabin, resting, according to Lianna.

"I know better than to ask."

Everyone was crowded around the airlock. Marissa and Lianna, the cargomaster sporting a deep scowl, the captain looking more tired than anyone Ori had ever seen; Lart on an upturned storage bin, his skin gray and lifeless as he stared at the deck, bony hands folded in front of him. Zarr lounged against the bulkhead beside him, avoiding all eye contact.

The ship shuddered again as the airlock engaged with the dock. Van swung open the hatch as soon as the light turned green, only to be roughly shoved aside by a troop of armed men.

"What is this?" Marissa demanded as the intruders took up position, flanking either side of the hatch. Ori caught Zarr's terrified face; she took a half step back, the mesh prickly and hard under her skin.

"There! That's her," screamed Jwali from behind her. Van swore, an obscenity worthy of Rossim himself. Weapons came up, centered on her.

"No," screamed Zarr, leaping toward her, his progress abruptly halted by Lart, who grabbed the boy and pulled him back tight against him. Zarr wriggled furiously until a well-aimed blow forced him into submission.

"I don't understand," said Marissa. "Ori saved us, and the crew of the *Venture*, and the refueling station. Why are you here?"

"I asked for them," said Lianna. "She's the one who's been sabotaging the ship. She's a danger to all of us, and you refuse to see it. You're too interested in her pretty face."

"That is insane, you know it's Jwali. He's the one who screwed up the jump."

Chaos erupted as Lianna and Jwali pointed fingers and demanded Ori's arrest, while Van and Jen vehemently defended her.

Jen was the first one to see her. They all fell silent as a woman in the gray uniform of Tersen Port Authority, stepped through the hatch. Ori noticed she made no attempt to restrain the armed men. Behind her were another three men, all in gray, carrying sheets like they were weapons.

"Who is the captain of this vessel?" demanded the woman, in the tone of bored bureaucracy. "I am Port Investigator Deina. I have a complaint of sabotage, and possible drug smuggling against a Oryelle Tey." Deina looked Ori up and down as if surveying an animal at the market. "I assume you're her."

"I am Captain Marissa Nera ve Sero, and I demand to know why there are armed security on my ship."

The woman ignored her. "And Cargomaster Lianna ve Dev?"

Lianna stepped forward, malice radiating from every pore, Jwali close behind, grinning triumphantly.

"I'm Lianna. I'm the one who lodged the complaint."

The pain on Marrissa's face was palpable. "How could you do this? You know it isn't true."

"I am the engineer, Ilsa Van. I can assure you; she is innocent."

"I don't care. I have an official complaint lodged and she will have to answer for it." Deina gestured to her men, who advanced on Ori. "And I have a detention order for Jwali ve Dev the navigator."

It was almost worth it, to see the blood drain from Jwali's pinched face. Better still to see Lianna also go quite white.

"Arrest? What for?"

Deina didn't answer, merely made a tiny gesture with one hand. One of the retinue leaped forward and read from his sheet, held out before him as though he was announcing a great event.

"Jwali ve Dev, registered navigator on the Light Freighter *Avadora*. Charged with willful negligence, endangering vessels and crew, and endangering the refueling station Alpha 4. Jwali ve Dev must answer these charges before the Tersen Port Authority tribunal."

The armed security moved in, swiftly surrounding Jwali and pushing him, none too gently, toward the hatch. Ori, far more conversant with the ways of prisoner escort, moved of her own accord.

"Take care of the boy," she murmured as she passed Van, "and yourself."

The guards herded them both into the airlock. Jwali tried to put as much distance between himself and Ori, and found himself roughly shoved back to almost touching.

"You would do well to behave yourself. Or you may find yourself accidentally falling down some stairs, or crashing into a hatchway," Ori advised him. The guard behind her jabbed her sharply with the butt of his weapon. She could kill them all within seconds if she chose, but the satisfaction would be short lived. Soon, Rossim would be informed of her arrest. Retribution would arrive swiftly.

The cell they pushed her into was the same as every other cell she had been held in. Small, cold, and reeking of previous inhabitants. The mattress was marginally better than the one on Central, but there was no pillow or blanket. Perhaps they were concerned she would harm herself. The waste unit in the corner looked like it hadn't been cleaned in months; dark streaks of fecal matter striped the bowl and sides. Having existed in far worse conditions, Ori ignored all the filth and folded herself down onto the floor, back hard against the cold metal wall. Who would get to her first? Rossim or Reinnor?

The Sleeping Princess dropped into Tersen space with her drives redlining and carrying so much inertia the ship's AI had to fire the thrusters on full to keep the ship from overshooting her designated slot. "Sorry, darling," Reinnor murmured, patting the navigation console. "I'll make it up to you, I promise."

"New vessel, what the fuck was—"

There was a strangled gasp, followed by a brief period of silence as his ship's ident hit the port AI, and *The Sleeping Princess*'s registry details became available, and then another voice took over comms.

"My apologies, Excellency. How may Tersen assist?"

Polini aristocrats, let alone high-ranking Central bureaucrats, did not generally favor the outer reaches of Republic space. The moment the port AI digested the ship's ident, the fawning began and continued right up to his first inquiry concerning Ori.

From that moment, the port authorities did everything in their power to deny any information on Ori, or her whereabouts. On Rossim's orders, he assumed; it wasn't often that he ran up against this sort of resistance. Usually, his obvious wealth and Polini accent was enough to open nearly any door.

His persistence had finally brought him here, to Port Investigator Deina's office, although calling it an office was a stretch. Jak had seen bigger storage lockers. At this level of the docks, you could feel the vibration of the life support systems work their way up from your feet to almost rattle your teeth.

There was barely room for a tiny desk and two chairs. The woman didn't even rate a holo-wall, which at least might have given the cramped, stuffy office the illusion of space. She waved him to the empty chair, her tight smile barely concealing her annoyance. Jak noted the woman wasn't startled to see him, which meant someone, probably a superior, had warned her in advance of his arrival.

Jak Reinnor settled himself, tugged his cuff back into position, covering the discreet AI monitoring bracelet, and tried not to let his irritation show. It had taken all day to get to this point, and he didn't know how far behind Rossim's people were.

"Thank you for seeing me, Investigator." The indicator on the bracelet remained dark, meaning that there was no active AI in the area. How fortuitous.

"It is a courtesy, nothing more. This is an internal matter. It will be dealt with by the Tersen legal system."

It was the same story he had heard repeated countless times in the last six hours.

"Investigator Deina, with all respect," he said, patiently, "under Republic law she is entitled to receive legal advice. I am here to provide that."

"And equally, sir Reinnor—"

"Excellency," corrected Jak, "I am Xi Liaison. The correct address is 'Excellency'." Deina went an unpleasant shade of red. Blessed Mother; he shouldn't take so much pleasure in humiliating a subordinate. "I have no wish to undermine your authority, but the woman is known to me. I'm sure this is a misunderstanding that can be resolved."

He had tried diplomacy and rank. Now it was time for cruder methods, easier now he knew he wasn't being surveilled. One hand circled in a graceful gesture, encompassing the sad little office, its dingy, dented furniture and stifling air.

"Surely," he said, in a tone of light inquiry, "someone of your talents, and competence must find these facilities..." He paused and made another motion— "Limiting?" and was rewarded with a glint of interest behind Deina's suspicious frown.

"Why do you care about my facilities? Can you conjure up a new office in the upper levels? Excellency." It sounded mocking, but her voice held a thread of interest. Good, he could work with that.

"I don't imagine that Tersen Port Authority pays well?"

Jak could almost see her mind calculating the deal. "I can't simply hand her over to you. I have orders."

"I don't expect you to. Let me speak to her."

"That's all. You just want to see her?"

He really didn't have time for all this. "Of course." Her superiors had proven annoyingly resistant to corruption, but Jak knew you only had to find the right individual. A sufficiently large enough sum, discreetly routed, should do the trick. And if the Tersen authorities found out after he left, well, that would be unfortunate. For Investigator Deina.

Five

She chose to sleep on the cold metal floor. After weeks of clean bedding, the mattress, stinking of piss and vomit, repelled her. For the last four days she had seen no one except the guard who brought food. Once, she could have sworn she heard Zarr's raised voice, but it might have been a dream. All those years of imprisonment should have inured her to such privations but enduring it in front of the boy, seeing his distress, was a humiliation she'd never thought she'd experience.

That they were arresting Jwali as well was the only compensation. She would probably never see the boy, or Van or Jen, again. Rossim would send the Guard for her. Or just as likely an assassin, more competent than the one on Corelli.

When they ordered her from the cell, Ori expected to be handed over to the Imperial Guard. The restraints were standard issue; she could break them easily enough, kill the guards and escape. Escape to where, though? If it was impossible to escape detection on a planet, getting anywhere on the orbiting dock was truly pointless, so she allowed herself to be marched along an endless succession of gray corridors and didn't bother trying to conceal her surprise — and relief — to be pushed into a small room containing Jak Reinnor.

"Ah, at last. You have no idea of the day I've had, trying to see you."

Threat analysis? Concealed AI monitoring point in top left corner.

"Unless you have some magic power that will get them to release me, I can't see the point. You know what they're waiting for." No doubt someone was listening to every word, watching their every movement. Hoping that Reinnor wasn't a complete idiot, she raised one eyebrow toward the overhead and was surprised when he casually rotated his wrist to display a personal security monitor designed to detect, and neutralize, AI surveillance. So, maybe not a complete idiot.

A small metal table, with a seat on either side, was the room's only furniture. She pulled out one seat and sat, the restraints clanking loudly against the metal. The security point, an ovoid button in the center of the table remained inactive.

"What are the charges?" Reinnor sat too, black-silk-encased legs neatly crossed, the sweep of his gray jacket grazing the metal deck. "I know we are on a strict timetable."

So, he knew that Rossim was behind this. "Drug possession, sabotage and assault." How close was the Guard? Were they already in system? On this orbital?

"Hmm. And these charges are false, I assume?"

If she admitted to hitting Jwali, on video, she would never escape. "The navigator, Jwali, is jealous and paranoid. He made the accusations. But it will never get to a hearing, we both know that."

Reinnor's fingers drummed softly on the tabletop. "I have access to my family's legal resources."

"And why should I trust your legal resources? You lied to me from the beginning."

He didn't even look surprised.

"There were things I couldn't discuss at the time," Reinnor replied, with a discreet motion with one finger at the AI.

"Like the *Ava's* fuel tanks? And your actual job title?"

The anger surfaced, just for a second, before Reinnor resumed his bland expression. "Perhaps this is a conversation for another time," he said, adjusting his cuff with minute, precise tugs.

Oh, I will look forward to that conversation, Xi Liaison.

"Perhaps it is."

"And speaking of conversations, may I remind you of the last conversation we had. I wonder if perhaps you might have changed your mind."

So, he wanted assurances that she would go to Ma'al before releasing his lawyer on the Port Authority. His gaze never wavered and Ori was certain that nothing less than her absolute acceptance of the mission would satisfy him.

"I changed my mind weeks ago," she said. "You were right. I do need to do this. I will decide what to do from then onwards." This time, she was gratified to observe, there was more than a hint of fear behind the professional smile.

"Good. I knew I could rely on you." Reinnor pulled out a sheet, unfolded it and began tapping away. "Give me a few minutes and I'll confirm your new berth."

"No."

Reinnor looked up, surprise spreading across his face. "What?"

"I'm not taking a new berth. It's the *Ava* or nothing."

"The *Ava* is a wreck. The drives are scrap, a quarter of her cargo is destroyed or damaged. You are here, that piece of shit navigator is in another cell." Reinnor made a dismissive motion with one hand. "Forget them, they're not important."

Reinnor barely had time to let out a squeal of protest before Ori's fists clamped onto his jacket and she dragged him bodily across the table. "How dare you speak of them like that," she spat as she threw Reinnor to the floor with a heavy thump. "Yes, Jwali is a predator, and his aunt a fool, but the others are only trying to survive. I will not go anywhere without them."

"All right." Reinnor held up his hands in surrender. "You only had to say so."

"So, you will help, you will find the money for repairs, get the ship released?" Ori heard the crash of hatches, and raised voices.

Reinnor sighed, and dropped his hands down to encircle Ori's fists. "If it will get you to Ma'al, I'll do it."

Six

Van stepped out into the corridor, deep in thought, and almost tripped over the boy, lurking right beside the hatchway.

"Zarr," he sighed, "what are you doing here?"

"You have to help me. You have to help me rescue Ori."

"What? Ori? She'll be fine. The Tersen authorities are dicks, but they'll soon work out she's innocent." In the name of the Mother, what was wrong with this boy?

"I should have done something. I should have stopped them from taking her away. Now they'll be able to get her."

"For fuck's sake, what do you mean? I've got both drives fried, our navigator is in prison, and Davey's dead. I don't have time for this."

Zarr stood there, hands jammed as usual into the pockets of his overalls, head hanging, his face set in stubborn determination. Van reigned in his irritation.

Try and remember you were young once. First love is a bitch.

"Listen, I'm sure she'll be fine. Before you know it, Ori will be back here, giving orders."

Zarr shook his head. "You weren't there. On Corelli. We weren't injured in the riot, someone stabbed her, tried to kill her. She was bleeding everywhere." He stopped, as if trying to find the right words. "And when she needed me, I failed. I failed to warn her about Jwali, and he hurt her, and now she's in prison. What if they come for her again?" His voice rose in volume, and then he collapsed, sobbing onto the deck.

"You can't protect her from everything," Van said, kneeling beside him. "It wasn't your fault about Jwali. The man is a fucking amoral, evil predator, and someone should have smashed his head in years ago." He should have smashed Jwali's head in. He should have gone to Marissa and made her listen, but no, all he'd cared about was disappearing into the next flask of booze. He was no better than Jwali. And what was this about an attack?

"What stabbing? You never said anything about a stabbing."

"She made me promise not to tell." Zarr sniffed, wiping his nose on his sleeve. "She said it would only worry everyone. But there was this medic who turned up out of nowhere. He said he was from Six, but I swear he was some rich nob from Central, and he knew Ori."

"Zarr." Van paused, searching for the right words. "I don't think Ori has told you the whole truth about who she is."

For a moment, a strange look swept across the boy's face, then he shook his head. "I don't care. We have to help her. Whatever she's mixed up in, she's in danger. We're her crewmates."

That their new crew hand possessed a much longer list of skills than expected from a simple navigator, Van accepted. But assassins, stabbings in broad daylight, and mysterious friends from Central hinted at something much darker. "I think she's maybe an ex-Marine or something similar," he said, trying to pick the most innocuous way to convey the danger. No way was he going to voice the opinion she was Directorate, or possibly something worse, some black ops specialist. What had the *Ava*'s crew been drawn into?

"Whatever," Zarr said, dismissing Van's concerns. "Are you going to help?"

"Look, Zarr, even if we can fix the ship and get Ori back, I'm sorry, but I don't think she'll stay on the *Ava* long. You should be careful about getting too close to her." He suspected that as soon as they hit Ma'al, Ori would disappear, leaving the heartbroken boy behind without a backward glance. "Don't become too attached. You're going to end up hurt." Advice he should take himself.

The boy's face closed and disappointment hit Van. He remembered when he was young, every emotion sharper and more intense — love, hate, fear, joy — and stubbornly intent on ignoring the warnings of older, wiser heads. How many times since had he he regretted not listening? Though he couldn't really blame the boy; Ori's physical delights would blind anyone, subvert the strongest person's judgment. All Zarr saw was someone needing protection and love, not the soldier with elegant, competent hands who moved like a dangerous animal and spoke of interrogation with the ease of long familiarity. Van knew others like her; trained and deadly, who weighed everything in terms of risk and reward, with a long trail of bodies left in their wake.

"Look, she'll find a way to get back to the *Ava*," he said, trying to be kind. "She's saved all our asses; have some faith."

Zarr nodded and turned away, heading back toward the crew quarters, a picture of misery. Van shook his head in a mix of irritation and compassion.

By the Blessed Mother, I am so glad I am too old for that crap.

Seven

"I can't believe my ears," Lianna screamed. "What do you mean, you won't find a lawyer for your own family?"

Marissa dropped her head into her hands, partly out of weariness with this endless argument, and partly so she didn't have to see Lianna's face, twisted in rage, as she paced up and down the cabin, her hand flinging out wildly with every word.

"We can't afford it," Marrissa said, trying to maintain her patience. The yelling had started the moment the hatch to their quarters clanged shut, and had been going on now for what seemed like days. Marissa took a deep breath, scrubbed her tear-filled eyes, and tried again. "Baby, we have no money for the drive repairs. Insurance won't cover it. It will take months before the damage assessment on the cargo is finalized, and there's no guarantee they'll pay the insurance out either, since it's your nephew's fault we nearly killed ourselves, the crew of the *Venture* and almost wiped out a main refueling station. Don't you understand, I could lose my license for this. Lose the *Ava*."

Lianna's fists hit the table, rattling the bolts that kept it connected to the deck. "Oh, I see. Suddenly he's 'my nephew', and it's his fault. Not that whore you've been getting all wet over since she came on board."

"Lianna, that's unfair. I've never been unfaithful, ever. And I certainly wouldn't with a crew member."

"Don't lie to me," Lianna howled. "He told me. He told me you said she was beautiful. He said you wanted her."

What poison had Jwali been feeding her wife? Marissa rose, and took Lianna's hands in hers.

"Baby, I've never said anything like that to Jwali. Ever." Shame and anger warred within her. All these years Marissa had believed Jwali and Lianna's versions of events. She, as captain, had dismissed all the complaints, all the rumors. The constant issues with getting and keeping crew, she'd put down to the deteriorating labor market and the *Ava*'s age.

Now Marissa faced the ugly truth. Jwali was a predator, a cruel, manipulative monster, who had destroyed everything Marissa valued.

"Lianna, listen to me. I never said anything to Jwali about Tey. I have never wanted anyone but you. He's lied to you, lied to both of us. We have to concentrate on—"

Lianna snatched her hands away. "You bitch. You've always hated him. Now I see the truth. You'll leave him to rot and wait for your whore to saunter back on board and replace me. Well, I still own half of this ship, and while that still stands, that slut is never setting foot on board again."

The hatch slammed shut with a clang that reverberated through their quarters. Marissa slumped to the deck, her body numb with shock and grief. After thirty-seven years, it looked like her marriage was over.

Eight

The door crashed open, disgorging a mass of Tersen security, followed by Port Investigator Deina. Ori did not resist as they dragged her off Reinnor, ignoring the man's protests that he was unharmed. Briefly, she considered breaking the restraints and killing them all, but the ever-present AI prevented her. It would be yet another justification for Rossim's attacks.

"I'm fine," Reinnor protested, again. "It was simply a misunderstanding."

"You said you only wanted to talk to her." Deina pushed one of the guards away. "It looked more like she was trying to kill you."

"If I wanted him dead, he would be," Ori said, ignoring Reinnor's head-shake of disapproval. "We were discussing something, and it got a little heated. I did not hurt him."

Two guards kept a vice-like grip on her arms, while the third pressed his handgun into her temple as if expecting her to attack.

"Return her to the cell. We'll add resisting arrest and assault to the charges," Deina ordered.

"I don't think so," came another voice at the doorway, the stolid Standard transformed into something close to music. It was ridiculous how everyone stopped and turned, like a scene from one of Zarr's e-feeds. The harsh lighting bounced off the glossy plait and silver rings, and slid across the dark-green silk and generous gold scroll-work. "If you could unhand my client," the lawyer added.

Since no one had dared lay a hand on Reinnor, their collective gaze swiveled back to Ori. To their credit, the guards did not release her until Deina gave an impatient nod of approval.

"Since when do freighter crew have the credits for an Eidress lawyer?"

"Hanjile Eidress has always supported honorable causes and freely give their talents to help the oppressed."

How the man managed to sprout such sanctimonious drivel with a straight face mystified Ori; clearly this was Reinnor's "legal resources".

System's port authorities may be gods of their own realm, but the entire Republic bowed, if unwillingly, to an Eidress lawyer.

"I have orders," Deina began.

"I have a court order," returned the lawyer; as if on command, Deina's sheet pinged.

The struggle was obvious, on one hand the woman was at the command of her superiors who wanted Ori kept imprisoned, on the other hand, here was the embodiment of Republic law in five years' salary's worth of green silk. Ori could almost feel sorry for her, trapped between two opposing and equally inimical forces. In the end Deina surrendered, handing Ori over to Reinnor with a sour look, no doubt already rehearsing to herself the substandard excuses that would not save her career.

Ori hoped Reinnor's bribe was generous; the woman would need every credit.

"There is still an investigation," Deina tried vainly, one last time.

"And my client will make herself available when and if the tribunal hears the case."

After that, it all proceeded quickly and without incident. Technically, Ori could not leave the system until a decision had been reached on the investigation, but the *Ava*, in her current sorry state, wasn't going anywhere.

"You will keep your promise?" Ori pressed, as she and Reinnor stood in a side corridor of the docks, his pet lawyer having discreetly withdrawn from hearing range. Reinnor's two agents were also absent.

"The funds are being routed as we speak," Reinnor said. "I don't understand why, but if that's what it takes to get you to Ma'al, then I'll do it. Please, try and behave yourself for the next week or so, and be careful. Rossim will not give up easily."

"I have never understood his hatred of me, I was never a threat."

"Of course, you are. You're a constant reminder of the war, of the bloodshed, of everything his family lost."

"The engineered killed his family?" Ori had to admit, she had never wasted much time interrogating Rossim's motives. Up until now, the emotional life of eijen hadn't interested her.

Reinnor looked uncomfortable. "No. His ancestor backed the wrong side and he and his entire family paid the price. Rossim's branch is all that remains of a dynasty that could trace its lineage back to pre-space times. It has taken the last three centuries for them to regain fewer than half of the confiscated estates."

It did not excuse Rossim's treatment of her, but Ori found herself in the novel position of understanding the Lord President a little better. If the incident on Corelli had taught her anything, it was that dark currents of revenge and bloodlust still haunted the Republic centuries later.

"I will not stray from the *Ava*; once it is repaired, we can leave. They cannot attack me if I am on the ship."

That the *Ava*'s security system still accepted her ID shouldn't provoke such immense relief, but the familiar scratched and chipped corridors were a welcome sight after the loneliness of imprisonment. As she approached the mess, Ori heard Zarr and Van talking. They were speaking too softly for her to pick out the meaning, but the tone was of sadness and resignation.

Zarr was the first to see her, his eyes widening in surprise, joy flooding his face. She tried not to show any pleasure as the boy crashed into her arms, then backed off all red with embarrassment.

"See, I told you those dicks would have to let her go," Van declared, his face impassive but his eyes alight with need so intense, Ori felt her resolve wavering.

"They tried, but in the end, they had nothing," Ori agreed, choosing not to say anything about Reinnor. "So, what has happened while I have been entertaining Tersen Port Authority? Have you started on clearing out the holds?"

Zarr sighed theatrically. "Blessed Mother, Ori, you've only been back five minutes and you're already ordering us about."

"The port is sending in heavy lifters to shift the worst containers," Van said. "We're turning off gravity in that section, so I'd stay out unless your zero g training is OK. Then we can use our equipment to get the rest back up onto their rails. It looks like we didn't lose as much cargo as first thought, which is a blessing."

"I will report to the captain, and then check on the cargo. My zero g training is excellent, by the way."

"I don't doubt it. But I'd be careful, talking to the captain," Van said, dropping his voice. "Her and Lianna have had a real falling out. Marissa hasn't come down here in days."

"She is better off without her. And we are all better off without her and that useless piece of filth, Jwali. If I ever see him again, I will rip his throat out."

"I must say I'm very disappointed, Jwali. I thought you better than this." The man, the agent from Corelli, perched on the edge of the table, completely at ease.

The guard pulled out the one seat and pushed the navigator into it. Jwali's arms jerked sharply forward as the security lock, embedded in the table, engaged with the restraints, pinning him in place.

"I did everything you—" The blow rocked Jwali back, snapping his arms nearly out of their sockets as blood splashed across the metal tabletop.

"I gave you simple, straightforward instructions." The man resumed his perch, wiping his bloodied knuckle on his trouser leg. "And yet you managed to fuck it up. Again."

"I'm sorry," Jwali whimpered, the blood dripping down the front of his clothes. The guard smirked with the enthusiasm of a pet trying to please its master. "I tried, I really did. But the bitch always managed to find some way out of it."

"So, you decided to kill her, and your entire crew, the crew of a heavy freighter and a refueling station?"

Jwali said nothing. It had all been a serious miscalculation. All he'd wanted was to get the *Ava* held by the authorities, long enough for whoever was orchestrating his blackmail time to act. Instead, that bitch tremmie had pulled off a maneuver no one had seen outside of a textbook, and had come out of it a hero, again. There had to be some way to get to her.

"I have an idea," he said, "a way to get to her, easily." The words tumbled out, lashed on by terror. "The bitch has a little pet. Zarr, the junior cargo hand. You snatch him, she'll come off the ship to rescue him. Guaranteed."

The agent gave a very good impression of someone gravely considering a weighty conundrum.

"And how do I get this pet off the *Ava*?"

"Get me out of here and I'll do it. I promise, I won't fuck it up. I'll get Zarr out onto the docks, you can snatch him."

"An interesting proposal. What about afterwards? You know we can't simply let him go."

"Fucking torture him as far as I'm concerned," Jwali snarled. "Make him watch you do over the whore, then kill him."

"Ah, Jwali." The man laughed, ruffling the navigator's hair with too-rough affection. "You are an evil little prick. But I don't have to get you out of here; your delightful aunt has mortgaged her half of the ship to post bail. Get me the bait, and soon, or I may take up freighter ownership as a hobby."

Nine

"You look nice," Zarr whispered. "That color suits you." His hand sketched a rough line in the air, encompassing her outfit. "I was half expecting you to turn up in green, or worse still, black." The *Ava's* AI had supplied a brief rundown on the mourning customs of the Republic. Zarr might overlook her ignorance of clartis-berry pies, but no one would forgive her turning up to Davey's funeral in the wrong outfit.

"It is the clothing from Corelli," Ori whispered back. "I am just not personally acquainted with every single cake and pie available in the Republic." The dark blue pants and matching high-collared shirt was the most elaborate dress she had worn since her capture, and she had to keep resisting the impulse to tug at the sleeves. At least it lacked the ruffles and ribbons of Corelli clothing.

"Did Alise ever message you?" she asked, all innocence. Zarr went bright red.

"Will you two shush," admonished Van, leaning over from his spot further along the pew. "This is a funeral, not a social club."

Chastened, Ori and Zarr subsided. The small chapel, just off the main docks, was not quite as pristine as the *Ava's* prayer room, carrying the ambiance of well-worn use. Jen sat next to Van, her hands clasped around her pendant, eyes closed, lips moving in prayer. The space was roughly oval, painted in a uniform soft white, with three rows of benches set around the central flame. Unlike the *Ava's* little holographic flame in a simple bowl, this chapel boasted a beautifully carved sculpture of two hands forming the traditional cup, in which the flicker of flame sparkled in the dim light.

Ori twitched her collar back into line and tried to look like she knew what she was supposed to be doing. Beside her, Zarr bowed his head and mumbled something under his breath. The AI offered the words to most of the common prayers, but she had rejected it. Somehow it didn't seem right, mouthing the words of faith when she had none.

Marissa sat two pews down with Lart, and there was no sign of Lianna. A handful of people, freighter crew and dock workers by the look of them. sat scattered on the rest of the simple wooden benches.

"That guy fancies you," whispered Zarr. "Last row, about 40 degrees. He keeps checking you out."

Ori leaned on her forearms, feigning grief. Zarr was incorrect. The man was watching them both. At first glance he could pass for freighter crew or a dock worker. A second glance revealed body language that was ... off. He sat too straight, held his body too rigidly, looked around far too intently. And that haircut. Too crisp, too precise. Too new. Another of Rossim's assassins?

"I'm not interested," Ori whispered.

Marissa stood, cutting off any further discussion. Ori's brief research showed that the Republic's main religion had no priestly hierarchy; there were Brothers and Sisters, serving as caretakers of chapels, and informal spiritual advisers as needed, but any services were loose, unstructured affairs, led by the congregation itself. The captain had clearly taken on this responsibility herself.

The congregation stood, leaving Ori once again a few seconds behind. Zarr gave her an annoyed look. Everyone held their cupped hands before them and this time Ori kept up.

"Blessed Mother, your children are here, united in sorrow. Comfort us, Blessed Mother," Marissa intoned.

"Comfort us, Mother, for we are lost," responded everyone, except Ori, who now regretted refusing the AI's information. That could be remedied though. She reached out to the port AI, to find her access blocked.

Network access is not permitted from chapels and other places of worship.

One of Rossim's more blasphemous curses came to mind. She would just have to pretend. As the rest of the crew recited the responses, Ori mumbled along, relieved when a pattern emerged and she could raise her voice a little.

As the prayers ended and Ori resumed her seat gratefully, Zarr's elbow dug into her side.

"You could at least look like you care Davey's dead," Zarr said, anger shading his voice. "Or at least try to learn the words. Someone will notice."

"I do care," she replied, a little too loudly, as both Van and Jen turned to look at her, disapproval apparent at the disturbance. "I'm just not religious, that's all."

"This is a funeral. You don't have to be religious to say the words. You must learn to fit in." And with that Zarr stood up and pointedly moved to the next row. Van raised an eyebrow in inquiry, but all she could do was shrug.

Marissa stood again, Ori began to move, but it seemed this part of the service didn't require anyone else to stand.

"Davey was part of my crew for over six years," Marissa began.

What was wrong with the boy? She didn't need to "fit in". Across the other side of the chapel, the man appeared to be listening to Marissa as she cataloged Davey's short and uneventful life, but Ori could almost feel the intensity of his interest.

"His death was a tragedy, and I know that all of us grieve with his parents, who he loved," Marissa concluded.

That Davey had parents didn't surprise her; that he loved them did. She had dismissed the young man as lazy, feckless and sex-obsessed, yet he had people who loved him. What must it be like to be wanted? To be loved for just being yourself, rather than merely a tool, a weapon in an endless war? The grief hit her; the neuro-suppressors too slow. She had been wanted. Tszcienna had told her so. That she was special, that he had designed her himself, that she was his, not the Line's.

"Are you OK?" Van slid in beside her, concern etching lines between his brows. "It's time for the Prayer for the Dead. Are you sure you're all right?"

It had been a stupid, childish fight over a toy that, in hindsight, neither Ori nor her sibling had really wanted, but it was only two weeks until the trainers arrived and fear had permeated the entire nursery. And in her fear and anger she had blurted out the secret, not knowing it was forbidden. That she was special, not like the hundreds of other Command Lines in the nurseries. Designed for a person, not a purpose.

The next morning, they dragged Tszcienna into the main hall and executed him. She watched the round explode his skull, his body falling lifeless to the floor, the blood spreading out in a scarlet pool, and not by the merest flinch or noise did she betray the slightest emotional response.

"I'm fine," she said, with all the conviction she could muster, despite the tears gathering behind her eyes and the weight pressing down on her chest. She was fine.

Van didn't look convinced, but didn't object when she waved away his assistance. She could stand by herself. The congregation once again held out cupped hands and bowed their heads. Ori looked around in sudden panic — the seat in front of her was empty.

"Van," Ori whispered, "where's Zarr?"

Zarr scrubbed at his face with his sleeve and shoved both hands deep into his pockets until the grief passed.

"Hey, are you OK?"

Zarr whirled, panic-stricken, then relaxed. It was the guy from the chapel, the one who was checking out Ori.

"Yeah, just ..." Zarr shrugged, trying to look unaffected. "You know, funerals." As if that covered everything.

The man nodded sympathetically. "I understand. I did a couple of runs with Davey. Sorry to hear how he died. Freighter life, eh," he replied in a rueful tone, leaning against the bulkhead with one outstretched hand.

Zarr became uncomfortably aware that the exit from this small corridor was now effectively blocked. Behind him was a storage hold, locked, the red warning of the access panel obvious. He could see the constant traffic of people in the main concourse, but none gave the two men more than a cursory glance. Everyone knew how to mind their own business.

"So, you knew Davey?" Zarr managed to get out, and took a half step back.

"Yeah," the man replied, sliding a little closer. "On the Nax'tl run. This was years ago, though."

Davey had never been further than Six. Zarr's palms went slick with terror as his bowels turned to ice water. This man wasn't checking out Ori. He was one of them.

"Can I help you?" Ori appeared, seemingly out of nowhere. For a second, Zarr caught the flash of rage on the man's face before he turned, his voice smooth and confident. The vat- cultured leather jacket, in a soft tan, didn't fully disguise the bulge in the small of his back.

"Just having a chat."

"Then chat to someone else. The boy is mine."

"Hey, I'm not yours," Zarr protested, trying to push past, only for a hand to clamp down on his shoulder.

"Seems like he's with me now."

Zarr struggled to escape, but the stranger's hand just tightened further, fingers digging into his flesh.

"I would let him go. Now."

It was not a request. That was an order. An order given by someone he didn't recognize. This wasn't Ori, this wasn't even the vision in an officer's uniform that still haunted his dreams. No, this was the very thing he'd been terrified of. Abomination. Her face was now a mask of cold, ruthless power. He felt the shudder run through the stranger, the whispered obscenity. Then Van was there, reaching for him.

"Come with me," the engineer hissed, his hand tightening on Zarr's arm. "Now."

He should stay. He should tell Ori that he wasn't her property, that he didn't need protection. That the man was armed, with something big. But then he realized. It was the stranger he should warn.

"Possessive, aren't you."

Rossim's thug held himself with the easy confidence of the trained soldier, his hands loose at his sides. The weapon would be tucked into his waistband, at the back. It would be one of those big silk and graphene composite types; powerful, but noisy. The trick would be to disable him before he had a chance to pull it.

"The boy is a crewmate. But you know exactly who he is." The mesh activated, running hard and prickly under her skin, her bloodstream awash with chemical enhancements. "And who I am."

His hand moved a fraction, and for half a second Ori toyed with the idea of letting him try, just to make it a little more interesting, but there were bystanders only a hundred meters away, and they wouldn't ignore a real scuffle, or a gunshot. The crunch of broken bones and the bitten-back squeal of pain as his body hit the storage locker hatch was satisfyingly loud in the confined space, followed swiftly by the dawning comprehension and terror as the man realized he couldn't get away.

One hand held him securely against the cold metal as her other intercepted his desperate attempt to reach the gun.

"Now, don't struggle. I don't have time to draw this out. You should be grateful for that," Ori whispered, as bone by bone, she methodically crushed his hand. His body thrashed against hers in one last futile effort to escape, but the nanites were already at work. The microscopic machines slipped into his body, navigating the layers of epidermis and muscle as easily as she piloted a ship, heading for the brain stem. His pulse slowed, then stumbled, becoming more erratic as the nanites attacked. He took in one ragged, desperate breath as his heart stopped, then his body slid lifeless to the deck.

Let that be a warning to Rossim.

```
[Subroutines initiated.
Data processing from nanite incursion underway.
Comparing to programmed parameters.
Mission unsuccessful. Parameters not achieved.
Information shunted to secure storage.
Accessible memory erased.]
```

Ten

After dragging the protesting Zarr back to the safety of the *Ava*, Van waited by the main hatch trying not to look like someone consumed with anxiety, but he was sure his sigh of relief could have been heard on Central when the airlock cycled green and Ori stepped out.

"Are you all right?" he asked, then berated himself for how needy that sounded. She seemed unharmed. No sign of a fight. Which was good, wasn't it? The guy, whoever he was, had obviously backed off. Except he hadn't looked the backing-off type.

And there was this: *I would let him go. Now*

Van hadn't seen Ori's face, but he had seen the blood drain from Zarr's. Even now, just thinking about it, the threat present in those few words sent cold shivers up his spine.

"I'm fine, Van," Ori replied, interrupting his thoughts. "Where is Zarr?"

"In his bunk. He's OK, a little shook up, but he'll get over it."

Now what do I say? Did she know how much he wanted her? Since that one fleeting moment in the prayer room, Van had struggled with, and lost, the battle to resist her.

Now she was looking at him, probably wondering why he was standing there like an idiot.

"Would you like some rakosh? I was about to get some." Blessed Mother, could he just stop babbling?

Her shoulders tensed, and he knew she was going to say no and stalk off down the corridor and leave him standing here. Then some emotion, as ephemeral as a Ma'ali summer, passed over her, and she shrugged.

"Yes. I would like that."

Van headed toward the mess, Ori falling in beside him without a word. Her head would rest comfortably on his shoulder, his brain told him. *Shut up, we're just having a friendly drink. That's all.*

The mess was fortuitously empty. Van waved Ori to a seat, found two clean mugs and filled them with the dark, spicy brew. He placed them both on the table, trying not to slop liquid everywhere.

"Thank you, Ilsa," Ori said, taking a sip, her long, elegant fingers wrapped around the mug. "For bringing Zarr back."

Van nodded, deciding silence would serve him better. Let her take her time. The silence stretched out again, warm and companionable. The tension between them melted away; Van refilled their mugs.

"I'm sorry. About, you know," he said finally.

"I hurt you," she replied. "In the prayer Room. I did not intend." She stopped, and Van saw how she struggled to put her emotions into words. "I was overwhelmed. It has been a long time since I have been with anyone I could ..." She stopped again. "Trust," she finished. Her storm-gray eyes held Van's gaze as though staring into his soul.

Trust. When was the last time anyone trusted him? Drunkard, unreliable, Ilsa Van.

"Do you want to talk about it?"

She shook her head, her hand reaching out to cover his. "No. It isn't safe. Just make sure Zarr stays on board in future."

All he could do was nod as she withdrew her hand, stood, and left the mess.

Eleven

The hatch closed behind her. Ori lowered herself to the deck, leaning back against the bench and staring into the holographic flame, caught in the flickers of light, her mind a swirling murmuration of conflicting thoughts and emotions.

She had felt that warmth before, or something very close to it. Ori didn't need to open digital memory to recall the scene; it was always there with her, a talisman against the pain. Tszcienna, his arms around her, his laughter. Soft lips seeking fruit across her palms, the juice sticky on her fingers.

Safe.

Loved.

Her head dropped into her palms, her tears splashing onto the deck. How could she go home now? Love, friendship, compassion — these were foreign, dangerous emotions. Siblings had been culled for fewer defects than this. Tszcienna had been executed for less. Her fault. His death was her fault. The voices were correct. She was damaged, imperfect.

The hatch crashed open, driving her to her feet, ready to attack. Jwali framed the entrance. "Well looks who's sitting in the dark. Prayer won't help you, bitch." Hands on his hips, a triumphant grin spread across his narrow face.

Ori fought down the urge to drive her fist through his skull. "How are you here? Did you think you could escape?"

"I'm not escaping, bitch, although I might say the same about you." He stepped into the compartment, swinging the hatch shut behind him. "I'm out on bail, thanks to my aunt. I hear you got yourself a lawyer. Must have whored yourself out good and proper."

Rage ran out of her, replaced by exhaustion. "What do you want, Jwali? You know I can kill you in an instant if I wish, so why this continual taunting? Do you want to die?"

"Yeah, you keep saying that; haven't seen any sign of it so far. Your little pet gets in one lucky shot and you both think you're some action hero." He was so close now she could smell him. "Lianna can twist Marissa around her little finger. Once my aunt's back on the *Ava*, you and your little bitch, Zarr, will be gone."

Jwali left the hatch open as he left. Ori sank onto a bench, filled with weariness. No doubt what he'd said was true — Marissa would not easily jettison so many years, and so much emotional attachment. Lianna would be back.

It had been four days since Reinnor had promised to fix the *Ava*, and still no word. She would have to go out and find him.

Ori slipped off the *Ava*, after telling Van she needed to do something. He protested, of course, pointing out her enemies — whoever they may be — were probably watching the docks. She pointed out, a little testily, that she knew this, and could take care of herself. All he had to do was make sure he and Zarr didn't leave the safety of the ship. Or Jen. Just in case.

"So, you care if I get snatched?" he'd said, teasing her.

"Of course, I do. The *Ava* would have to find another engineer," she replied, smiling.

Jwali tracked Jen to the maintenance compartment.

"Ah, just the person I'm looking for," he said, slamming the hatch loudly.

Sadly, the little bitch must have heard him coming, because she didn't even flinch, just laid down her tool, suspicion filling her fat, ugly face. "I heard you were released. I hope you are grateful to Lianna."

Fucking bitch, lecturing me like that.

"Oh, I am." Jwali smiled. "And I've learned my lesson. I made some mistakes, and I'm going to make amends."

"You're responsible for Davey's death," Jen snapped. "I haven't seen any amends yet. And what about all the equipment failures? Rumors are that you caused them."

Once that cunt is off this ship, I swear, I'm going to make sure you never get another berth anywhere.

"I don't know how you could believe such things, Jen." Jwali forced his expression into one of sorrow and hurt. "I'd never do anything to hurt any of you. My aunt and dear Marissa are on board; surely you don't think I'd do anything to endanger them, or," he added quickly, "any of you."

He could tell from the fat bitch's face he wasn't making much headway.

"And I miss Davey as much as everyone else." Meaning, not at all. Everyone despised him when he was alive, now everyone was crying over him. "It was an accident. I never meant anyone to get hurt." He took one of Jen's hands, although his skin crawled at the thought of touching her. "No one is beyond forgiveness. Surely the Blessed Mother knows my heart and will forgive me?"

She still looked doubtful, but didn't retrieve her hand.

"The Blessed Mother does indeed forgive all, Jwali," she said, patting his hand like he was some sort of pet, "and if I can help in any way, I will be happy to pray with you."

He had to swallow hard to keep the bile down. "Thank you, Jen. I look forward to that," he replied, forcing himself to return the pat. "Actually, I was looking for Zarr; Van wanted me to pass on a message."

"So why didn't he come himself?" she asked.

I swear, bitch, if you don't do as I tell you right now, I'm going to track down those fucking kids of yours and throw them off a building.

"He was going to, but I asked if I could deliver the message. I needed to come and apologize to you personally, and I guess I needed a reason."

"Well, I'll be happy to tell him, he's down in the starboard cargo bay, watching the container retrieval. Not much else to do at the moment. Does Van need help with anything?"

"No." Jwali adopted his most reassuring expression. "Just let him know that Ori has some errands on the dock and thinks Zarr should go with her, to help."

Once he's out there, it shouldn't be long before they grab the little shit. Then, finally, I can be rid of that bitch and everyone else on this ship.

Twelve

Zarr stepped back behind a bulkhead strut, barely avoiding being squashed. How was he going to find Ori in this crowd? If he didn't watch himself, he'd be swept up and lost in the melee. It would be Corelli all over again. The very thought made him shudder.

He hadn't quite believed Jen when she came bustling down to the cargo hold, but she assured him the message came from Van. Although the captain hadn't forbidden anyone to leave the ship, there was more than enough work to keep everyone busy. Especially since Davey was gone and Lart spent most of his time now either lying in his bunk or sitting in the mess, gnarled hands clutching a mug of rakosh gone cold hours ago. Still, it would be more interesting shopping out on the docks than watching the torturous extraction of containers. The insurance bill, according to Jen, was staggering.

The main corridor widened to a sort of viewing platform where you could see all the ships on this side of the docks lying in their repair cradles, and watch the drones and repair crew flit and dance through the superstructures.

She could have told Jen where I was supposed to meet her.

Zarr edged along the corridor, periodically standing up on tippy toes to try and see over the crowd, and was rewarded finally with a flash of blonde head, further along. He opened his mouth to shout, before remembering the guy at the funeral. He'd been waiting for Ori, Zarr was sure. Although, as usual, Ori wouldn't answer any questions about what had happened.

A cleaning bot, intent on its work, split the crowd for a second, and Zarr saw Ori clearly, up ahead. As he passed the machine, much larger than those on Corelli, Zarr gave it a pat, remembering the little bot he had kicked after they left the medical tent. "Sorry," he whispered, feeling himself redden with shame.

Ori was only a few meters away, threading her way through the press of sightseers to the window. For the most part, the crowd of haulers, mechanics, port workers and passengers let her through without comment, but Zarr saw the looks some exchanged as she slid past, and the crude gestures they made behind her back.

A pair of large mechanics in filthy overalls, stinking of coolant and machine oil, cut in front of him. When he found her again, she was standing at the window, obviously searching for something. Or someone. Ori worked her way along the platform before pushing her way through the crowd again and heading for the repair docks.

She's not shopping. What is she doing?

No one stopped her, or asked her for ID, as she approached *The Sleeping Princess*, out of Polinia and bound for Six Jump, clamped into her docking cradle. Ori briefly considered stealing it; the pain of an AI interface would be a small price to pay. The access tunnel from the central corridor to the *Princess*'s hatch was in place, empty of crew or repair crews or port officials.

"I wouldn't if I were you," came a male voice. She didn't need to turn around, she recognized Finn from Six. "It won't do you any good to steal her." In the tunnel, between her and the busy corridor, stood both the agents from the op on Six Jump, dressed as port workers.

"I could kill both of you now and be in control of the ship before your bodies cooled."

"I know you think we are filth," the female agent said, sarcastically, "but we're clever enough to make sure any vessel small enough to be a target has its drives disabled until the *Avadora* jumps."

Ori slid into the port's database, only to pull herself back out at the shift in Finn's expression. The tiny eye movements were usually only noticeable if she was undertaking a significant search. Had he seen? Worse still, did the agent understand what she was doing?

"Go ahead and *check*," Finn said, producing his weapon, a heavy, black model made of the same composite as the ship outside, "we're smart enough to hide that information."

She made a show of fumbling for her sheet, but the agent continued to stare at her, his weapon aimed quite obviously at her head, his gaze fraught with an almost visceral hatred.

"Will the three of you please shut up." Reinnor appeared from the ship's hatch, this time in a quite subdued suit of matte-black silk, the high-collared jacket reaching to his knees. "Thank you for coming. I know it's dangerous." He waved his hand toward his agents and they lowered their weapons with obvious ill grace, Finn's response notice-ably slower. "Do you want to come aboard?" Reinnor gestured toward the open hatch.

An enclosed space with two armed agents outside and, no doubt, security not far away? Ori shook her head. "No, out here is fine."

Reinnor gave one of his exasperated little sighs and waved Finn and the other one further up the access tunnel. "Go and guard something. I'm quite safe." The woman moved perhaps five steps up the tunnel, Finn remained where he was for a long moment. The intensity of his stare made her uneasy. Reinnor gave him an irritated look and repeated the order. Finn joined his fellow agent with obvious reluctance; Reinnor appeared to dismiss them from his thoughts. The idea that she was no threat rankled. Ori resisted the temptation to demonstrate how wrong he was. Maybe in the future an opportunity would present itself and she could enjoy watching the life drain out of him. Right now, she needed him.

"I know we agreed no contact, but why hasn't the money been transferred? You promised it would be."

Reinnor, either unaware of his future demise, or, more likely unconcerned, leaned against a support stanchion, a picture of nonchalance. "I know, but you have a prob-lem. In fact, you have two problems. I have intelligence there is a private team of — let's call them contractors — on the docks, and they aren't here to do construction."

"I have met one," Ori replied. "They must have found his body by now. There was an attempt to snatch a hostage — one of the crew."

Reinnor came away from his relaxed position. "You killed him?"

Ori shrugged. "Yes, it seemed like the best use of my time. And the second prob-lem?"

For a moment Ori thought he would launch into a lecture about unnecessary killing, but he simply sighed and moved on.

"How are you going to persuade your captain to take the money?"

Ori stared at him in confusion. "Me? Why should I have to do anything? Surely you can simply transfer it to her account?"

"And how do you think she will react? Thousands of credits turn up out of nowhere? Any sensible person would wonder where it came from and why. The first question your captain would ask is what it is going to cost her."

She had not thought of that. She had simply assumed Marissa would take the money gladly and not be concerned at its provenance. Ori had the uncomfortable realization that perhaps her constant underestimation of people was the reason her plans kept failing. Clearly, the transition from eijen to human was more than just semantics.

"What do you suggest then?" she asked, and was rewarded with Reinnor's infuriating smile.

"You know her better than I do. Go and speak to her. Persuade her to take the money. But quickly. Rossim isn't thinking clearly; he's quite willing to defy the Xi to destroy you."

"I am not sure I can persuade her. It is not something ..." Ori paused, feeling herself blush with embarrassment. She was getting as bad as Zarr. "It is not a skill I have had to acquire," she finished, sweeping away the discomfort with a wave of neuro-suppressors. "As for Rossim, he is insane if he thinks the Xi will allow him to defy them. Trust me on this Reinnor, they demand total obedience. I have learned this through much pain."

She expected him to tell her she deserved it, or that he could handle the Xi, or some other nonsense, but instead, he stepped forward, and laid his hand on her arm, with only the slightest hesitation.

"What they did to you, what we did to you, was unconscionable. Unforgivable. My only hope out of all this is that if we can discover what the Xi want, you can go home."

This was not some sort of trick to gain her confidence, or faux concern. Ori could see this strange little man, steeped in privilege and power, whose head barely reached her chin, meant what he said. The feeling came back, the same one that had overwhelmed her on Corelli. *People*. She had slaughtered millions of people. If Reinnor knew what she was, what she had done, would he be so sympathetic?

"And yet you lied to me. You let me believe you were Directorate. You manipulated me so I was forced to take the *Avadora*. You knew she couldn't make the border."

At least he had the courtesy to look contrite. "I'm sorry, but I had to do what was best at the time. I knew you would try and escape. I would have done the same, under the circumstances, but you must admit, I did try to gain your cooperation."

The beautifully cut clothes, shimmering under the harsh station lighting, could buy a small town. He had no need to court her understanding.

And yet, here they were. Others had tried to reason with her — the Hubnae, the Xi, even Garrett, in the beginning. She had fought every single one of them, believing herself superior.

It felt like the ground was opening under her, catapulting her into a strange new landscape. "I am not an innocent, Reinnor. You would not be so forgiving if you knew me."

"Perhaps not. But all of us have done things we regret, Oryelle."

"I think that is where we differ. I am not sure I have moved to regret. Yet. I have moved, though, to classifying those I encounter into enemy or ally."

"I would be honored to be an ally," replied Reinnor, executing a faultlessly elegant bow. "And call me Jak."

"Oryelle is the name the Xi gave me. Allies call me Ori."

"Then I have a question for you, Ori. Have you ever heard of Carillon D'e?"

Thirteen

Zarr followed Ori along the corridors and down through the repair cradles to an access tunnel. He backed up until he found a port where he could see. The ship was beautiful, a private yacht by the look of it. Glossy black composite hull. Surely, she wasn't going to steal it? He peered around the corner, hastily flattening himself when two port workers turned and headed down the tunnel. Although he couldn't hear the conversations, it was obvious Ori knew them. Not as friends though, the weapons they produced confirmed that. What was she doing? He crept closer, trying to hear the conversation.

A hand clamped hard over his mouth and something heavy poked into his ribs.

"Don't make a noise," a voice whispered, "and you won't be harmed." Whoever it was, they were big, and stank of sweat and coolant. He got his teeth around a dirty finger and bit down. Whoever had him cursed and their grip loosened. Zarr struggled, flailing out with his fists and feet, then he felt the cold, slimy press of a medi-patch on the back of his neck and darkness claimed him.

"Ilsa, are you down here?"

"Is that you, Ori?" His voice emerged from the other side of the curve of the primary housing.

"No one else would be mad enough to come down here. What are you doing?" It looked like the engineer was stripping the main drive down. Perhaps Marissa had changed her mind?

Van appeared, wiping his hands on a filthy rag, overall sleeves knotted around his waist. His shirt stuck to his skin. "Stripping the drives down to usable spare parts. Captain's orders. We're going to sell what we can, use it to pay some of our wages, and hope the salvage is enough to cover the rest."

"No, don't do anything yet, I'm going to sort it out. The *Ava* will be repaired. I must talk to the captain."

"Repair? Ori, it's thousands of credits. You can't just make that appear. I mean, can you?"

She climbed up the scaffolding and peered down into the body of the drive. The scorch marks and pervasive stench of burned electronics signposted the devastation.

"I'm working on it. Have faith, Ilsa; I'll get the *Ava* going again." She took one more look at the drive and climbed back down. "Have you seen the boy? There is still chaos down in the starboard cargo area. The port needs to get their crew in to remove more pods."

Van shook his head. "No, I told him to go to starboard cargo hours ago."

"Yes," she said, aware of a thread of concern making itself felt. "I think I shall see if Jen has seen him. He'll be avoiding work somewhere." Which was untrue and unfair. Given the correct supervision the boy worked hard, and even showed some degree of discipline the rest of the crew would do well to follow.

Consciousness returned, bringing with it a skull-splitting headache, the groggy realization his arms and legs were bound, and he was upside down. Why was he upside down? He'd been snatched, he remembered now, as the fog of sedation slipped away. Whoever was carrying him — Zarr worked out he was slung over someone's shoulder — lurched slightly. And the stench! An eye-watering cocktail of coolant, sweat and some other odor Zarr really didn't want to know about.

"Confirmed. En route to position. I have the bait."

Everything lurched again. Silence except for the hum of the lift mechanisms and the asthmatic whine of life support.

"Fucking lift. No, not you, the lift is crap."

Lift. Zarr's brain supplied. Lift to where? And was he the bait?

Another long period of silence. His attacker was talking to someone.

"Yeah, I know what the boss said. Wait until we capture her, do the kid in front of her. I know what to do."

Ori. They were going to kill Ori, and kill him, too. Zarr opened his eyes slowly, trying to pretend unconsciousness for as long as possible. His arms hung down, his wrists tied, and his bound legs held firmly. Of his kidnapper, Zarr could only see a wide swathe of dirty overall.

The lift gave another lurch and stopped. The door chimed and Zarr could feel the body under him begin to move. Zarr raised his arms as high as he could, then brought his elbows down and into the man's back. The kidnapper grunted, and staggered slightly, as Zarr tore himself loose, crashing to the floor of the lift and half falling out into the corridor beyond. A hand grabbed his ankle and Zarr lashed out with both feet, his impressions of his attacker reduced to a looming figure in blue overalls, and hard, grasping hands. Zarr slithered back, trying to get distance, but his captor was onto him now.

"Let me go. Help!" Zarr screamed and kicked out. The Blessed Mother must have been looking out for him as his boot crashed into the attacker's nose. Blood spurted across his face and the kidnapper howled with anger.

Zarr's victory was short lived.

"Come here, you little prick," the man yelled, snatching hold of Zarr's arm and dragging him to his feet.

"No. Ori, help," he screamed, as terror drove him to frantic, ineffectual kicking at his kidnapper.

His attacker's face resolved into a blood-splattered visage and a shock of dark hair. A large, thick-fingered hand closed around Zarr's throat, cutting off his screams.

"Will you shut up," the man snarled and slammed Zarr's head into the lift door.

Fourteen

J wali. She was going to rip his throat out when she got back. How could Jen be so stupid— No, there was no point in blaming her.

The boy wasn't on the *Ava*, or in the immediate area of the docks, or in the recreation areas either. Ori found herself following the path she'd taken earlier, trying without much success to push down a growing sense of unease. He wasn't answering her messages, either; she'd tried calling his sheet, with no success, and searching the entire dock was impossible. Raising her concerns with port security would put a target on herself. The only other option, to try and hack into the port AI, wasn't a course of action she relished.

Ori stopped near the observation platform, searching the crowd, as if wanting it could make Zarr appear. Perhaps he had jumped ship? No, he wouldn't leave, not without telling her.

The same anxiety she felt on Corelli hit her like a thousand insects crawling under her skin. The mesh activated in response; neuro-suppressors unable to control her fear.

The crowds thinned a little as Ori searched corridor after corridor. Intent on her search, her sheet had to ping twice.

Missing someone? Deck L Compartment 1145.

The message stared back at her. Rossim's contractors had taken the boy. They were going to regret that.

This wasn't like Corelli. Yes, the fear was there, eating away at her, the mesh hard, but the rage... It burned in her, a dark, cold fury. They had taken Zarr.

Ignoring the muttered curses of a knot of gossiping port workers, Ori pushed past and made her way to a cubicle at the end of the ablutions block. Once inside, she slammed the door closed and touched her chip to the access panel, granting herself fifteen minutes of privacy. The cramped space contained a leaky shower head in one corner, a waste unit, and a sink on the opposite side, all illuminated by harsh industrial lighting and suffused with the smell of cleaning chemicals.

Ori reached out to the dock's public AI network, her interface projecting the search screen onto her field of vision. Using a series of mental nudges and tiny eye movements, she navigated the virtual maze of the network. To an onlooker, her movements would have appeared as a disconcerting series of tics and twitches, guaranteed to attract unnecessary attention in a public space.

Her search finally unearthed a schematic of the lower decks including L, a floor of partly abandoned storage units above the dock's life support machinery. It appeared a solitary lift serviced the entire section — a solid strategic choice. If she were Rossim's crew, that's where she would put either a lookout, or even better, an autonomous sentry gun. Anyone stepping out of the lift would be mowed down almost immediately.

What she needed was another way in.

The schematics led her to a maintenance compartment off the main concourse; the lock no match for her rage. Inside, the compartment was empty, the entire space dominated by a huge curving bulkhead, inset with a large access hatch — a small section of the ventilation shaft running from the lowest to the highest decks, pulling fresh air from the life support system up through the docks.

As Ori drew closer to the shaft, the muted thunder became louder, the vibrations of the deck stronger. Signs attached to the bulkhead warned that entering the shaft when the system was operating was an extremely bad idea. The handle buzzed in her hands, as she opened the hatch; her hearing protection protocols activated, reducing the deafening roar of the fans. She leaned out into the void, and was nearly knocked off her feet by the up-rushing air. This wasn't going to be easy.

Ten meters below, the first of the massive fans spun, its blades a blur. Ori stepped out onto the tiny maintenance platform, designed only to be used when the fans were off, flicked over into thermal imaging and dropped, keeping as close to the side of the shaft as possible; the air flow was strong enough to blow her into the overhead screen if she wasn't careful. The grating covering the fan shuddered under her impact. The vibrations shook her entire body; the up-rushing air threatened to rip her clothes off, its intensity a physical bludgeoning.

To one side, a small maintenance hatch allowed bypass of the fan, although it was never supposed to be used when the fan was in operation. The huge metal vanes, spinning so fast as to a blur, were only a few centimeters from her face as she squeezed past. She dropped to the next fan, her carbon-fiber reinforced tendons and bones absorbing the shock. Two more to go.

The exit hatch opened reluctantly; its squeal lost in the background noise. Ori climbed out into a poorly lit compartment strewn with rubbish and smelling of grease and coolant, shoving the hatch closed behind her. She stepped silently across a minefield of rusting parts and unidentifiable rubbish to the hatch, took hold of the handle, and turned it as quickly as she dared. The thundering pulse of the dock's life support systems under her feet would cover most small noises, but she still didn't want to give her position away.

Compartment 1145 was at the end of the corridor to the left of Ori's current location. To her right, the corridor stretched in a straight, empty line to the lift. There were no sentry guns, no ambushing agents in sight, but it didn't mean they weren't there.

The Tersen Port Authority must have thought security protocols on lifts unnecessary. Ori slid into the AI network and subverted the lift commands within seconds. The lift chimed softly, the doors twitching back and forth as the AI tried to overrule Ori's control. No more than two meters in front of her, a woman stepped cautiously out of an alcove. Her weapon, a big, high-caliber composite like the kind used by Reinnor's thugs, tracked unwaveringly to the empty lift. A second agent, a thin, sharp-faced man, peeled out of his hiding place, his weapon also trained on the malfunctioning door.

Two steps and Ori was behind the woman. The crunch of cervical vertebrae barely registered against the background rumble. The other agent, his attention fixed on the lift, didn't notice his companion was dead until her body hit the deck. His weapon swung unerringly to point at Ori; only to see it fly across the corridor, landing with a clatter before spinning out of sight.

There was a second when he hesitated, caught in the fight or flee decision. Neither option was ever a possibility; in a heartbeat Ori had him around the throat and crushed against the bulkhead, his feet kicking uselessly in the air.

"Where is the boy?"

"Fuck. They warned us you were dangerous. You're too late. He's dead. Dumped into waste disposal."

"Wrong answer."

The nanites were already in his brain stem. The interface flicked over, physiological data streaming across her vision. A mental nudge paralyzed his vocal cords, rendering him mute. His eyes bulged in terror as he struggled futilely in her grasp.

"How many are waiting for me?"

A violent shake of the head. She couldn't drag this out too long, there would be others, waiting for a signal, or shots.

She sent the command. His body spasmed in agony as the nanites, hijacking his central nervous system, activated pain receptors.

"Where is the boy?"

He was going into shock. She released vocal control, but tightened her fingers around his throat, digging into the muscles.

"He's ash by now, with all the rest of the garbage," he croaked out.

"I don't believe you."

The man made a nod toward the lift, still caught between Ori's control and the dock AI. "Look for yourself. There's enough blood."

She dropped him to the deck and strode to the lift. Blood splattered the door frame, more covered the deck in large, drying patches. Her fingers touched one large pool of rusty red, the nanites making contact immediately. It was Zarr's blood. Her systems recognized his genetic profile.

"See. I told you."

His head exploded, her foot driving through his skull, brain and blood and bone fragments spraying across the bulkhead. Arterial blood pumped once, twice, before slowly subsiding as his body sagged and collapsed to the deck. Ori scraped her boot clean on the still twitching body.

"You should have listened to them when they warned you about me," she said to the dead man. "And now I am going to find the rest of your team and I am going to kill every one of you."

She picked up the discarded weapon and checked the power levels, moving down the corridor and shifting to infrared. Two bodies, in bright orange and purple, were inside, close to the compartment's hatch. Her sub-dermal mesh activated, prickly and sharp, enhancers racing through her bloodstream. The door burst open under the force of her kick, slamming into one opponent. Her first round took his companion just above the right eye, the second through the throat. He was dead before his body hit the floor. The other agent, reeling back from the door, got off one shot, the round speeding past her ear to ricochet off the bulkhead. Two shots, both center forehead, and he sagged and fell.

```
[Subroutines initiated.
Data processing from nanite incursion underway.
Comparing to programmed parameters.
Mission unsuccessful. Parameters not achieved.
Information shunted to secure storage.
Accessible memory erased.]
```

The only sound was the distant rumble of machinery. An expanding pool of blood spread across the deck, subsuming dirt, and rubbish as it went.

A fan started up somewhere, missing a bearing or two given the squeal it made.

What would she tell Ilsa or Jen? How could she go back to the *Ava* and tell them Zarr was dead? She didn't even have his body.

They threw him into the waste.

No, she would tear this entire dock apart before she accepted that.

The fan stopped and there was only the machinery noise.

Weapon raised, Ori checked the compartment. Apart from the bodies, the entire area was empty except for a pile of rubbish in one corner. Unrecognisable items ricocheted around the compartment as Ori tore the pile apart. No Zarr, or sign of him either. He must be somewhere else. *He must be.* Out in the corridor, the other agents' bodies lay where she left them. Ori reached into the dock AI and overrode the lift controls again, disabling access and logging the lift as disused. That should stop anyone stumbling onto the scene accidentally. Or deliberately.

According to the schematics there were three more compartments down here. The first was no more than a large storage compartment, and totally empty. The second held what looked like a pump assembly and two other large pieces of equipment she didn't recognize, but no Zarr.

Yet, as she headed toward the last compartment, some part of her *knew* he was still alive. The persistent itch in her mind would not let her rest until she found him. The small access hatch opened smoothly, on well-greased hinges. Her weapon snapped up.

The lights, which had come on automatically in every other part of the dock, remained off. Ori switched to thermal imaging and everything shifted into a gray-green landscape of boxes and looming mountains of unknown contents under syntheplaz covers. The compartment was enormous, stretching into the distance; it had to take up at least half the level.

I will never find him in this.

Even as she thought it, she moved toward the far aisle, stepping cautiously along the piled containers, weapon ready, her feet taking her unerringly toward the end, where the organization gave way to jumbled piles of machine parts, and rusting metal.

"Zarr," she called. "Zarr, can you hear me?"

Zarr opened his eyes to darkness. And to pain. Blessed Mother, his head hurt. Where was he? His arms and legs were numb, he couldn't feel his hands at all. And something stank, really bad. He tried wriggling around, to get his head out into fresh air, but the slightest movement made his head scream with agony.

He was very tired. Zarr let go and darkness swallowed him.

Something dragged him back to consciousness. But he couldn't work out what. Everything was blurry and unfocused. He couldn't remember anything. He felt sick. And too hot. And too cold. He should get up. Go home. His parents would be worried. No, that wasn't right. They were on Six Jump. So where was he?

Darkness again.

The pain was worse this time. Why couldn't he move? He needed help. He needed...Ori! Where was Ori? He was supposed to be the bait. Zarr tried to move, the world swam and spun; he threw up, vomit plastering his face and clothes. Terror gripped him. He was going to die here, wherever here was. Alone.

"Ori," he called, as the tears ran down his face, and consciousness fled.

Ori stopped. Had she heard something? Hard to tell over the incessant rumble of machinery. Vision flicked over to infra-red, but no tell-tale blooms of color appeared. She crept down the aisle, weapon steady in her hands.

He's dead.

Despite that, the feeling continued to tug at her, driving her forward. Whatever it was, it would not let her turn around and leave. The row ended, the machinery and stacked boxes petering out to a pile of discarded packaging and unrecognizable lumps of syntheplaz, partially covered with a vile-smelling blanket.

A blanket that moved.

Ori took hold of one corner and flicked the blanket off the pile, reeling back at the stench.

Blood and vomit plastered the fine brown hair to his scalp where a deep, curving laceration cut across the top of his skull. Tear tracks meandered across his cheeks. Restraints bit into flesh at his ankles and wrists.

She should not have killed them so quickly.

"Zarr, it's me. Can you hear me?"

The only response was a feeble moan; his face twisted in pain as she cut his bonds.

"The feeling will come back soon, it will be painful for a few minutes," Ori reassured him, pulling her shirt off and wiping away the blood and filth. The ragged and dirty top underneath would have to do until she got back to the Ava.

I should have brought water.

The nanites activated the moment Ori touched him, flooding into Zarr's bloodstream and beginning the repairs without much input from her. A disconcerting experience. Granted, Ori had never shared nanites with anyone before this, not even her siblings. Such an intimate act was usually reserved for a mate or some other close bond, something, Ori realized, which had always eluded her.

"You have to stop running into hard objects with your head," she said in a whisper, wiping the boy's face. "The nanites will repair your brain cells, but they can't replace damaged memories."

Zarr stirred, opening his eyes.

"Where are we?"

"Still on the level above life support," Ori said, slipping her arms under his body, lifting him with ease. "Come on, let's get you back to the *Ava*." And past the carnage, before he became aware of his surroundings.

Ori carried him back out of the compartment, down the corridor and past the rapidly cooling bodies with their thickening pools of rust, to the lift. The machine responded to her commands, the door slid closed and the lift began to ascend. In the confined space, the smell was overpowering.

"Are we on Six?"

"No, we are on Tersen docks. Don't you remember?"

He shook his head. "No." Then. "I'm feeling better. Put me down, please. I'm not going to get carried through the docks like a little kid."

The interface assured her repairs were well underway. Reluctantly, Ori stopped the lift and lowered Zarr to the floor. He pulled himself up against the wall, blinking in confusion.

"I was trying to find you, and this guy snatched me."

Ori crouched down, leaning back against the opposite wall. "You should not have left the *Ava*. More of Jwali's interference again. He somehow persuaded Jen the message came from me."

"Don't blame Jen, she thinks the best of everyone. And that prick can be persuasive when he wants something. I thought I was going to die."

"I would not have allowed it. I'm not going to do cargo handling by myself." The wan smile warmed her more than she expected.

He felt through his scalp, where the nanites, efficient little machines, were repairing the torn and bloody skin.

"It doesn't feel too bad now."

Her hesitation must have alerted him.

"What did you do?"

"I used my nanites to heal you. Your injuries were severe."

"Hey, don't say that out loud," he hissed, pointing at the ceiling. "They'll hear you."

Ori shook her head. "No, at the moment I am hiding this lift from the AI. It is temporary; if the network was actively searching for me, I could not resist it. But for now, we are invisible."

She had no idea if any more of Rossim's agents lurked on the docks, or if they were capable of subverting Tersen's AI network, but the prudent course was to get back to the *Ava* as quickly as possible.

"You can do that? Wow. So, I'm going to turn into you?"

The question caught her unawares. "No, of course not. They will repair the damage, and then self-destruct. You won't know they were there." Of course, he wasn't turning into her. No amount of nanite exchange could do that. It still left the question, though. How had her systems known he was still alive?

"You did this before, didn't you? When I hit my head on the bunk. I thought I was out for longer than a few minutes."

"I didn't realize it was you, when I hit you," she replied, a little defensively. "You started seizing. The *Ava* does not have the medical equipment needed to save you." Although Ori knew she shouldn't pursue this, a mix of curiosity and concern drove her. "Are you aware of them? The nanites," she clarified, at Zarr's confused face.

"No, well." He paused, thoughtful. "I always knew you would find me. But, I mean, I knew you wouldn't abandon me. Not sure that's the nanites, or you know ..." He reddened, scarlet rushing up to his ears.

Friendship. He knew you would come for him because you are friends. Not a sibling, not a superior, not because it was required, or demanded.

Ori nodded slowly, understanding what he meant. It had been more than just physical proximity that led her back here; there had been an unmistakable pull toward Zarr she'd been unable to resist.

"We must return to the ship before someone starts missing us. We do not want questions." The lift jerked into life.

"I know what you are, Ori. Those guys would have killed both of us. I don't care they're dead," he said, climbing to his feet, the blood and vomit-stained clothing the only reminders of his ordeal.

"Then you should. I am not someone you should emulate. Being around me is dangerous. This is why I wanted you to go back to Six."

"Maybe. But I also know you need someone to watch your back." He held up his hands. The lift doors opened, and Zarr stepped out. "Your secret is safe with me," he said. "But what about the Captain and Van? Won't they want to know where we were?" He tugged at his soiled clothing with distaste. "How are we going to explain this?"

"Let me take care of the Captain and Van. You make sure you stay on the *Ava* from now on, no matter what anyone tells you."

"Yes, Commander," Zarr said, resignedly.

Fifteen

Ori's fear that it would be difficult to get back on board unchallenged proved unwarranted. No one lurked at the airlock hatch to accuse them, and the corridors of the *Ava* were mercifully empty, the rest of the crew clearly occupied elsewhere.

"I'm going to talk to the captain," Ori said, pulling on a shirt, as Zarr rummaged in his locker for clean clothes. "If anyone asks, you found me, and we returned to the ship without incident. And stay away from Jwali. I'll deal with him."

"Yeah, well, good luck with the captain, she's not in the best of moods right now."

According to Van, the captain had spent most of her time on the bridge since Lianna left. Ori felt an unexpected twinge of sympathy for the woman, who was a decent captain, just a poor judge of people.

The bridge hadn't changed much since the last time. Rubbish and filthy mugs still littered the nav console, a further layer of dust shrouded the netted piles of miscellaneous junk. Marissa sat in the command chair, staring blankly at the bank of dark screens, a mug of congealing rakosh clasped in both hands.

"I'm busy," the captain said, without turning around.

"I can see that, ma'am," Ori replied, taking up the position she had so often occupied, hands clasped behind her back, solid and unmoving beside her commander. Until she'd had a command of her own and another sibling stood in her place.

After a long moment of silence, Marissa made a small noise of exasperation. "What is it?"

"I wanted to discuss the repair schedule, ma'am."

"Repair schedule?" Marissa rounded on her. "The *Ava* is dead. My marriage is dead. I've been protecting a man I thought was family, and now..."

"I can help."

Marissa's fingers were white with strain as the captain clutched the mug tightly to her chest. Ori leaned over and gently prized it from the other woman's grasp, setting it down on a handy netted pile.

"Captain, listen to me. I can help. I have money—"

"What use is money? Don't you understand. I've lost Lianna. And Jwali— I can't even begin to make amends for that. All the people he hurt. You, Zarr. That poor boy." Marissa began to weep, great sobbing gasps of pain and despair that Ori recognized all too well.

What would she do for family? Keren had risked his life to free his obviously guilty brother, even Rossim raged against her and all the engineered because of deep-seated family guilt. And what had she done? Fought alongside her siblings, slept with them, ate with them, trained with them.

But never loved them.

"You still have people who need you. Jen, and Van, and Lart. They all need the *Ava*, they need you. And you can make amends to Zarr by not throwing him off."

Marissa shook her head. "I know. I'm sorry. I should have spent more time with you all, instead of leaving it to Lianna. But it makes no difference, even if we repair the *Ava*, Tersen won't let us leave until the investigation is complete. They are bound to find Jwali guilty. He'll be sent to prison. Lianna refuses to leave here until the case is resolved, and as half owner, I can't take the ship without her. Which may take months. Not to mention the border issue is still unresolved."

Which was the least of their problems. However, what Marissa said was correct. Repairing the *Ava* was only part of the solution.

"If I can find a way to get Jwali out of major prison time, will you start the repairs?"

"Yes, but how will you do that?"

"There is a solution. It requires ... courage to implement. But it will save the *Ava*, and you. So long as you can persuade Lianna to let the *Ava* leave."

Marissa tilted her head, narrowing her eyes with suspicion. "So, you're going to give me thousands of credits and keep Jwali out of jail, just out of the goodness of your heart? This latest debacle will end my career and no one will ever employ me again short of a janitorial position. You could leave now, go down to Tersen. After pulling off that maneuver, ships would be lining up to take you. You don't need me."

Ori shook her head. "No. I'm going to pay for the repairs, and solve your problems with Jwali for my own reasons. Which do not concern you. Do this, and you have your ship and your reputation back."

For a long moment, Marissa said nothing, staring at the curving bank of screens as if trying to read the solution in them.

"Lianna and I have been together for over thirty years," Marissa said slowly, leaning back in the command seat. "We needed a navigator, and Jwali was fresh out of training and needed a job." She looked away, staring at the empty, lifeless nav panel. "Finding crew, keeping the crew, is impossible sometimes. The *Ava* is old and slow, and I can't pay as well as some of the other captains." She folded her hands into her lap and transferred her gaze to them. "It was all right in the beginning, and there were complaints, but Lianna persuaded me they were willing, that it was only the usual crew bitchiness."

"We were not willing. I tried to tell you what he was like."

Marissa sighed, long and despairing. "I should have listened to you, to Jen, to Van." She looked up, holding Ori's gaze. "What are you going to do to him?"

"There are desires and there are necessities, and to save you, I must..." She stopped, trying to find the right word. "Moderate my response. He will lose his license and probably never gain a position off-world again, but you will retain your ship, your license, and your reputation. Tersen will let us go. If you use the money to get the repairs finished."

Marissa nodded, no doubt weighing all the possibilities and the possible traps. "What do you need?"

Ori smiled. "The access codes to the AI. Leave the rest to me."

Sixteen

The cargo bay was the quietest place on the ship, where she could be sure no one would interrupt her, or creep up on her unawares. The state of the console surprised her. Someone had replaced all the data cables, replaced the door, and cleaned every surface to a standard not seen elsewhere on the ship.

This was the boy's doing. He had seen what needed to be done, and carried it out flawlessly. Perhaps it would be strategically advantageous to have someone she could rely on, someone more familiar with the nuances of Republic culture than herself.

The cargo console booted up without incident this time, and the AI accepted the codes without issue. She commanded the ship now, except the *Ava* couldn't go anywhere. Time to fix that.

Ship, give me access to the medical logs.

The crew's medical files appeared on her interface screen. Adding an extra entry or two presented few problems; the skill came in crafting the information to make the lies seamless with the truth. Interesting. Jwali needed treatment for headaches on a semi-regular basis, no doubt due to floess withdrawal. It would make it so much easier to craft a convincing story. In truth, this level of realism wasn't necessary; the story only needed to hold up for a week or so. She brushed off such concerns. It would hold up to any scrutiny short of a full forensic sweep. Finally, everything was ready. Now to find Jwali.

The hatch to Jwali's quarters swung open without a sound. Unfettered access to the AI meant inconveniences, such as locks, disappeared. The lights were off, so she shifted into thermal imaging. Jwali lay on his bunk, his back to her, curled up under a blanket. Her bare feet made no sound on the cold deck as she moved closer to the sleeping man.

Rage warred with logic. It was imperative his body have no other injuries than those consistent with the altered medical records, but her mind howled for vengeance. *Soon,* she whispered to herself. She pushed the rage back down, calmed herself. Jwali murmured in his sleep and settled again.

Others might have surveyed the sleeping form and perhaps hesitated, burdened with doubt that an attack now, when he was the most vulnerable, was moral. Ori harbored no such doubts, no hesitations. The nanites collected on her fingertip, an invisible thread from her finger to Jwali's neck. The microscopic machines slipped into his body, racing for his spinal cord. The interface relayed the nanite's position and Ori initiated the link. Jwali's body jerked suddenly.

"Wake up, Jwali," she whispered, rolling him over to face her. His eyes flew open, his chest heaving. "You are paralyzed," Ori said, her voice dripping with venom. "You can't move, can't speak." She tilted her head, examining the data scrolling across one of the screens. "Hmm, I can also do this." His eyes flicked wildly back and forth in terror as his breathing stopped. Ori monitored the falling oxygen levels, before releasing control. Jwali drew air in deep ragged breaths. "Do not pretend you do not know why I am here. I warned you. You did not listen." She grabbed the edge of the blanket and jerked it off his still body.

"I have killed many, Jwali. Those who thought me at their mercy, those who thought I was powerless." The navigator's eyes bulged in terror, the whites standing out starkly against his skin. "Unfortunately, I cannot kill you today. But I am going to make you suffer."

She consulted the screen again. Blood pressure, heart rate, cortisol levels all rising toward critical levels. If she was not careful, he could have a heart attack or stroke under these conditions. Not what she wanted. She released control a little and he thrashed back and forth on the pillow as some movement returned.

"Jwali, there is no point in resisting. This is going to happen, one way or the other. Now, I'm going to release voice control, but if you scream, the pain I will inflict will be nothing like you have ever experienced." A mental nudge and the paralysis of his vocal cords dropped. She slammed back control as the first squeak emerged.

"Jwali." She shook her head in mock disapproval. "What did I say?" His mouth opened in a silent scream as the nanites stimulated pain receptors, the levels of stress hormones rising sharply. She cut the stimuli as his body was reaching critical again. His mouth and eyes closed, tears leaking out from the corners.

"Now, will you obey?" she asked. After a moment he nodded. This time he did not attempt to scream, instead, he watched her warily. "Good. See what obedience gets you? Now, firstly I want to know how you managed to screw up such a simple task as dropping us into Tersen space." His mouth opened and closed again, and he swallowed.

"What are you?" he croaked.

"Command Line," she replied, evenly. "One of the Khatjarit." It felt oddly satisfying to say it out loud. "I would give you my Line designation, but it wouldn't mean anything to you." Jwali closed his eyes tightly and she could almost hear him willing himself to wake from this nightmare. "You are awake, there will be no escape." He didn't open his eyes, but he did answer her.

"What do you want?" he rasped.

"Tell me what went wrong." He turned his head away, his face flushed with anger. No, shame.

"Zarr keeps boasting to everyone how great you are." His face remained turned away from her. "Pod handling, navigation, engineering. That little bitch thinks you can do anything. I wanted to show everyone I was as good. I bypassed the AI control. Entered the string manually."

Zarr, you stupid boy. You came close to getting us all killed.

"It does not excuse your assaults on him, on me."

Jwali's expression abruptly closed. "Fuck off. Do whatever you want. They'll catch you," he said through gritted teeth.

"Catch me? Who?"

Jwali sneered, and turned his head away.

The Directorate.

"Did the Directorate of Protection coerce you into this? Into attacking me?" His expression didn't change but Ori knew what had happened. "Did they blackmail you?"

"I did six months of rehab. I was clean. I had a chance to get away from this rusting piece of garbage. Then the cops on Six decide to stop me one day, and look, I'm carrying. Hadn't touched a single flake since before rehab and suddenly I'm carrying enough floess to buy this heap of shit and two more besides."

They wouldn't have told the navigator the truth. It was unlikely he'd believe it anyway. What story had they spun? Escaped criminal? Enemy of the state?

"What did they tell you? Whatever it was, it was all lies." It was a strategy older than space travel. She released control a little more and saw how he relaxed. "I am sorry they used you to get to me. But that does not excuse Zarr."

"Zarr?" Jwali gave a sort of strangled laugh. "He knows the deal. He's bottom of the heap on this ship. That makes him fair game." Jwali snapped his head back to face her. "He wants it, he just gets off whining about it."

The rage came boiling up again, and this time she made no attempt to control it. Jwali silently screamed for two minutes before she released him. "I would choose your words with more care." Blood-flecked saliva bubbled out of a corner of his mouth. The last thing she needed was him choking on his own blood. She grabbed hold of his shoulder and rolled him to his side, holding him there as he cleared his throat. Then she pushed him back down.

"Why?" he croaked. "Why are you doing this? You don't care for him, or like him. Look how you treat him, talk to him. You're only pretending to be angry so you have an excuse to hurt me."

His words hit her, almost physically rocking her back.

Why indeed, asked the voices. *You were going to kill the entire crew only a few weeks ago, yet you torture Jwali for what? Touching a boy, you have no concern for? Or were you going to take him as a battle trophy? Have him kneel at your feet, follow you around like a trained animal? Is this what you are angry about? That he took something that was yours?*

"I'm sorry. I should have kept my hands off him." A rough, thick sob escaped Jwali. "It's the floess, I take it, and all I want is that feeling. He wants it too; I swear he does. I didn't think it would matter; they only wanted you. To stop you. They said you'd be intercepted at Corelli if I pushed you enough." Bloody tears rolled down his cheeks. "Please, no," he sobbed. "I'm sorry."

Ikaluos, he was going into shock. Successful interrogations required skill, control, focus, and not letting your emotions run away with you. She forced the anger back down, ignoring the sullen red warnings pulsing in the corners of her screens. She sent a swift command to the nanites and Jwali slumped into unconsciousness. His medical files popped up on one screen, while the information from the nanites covered the other. She took a long moment to compare them. The tearing in the throat could be explained by his meltdown on the bridge. The remaining physiological damage would require a few minutes of work, beginning with repairing the damage to his heart. There were no other obvious injuries, not physical ones, at least. While the nanites worked, Ori rolled Jwali back into the same position she had found him, retrieving the blanket from the floor and painstakingly tucking it in around him. She took a step back, examining the scene, before placing her hand on his head, on the exact site of the injury logged in the files, and pressing.

Jwali didn't move as she continued to apply pressure until there was a small, but audible crack. A smear of nanites completed the procedure. They would heal the surrounding flash, making the wound look a week old and, at the same time, destroy the underlying brain tissue. The resulting cerebral hemorrhage would be enough evidence for any port medic. She gave the nanites one last command — to remove all traces of the drug from his system, before closing the hatch quietly behind her and reengaging the locks.

Van almost jumped at the first screams for help. Ori, sitting across from him in the mess, didn't even flinch.

"What have you done?" he hissed.

Those unwavering gray eyes stared back at him. "Nothing irreparable. He will live."

Jen bolted into the mess, red-faced and flustered. "Jwali is sick, really sick. Marissa has called for a medical crew."

By the time the crew arrived, Jwali was conscious, though only marginally coherent. The hemorrhage had had the desired effect — slurred speech, disorientation, nausea. A medic ran a portable scanner over Jwali before declaring a medical emergency.

"What did you do?" whispered Zarr, sidling up beside her.

"Nothing he didn't deserve."

Lianna arrived two hours later, white with fear, and swept past Ori, Van, Zarr and Jen without a word. The hatch slammed shut on the captain's quarters.

"Now what?" asked Zarr.

"Now we make a repair schedule, and a list of parts required," said Ori.

"I have already," said Van.

"Good, I suggest we get started with pulling the drives down."

The drive room stank of coolant, fried electronics, and sweat when Marissa stepped through the hatch. This time Ori did not need reminding before stopping work and standing respectfully with Van and Zarr.

"I have received word from the port authorities. Jwali will make a full recovery, eventually," Marissa began, her expression unreadable.

"Can't have everything," whispered Zarr.

"It seems his original injury was misdiagnosed and was more serious than anyone sus-pected. The port has determined this injury led to Jwali's momentary lapse of judgment and subsequent collapse."

Beside her, Van grunted, covering his amusement. Jwali's 'original injury' being Zarr laying the navigator out cold with a length of pipe.

"Jwali has been declared medically unfit and his navigator's license has been revoked. I have been fined a significant amount for not reporting his injury. Cargomaster Lianna will be re-joining the ship. I have been informed that the border has opened, and all vessels enroute to Ma'al will be permitted to leave as scheduled. Most of the cargo has been salvaged, so while we won't make quite as much as we expected, no one is going to starve. We are waiting for confirmation of our slot. So, I expect a repair estimate within the hour, Engineer."

"It will be ready, Captain," Van assured her.

"Good. And Tey?"

"Captain?"

"You are the navigator. Effective immediately."

Seventeen

Ori brushed the last residue of food scraps into the disposal unit and allowed herself a small measure of satisfaction. Finally, the bridge was clean and ready. For the first time in over a decade, she was in a position of authority.

Ori slid into the navigator's position and swept her hand gently across the panel. Fifty-two minutes until their slot opened and the *Ava* could leave. The panel sprang to life, displaying a holographic view of the Tersen system and its immediate environs. The four main planets each sat in a golden cloud, every mote representing a ship, satellite, or space dock. Further out, an arc of blue delineated the dense asteroid belt. Ori touched a control and the view shifted to the space dock, in orbit around T5. The tiny particles appeared and disappeared as ships dropped in and out of normal space, or shifted orbits as the port controllers ordered.

This was the closest system to the frontier. Once, only weeks ago, she wouldn't have hesitated, wouldn't have thought twice about inputting the coordinates, never concerned herself over the deaths of her crewmates. *You could still go,* the voices said, though more faintly now. *You can dump them in the shuttle, close to rescue. They wouldn't die.*

Perhaps not, but Ori now knew escape had always been a mirage. And now the idea of Van, Zarr, Jen, waiting for rescue in the darkness, as she had waited all those years ago, provoked a response so violent it took nearly a minute for her to regain some measure of control.

The hatch opened behind her and she killed the display with shaking hands.

"Hey, Navigator," Zarr called. "Can I come on the bridge?"

"As long as you don't touch anything," she said. "I finally have everything clean."

Zarr looked around with a mixture of approval and alarm. "And the captain let you?"

Ori didn't answer. The captain understood how much she was beholden to her new navigator.

"You know, I've been on ships for nearly two years now. I know what to do," said Zarr, putting down the mug with exaggerated care. A mug with a chip on the edge, and "I (heart) Maal" on the side.

"I brought you rakosh," he said, unnecessarily. "I thought you might like some." The tips of his ears burned scarlet and his fists buried themselves, like some sort of animal seeking sanctuary.

"Haven't you got work to do?" she said, because even now she didn't know the right words. As far as peace offerings went, the mug represented a significant gesture.

"Yeah, but..." He paused and shrugged. "Can you show me how it works? I've never seen the nav panel working. I was never allowed up here before."

"So long as you're gone before the captain comes back." Ori saw little point in aggravating Marissa unnecessarily. "Here, this is Tersen system." Her hands moved across the display and the cloud of ships appeared again.

"Where are we?" asked Zarr.

"Here." She zoomed in, the dots resolving into icons with the ships' names, registry indents and captain's name hovering beside it. "And there is the *Trailing Venture*, probably still cursing our name after our near miss."

"Yeah, they're never going to forget us," Zarr said, with a rueful smile. "But at least they'll be alive to hate us." Zarr pointed at the cloud, to the large dot that had appeared. "What's that one? Why is it red?"

Red. Red was Fleet. Her fingers flew across the display, bringing the resolution into maximum view. The tag with the ship's details floated over the pulsing red spot. Ori felt her blood run cold as space.

"Wow," said Zarr, almost squealing in excitement. "The *Kenthu Zen-ii*. What's she doing here? I never thought I'd be this close to a warship." He caught her expression and his voice faltered. "It's them, isn't it? They're after you."

"You should go," she said, "get to somewhere safe." It was a stupid suggestion. If the *Zen-ii* fired, there would be nothing left of the *Ava*.

"No, I'm staying here," the boy replied, although she could hear his terror in every word.

The view on the nav panel shifted as Ori manipulated the orientation to show the *Ava* in respect to the warship. Slowly, steadily, the cloud of ships between her and the *Zen-ii* were shifting in response to a stream of orders from the Port Authority. It would not take long before the warship had an unobstructed line of fire to the *Ava*.

Ori stared at the glowing marker as though willing a connection between herself and hopefully Commander Haruichi, although she had no idea if the woman was still in command of the warship. Ori had not seen her since the mission to Nianah Four. It was, as she had told Van, a warm, tropical world, with long strings of islands, the tips of drowned mountains. The small moons didn't exert enough gravitational force to produce much in the way of tides. It was a gentle world — the sort where you could find yourself an island and live out your life without seeing anyone from one month to another. The indigenous population of pre-tech fishermen had long since ceded control to the Republic. Now they fished the shallow seas in wooden boats reinforced with carbon fibers and navigated using the planetary AI.

It had been a straightforward mission — join in with the month-long party held at one of the most exclusive resorts. Have fun, eat, drink and sleep with whoever you choose. So long as those choices included specific individuals. She had obeyed. After three years of prison, the wide blue skies and soft breezes had been almost overwhelming. She had eaten and drunk and slept with every name on the list. Then she'd stolen a boat, taken off across the shallow seas and found a tiny, remote island, and thought herself safe.

It hadn't taken long for them to hunt her down. There was nowhere in the Republic she could hide from the AI network. The Directorate agents tasked to watch her were less than pleased; the Imperial Guard was given free rein to enforce that displeasure. Ori had been dragged back, close to death, onto the warship the *Senglis Ji* with Commander Haruichi as her captain.

"*Avadora*, this is Tersen Port. Please confirm your jump coordinates. "The speaker had the crisp, clipped accent of Central. The port already had their coordinates, the *Ava* was cleared for Ma'al. This was a warning. *We are here, and you will not escape.* She had indeed underestimated Rossim's hatred.

"Tersen Port. This is the *Avadora*. We are cleared for Ma'al. We're going to Ma'al."

If she activated the drives now, it would take forty-five seconds for the jump point to open. Of course, the *Zen-ii* could simply prevent them from opening a jump point; all warships carried jump suppressors. The *Ava* would be helpless. She did not doubt at all the warship's AIs had acquired a weapons lock on the *Ava*. Would they fire through the remaining ships? Would Rossim sacrifice so many to kill her? Would he defy the Xi so he could have his revenge? This was what Reinnor had warned her of, and once again she had underestimated an opponent.

Zarr's mug sat on the console, the red heart glowing in the bridge lights.

The brig of the Senglis Ji *was small and cold. She watched her blood seep across the metal deck almost dispassionately. At first the shouting had barely registered, unconsciousness called to her, the seductive lure of oblivion, and end to the pain. Then the angry voices and the sound of a sustained scuffle dragged her back into awareness. The hatch slammed back with an impact that jarred her broken bones. Hands were on her, and she flinched, expecting more pain; instead, a woman's voice spoke gently, from close by.*

"Lay still, my medic is here, she will take care of you." A hand patted her arm. "No one will hurt you, not while you're on my ship."

She didn't have the strength to tell this unknown woman to leave her to die, but it didn't matter, there was the sharp sting of a hypo spray and darkness finally claimed her.

"Tersen Port, this the *Avadora*. We have a crew of nine. Acknowledge." The protective cloud of ships thinned further; the *Ava* had only a few minutes before they were vulnerable. The *Zen-ii*'s weapons systems would already be programmed to fire the moment the drives activated. Ori needed Van. She might have access to the *Ava*'s navigational systems, but Marissa was not stupid— any competent captain would make sure their newly acquired navigator couldn't get creative.

"We know how many are on board," came a different voice, on a different channel. This was coming straight from the warship. It wasn't Haruichi.

"Don't fire. They haven't done anything."

She needed access to the drives, but if she tried to tell Van, over the comms channel, anyone could hear, with the real possibility they might try and stop her. "Run. Run to Van and have him turn over control of the drives to me. Go, Zarr." The boy nodded, face white with fear, and fled.

When consciousness finally returned, Ori found herself still in the small brig, but this time on a bunk, under the comforting bulk of blankets, and in no pain. Commander Haruichi had promised her she would not be harmed, and for the four days it took to get back to Central, Ori had the luxury of decent food, and a warm bed.

She stared at the nav panel again, at the glowing red dot. On the console the red heart seemed to pulse in unison. How long would they wait if she did nothing, just sat here?

No. Rossim would not risk a stalemate. What had her trainers always had to beat into her? Do not let your emotions rule your decisions. They would be bitterly disappointed in her.

A chipped mug. A red heart.

The guards waited until she was back in her prison before exacting their delayed revenge. All Hauirchi's kindness undone in a few hours.

"I surrender," she said, in the hope they would be content with only her. "I'll use one of the escape pods. You can pick me up. I won't resist."

Please, Zarr, be quick. Please, Van, believe him.

"I have orders," the voice replied, but a little hesitantly, as if not expecting this response. What had they told him? That they were terrorists? Traitors?

"Please." Ori swiped at the tears with one sleeve. "I promise. I'll surrender. I won't resist. You can do what you like."

How long? How long did they have? The cloud of ships was dissipating before her eyes. Did they have minutes? Or seconds?

"Drive control routed to navigator's position," the *Ava*'s AI informed her. Forty-five seconds. Her hardware slipped seamlessly into sync with the *Ava*. The drives came online.

"Do not attempt to jump," warned the warship.

Three vessels still blocked a direct line of fire, and they were taking their sweet time moving into their new positions.

Twenty seconds. The *Zen-ii* couldn't use the jump suppressors with other ships within range. Ori felt the pulse of the drives as they turned up to maximum.

A hand slipped into hers. Zarr. The commander of the *Zen-ii* must be screaming with frustration by now. Who was it? Someone who wouldn't question firing on an unarmed civilian freighter in a commercial system.

Fifteen seconds. Would they fire with civilians still between them and the *Ava*?

Ten seconds. The last ship began to move.

Prepare to jump.

The Kenthu-Zenii *is powering weapons.*

I know.

Five. Four. Three.

The Kenthu-Zenii *has fired.*

Too late. Too late. Death is coming.

Ori squeezed the boy's hand. At least it would be quick.

The writhing energies of an opening exit point filled the screen. The measured tones of the Tersen Port suddenly changed to frantic commands as the blue-white tear in space time licked at the warship.

Ori. GO!

Two.

One.

Jump.

Eighteen

J ak Reinnor leaned back in his seat and let out a small, restrained sigh of relief. For a moment there, he'd thought she would run, or worse still, not be quick enough to jump. Rossim was wrong. She wasn't a threat, she wasn't an unfeeling killing machine, devoid of emotion. Given the right environment she could have been their weapon. Unlikely that would happen now; too many years of cruelty for her to forgive.

The comms filled with the curses and shouts of both the commander of the warship and the port. No doubt there would be questions. Rossim's anger would be monumental.

Reinnor activated the nav panel of *The Sleeping Princess* and entered the coordinates for Central. He would prefer to be in Ma'al space when the ancient freighter dropped out, but getting the clearances would attract too much attention. Anyway, once Ori was on Ma'al his contacts in the Directorate would keep an eye on her. As an off-worlder she would be confined to the general port and Main Dome, so there would be some constraints on her movements.

Which brought him back to the never-ending question. What were the Xi up to? They weren't known for their forgiving natures, and Ori had certainly provoked them often enough. They wanted her for something. Reinnor glanced back at his two agents. Mardia was trying to look professionally unimpressed at the yacht's luxurious interior, while Finn... What was wrong with the man? Jak was used to his agent's impassive demeanor, but lately he'd seemed far more withdrawn than usual.

Well, Jak didn't have time to sort it out now. He had to get back to Central. On the way, he'd have to come up with a plan to handle the Lord President.

Betan Casar swept down the corridors of the palace, his retinue struggling to keep pace. As they approached Rossim's office, they scattered as if compelled by some primeval instinct, coalescing into small groups in strategic alcoves. No one would disturb their master, not while Betan's staff occupied the hallways.

The doors slid open at his approach and slid closed silently behind him in AI-controlled efficiency.

"Lord President." Betan gave a minuscule bow, surprised to see Rossim slumped in his seat and not at the window.

"What is it?" Rossim dragged himself upright. "It had better be important."

"Important? The First Secretary of the Directorate of Protection has disappeared. There is a real danger our little plan has been discovered. We could be arrested at any moment."

The sudden and mysterious disappearance of the head of the Directorate was the talk of Central. The news feeds were overjoyed to find another scandal to report on just as the inquiry, and interest, into the riots was winding down. Before Imsu's disappearance, the average citizen wouldn't have known Pesek if they'd passed him in the street; now his image, life story, and theories about his fate were all anyone talked about.

Rossim waved a hand toward a seat. Betan sank back into the enveloping plumpness. It was then he noticed how empty Rossim's desk was. Usually, it was covered in a variety of objet d'art, obtained, Betan suspected, from less than scrupulous sources.

"We'll appoint someone in the interim; he'll turn up."

What was wrong with the man? It was obvious Pesek was never going to reappear, unless it was as body parts. "It's too late. The Senate is appointing Mu'asa Wi'jlar as Head of the Directorate."

For a second, Betan thought Rossim hadn't heard him.

"Wi'jlar?" Rossim waved a hand dismissively. "No, they can't. Pesek will be back. The plan must continue."

Betan stared at Rossim incredulously. "Rossim, in the name of the Blessed Mother, listen to me. Wi'jlar has been appointed. The plan is dead, as dead as I suspect Pesek is. Someone with a great deal more power than us has removed him, and we could be next. If they arrest us, rank and money won't protect us. I don't know why I let myself be talked into this. The whole thing was madness anyway."

"No, I'm not going to give in. I'll find someone else. We can still do this, Betan."

"Take my advice, Tel, cut all ties with anyone connected to this. Destroy any evidence. Forget you ever thought of this. I'm returning to my estates, and intend to keep a very low profile until everyone loses interest. You'd better hope whoever you have on Ma'al is sensible enough to do the same."

MA'AL

One

"**F**or those of you on your first turn of this loop, listen up."

Van leaned back on the compartment bulkhead, his arm resting against hers, the warmth of his touch reaching her through the jacket sleeve. Zarr sat beside her on an upturned storage bin, fidgeting, clearly bored with having to sit through Lianna's rambling safety briefing. Jen and Lart sat side by side on an empty packing crate, Jen's hand enclosing the old man's own. Davey's death still sat hard on him, but lately he would come down to the cargo bays, or up to the bridge, when it was her watch, and talk about his days in Fleet.

"Current surface conditions on this ball of ice are hitting 200 degrees K, with a wind chill that will drop the temps down at least another thirty degrees. So, the port's underground, like everything else on Ma'al," continued Lianna. "No one with any sense goes out on the surface unless you like freezing to death in minutes."

No doubt Lianna was imagining that fate for Ori. In the fifteen days since the *Ava* had left Tersen, the cargomaster had spoken less than a dozen words to her. Ori was sure, if it hadn't been for Marissa, Lianna would have dumped the entire crew at Tersen rather than have Zarr and herself back aboard.

"That's not true," whispered Zarr. "I know of people who go out all the time. If you have the right gear, it's OK."

"Pay attention," Ori ordered.

"Yes, Navigator," he muttered.

The captain had not been impressed when she discovered the *Ava* had jumped without her permission, but had no choice other than to accept Ori's explanation, backed up by Van, that the sudden arrival of the Republic's largest warship had forced the port authorities to reshuffle exit slots on the fly.

It was telling that no news feed carried any mention of the *Kenthu Zen-ii* firing on a civilian vessel, or a near miss in Tersen space.

While Lianna continued with the obligatory warnings about industrial espionage, scam artists and an update on the latest security measures, Ori checked again for any messages. Apart from confirmation of a room, booked and paid for, in the port dome, there was nothing. Perhaps Reinnor would wait until she was dirtside before sending through the orders.

Finally, Lianna came to the end of the briefing and they could all file into the shuttle.

"Prepare for shuttle drop," intoned the AI.

On the ride down, everyone logged in to their sheets to watch the feed from the shuttle. From space, Ma'al was a uniform white, with a heavy cloud cover. Ice covered the entire surface, with only the bare mountain tops to give any hint of color. The one landmass, straddling what would be the equator, barely covered two million square kilometers. The rest was a thick, saline sea, trapped under a kilometer-thick ice floe that never melted. Even the moon consisted of an amalgam of ice and rock welded together by gravity. No wonder the Imperium had classified the system as a Marginal and dismissed it from memory. There wasn't even an asteroid belt to mine. Cimmili must have been glad to get rid of it.

As they approached the surface, Ori could make out the high spine of mountains running parallel to the equator. The surface appeared empty; the only artificial structures were the landing beacons strung out between the general freight port, and Ma'al central port, where they loaded the silk. The briefing material had emphasized the level of security surrounding the central port. Even Reinnor could not guarantee her false ID would pass Ma'al security if she ventured over there.

"Hey, Ori, we're coming up to the irises now." The feed showed five enormous circles, dark against the snow. The shuttle pitched and rolled in the crosswinds the closer they got to the surface. Flying would be a nightmare in this atmosphere.

"Is it always this rough?" she asked Zarr, as the shuttle dropped and lurched sideways, before recovering.

"Nah, this is good. Bad days, they have to suspend traffic completely. Even in good weather they still get crashes."

Synced directly into a craft via her neural port, she thought she would be able to handle these conditions, but it would be impossible for normal humans relying on unengineered reflexes to survive. No wonder the port AI controlled all the shuttles.

The shuttle dropped closer to the surface and the feed showed the irises opening and closing as cargo pods and shuttles entered and exited. The iris opened and the shuttle dropped into the airlock. The only sound was the shuttle engines, almost silent after the screaming wind outside. The second iris opened and the shuttle lowered into its designated landing spot.

"Welcome to Ma'al," said Zarr, with a smile.

TWO

The Matriarch settled down onto her folded legs, and sighed with relief. It had been a long trip back from the peace talks and she was grateful to be back in the safety of the Nest.

Beside her, on a bed of rumpled magenta silk, the spent male twitched and chittered in his sleep. She lowered her triangular head down onto the pillows and watched him with something approaching affection. It was a shame they didn't live long; this one had been quite entertaining in its own way. Still, there was never a shortage of males. There would be others.

And now the Brightstar was finally on her way to Ma'al, perhaps this plan, as tenuous as silk, might be underway. Although the opposition from within the Nest was gathering, even as the danger moved inexorably closer, and she feared the whole project could still go horribly wrong. The new Liaison, Reinnor, was proving surprisingly effective, despite his disability. Whether he let his ambition override caution was yet to be seen. She would deal with that when and if it was warranted. Humans had accidents all the time.

Success wasn't guaranteed, unfortunately. Humans were difficult, unpredictable creatures, and the engineered one doubly so. If the Meians or the Hubnae discovered the truth — that she had been lying to them from the beginning — war, real war, would be inevitable.

So many threads to keep track of. Which brought her back to that fool, Rossim. Did he think his petty machinations had gone unnoticed? He definitely needed disciplining. She would give the job to one of the younger sisters. It was good training.

Ma'al was the last possible hiding place. In the beginning she had believed success might come quickly, but as the years went by, hope had begun to fade. If there were no successful hits from the covert nanite program, she might have to openly oppose both the Hubnae and the Meians. And despite all their talk of peace, the Hubnae military strength matched that of the Xi. If the Xi's allies joined forces against them, it could get very messy.

She reached out with one palp and gently stroked the restless male. Perhaps it was time she stopped calling her Brightstar. Carillon's daughter/clone. Orestria D'e, last surviving member of the Imperial House. Somewhere, out there in the dark reaches of interstellar space, the refugees from Da Chet had survived, at least for a time. She had kept her promise to her friend: she had given them a chance.

As sleep overtook the Matriarch, she made a mental note to check the latest intelligence from the probes. The last thing they needed was their enemy sneaking up on them.

Epilogue

Keren leaned on the railing and tipped his head back as far as it could go. Hundreds of meters above him, the faint outlines of millions of panels covering the curve of the dome were almost visible, if you knew what to look for. Or you could simply admire the sweep of blue sky, dotted with clouds, and bask in the full spectrum light of a heatless, artificial sun, all generated by millions of holographic panels and a sophisticated AI digital program. Across the artificial lake, complete with synchronized fountains, the meticulously landscaped lawns and gardens blended seamlessly into the holographic mountain range on the far wall of Main Dome.

Keren was calculating the cost when the sound of giggling abruptly brought him back to reality. A group of young Ma'ali in the colors of Hanjile Toachi's medical division, were clearly finding his activities amusing. Keren adopted his professional face and bowed; as one, the group returned the courtesy, before darting away in a whirl of pale-blue silk, the musical tones of the Ma'ali language floating back to him. He hoped they were being kind.

Abandoning the math, Keren headed along the genuine timber walkway circling the lake. Water lapped rhythmically under the boards, a breeze (artificially generated) ruffled the water and bent the stands of reeds dotting the edge. It took him longer than it should have to comprehend there were no insects flitting about, no fish or any other creatures in the water.

A few Ma'ali citizens passed him, all dressed in ordinary day wear, only an ineffable aura of maturity marking them as much older than the Toachi youths, their glossy lengths of plaits and silver jile rings glowing in the bright, artificial sunlight. The occasional off-worlders like himself made no eye contact, passing without any acknowledgment. He wondered how Ori was, whether her ship had reached Tersen yet. He imagined meeting her at the port, showing her around the delights of the Enclave, before common sense reasserted itself. Whoever had tried to kill her on Corelli would try again; there would be no rendezvous, no cozy chats in elegant cafes.

From somewhere came the scent of cooking food and Keren's stomach rumbled in response. "I have no self-control," he mumbled to himself. "You had breakfast only a few hours ago," he reminded his stomach. Still, it did smell good, and he had walked at least halfway around the lake. A small snack wouldn't hurt.

Wooden steps led from the boardwalk up a small grassy slope, planted to resemble a wild meadow, to a road of fake cobbles lined with shops and eating establishments, most of them closed. His sheet vibrated with "For Sale" notifications as he passed. The tightened security measures were affecting small businesses, never a good sign.

Keren's stomach led him to a small café, almost empty, where a bored young man showed him to a table on an otherwise deserted balcony overlooking the boardwalk and foreshore. His sheet pinged as the café menu loaded automatically. Ignoring, for once, the demands of his appetite, Keren ordered only rakosh and a small plate of draci cakes. The ones with the pink icing. Only three, though, so it hardly counted as a snack. After further perusing the café's menu, Keren decided to pay for his food with a tap of his chip, before temptation got the better of him.

Temptation nearly won, once his order was delivered. The cakes were delicious and Keren discreetly licked the little cakes clean of their pink goodness, imagining Sylvie's horror at his lack of decorum. In public, no less.

The cakes satisfactorily devoured, Keren nursed his rakosh, content to watch the flow of people along the path. Four off-worlders appeared, port workers or freighter crew, Keren guessed from their dress and cropped hair. The men lounged against the boardwalk railing, at one point replicating Keren's survey of the dome roof. Seeing all four faces upturned, frowning in concentration, made him smile.

Three more figures arrived, this time in the gray and black of SK security. As an invited guest of Hanjile Eidress, Keren's interactions with Ma'al security were unremarkable. Everyone was thorough, but respectful, and he had been ushered through the security checkpoints politely.

These three were different. They reminded him unpleasantly of the guards at the house, carrying their weapons as if expecting trouble, and making a direct line to the four tourists immediately upon spotting them. All thoughts of more cakes fled as Keren watched the troops move in. One of the men made a half-hearted plea, raising his hands in supplication, to no avail. A weapon swung up and its butt slammed into his head.

Keren didn't remember making the decision, but there he was, out of the café, down the stairs to the boardwalk, as another security guard turned his weapon on the other three men, driving them back from helping their fallen comrade. He hadn't intended to hit anyone, only intervene. The shot was shockingly loud, followed by a scream.

His arm didn't work. Strange. Someone was yelling, loudly. Keren watched, in total disinterest as the rifle butt swung again.

Then there was nothing but darkness.

Acknowledgements

Thank you to the following:

- Abigail Nathan at Bothersome Words. Thank you for your patience and excellent editing.

- Kat Betts at Elemental Editing for Beta Reading

- Lori- Jay Ellis and all the staff at the Queensland Writer's Centre.

- Miblart for their wonderful cover art designs.

About the Author

D.E Cheers has been reading, watching, and writing science fiction since childhood. Her short stories have been published in the Zodiac Anthologies (Capricorn and Aquarius) And the Wandering Stars Anthology- The Best of the Zodiac series.

This is the first novel in the Abomination Series. In real life, she has worked on a farm and spent four years sailing up and down the Queensland coast. Currently, her work takes her to some of the most remote areas of Australia. She lives in Brisbane, Australia, with her two cats.

Contact me at decheersauthor@gmail.com

www.ingramcontent.com/pod-product-compliance
Lightning Source LLC
Chambersburg PA
CBHW030624250626

47154CB00006B/1916